SEA

OF

CRIMSON
SILK

A BURNING EMPIRE NOVEL

EMMA HAMM

SEA
OF
CRIMSON
SILK

A BURNING EMPIRE NOVEL

EMMA HAMM

*For the fat cat who stared at me with judging eyes
the entire time I was writing this book.*

This one's for you kid.

You're kind of a dick.

the
CRIMSON
PALACE

Glasslyn

Misthall

Falldell

Bymere

SIGRID

"SIGRID OF WILDEWYN, FOR WHOM DO YOU SPEAK?"

She knelt before a crowd of masked women, her knees pressed against soft furs. A curl of smoke wafted from a bowl of incense set on an altar before her. Pale as a ghost, the smoke twisted in the air, coiled around her wrist, and left behind the faint scent of birch bark with an ashen smudge. "I speak for myself, as there are no others to speak for me."

"What promises do you make to the gods?"

Ceremonial words burned her throat and made her voice a quiet rasp. "I vow to honor this earth, and all who stand upon it."

One of the women reached forward with delicate fingers and touched a small dot of gold wax to the center of Sigrid's forehead. Her skin heated the bead, which dripped down the bridge of her nose.

"I vow to battle for justice and honor as long as there is breath in my body."

Sigrid's eyes fluttered shut as the masked woman swiped more wax down her left brow, over each eyelid, and the bottom of her lip. Each mark slid down her skin, leaving long lines of color behind.

"I vow to hold true to my oaths and never be ashamed of my people or my birthright."

Another line trailed down her opposite cheek.

The final words of her vows vibrated deep within her being and rose from her belly with the rumble of thunder. "I vow to impress the gods with all I do."

The vows were the first of many tonight, and the most important to *her*. She whispered prayers to the gods every night, wishing for a future that would cast meaning upon her body and soul. Now, the gods had given her purpose.

It was a shame she did not want it.

One of the many masked women offered a small wooden bowl. Burned runes decorated the sides, symbols representing happiness, health, virility—all important for this new chapter of her life.

She took the cup, held it cradled in her hands as so many women had done before her, and took a small sip. The nettle and dandelion tea made her salivate. Bitter and biting, she hoped it was not an omen for all to come.

"You're doing well," her closest friend whispered. "Just a few more rituals and then you will be free."

Instead of replying that she had never wanted to be free, she smiled and inclined her head.

"Don't look so glum." Camilla laughed. "It's your wedding day! You must learn to smile more convincingly if you're to fool your husband."

A strange thing, marriage. Sigrid had never thought she would see the day. As a child, she had always known it was a possibility. The species required women to marry, to have children, to bring new life into the world. She just hadn't thought it would arrive so soon.

"Come on. We have to get you into your wedding gown."

Camilla reached out a dark hand. Her fingers were long, graceful, and tipped with the faintest of claws. Fitting, considering Camilla's other form was an owl.

Gold bangles jingled on her wrists as Sigrid reached up and placed her ghostly pale hand in her friend's. They were two sides of the same coin. Where Camilla was dark, Sigrid was light. When Camilla laughed, Sigrid frowned. But for all their differences, a warrior's soul burned bright inside them.

"They will expect your happiness," Camilla advised. "You must hide your emotions better. Even I can see how angry you are."

"They will be disappointed if they expect me to smile through this entire ordeal."

"Dalvin is a good choice. He'll be a kind husband and a good father. What more could you ask for?"

Sigrid's mind flew with all the things she desired. Adventure. Whispered promises of heat on their wedding night. Flickers of wickedness in his gaze, a sign he understood her desire for the hunt. All this, and more.

Sigrid's brows drew down. She frowned at Camilla but couldn't force the words past her lips. It was unreasonable to desire all those things. Husbands weren't close to their wives. They worked side by side, and they desired the same outcome for their children. But passion was unnecessary. It would come in time, or she would learn to respect him for who he was.

She sighed. "I will try to smile more."

"Good, because they're all very excited for you."

Camilla led her down the darkened hall. Small slats in the walls revealed the sun had set and flames flickered through the stretched leather skins.

They reached stone doors carved with hunting scenes. Women with strong bodies, tall and powerful, racing through the forests. Some remained on two feet, wielding spears made of twisted metal. Others had already changed and ran on all fours, on wings, and through the rivers.

Beastkin, the humans called them. The rarest and most exotic creatures in their world. They were women who hid an animal inside their bodies.

Light reflected in Camilla's eyes, changing them to eerie silver before returning to her dark gaze. "Be happy for *them*. It's been a long time since one of our own married."

She opened the doors and revealed the hidden world beyond.

Emerald green carpet covered the stones beneath their feet, mimicking moss covering a forest floor. The walls were painted with dark and light strokes as if sunlight were filtering through trees. Gilded frames outlined the ceiling. Each frame contained a hand-painted scene from the memories of the Beastkin. The first moment they came from the mountains, the first man they ever met, the first of their sisters to step foot in a human village.

It was an incredible room full of wealth and immense talent, and yet it was still a gilded cage.

Birds sang in the rafters, some Beastkin, and some animal. A deer lifted its head to look at her. A lizard crawled towards her, and so many more beautiful faces froze as they stared.

Sigrid was the first woman the Council had requested to marry in many years. They all worried that their kind would die. The Earthen folk had captured them long ago, and there were too few Beastkin to challenge them. They were ruled by human men and women who kept their numbers limited.

However, no man had ever stepped foot in their sanctuary. They had made it a replica of their lost home, a hidden place human eyes would never see.

"Sigrid?" A voice lifted into the air.

She took a deep breath and squared her shoulders. "I am to marry this day."

The cheers of her sisters lifted her spirits. She could do this. It was not an impossible task. Training for hours on end to learn how to fight with a spear instead of claw, that was impossible. Forcing her body to remain in its soft, fleshy prison without shaking, that was impossible.

Marrying a man was nothing more than a duty.

As her sisters dragged her to the center of the room and draped white fabric over her shoulders, she thought of Dalvin.

He was a simple man. His eyes twinkled when he laughed, and deep grooves had formed on his cheeks because he was always smiling. Dark locks fell in front of his eyes, curly hair so soft it didn't belong on a man. His arms were overly long, his legs too lanky to be graceful, and he tripped over himself at every opportunity.

She would need to watch out for him. It was like marrying a baby deer. Except this man was already full grown, and she feared she would spend the rest of her life worrying whether he'd fallen into a mire somewhere and couldn't get out.

13

Wildewyn was full of dangers. Their forests were dark, their beasts horned, their nights rang with the cries of predators. And humans were weak.

Sigrid curled her fingers into fists. She was not a caring person. Her nature was to fight, battle, and taste blood on her tongue. Now, she must become a meek creature looking after the fragile man she had bound herself to.

What if her daughter shared more of her father's traits? How could she train a Beastkin with legs like a foal?

"Sigrid?" Camilla whispered.

Schooling her face back into the serene expression her sisters would expect, Sigrid nodded and allowed them to slip her into the wedding gown. They had spent many nights sewing it. She should respect them enough to appreciate it.

Silk so white it looked as if they had dipped it in the moon slid down her body. They settled a golden corset around her ribs, the metal heavy and sturdy. Around her biceps they secured swirls of gilded leaves that tangled around her arms, forming armor both beautiful and strong.

They deftly twisted her waist-length white hair upon her head. Most of it remained loose, but pulled back from her face with braids so intricate they could never be replicated. With whispers of encouragement, they spun her around and let her see her visage in a mirror.

She was beautiful. But more than beautiful, she was dangerous. Her eyes flickered gold and her gaze turned toward Camilla, who had painted half of her own face white. Patterns of swirling lines gave her an otherworldly look.

Camilla held in her hands the one thing Sigrid both loved and hated. A golden mask carefully made by the most talented artisans. She held it out and placed it in Sigrid's waiting grip.

"Remember sister, you come from a line of ancient blood. Your skin is armor, your beauty is a blade, and your voice rings with steel. Go to your marriage knowing our ancestors will always guide you."

Sigrid lifted the mask in her hands and affixed the prison to her face. Hands helped her hide the ties beneath the weight of her hair. The beast inside her sighed, drifted into the corners of her mind, and was laid to rest. As always, the mask calmed it as nothing else could.

She turned and stared into her own eyes in the mirror.

A golden dragon stared back.

"Are you ready?" Camilla asked.

Sigrid nodded, followed her sister out of their haven, and strode towards the village of man.

She marveled at how many times a woman died in her life. Her first blood, her first love, her first marriage. Every instance bringing about a new person whom she had never met.

Who was this new version of herself? A married woman looking after a soft, clumsy male who would never be worthy of the creature within her? The dragon wanted to claw its way out of her skin. To breathe fire upon the village and remind them all what powerful creature she hid away from the world.

It would do no good. She would have to return to this form eventually, and they would find her. Thousands of armed men could quell a single dragon easily, though not without casualties. And she'd seen too many Beastkin die because they rebelled.

Small fires appeared at the end of the path, guiding them towards the ceremony. They walked together until they saw the circle of fire and the many people standing around it.

Camilla tugged on Sigrid's arm one last time. "You will visit?"

"I cannot return to the enclave, but you can fly on wings of night to see me anytime you wish." Sigrid leaned forward and pressed her mask against her sister's. "I will miss you, my dearest friend."

"You're afraid?"

"No." She shook her head and took a step back. "I'm sad."

Humans stood outside the first fire circle. Only family could step through to the second circle where a few people stood. Delvin had little family, and Sigrid had none. Therefore, many of the Council had replaced them.

She saw the old men and women—wrinkles lining their skin, smiles on their faces—and wondered just how much they knew. Beastkin were an anomaly, a blessing, but they remained in cages until they were deemed useful.

She passed through their ranks to the inner circle where a bonfire blazed. Dalvin stood beside it, waiting for her.

His hands opened and closed as if he didn't quite know what to do with himself. A man should know. A man should reach forward and take what was his.

Pity bloomed in her chest. He was young, like her, barely twenty summers. Neither of them knew each other well, and they had no choice in this matter. She had never considered he might not wish for this union.

With her cold mask hiding her expression of disdain, she held out her hands for him to take. "Dalvin of Wildewyn, I offer myself to you, willing and free of chains."

A smile split his face, sending stars dancing in his eyes, and grooves appeared on his face. Working hands took warrior hands, and she marveled at how different they were. She had trained to fight. He had trained to work the land and eventually join the Council. They were a good match.

He leaned forward, asking, "Are you sure you're free of chains?"

How could she respond? No, she wasn't free of chains until she was flying in the air above the forests where no one else could find her. Marrying him would only add more weight to the hundreds of chains which already bound her. But what was one more when she was already pinned to the ground?

She gave him a curt nod.

"I hope, someday, you will feel comfortable enough to confide in me." He reached forward and placed a palm against her mask. "It's a hard enough life without having to battle the days alone."

He didn't deserve to be married to a Beastkin. They were selfish creatures, and Sigrid was the worst of them all. She had to be. She was the last of her kind.

Gods, how she wished she could love him. Dalvin was a man worthy of love. He would give everything he could to his wife until she drained him; and even then, he would thank her and give more.

The ice in her chest cracked just enough for her to reply, "I'm always alone."

Drums beat, the echoing call resounding throughout the forest. Their families hummed, those who watched the hand-fasting quickly following suit. They had little time to speak now. Soon, they would be married before the eyes of their people and the gods.

Dalvin looked as though he wanted to say more, but she shook her head. He could ask further questions when they were bound. A Beastkin must hide their true nature from everyone but their family. He had to wait only a few moments before she could tell him everything.

The drums drew to a crescendo and birds flew from the trees above them into the night sky. She tilted her head back, a breeze slipping beneath the bottom of her mask, cooling her heated flesh.

"Join us in hand-fasting these lovers," an aged voice broke through the sound of drums. Hallmar, the King of all Wildewyn and the Keeper of Beasts.

Sigrid's gaze cut across the crowd and found him. White hair was pulled tightly back from his skull in a magnificent braid. His voice was still strong, but she sensed a weakness in him. His body withered from an illness she could not pinpoint.

He strode through the circles of flames into the center where he brandished the rope in his hands. "Come forth, chosen of these lovers. Guide them into the next part of their lives."

Camilla stepped into the circle with one of Dalvin's brothers, his name unimportant although Sigrid now wished she knew. They each held a garland of flowers which they placed atop Sigrid and Dalvin's heads.

Hallmar knotted the rope into a small noose, leaving a long tail, then looped it around their hands. She knew what to expect now, knew the words that sang in her mind until she could think of nothing else. She opened her mouth to speak, jaw working but not even a breath escaping her lips. Strange how they the words caught in the back of her throat.

Her new husband squeezed her hands and smiled. "I choose you, to be no other than yourself."

So, Dalvin had a spine after all. He had spoken when she hadn't been able to. Hallmar looped the rope over their wrists with each line spoken.

Sigrid cleared her throat. "I will love what I know of you," she replied, "and will trust who you become."

"I will respect and honor you, always and in all ways."

Gods, what was she doing? Marrying herself to a mortal man when she was something so much more. They could have chosen Camilla. She would have been perfect for this quiet, kind man who looked at her as if the world was reflected in her soul.

Sigrid would destroy him. Why couldn't they understand that she was a beast in fragile flesh? That she dreamt of blood and fire? That every moment was a battle? He deserved a wife who could see him as a man.

Not as a meal.

Her words thickened in her throat. "I take you as my husband—"

A whistling sound interrupted her, followed by a quiet thud, and then the drums silenced. The faint crackle of the bonfire snapped, and the quivering fletching of the arrow embedded in Dalvin's throat sang a quiet dirge.

He let out a quiet, choked sound. His hands lifted, bringing hers with them, as he tried to stop the blood from spilling out of the wound, soaking his soft, white tunic.

Sigrid ghosted her fingers over the wound and stared at the red smear on her fingertips. She knew it would smell metallic, but the mask hid the scent. She lifted her gaze to his shocked expression as more arrows whistled through the air.

Three struck him in the back, sending him reeling into her. Sigrid held her ground. He sagged, tilting his head back to look up once more, and the life drain slowly from his eyes.

Sparkling laughter disappeared forever as war cries filled the glade.

Heat filled her body, embers sparking to life. Sigrid lifted her head as brightly colored warriors raced towards them. Shrieks echoed from the crowd that spun and ran like the cowards they were.

"Sigrid!" Camilla shouted.

There were no words between them, for they were warriors at heart. She spun towards her sister and held out her hands still bound to Dalvin's limp ones. A blade arced and sliced through the bindings. The hand-fasting was not yet finished, but she still sent a prayer to the gods for their forgiveness.

"Here," Camilla thrust another blade towards her, small but enough to injure.

Jewels encrusted the hilt and Sigrid wrapped her hands around it, strong and firm. The metal was flimsy and would break if she pushed too hard.

"I'm sorry," Camilla started, "it's your wedding day —"

Sigrid held up a hand for silence. "It's the gods will that I fight."

Another arrow flew, pinging off the edge of her armored corset. She spun on her heel toward the advancing warriors and let out a war cry of her own. The sound carried, echoing through her mask and out into the glade until it reached the armored men. The first few faltered when the piercing sound echoed.

She traced her fingertips at the edge of the mask until Camilla's voice cut through the haze of rage covering her vision.

"Sigrid, *no*. Not now."

"The dragon has awakened."

"And she will remain enchained. Fight as a woman, not a Beastkin."

Sigrid bared her teeth in a grimace no one could see, but her hands fell away from the clasps at the edge of her mask. If her sister wished her to fight as a woman, then so be it. These warriors did not know what they were attacking.

The first man reached her. She struck his shoulder hard, grasping the leather strappings of his arm and whipping him towards Camilla who sank her blade between the plates of his armor. He froze, let out a dying gasp, and dropped his sword into her sister's waiting hands.

A curved blade. Earthen men carried broadswords, their heavy hands and strong bodies capable of swinging a deadly blow. At the least, they carried a short sword. But never one like this.

Camilla glanced up, shifting the blade from hand to hand. "Bymerian."

"They haven't attacked in months. Why now?"

"Perhaps their boy king grows too comfortable upon his new throne."

"Perhaps."

Footsteps slammed into the ground near her and she spun to stare down the soldier leaping toward her. Their armor was strange, leather instead of metal. It allowed for smoother movements, but still they did not know how to fight a woman in a dress.

The warrior hesitated for the briefest moment, and she saw her opening. Sigrid darted forward and slid her blade across his throat. The spurt of blood sprayed across her dress, but they could never use the fabric again. Death had already marked it.

Wildfire raged through her veins. The boy king would dare attack *her* wedding? He would dare kill a groom who had almost become a husband?

She stepped over Dalvin's body and let out a scream of rage. More warriors attacked. She did not count their numbers in men, but in deaths. Each garbled word, each gasp for breath, became a chanting call to the beast inside her.

Camilla stayed close. She was a whirling arc of movement, the curved blade lifting above her head and glinting in the moonlight.

The jeweled hilt glimmered in Sigrid's hand, blood dripping down the crystals and pooling in her palm. She held a man close to her chest, arms trembling as she kept the blade still inside his heart.

Their gazes met. His eyes were brown and yellowed at the edges. Long lashes framed them and he stared at her in fear.

"You've heard the rumors of Earthen women?" she asked. "How the blood of animals runs in our veins?"

He nodded, blood trickling from his lips.

"All these rumors, and more, are true." Heat burned the backs of her eyes, a sign the dragon looked out at him. "Consider yourself lucky, warrior. You met the woman when you might have met the beast."

She drew the blade from his chest and allowed his lifeblood to seep from his veins and douse the earth with his essence.

Someday, a tree would grow where he died. Wildewyn took what she wanted from men and women alike. Their souls sank into the ground and grew branches.

Screams echoed from above, and birds descended upon the remaining warriors. Some remained hawks and eagles, their silver talons digging into eyes and soft skin. Others transformed in the air. Nude women fell from the skies and landed upon soldiers who did not have time to make ready their weapons.

Sigrid let loose a shrill whistle, ordering her sisters to free a single man. He could leave, racing from the glade with fear nipping at his heels. She let him return to his master with stories to tell. Creatures, the likes of which Bymerians could never understand, protected the Earthen folk.

Soon, blood saturated the glade. Dying men gasped their last breath, others groaned as their lives ended with the swift swing of a blade.

None would live without Sigrid's permission.

She stood alone, the bonfire heating her back, and stared at the surrounding carnage. This was a hand-fasting. Happiness and the bright promise of the future should glimmer in the air like torchlight.

Had she brought this upon herself? Had her dark thoughts somehow traveled to Bymere and incited their boy king to send yet another attack to plague her people?

"Sigrid?" Camilla called out. Blood dripped from her blade to her fingertips. "Do we return to the enclave or follow the man you released?"

Sigrid looked out over the crowd of her people. Some stared at her with apprehension, others with gladness that she would still be with them for a little longer.

The leader of their tribe was always the most powerful. The strongest, the matron who would take care of them all. Sigrid was the last dragon. She would always be their matriarch, regardless of their age.

"Send a sparrow," she replied. "But keep it quiet. I don't trust the Earthen folk to tell Beastkin the whole truth."

"They said the war with Bymere was over."

"They were wrong." She held out a hand for a sparrow to land on, human eyes staring back at her. "I want to know what the boy king plans to do. Bring me his words, little sparrow, and keep yourself hidden from sight."

NADIR

THE ROAR OF THE CROWD CRASHED DOWN FROM THE SKY, ROLLING
over the advancing royals. Poppies rained down upon them and coated
the streets in a perfume so intoxicating it made many stumble as they
made their way towards the coronation.

Nadir liked to pretend they cheered for him, but he knew who they
really reached out for.

His older brother was a man unlike any other. He stood a head
taller than the crowd and just a few steps ahead of Nadir, but he was
easy to pick out no matter where he was.

Shoulders broad enough to carry the world parted the teeming
masses like a wave and his long, ebony hair swung free to his waist.
Crimson fabric spilled from his form and slid through the poppies like
a snake.

The people were blessed to be in his presence. Hakim, the golden
prince who would soon be emperor.

Nadir watched as hands reached out for his brother, their
fingertips stained red with clay, and gold bangles dancing in the light.

Delicate, like a dancer, they would touch the edges of his sleeves, then retreat as though the rare moment was a gift.

And was it not? How many could say they had touched the blessed sultan?

They reached the dais where the advisors waited for them. Each was more honored than the last, but it was Saafiya who captured Nadir's attention. No other woman could ever hold a candle to her beauty.

Her caramel skin was burnished gold in the sunlight, dark kohl rimmed her large eyes, and she batted her lashes at his brother with a spark of mischief that promised adventure. Henna tattooed her hands in swirls and dots that told a story, but he wouldn't be able to focus on the words if she told him. She was too pretty, her dark eyes too powerful for him focus.

An arm hooked around his shoulders, shaking him firmly.

"My brother, pay attention. It's an important day for both of us."

"For you," Nadir replied, shaking himself free from Hakim's grasp. "You're the one who will be the sultan."

"And your brother will be the most powerful man in all Bymere. You should be happy."

"I am."

"You don't look it."

Nadir shrugged, but stared off into the crowd. His golden eyes flicked towards their home. The red palace loomed over everything and could be seen for miles. Crimson stones made the towers and the circular peaks look more sinister than he could ever recall his home being.

"Nadir," Hakim growled. "The coronation?"

"I'm here with you."

"Smile a little more. The people want to think you're happy for

me, not jealous."

"I'm not jealous," he answered honestly. Nadir had never wanted to be sultan. Instead, he wanted to fight in battles, wield the deadly scimitar, travel the sands, and find new lands. Sitting on a throne whilst listening to other people complain held little appeal.

"Then smile."

He forced a grin and turned towards the crowd as another cheer rose into the air. He reached for his brother's arm and lifted it high above their heads.

There, they stood at the bottom of the dais where their lives would forever change.

"A sultan," he muttered and shook his head. "Of all things, did you ever expect to become this?"

Hakim arched a dark brow. "We've been princes our entire life."

"But I never saw us here."

"Premonitions? I thought you renounced all magic."

Nadir shook his head again, then turned them both towards their advisors. "Just go to the top and become sultan, would you? We both know your ego could use the favor."

"You'll stand beside me?"

"Without question." He nudged his brother forward. "I'll always be beside you brother, no matter how bad a sultan you are."

They teased, but Nadir was immensely proud of Hakim. They had grown up in the palace where every desire was met without question. While Nadir took advantage of such a lavish childhood, Hakim had worked every moment of his life to be a good king.

Being an older brother was not an easy job, especially when Nadir was such a troublesome eight-year old. He had a lot of responsibility on his shoulders, and not many people saw beyond the stern exterior. Hakim would be a sultan that would go down in history for making his people happy, his kingdom rich, and the land would prosper every moment he was on the throne.

Nadir puffed out his chest with pride and remained at the bottom of the stairs. Tomorrow, he would begin his training as the captain of the guard. It would be his duty to ensure Hakim stayed alive.

It wouldn't be a hard job. Who would ever want to kill his brother?

Hakim lifted a hand and smacked it against his neck. The bugs this year were horrible, worse than years prior. Nadir already knew the advisors would send him to the outer province where the beasts were devouring cattle. The promise of adventure sang through his veins until his leg bounced.

Soon, he would leave. Soon, his life would start anew. No longer a prince, no longer protected. Just a boy with nothing but the sand to keep him company.

Hakim stumbled. He righted himself, although it must have been embarrassing. A sultan never stumbled.

A frown wrinkled Nadir's forehead as his brother did it again. Yet another trip sent him to his knee on the steps.

"Hakim?" he called out.

"I'm fine." But his voice was weak. "I'm fine, I just – "

The breath in Nadir's lungs rushed from him as Hakim fell against the steps and did not rise. Time seemed to slow as he raced towards his brother, touching a hand to his back and rolling him onto his side.

White foam collected in the corners of Hakim's dark lips. His eyes rolled back in his head even as Nadir shook him.

"Brother," he frantically called out. "What is wrong? What dark magic is this?"

Hands pulled him away from the would-be king, and he fought for all he was worth. He might be young, but his body was made for war. Nadir struggled until the aged captain of the guard pinned his arms against his sides.

All he could do was watch the advisors gather around his elder brother, his last remaining family, and try to still the seizure that spasmed through Hakim's body, sucking the life from him.

The dream melted away as Nadir lurched forward in his bed. Dark locks of hair fell in front of his eyes, still sticky from the sweat clinging to him.

Such memories had not plagued him for years. What had changed?

Nadir pushed back the mass of his long hair and attempted to ground himself in the present. He was not on the dais watching his brother die. He was in his bedroom in the Red Palace.

Gauze fabric hung from the ceiling, obscuring his vision of the room beyond. Embroidered pillows surrounded him, each more opulent than the last. His pale, tunic was tangled around his form. It was no wonder he had overheated. The damned material was enough to smother him in his sleep.

He pushed aside the curtains and stumbled away from the bed. The braziers still burned with red coals that winked at him, the promise of pain almost too tempting to ignore.

Cold marble soothed the soles of his bare feet. He padded through his room, pushed open his door made of solid gold, and rushed into the private hall just outside his rooms.

Here was sanctuary. The polished, white marble floor looked like a mirror. Columns from floor to ceiling were the only embellishment to the entire room, and they touched the edge of the palace that fell hundreds of feet towards the ground.

Starlight reflected across the floor, and the sliver of the moon danced at the tips of his toes.

He smoothed a hand over his slick chest, the tunic parting to reveal the broad planes of his body. His fingers came away gritty with the remains of henna which stained his skin from collarbone to hips.

One of his concubines had thought it was entertaining to mark him, and he'd been half drunk on spiced mead and her beauty, so he had let her.

Nadir made a face when he saw the patterns in the meager light. What had he been thinking? His advisors would never let him live that down, no matter how few people saw it. His guard would think him foolish.

Perhaps, he was.

He stepped forward, tugging a curtain from the wall and flinging it over his head. Though it was not as warm, nor as soft, as a blanket from his bed, it was comfortable enough. The pale orange fabric gave him a sense of security as he leaned against a column.

He flirted with the edge of the stone, toes barely hanging on to the edge of the mirror floor, the gulf of a dark abyss just beyond. He leaned against the column and breathed out a sigh of relief.

Life coursed through his veins. He had survived, although he would never know why the assassin had killed Hakim and left him alive. If their purpose was to kill the royal family, then they had failed. Nadir was nineteen years of age and his lungs still drew breath.

But what if they had intended something else?

Such thoughts would plague him for as long as he existed.

Nadir had never believed the assassin had left his kingdom. It was too simple. Killing two princes should have been just as easy as killing one.

He pressed a hand to his forehead.

Dwelling on such thoughts would only send him into another spiral. He could hardly think straight. Too many drinks, far too many herbs, and a night with too many women made his head spin.

And that dream.

That nightmare.

He wouldn't sleep tonight, knowing what waited in the realm of sleep. Hakim would stare back at him, slowly withering away until he was nothing more than a corpse.

His brother had always been determined. In those last moments, he had refused to die. It had only prolonged his pain in the end.

Sixteen days of suffering. Sixteen days of unimaginable agony as his body ate itself alive until he heaved his last breath in Nadir's arms, while staring at the sun.

A shiver skittered down his spine. Death had always seemed so implausible when they were younger. Nadir had been just a boy back then, dreaming of becoming a captain of the guard. If only he had known all those years ago that he would become sultan instead.

Would he have prepared better? Would he have listened to all the tutoring that his brother had so diligently mastered?

Likely not. Nadir could hardly stand still now, let alone when he was younger. It would have been an impossible task to still the inferno of his mind.

"Your Majesty?" A deep voice sliced through the darkness.

"Your advisors wish to speak with you."

"It's the middle of the night, Raheem."

"And still, they have requested I bring you to them."

He turned towards the one man he might call a friend. Raheem had appeared out of the darkness one night. Nadir had only been sultan for a few moons and had yet to choose the one person who would protect him.

There had been no choice when Raheem had offered the boy king his own sword, placed it against his throat, and requested Nadir either kill him or take him into his guard.

He was a beast of a man with skin tanned by the sun, silver loops sparkling in his ears, and head shaved so close it looked as though he couldn't grow hair at all. Muscles bulged from every part of his body, but he moved with surprisingly light feet. Every person in the room had gasped when he placed his life in the boy king's hands.

It took a strong man to put himself in a situation where he might die. It took a stronger man to give that power to a child.

Even then, Nadir had known this man was worthy of being a captain. Despite his advisors' complaints, he had offered the role to Raheem in that moment. Not once had he ever regretted his decision.

Nadir sighed and pushed away from the column. "What do they want now?"

"I suspect it has something to do with the raid you ordered."

"How did they find out about that so soon?"

Raheem shrugged a large shoulder. "Did you mention anything to your wife?"

He had forgotten about his wife. Nadir sighed and rubbed

a hand against his shoulder. "I might have mentioned something while in her presence."

"Then that's how they know."

"A conversation between a man and his wife should remain private," he grumbled.

"But she's not just your wife." A bright flash of a grin split the darkness in two. "She's also your most esteemed advisor, and the guardian of Bymere."

Titles and semantics. His entire life was based upon them.

Rolling the tight muscles in his shoulders, Nadir pushed past his most trusted friend and stalked down the halls of the palace. He had words for his wife. Words for his advisors.

Hell, if he could have screamed at the gods themselves he would have. This was supposed to be a quiet night of revelries as he rejoiced in the bloodshed of his most hated enemies. Why couldn't they all let him be?

The flashing of burning torches caused an ache to bloom behind his eyes. Great swaths of gold fabric billowed from the windows as the winds stirred to life. Moonlight chased the air, spearing light across the endless halls and reminding him that no matter how much wealth he had, Nadir was still very much alone.

Every step set fire to the simmering anger in his breast. She had told them all about the raid? She dared to tell others something said in private. In his own bedchamber! Was there no sacred place left?

He pressed a palm against the door to his advisors' hall and shoved so hard it slammed against the wall.

Six people jumped, spinning on their heels to stare at him with wide eyes. They knew to be worried when the sultan grew angry, and in this moment, he was furious.

"You dare to summon me?" he growled, stalking towards the center table. "In the middle of the night, my advisors dare to summon me?"

His wife stepped forward, the golden hoop in her nose gleaming. "Nadir—"

"Sultan," he snarled. "In this room, I am sultan. You overstep your bounds, wife."

The color drained from her cheeks. Perhaps now she understood his anger, his embarrassment. He knew it was his wife who had bandied his secrets so freely.

Nadir wished he could say she had no right, but she did. This was the punishment he must bear for marrying a woman who was also an advisor. For falling slave to the harpy who had seduced a young king and become the most powerful woman in the kingdom.

It was a pity he still loved her.

Another of his advisors stepped forward, an aged man with a trim white beard and a frown. Black linen stretched over his broad shoulders, gold embroidery emphasizing the latent power his age hid. Abdul liked for others to think him aged. Nadir knew better.

If there was anyone in the kingdom who could battle against Raheem and Nadir, Abdul was the only one who could put up a fair fight. He had started countless battles, won them, then brought their severed heads home as trophies.

Nadir always watched his back when Abdul was in the room.

"The raid upon Wildewyn was not something we spoke of, Sultan," Abdul began, his voice calm and serene. "Perhaps, it might have been better to consult with us before wasting our resources."

"Wasting? I was unaware it was a waste when attacking the neighboring kingdom that *murdered my brother*."

Nadir's hands were shaking, the dream too close to the surface, making it difficult to think. Stalking toward the table, he brushed aside Abdul and shifted a small figurine forward on the table, where a map of their world was painted.

He jabbed at the vellum. "This was the last remaining stronghold for Wildewyn. All others already have spies, and now we have an entire force of trained assassins at the ready. At my order, we can take the entire kingdom."

Saafiya cleared her throat. "They're all dead, Sultan."

He chuckled. "The Earthen folk? Of course they are. That was the point, wife."

"No, husband. The assassins you sent to Wildewyn. They're all dead except for one man who returned. He told us a tale before he breathed his last."

"Dead?" Nadir shook his head. "No, that's impossible."

She reached out and stroked a hand down his arm, trying to calm him down. "The survivor spoke of impossible things. We think it likely the Earthen folk poisoned him, like your brother."

His head was reeling. He couldn't hear her words over the ringing in his ears, couldn't see past the haze of red obscuring his vision. "How? How did they die?"

The advisors hesitated a moment before Abdul responded. "The soldier claimed that women wearing the shape of animals ripped them apart."

"Women?" he scoffed.

"He said they were the most beautiful creatures he had ever seen. Like angels falling from the sky and growing talons that ripped out his brethren's eyes. He only returned, because one woman allowed him to." Abdul cleared his throat. "He said she was made of iron, and that she was pale as a ghost."

"Impossible." Nadir shook his head. "Magic no longer exists here. We've destroyed every lingering bit."

"Not all of it." Saafiya pointed to a small corner of the table, indicating a small portion of Bymere they all liked to pretend did not exist. "There are some who still survive."

"I will not speak of them."

"Not even now? If Wildewyn has creatures such as that—"

"Silence." His voice boomed in the Council Room. "I'll hear no more from you."

Abdul trailed his fingers along the edge of the table and made his way towards Nadir. "There is much we can do to prepare, but I fear you have broken any alliance we may have made with Wildewyn."

"Why would we ever want to ally ourselves with the people who killed your king?"

Saafiya reached for him again. "If they have beasts who can turn themselves into creatures of legend, then we must consider that they are a dangerous enemy best held close."

Her perfume clouded his mind. The scent of clementines and apricots reminded him of days when he hadn't worried about bloodshed and violence. They had spent his first few years as sultan wrapped in each other's arms. She knew how to twist him around her beautiful fingers far easier than she should.

Nadir sighed. "How would you propose to do that?"

It was not his wife who responded, but Abdul. "We offer them peace and in return, they give us their greatest treasure."

"What treasure do I not already have?"

"A woman made of iron, who controls their armies of beasts." Abdul picked up a small female piece from the map, pressed his thumb against her head, and snapped it off. "Cut the head off the snake, but save her venom for later."

Something felt wrong about the plan, but he couldn't think straight. Smoke filled the Council Room, cloying and making his mind whirl. Was it the right choice? If his advisors said so, then it had to be. He wouldn't know what to do without their esteemed advice.

Nadir shook his head but relented. "Reach out to the Wildewyn king. See what you can do."

Abdul bowed low. "As you wish, Your Majesty."

His advisors shared a look as they left the Council Room. Perhaps, they thought he wouldn't catch the sly glance, but they never gave him enough credit. Their fault was thinking that Nadir didn't understand they were controlling him. In reality, he just didn't care.

He placed his hands on either side of the table and stared down at the map of his homeland.

Nadir had never wanted to be sultan. This land deserved someone better. It deserved his brother, a man who had devoted his entire education to knowing exactly what Bymere needed to prosper.

Under Nadir's rule, the cities floundered. They feared him rather than loved him. When he tried to bolster their confidence, they ran. When he tried to convince the traders to lower their prices, the kingdom assumed the royal coffers ran low. Repeatedly, he failed as a sultan.

Hakim would not have failed his kingdom.

"Sultan?" Raheem murmured from the shadows. "What plagues your thoughts?"

"Have you heard of these beastly women?" he asked. "Are the rumors true?"

"There is always merit in stories."

"But have you heard of them?"

Raheem hesitated and then spoke the words Nadir needed to hear. "I have heard of them, but they are little more than myth. When I was last in Wildewyn, a trader told me a story. He said he had gone to the castle Greenmire and was asked to bring jewels to secret rooms beneath the castle. He said the king kept the most stunning creatures he'd ever seen locked away as if they were animals. But they seemed happy, and they loved his gifts."

"That doesn't reek of magic to me."

"Women turning into animals? What other explanation is there?"

Nadir did not have an answer for his friend, but his mind grew troubled. He lifted a hand and waved away the captain of his guard.

While the rest of the palace slept, Nadir stared at the map until the lines moved on their own. They formed patterns he couldn't recognize as if someone was reaching out to him from afar.

What would one of these beast women say to him? Would they fear him? Unlikely, for what did a beast have to fear from a man?

And then there was their leader. A woman? Unusual, but not unexpected. Wildewyn was progressive in their practices. He couldn't say it surprised him that their magic came from the fairer sex.

He clenched his hands into fists and pressed his knuckles against the table until the grooved lines remained engraved on his flesh.

Nadir vowed to discover the truth. Perhaps meeting the Sultan of Bymere would strike fear into the heart of this mythical iron woman.

SIGRID

"HAVE YOU HEARD?" CAMILLA ASKED, HER VOICE ECHOING IN THE quiet chamber.

"I've heard many things today."

"Sigrid."

"I'm not a mind reader, Camilla. You must be more specific."

Her sister let out a long-suffering sigh. She had little patience, even in times like these.

Sigrid knelt on a small cushion deep beneath Greenmire castle, her gold dragon mask in her lap. She was already dressed for battle as many of the Beastkin were. A metal corset covered her entire torso, hammered edges blending into the heavy brocade of her midnight gown. Dark beading embellished the lines of her hips and accentuated her hourglass form.

They sat within a spider web of tunnels, each extending into the heart of the earth itself, so deep that all sound ceased to exist. It was here Sigrid found her greatest peace.

At least, until her sister found her.

Before them was a small statue, barely noticeable nestled in the stone wall. The first matriarch had carved a dragon and woman intertwined. They remained here for any who lost their way, in body or mind. Sigrid wasn't certain which one she had lost.

"The councilmen have summoned representatives from Bymere to explain the attack."

Sigrid's fingers curled around the edge of her mask. The metal bit into her fingers with the sharp edge of frustration and anger. "Why?"

"Politics. They wish to stop the war, which we all know won't happen, but that's not the exciting part! You'll never guess *who* is coming with the Bymerian advisors."

"Camilla, I've little patience for this."

"The sultan!"

Sigrid whipped around to stare at her friend, the mask tumbling from her lap to land on the ground with a dull thud.

"What did you say?"

Camilla's dark eyes flashed with excitement, but her expression remained hidden beneath her silver owl mask. "The entire sultanate, including the sultan himself is coming to our doorstep, sister."

"Why would he do that?"

"Perhaps, he truly desires to end this war."

"He started it," Sigrid spat. "He desires the bloodshed, and will stop at nothing to avenge his brother's death."

Camilla's excited expression fell.

Her sister had always hoped that the war would end. She

41

saw beauty and kindness even in the darkest times. And while Sigrid admired that trait, she also knew how damaging it could be. There was no light in war.

"No one proved him wrong," Camilla murmured. "The poison that killed his brother was derived from a plant native to Wildewyn."

"Don't you think someone would have come forward by now? They would be a legend in Wildewyn. The hero who tried to end the villainous line of Bymerian kings. Why wouldn't they tell any of us what they had done?" She shook her head. "The assassin wasn't from Wildewyn."

"You think it was his own people?"

"I think it might have been one of ours who now lives there. It might be someone close to him or his brother. It could be anyone, but it wasn't one of the Earthen folk. They wouldn't have taken such a grave risk."

Wildewyn was not known for adventurous people. They liked to stay in their routines. Rise in the morning, tend the fields and flock, then return home to their safe beds where they could relax. They were predictable folk who enjoyed being predictable.

They were not murderous by nature. She had yet to meet any Earthen folk who would not have been wracked by guilt and then come forward.

The Beastkin were another story. Her own people could murder without guilt as their animals took over in times of blood and anger. But she would know if one of her sisters had killed the king. They shared even their deepest thoughts with Sigrid.

Camilla waved a hand in front of Sigrid's face. "Enough

contemplating. Let's go and see the sultan!"

"When is he arriving?"

"Right *now*. That's why I'm here. I thought you wouldn't want to miss the spectacle of the century. Do you think he'll ride in on an elephant?"

"I don't think they could get an elephant through the mountains."

"It's happened before." Camilla grasped Sigrid's elbow and tugged her to standing. "They rode elephants in the first war between Wildewyn and Bymere."

"How do you know that?"

"The murals depict giant beasts with tusks larger than a man. I would very much like to see them in my lifetime."

So would Sigrid. Though she was uncomfortable in the presence of humans, she found the company of beasts much easier. She would like to meet the animals that made even the strongest of men tremble.

She was jealous of them in a way. They were free to be who they were, without question. She hid behind a mask for most of her life, because the Council refused to allow her freedom where others might see.

What would people think if they saw a dragon in the flesh? They would run, then riot, then hide their families, and the entire kingdom would fall into ruin. Sigrid must keep her true nature hidden, but threaten the possibilities with her mask. They would only allow her freedom if the war became so dangerous that they must beg the dragon to save them.

A small part of her soul hungered for war, if only for a few moments of freedom.

Sigrid stooped, lifted her mask, and fastened it back to her face. Heat burned in the back of her eyes as the dragon rebelled for a moment before the cold metal pressed against her skin.

With the weight of her self-imposed prison settling on her shoulders, she followed her sister out of the winding tunnels. They slid along the intricately carved white marble walls of Greenmire Castle, and up into one of the towers that always made her dizzy.

"Quickly!" Camilla called out. "If you don't hurry, we will miss him."

"We won't miss him," she grumbled. "They'll drag us in front of him like prized pets."

She despised the ritual but knew the Council would insist upon it. Sigrid would stand in front of important figures, allowing them to look her and talk as if she wasn't in the room. Then one of her sisters would transform.

Dignitaries wanted to see something pretty. A peacock, a sparrow, a lithe cat who twined between their legs. They didn't want to be frightened. They wanted a show.

Sigrid reached the top of the tower and let the wind shove at her back. She tilted her head, enjoying the cold bite of Wildewyn wind.

"Look," Camilla pointed off into the distance. "See, I told you he was coming."

Sigrid narrowed her gaze and frowned. He didn't ride an elephant as her sister had so desired to see, but still, it was hard to miss him.

He rode ahead of his army, a vibrant spot of scarlet against the waving green tops of trees. His horse was a brilliant white and nearly blinded her as the sun peeked out from behind the clouds to illuminate his journey. Arrogance played across his shoulders, both broad and too straight.

He was posturing, she realized. Like a male peacock trying to impress a mate, he had puffed his entire body out until he looked ridiculous.

What looked to be the entire kingdom trailed after him. Countless armored men, horses, and square boxes carried by slaves. Were there people inside those flimsy things?

She arched a brow. "Well, that's not a sight you see every day."

"Isn't it beautiful?" Camilla sighed.

Beautiful wasn't the word that Sigrid would use. Ostentatious, ridiculous, garish were just a few of the words she would choose to describe the train of Bymerians. They obviously wanted the Earthen folk to not only see them arrive but also understand that they considered themselves to be wealthier and far more beautiful.

Sigrid turned her gaze towards the forest instead. Emerald green leaves waved in a delicate breeze. Small rivers wound down from the mountains peaked with snow. Everything here was vibrant and still. It didn't need gems or loud noises to make it beautiful. Instead, Wildewyn was how she was born to be. And she was lovelier for it.

"What do you think the Council members will say to him?" Camilla asked. "They must have some kind of expectation for such an unexpected visit."

They would argue with him, most likely. Sigrid had seen them turn red in the face shouting at each other and fixing nothing. She wondered what would happen when two walls met each other, shouting until the other fell.

She arched a brow. "Why don't we watch?"

Camilla spun on her heel, the long tail of her braid whipping around her. "What secrets have you been hiding?"

"Not hiding," Sigrid twitched her skirts and turned back down the tight stairwell. "It's common knowledge if you look at the building plans of the castle."

"Which are hidden in the depths of the library."

"But not locked away."

The billowing edge of her gown made it difficult to see the steps, but she had traversed these stairs many times. Sigrid could wander the castle with her eyes closed and she would still end up where she intended to go.

They casually strode past guards, nodding to the armored men who waited for the sultanate to step foot into their home.

Smoke fell from the ceiling where sconces had been lit, fragrance billowing down along with the white wisps. They had already filled the entire castle with sandalwood and lemongrass. She hoped the sweet scent was too cloying for the sultan and his men. Headaches would be the least of the curses she would like to fling upon them.

"Here," she murmured, pausing in front of a tapestry.

Footsteps echoed down the corridor, and Sigrid gave her sister a look. They knew how to hide their mischief from the guards. Camilla dropped to a knee, reaching forward and smoothing a hand down Sigrid's skirt. "You should take better care of this, my lady. The fabric was a gift from the high councilman."

"Quickly then, I'm feeling faint and would like to return to my room."

The guard coughed, hiding his smile behind a hand as he passed them. Let him think they were weak. It was better for them all if the Earthen folk underestimated the beasts they had captured.

Sigrid waited until he rounded a corner before she brushed aside the tapestry. Camilla shoved her shoulder against the stone and the hidden door gave way without a sound. They rushed into the space between the walls, closing the door behind them and sealing themselves in darkness.

"The Earthen folk use this?" Camilla asked. "How could they see at all?"

"Torches, Camilla."

"It would be fairly obvious if someone is walking around the castle with a torch in the middle of the day."

Sigrid's lips twitched into a smile behind her mask. "Then it's a good thing we can see in the dark."

She watched as Camilla's gaze glowed green. A small sliver of light reflected from a hole in the wall, and her eyes turned molten before they moved on. Quietly, they made their way through the hidden tunnels of the castle until they could peer through the slats of an embellished partition inside the Councilman's private chamber.

The sultan had not yet arrived with his entourage, but the Wildewyn council was there. They sat in a small circle, pouring over parchment paper laid out on the white marble table. Clean and effortlessly beautiful, the room had an open ceiling with green vines dangling into the room. Someone had swept fallen leaves into the corner, but she could still hear their feet crunching on a few that had blown towards the center.

"Jacques, I'll remind you again. This could lead to our ruin," one of the Council members said. "Once we make this decision, we cannot control what he will do."

"It is an act of peace," Jacques growled. "We must make sacrifices, and we cannot lose any more of our people to this tyrant's whims."

Hallmar, the King of Wildewyn, placed a stone on the corner of the map and sighed. "There will be no more arguments. I've made my decision."

"Highness, I implore you —"

"Enough." Exhaustion laced his words with defeat. "We have no other choice. He has too many spies in our lands, and this is our only option. If it doesn't work, if *she* does not do her duty, then we will consider our other options."

"And if he uses her to his advantage? We cannot defeat her if it comes to war."

Sigrid's spine stiffened.

"Sigrid would never fight against us. While she may be dangerous, she is also loyal. Wildewyn is her home. She would never betray us."

"Are you certain of that? No one can predict the actions of an animal."

When Hallmar did not respond, Sigrid let out a soft sigh. She should have known they wouldn't trust her. They didn't understand her, so how could they consider what she might think?

A warm hand surrounded hers, strong, familiar, and beloved. Camilla squeezed and interlocked their fingers. For all that the Earthen folk would never understand Beastkin, they would remain each other's strongest supporters.

The door banged open and the entire sultanate poured into the Council Room. She couldn't make out individuals in the flurry of color filling the room. Fabric twirled, hair intertwined with dark silk, and Sigrid's mind whirled. It was too overwhelming for her to pick out individuals.

Except him.

The sultan stood in the center of the madness, calm as the eye of a storm. He strode towards Hallmar and did not stop until they stood face to face.

"High King," the sultan began.

Sigrid shivered at the sound of his voice. It was powerful and deep. He was young, far younger than she thought he would be and though his face was free of lines, he might have appeared older if he'd somehow hidden his face.

"Your Majesty." The entire council bowed as Hallmar replied, "We welcome you to our city."

"Not much of a welcome. I see few of your people in the streets. Have you lost them?"

The sultanate chuckled behind their leader, and Sigrid saw red. He thought it wise to enter another kingdom and then mock the king? What kind of madman was this?

Hallmar, to his credit, laughed with the others. "No, Your Majesty. It's likely they are preparing for the feast tonight. But we have much to discuss beforehand."

"Ah, yes. Your treaty." The sultan shook his head. "I have little interest in this. What could you possibly offer *me*?"

"Peace."

"I don't need peace, Earthen king. I already have you under my thumb. All I have to do is press down."

"I believe you've heard of the creatures we keep under lock and key?" Hallmar continued as if the sultan had not spoken. "Perhaps, your man claimed they were animals wearing the skins of women?"

"Myths and legends."

"Truth, and I am willing to offer you our most precious Beastkin woman. She is unlike any of the others. A rare treasure."

The sultan scoffed and held his hand out to the side. One of his people rushed forward and placed a small knife in the center of his palm. He used the blade to clean underneath his nails. The very picture of calm.

"On the off chance I even believe you, what kind of creature would this woman be? A lioness?" Again, his entourage laughed. "I'll place her in the cages with all my other beautiful animals. I have no desire for more pretty things. I have plenty."

"Our own people don't know what her true nature is. We have hidden her for years, and now I willingly offer her to you." Hallmar paused dramatically. "She is a dragon."

Sigrid flinched. A part of her had hoped he would come to his senses, or choose one of her other sisters. It was a cruel thought. She had never desired to hurt another of her sister's before, and certainly this was a fate worse than death.

But they were speaking of her. Wildewyn offered their most powerful asset to their enemy, freely and without stipulation. They offered her to the man who had ordered the death of her intended husband and countless others.

Her icy eyes caught on the sultan's shoulders which had stiffened. His eyes narrowed on the king. "A dragon? Even when the Beastkin roamed these lands, there was no such thing as a dragon shifter."

"She is the last of her kind, and infinitely precious."

"Show me."

His eyes were yellow, she realized, and ringed with kohl. Tiger's eye agates set in a face burnished from the sun. He was handsome, in an aggressive way, but she could never see him as anything other than a tyrant who laid waste to all that was beautiful.

Hallmar coughed. "Show you? It's obvious why we cannot do such a thing, she—"

"Show me," the sultan repeated, his words stronger as his voice whipping across the room. "I know well how the Earthen folk lie, and I will see this Beastkin before I decide to have her at my side."

"There are stipulations."

"You misunderstand me." The sultan stepped forward until he was toe to toe with Hallmar, neither man backing down. "I have my sword at your throat, belly, and groin, Earthen King. You may test me if you wish, but I can destroy you with a wave of my hand."

"And *she* can destroy you. I will not give you our greatest weapon without a few assurances."

A prestigious looking man with silver hair stepped forward and placed his hand on the sultan's arm. "Your Majesty, perhaps we could convene without the Wildewyn council. This is a matter of great importance to all of Bymere. Your advisors have much to say."

She watched the sultan let himself be pulled away and wondered at the boy king who couldn't make his own decisions. Did he rely on his advisors for everything? This wasn't a monarchy; this was puppetry.

Hallmar seemed to come to the same conclusion as Sigrid. She recognized the calculating expression on his face as he watched the sultanate envelope their leader. They poured from the room like water from a tipped vase, even their steps echoing at the same time until Hallmar called out, "Sultan!"

One man in the rush of bodies slowed.

"There will always be a time when a sultan, king, or emperor needs to decide without the advice of others. A king chooses. A slave waits for orders."

Sigrid felt the power coursing through the king's words. They echoed through the room until it vibrated with the audacity that a royal would so blatantly observe that the boy king was not a king at all.

Slowly, Camilla pulled her hand away from Sigrid and reached for the edges of her mask. Sigrid quickly followed, wondering what would happen if she transformed within the walls. The dragon could shatter stone, even rend this building to the ground if it wished. But was that what she wanted? Was now the time to reveal her true nature?

The sultan looked over his shoulder, yellow eyes surveying the Earthen king. "What are your requests?"

"Marry her. Make her your queen and unite the kingdoms."

"I have a wife."

"Your people have never remained monogamous. A second wife is still a queen. Make her a royal to your people, shelter her, give her a good life, and consider the kingdoms united in every way."

The sultan's brow lifted. "You're asking much for a country with few options. I could start the war right now and end it all."

"We both know that's a bluff. With a dragon in our army, there is little your men could do. Or have you forgotten the assassination attempt you recently tried? Those were our Beastkin warriors, and there are more than just the few in that crowd. Take the offer and save many from certain death."

"Sultan," the silver haired man called again. "Let us speak."

Sigrid saw the exact moment the young sultan decided. His shoulders straightened, his yellow gaze heated to orange embers, and he nodded. "It is done. Write up your documents, Earthen king. I'll marry your dragon woman, but I will meet her tonight."

"You'll *marry* her tonight."

"So be it."

They swept from the room, the entire sultanate filtered out of the Council Room as if they hadn't just decided her future. The last bright color disappeared out of the pristine white room like the last drop of blood draining from a wound.

Silence reigned in the Council Room. Sigrid held her breath in fear they would hear her ragged gasps.

"Gods forgive us," Hallmar said. "We have sacrificed our greatest treasure to a child."

"You take a grievous risk."

"I believe there must be a man underneath that childlike demeanor." He pressed his fist against the table, staring down at the map. "Bring me the girl."

"Is that wise? Perhaps we should tell her outside the castle."

"Sigrid has always remained poised no matter what we have thrown at her. I would like to tell her in person."

"What will you tell her?"

She watched the king with rapt attention, her eyes locked

on his form. Hallmar's head lifted, and he stared directly at her through the slats in the wall.

"She will be our greatest weapon in this war. And make no mistake, we are at war with Bymere."

Sigrid had been a sword hanging in a closet for so many years that the thought of active warfare made her shiver.

Did he want her to kill the sultan, or worse?

NADIR

"WHAT DO YOU THINK YOU'RE DOING?" ABDUL HISSED, HIS footsteps echoing in the cold stone halls. "That was a decision we should have made together. They could plant a spy in our home. They *are* planting a spy. Why else would they offer her up so easily? Do you ever think at all?"

Nadir let the words wash over him. His advisors could shout as much as they wanted, but his gut knew this was the right decision.

The King's words unsettled him. A slave waits for advice? When had he ever faltered before deciding?

Besides, this was the better deal. A war would affect them all, and though Nadir had no intention of retracting his spies or failing to replace Wildewyn's head officials with those he trusted, now he also had their most powerful weapon in his own home.

"Are you listening, boy?"

Nadir whirled, hand on his hip where a jeweled blade

rested. "Are you questioning my decision, advisor?"

"Absolutely."

"And who gave you the right to question your sultan? Royal blood runs in my veins. Tell me again, Abdul, from where do you hail?"

The entirety of his entourage hesitated, glancing at each other in unease. His blood heated, his vision blurred, and all he could focus on was that Abdul was trying to control him. Coerce him. Again.

When his advisor did not respond, Nadir growled, "From where do you hail?"

"Misthall."

"Where in Misthall?"

"The plains of Whitehaven."

"And what do they do in Whitehaven?"

A muscle in Abdul's jaw ticked. "They are farmers, Your Majesty."

"Remember that." Nadir could feel the tentative hold on his temper slipping. "Remember that you came from nothing, and that it was my family who gave you every shred of power you hold. I can take it away just as easily as they gifted it."

He thought for a moment that Abdul might strike him. Nadir almost wished he would. This advisor had walked a fine line since the beginning. All he needed was a reason to have him killed, and he would relish the moment Abdul's head struck the ground.

A gentle hand settled on his forearm, stretched forward from layers of silken fabric. "Husband. Shall we retire for the night?"

Saafiya, with her endless well of patience. She always knew how to calm him, but he didn't want to let go of his anger. Not this time. There was something to prove here although he knew not what.

She smoothed her hand down his arm again, and he swallowed. It wouldn't hurt to go with her. He could relax, lose himself in her body, think about what he had agreed to do. And if she had other ideas, then he would listen. They were older, had all been advisors of his kingdom for a very long time, and knew more than he did.

She would know what to do.

"Your Majesty?"

He glanced down the hall towards the tall guard dressed in silver armor. "What is it?"

"King Hallmar has requested you join him in the great hall where he will introduce you to your new bride. The Beastkin have prepared themselves for your arrival."

Saafiya's hand clenched hard around his forearm.

So, his wife was jealous of the new addition to their home. Nadir forced himself not to roll his eyes. Saafiya cared little for him. There was no question about that. Her position as sole sultana of their people would now change, and that was the only reason she bristled.

She had his ear, and she knew that. He wouldn't be surprised if another woman walking into their life and disrupting such control made her skin crawl.

It should. He fully intended to spend too much time pulling apart this little "dragon" and seeing what she could do. If the Earthen King was telling the truth, then there was much he had to learn.

He reached down and peeled Saafiya's hand from his forearm.

"I hadn't expected your king to react so quickly to my request," he replied to the guard.

"The Beastkin are always at the king's beck and call. If you wish to see them, then they will come."

"I like the sound of that. Lead on."

He ignored the grumbles of his retinue. The journey from Bymere to Wildewyn was long and tiresome. Their backs ached, and they wished to rest in whatever luxuries the Wildewyn city could offer them.

Nadir understood their complaints. He felt the same way, but there were things a sultan must do before he found his bed.

He led his people through the halls, following the guard with a wary gaze. This castle was unlike anything he had ever seen before. The corridors were filled with splendor, yet felt as though they had been abandoned with leaves fluttering in through the windows and twigs littering the floor.

Perfectly polished, white, marble floors shone underneath his feet and reflected their movements when he could see beneath the debris. Every inch of the walls depicted carved images of hunting scenes. They covered the entrance hall with images of the forest.

Nadir wondered if every hall in this castle was so opulently decorated. An infinite amount of time and energy had gone into carving every inch of this cold castle, and yet still leaves blew over his feet, whisked by a wind that never ceased. Tree branches poked through the thin slats of windows. Birds sang in the rafters and took flight as they moved past.

Not a single citizen walked past them. It appeared that only ghosts inhabited the strange city. A shiver trailed down his spine at the thought. If they had captured shifters, what otherworldly creatures did the king also keep?

The guard paused, extended an arm, and gestured towards an open doorway. "The king awaits, Your Majesty."

"Kind of him," Nadir grumbled.

Perhaps he was needlessly rude to these people, but every pale face he saw made him wonder if *they* were the ones who had killed his brother. He wanted to shake every person and ask if they knew the art of poison.

If they had ever killed a king.

A checkered pattern of gold and silver embellished the floor of the great hall. White walls carved with beautiful women stretched up to meet a glass chandelier that sent rainbows skittering across the room as torchlight struck it.

Every detail was meticulously groomed, and yet completely unfeeling. Even the carved women lacked expression.

The king sat on his gold throne, navy blue fabric draped over the poured metal. He sat straight as a board, staring at Nadir and his people as if he might draw his sword any second.

Good. The feeling was mutual.

Nadir understood they were out of place here. All these people with their pale faces, their heavy brocade clothing, their ice-colored eyes, paled in comparison to the vibrant colors of his homeland. It had only been a few weeks, and already he desired the splash of orange and pink, the crimson stones, and the rainbow of colors on everything the eye could see.

Here, they valued winter tones. They were made of iron and ice, and he wanted nothing to do with them.

"You left before I could invite you to meet my Beastkin," the king said, a small smile carving grooves into his cheeks. "Please, seat yourself next to me, Sultan of Bymere."

His advisors murmured behind him, but Nadir enjoyed the small bit of freedom. They would yell at him until they turned red in the face when he returned. But they would not embarrass their country by arguing in front of everyone else.

He strode confidently forward, his boots striking the marble floor, and made his way to the throne they had placed next to the Earthen king. He sank down and slapped the silver arm.

"Not quite as opulent as yours, King."

"You're in my country, it is only fitting I keep my throne."

A small voice in Nadir's head whispered to ask them to switch. Just to see. Would the king abdicate his own throne just to make the Bymerians happy?

The king arched a brow and then gestured towards the door. "The Beastkin, as requested."

He would have to wait then, Nadir mused. Perhaps later when he grew bored with whatever spectacles the king would show him.

A line of women entered the room, graceful and poised with every movement. They all wore silver masks on their faces. Some were birds; others were cats. A few even showed fish and lizards. And though the masks were lovely, their forms captivated Nadir.

They were dressed in icy colors. All the fabric was a shade of blue, some sky colored, others the deep midnight of ocean depths. Metal armor and chain links embellished their clothing as if they were walking into battle.

He'd never felt both intrigued and afraid before.

Each woman approached the thrones, dipped into a curtsy, and murmured, "Your Highness. Your Majesty," then moved on.

His eyes widened with each beauty that paused before him. The king kept a harem like this locked up? Nadir would too if he had endless access to women such as this.

"Why masks?" he asked, distracted by yet another lovely, silken-skinned beauty. "If their faces are anything like their forms, then these are rare gems."

"The masks contain the beasts. We don't want to surprise them and end up with an angry lioness in the castle." The king chuckled. "And it is their way. You'll discover soon enough, the Beastkin are not Earthen folk. They have their own rituals, their own expectations, that we must all follow to keep them in our lives."

"The one you give me will bend to Bymerian ways."

"She won't." The king let out a full belly laugh. "You're thoroughly underestimating our women. But you'll find out soon enough."

Nadir pointed at all the women lined up in rows on either side of the hall. "And which one is she?"

The king nodded towards the opening to the great hall. "*That* is our most prized Beastkin."

Nadir turned and his stomach tightened. The woman walking towards him, bracketed by two lines of masked creatures, was the most exquisite being he'd ever seen.

Nearly white blonde hair twisted back from her gold

dragon mask, the mass of curls creating a ridge down the center of her head entwined with gold filigree. The mask itself was golden. Accusing, icy eyes glared at him from deep inside the shadows.

Icy feathers fell from her shoulders in a cape that trailed behind her. They ended just below her chest, revealing a corset made of the finest spun silver. It accentuated her tiny waist and hourglass figure. Tiny chains hung from the end, swinging with her movement and blending with her azure silk skirt until it seemed opal droplets hung suspended around her.

She moved with a natural grace that was both intimidating and calming. Every inch of her wasn't human. She was barely feminine. Rather, she was an imposing figure of power and grace.

The king tapped a finger against his throne. "Close your mouth, Sultan. She'll only see that as a weakness to exploit."

If admiring her beauty was a weakness, then that explained why his knees shook.

Nadir placed his hands on the arms of the throne, pushing himself up slightly as if he would run towards her. But he didn't need to move. She made her way down the aisle and paused just before him.

Her gaze met his, and he felt the chilling throb of her anger.

"Your Majesty," she murmured. Her voice was quiet, simple, light as air. "It's an honor to meet you."

His tongue stuck to the roof of his mouth, but he managed to grit out, "The rumors of your beauty are far understated."

She ducked her head demurely, and he thought for a moment he knew what love felt like. She was *perfect*.

Abdul stepped forward, cheeks red. "Your Majesty, this

woman could be anyone wearing a mask. We need proof she is what her king says."

"You accuse me of lying?" The king growled.

"He has a point," Nadir corrected the other man. He waved a hand to the Beastkin woman. "She could be anyone and we would never know until we returned with her. An assurance is little to ask."

"We must build this relationship on trust."

He raised his voice, "And trust is earned."

This king took liberties that few would ever dare take with him. Just how far did he think he could push? Nadir had ignored the slights thus far, but he would not take a woman home with him if they promised a dragon.

He locked gazes with the king until Hallmar sighed.

The king lifted a bejeweled hand and waved at the woman. "Show him."

"Highness," she quietly replied, "it's improper to show any who are not our husband or family."

"I'm asking you to make an exception."

"We will need to speak amongst ourselves."

"All I can request is that you be quick."

The woman bowed, then retreated into the mass of her sisters who circled her until Nadir could no longer glimpse her shimmering gown.

"You give them too much power," he scoffed. "They should bow to your whims."

"You will soon find out that ordering a Beastkin is like punching a mountain. You can scream and shout as much as you want, but they are not human and they will not be treated as such. Beastkin are not our subjects. They are a kingdom within a kingdom wherever they go."

Nadir saw his advisors shifting. They were uncomfortable with this development, and he shared their concern. If the king ordered a subject in Bymere to perform, they would rush to please. Why did these women have rights that others did not?

The circle parted. Like a clam revealing a pearl, his new bride stepped forward in a single fluid movement. She inclined her head, bowing to the Wildewyn king until her forehead nearly touched the floor.

"If our king wishes proof, then we will ignore the Bymerian insult."

"Insult?" Nadir repeated, stunned. "You dare accuse me of such?"

"To question the truthfulness of an entire species without reason is an insult, Your Majesty. While there may be different rules in your kingdom, I will remind you now. You are in Wildewyn." Her gaze lifted, and again her icy gaze sent shards of bitter cold into his chest. "And you are in the presence of a dragon."

Something heated deep in his belly at the challenge. Any woman who would challenge him was a rarity, let alone one who stared at him like a warrior on a battlefield.

"I have never feared another being in my life," he replied. "I'm the Sultan of Bymere, with armies I could unleash by a snap of my fingers."

"If assassins are your protectors, then I will train them myself when I arrive in Bymere. They were far too easy to kill."

Again, she rendered him speechless. This frigid woman had killed his assassins? Why had she been outside the castle where farmers laid themselves to rest?

His brows furrowed as she stepped away. The wave of masked women parted to reveal a single, dark Beastkin standing at the end. She held a small chest in her hands, its wood scratched and marked from years of use.

He watched, fascinated, as his new bride reached into the chest and pulled out another mask. This one would only cover the top half of her face. He held his breath as she lifted her hands to remove the one affixed to her face.

The women shifted, surrounding their companion, and no one in the room could see her change masks.

Nadir drummed his fingers on the throne. Just how long would this take? She was only changing a mask, which seemed to be entirely unnecessary. All he wanted was proof.

His line of sight shifted, and again his new bride stepped forward. This mask lacked the solid form of the other. Instead, her face was exposed from the nose down. It still mimicked the face of a dragon, scales climbing up her forehead and disappearing into her hairline.

How many of these masks did she have?

She nodded towards her king. "If it pleases you."

"Watch the ceiling," Hallmar murmured quietly to Nadir.

Nadir didn't have time to contemplate how strange a request that was before the woman lifted a hand to her mouth. A deep rumbling sound echoed from within her chest. It was strange, like the echoing call of a beast to its mate. The guttural sound continued until the woman opened her mouth and a fountain of flame poured from her lips.

Fire lifted into the air, dancing and twirling. It tangled in the chandelier which turned red hot, only cooling when the woman lost her breath.

Silence stung his ears. She bowed her head, laced her fingers in front of her, and waited for someone to say something.

It was the right posture, the correct thing for a woman to do after a performance, but she had just blown fire in front of them. That wasn't a performance. It was magic.

Abdul cleared his throat, voice wavering in the silence. "I've seen such parlor tricks before."

"I've seen a magician blow fire with alcohol in his mouth," Nadir responded. "But, I've never seen them create flame from nothing."

"She may have something in her hand."

"You think this is sleight of hand?" He scoffed. "I find that hard to believe."

Abdul shifted but finally shook his head. "I can't explain what just happened, Your Majesty."

"Neither can I," Nadir responded. He ran a hand down his chin, surveying the woman with a calculating gaze. "How do you explain it?"

"Beastkin women are born with two sides. I am both woman and dragon, the last of my kind."

"So, you don't claim it's magic?"

"I don't believe in magic. I believe in gifts from our goddess. I believe in the natural circumstances of our world, and I appreciate that my sisters and I are hard to understand. But it is not magic." She lifted her head and met his gaze boldly.

It was a challenge he would not turn down.

Nadir pushed himself from the throne and meandered

towards her, his steps slow and calculated. To some, it might seem as though he was giving her a chance to back away. But he wasn't, and recognition bloomed in her eyes. He was letting her measure him as a warrior might their opponent.

Let her get used to him. She wouldn't back away with all that pride glowing in her eyes, and he wouldn't want her to. She would be the first woman to fight him every step of the way.

The mere thought was thrilling. His heart pounded, his lungs heaved for breath, but he hoped he looked calm when he stopped in front of her.

Nadir lifted a hand and placed his thumb against her chin. Tilting her head to the side, he soaked in the hatred burning in her gaze.

"What is your name?" he asked.

"Sigrid."

"A good name," he mused. "Although not the one I would have chosen for you."

"Then I am grateful it was my mother's choice to name me."

"You don't trust my naming?"

"I don't trust you at all."

Her forwardness impressed him although it also grated on his nerves. He set his jaw and said through clenched teeth, "Why's that?"

"I find it hard to trust the man who ordered the murder of my husband."

"You don't seem like a grieving wife."

She swallowed. "My intended is dead. Your attack happened during my wedding vows."

"Were you married to him?"

"I would have been if your assassins hadn't killed him while he was pledging himself to me."

"Small miracles," he murmured. A twinge made his chest ache, but he refused to rub it in front of her. She didn't need to know how much it affected him, and it made him angry that he was so weak. Nadir leaned forward and pressed his lips against her mask, near her ear, and whispered, "Then we are even, dragon woman. Your people took my brother. I took your husband."

She didn't respond, but he could feel her shoulders tense and saw her hands clench. He had gotten through that icy shroud she wore. Small accomplishments. He intended to win many more of their battles.

Straightening, he cast a severe look over to his advisors. "Did that satisfy your curiosity?"

Saafiya was the only one who didn't nod. Instead, she stared at the other woman with black rage. He would deal with his first wife later. Until then...

Nadir nudged Sigrid's face towards him again. "I take it there are rituals to marry you? It seems your people like them."

A muscle in her jaw jumped against his thumb. "There will be no rituals. Not for you."

The dark woman behind her flinched. It was a barely noticeable movement, but he saw it for what it was.

He frowned. "I don't take kindly to insult."

"Neither do I."

She was feisty, he would give her that. Nadir glanced over his shoulder at Abdul. "Write up a marriage contract. We'll do this the Bymerian way."

His advisor frowned but nodded. Nadir returned his gaze to Sigrid, feeling as though he had won a battle. The fire in her gaze ignited a spark inside him, one he had thought long since diminished. "Ready yourself, wife."

"As you wish."

"Husband," he corrected. "It's appropriate to call me by my title."

"Husband," she growled through her teeth.

SIGRID

SIGRID FOUND HERSELF RUSHED INTO THE BEASTKIN'S PRIVATE
quarters. Her sisters pushed and shoved, their movements
frantic and their breaths puffing out in horrified gasps.

She knew how they felt. The arrogant, childish man whom
she was now engaged was less than ideal. He would be difficult
for the rest of her days, insulting her at every turn. He would
make her future a nightmare.

Camilla's reaction to Sigrid's crass declaration reminded
her just how far she'd fallen. Sigrid refused to go through the
Beastkin rituals of marriage. Not for that man.

Every gold line drawn in ceremony would be a shackle
around her wrists. The traditional marriage bound a husband
and wife to live out the rest of their days, willingly, with each
other. She could not perform such rituals when she knew she
would hate this husband of hers with every breath in her body.

Once the door shut behind them, a chorus of voices
chimed.

"You cannot marry him."

"We will *not* lose you to that fool of a man."

"He doesn't respect us, or even seem interested in learning our ways."

"*Never*, Sigrid. We will not suffer the embarrassment."

Camilla stayed at the edges of the crowd and watched her with dark eyes. They were more sisters than the others. So close, their souls intertwined. Sigrid knew what she was thinking.

"No," Sigrid said, shaking her head. "It's not my wish either, but it's what our king has commanded."

Brynhild stepped forward, the oldest of their sisterhood and a bear in her true form. "We will fight. We've been waiting for the right moment, and I'll not see you leave these walls. It's long pastime we rebelled against these fools."

"We will not fight."

"It is time, matriarch."

"I won't see bloodshed because I'm sent from your side." Sigrid reached out and placed her hands on Brynhild's. "It's too soon. Our emotions are too raw."

Camilla spoke up, her hands hidden in the folds of her dress. "There is always another choice."

Sigrid eyed where her sister's hands were, and her gaze narrowed. "I will not seek silence to escape from any man."

"It's not to escape from him. They're placing you in the most dangerous man's grasp, knowing he could use you against us."

She curled her hands into fists. "You think I am so easily controlled?"

"I think you're dangerous."

"Have I ever shifted because our king ordered it? Have I

ever given you the impression that if a war started, I would kill indiscriminately because another person told me to? How dare you think I am so easily convinced to murder just because they have traded me to yet another man?"

"You wouldn't be the first," Camilla replied.

She couldn't expect her sister to feel remorse in suggesting suicide, but she was still insulted. Sigrid prided herself on her abilities to make decisions based on her own morals. No man or woman would ever sway her when she knew something was right or wrong.

And yet, those yellow eyes haunted her.

Camilla pulled a thin blade from her side and held it out for Sigrid to take. "None of us would blame you, my dearest Sigrid. If this is where the drakon line ends, then I will be proud to have known you."

She wrapped her fingers around the blade, feeling the sharp edge cut into her fingers, but didn't take it from Camilla's hand. "This is not my path. Not yet."

Her sisters worried, and they had a right to. None of them knew what this boy king wanted. If anything. But she refused to show fear.

The Beastkin line had always been one of honorable women. They were known for their kindness, grace, and piety. She would not allow that to die with her.

Sigrid blew out a breath. "With great sadness, I must say goodbye to you all. I will miss you greatly, but know I will always think of you. My sisters. My family."

"You won't go alone." Camilla placed the knife back in the folds of her dress. "It would be an honor to accompany you to this strange world."

"Your loyalty may lead you to your death."

"It's mine to give as I wish. And I refuse to send you alone."

Her heart swelled until she thought it would burst from her chest. Slowly, Sigrid lifted her hands and removed her mask. Face bare for the last time in a very long time, she faced her sisters so they could see every emotion play through her eyes and across her face.

"Take care of each other," she said. "Camilla, see if you can pack my things while I say goodbye."

SIGRID STOOD OUTSIDE THE CASTLE WALLS FOR THE THIRD TIME in her life. The first time she had been a child, staring up at the cold white marble, wondering why her mother had brought her here. The second time was to marry a man who ended up dead, his blood warming her skin through the silken fabric of her wedding gown.

Now, she left with the man who had started it all. His war was the reason Beastkin moved from outside the city to inside its walls. His orders were the reason her intended husband was dead. And now, he had ordered her to return home with him.

Everything seemed to happen in circles. She always ended up back with the Bymerians who had started all this. It was strange how life could do that to a person.

Camilla reached out and placed a hand on her shoulder. "It's time to go."

"I know," she nodded. "I just wanted one last look."

"Will you miss it?"

Sigrid contemplated the castle, then shook her head. "No."

She was trading one cage for another. Why would she miss it?

The Bymerians waited for them. Some guards stood at attention, their hands lingering on bejeweled blades, crimson armor molded to their forms. Leather armor still escaped her understanding. Metal would be far more protective, and yet they insisted on something they could dye the color of their king.

Both Sigrid and Camilla wore Beastkin armor. The metallic corsets were uncomfortable to travel in, but they set a standard.

The nearest box opened. Small holes in the door allowed air into the confined space. A delicate hand reached out, henna dyed patterns waving in the air.

"Come, you are to travel with me."

Sigrid walked towards the voice. A woman was within the confines, her face bare and bells jangling at her ankles and wrists. There would be time for her to understand this female's purpose. But not now.

She shook her head. "Beastkin do not travel in cages. We will ride or walk."

Thundering hooves raced towards them. She looked up into the angry gaze of her new husband.

"You will ride with Saafiya," he growled.

"I will not."

He seemed taken aback. "I gave you an order, wife."

She hated how he used that term to try to control her. She lifted her head, the sun fracturing off her mask and reflecting its brightness into her husband's eyes. "I will walk, if I must."

His upper lip twitched. "Then you will walk."

He cruelly twisted the reins in his hands, forcing his horse to turn away. She winced at the mistreatment and was grateful he couldn't see her expression.

Camilla sighed. "That was foolish."

"He needs to understand that I will not break."

"Now we have to walk."

"You may fly, my dear friend." She reached out a hand and smiled. "Or ride on my shoulder if you wish. I'm perfectly happy to traverse these lands one last time."

Her sister arched a brow. "You wanted to walk, didn't you?"

Sigrid didn't respond.

Camilla shook her head, but left with a grin on her face to shift in privacy. Of anyone, she understood Sigrid's desire to be close to the land. She followed the tunnels deep inside the earth just to be close to the heartbeat she always heard. She would say her goodbyes to Wildewyn, one last time.

New footsteps approached, and it took every inch of Sigrid's patience not to lose her temper. She folded her hands at her waist. "I won't ride in the tiny box with that woman. Please, save your breath."

A chuckle boomed, so deep it sounded like thunder. "Then it's a good thing I'm not here to argue with you."

She turned and stared at a mammoth of a man. His dark skin glistened in the sunlight, shaved head tattooed with unfamiliar patterns. But she immediately saw the smile lines at the corners of his eyes, and the kindness reflected in their depths.

She dropped into a curtsy, spreading her pale blue dress

wide. "My name is Sigrid of Wildewyn."

"I am Raheem, the sultan's personal guard."

Her spine stiffened. "And for what reason has he sent you?"

"To be your shadow."

"And to report any unusual behavior, I assume."

The big man's mouth twisted into a wide grin. "That too. But I promise, I'll make certain it's behavior he needs to know about. Otherwise, your secrets are safe with me."

"I don't believe that in the slightest." But she appreciated the sentiment, nonetheless. "One small favor, guard. Please tell me his reaction when you regale him with what I'm about to do."

Raheem's brow arched.

She toed off her shoes, bent at the waist, and stowed them deep in the hidden pockets of her dress. Sighing, she lifted her skirts just enough to show the large man her toes wiggling in the earth.

His jaw dropped open. Though he could not see her wide grin, she hoped he understood the crinkling at the edges of her eyes.

"The only appropriate way to say goodbye to Wildewyn would be to feel her breathing underneath my feet."

He cleared his throat. "In this case, your secret is safe with me."

"A small miracle. How quaint."

The loud ruckus of Bymerians leaving heralded her last few moments. She didn't know how long the journey would take, but she was already dreading what she would find waiting for her in the deserts of this new land. A loud screech above them echoed.

She looked up to see Camilla fly past on silent wings. Her silver down feathers nearly blended into the clouds. She flew a distance before alighting on a tree branch and waiting for them to catch up.

Sigrid wished she could join her sister in the skies. She was too big to fly, people would see her, and no one knew how to react when they saw a dragon taking flight. So, she walked.

The guards sent her strange looks. She wondered what expressions they would wear if they could see her feet.

Her toes sank into the dirt with each step, mud squelching between her toes in the most glorious sensation she'd felt in a long time. Sigrid remembered running through these forests as a child. Her mother would call out for her to slow down, that she would disappear between the trees and no one would ever find her again.

Even when she was young, she'd always wanted to disappear into the forest and never return. There were too many rules among the Beastkin. Don't show your face to anyone but family. Don't speak too loudly or you might startle the others. Stand up straight, don't whisper, be polite, listen to the humans.

Her mother had whittled away at Sigrid's adventurous nature until she had created a being in her own image. Now, she was calm and quiet. Still water without a breath of air to give it life.

Sometimes, she regretted that change.

A breeze played across her shoulders, slipping underneath her mask to tickle her chin. Sigrid widened her eyes to fill them with the impossibly beautiful sight of her homeland. She wanted to brand every emerald leaf to her memory.

Raheem coughed into his hand. "Are you certain you wish to walk, my lady?"

"Yes."

"It's cold out. Perhaps, you should put your shoes back on."

"No."

He grunted. "If you get sick, I'm the one to blame."

"Are you my caretaker?" She glanced up at him, the mask chilly against her forehead. "I already have one if that's your role. You know nothing about my kind."

"I believe that is a critical part of my role," Raheem replied with a chuckle. "To learn about your kind without you knowing."

"You're doing a terrible job at it."

"I find it's easier to learn information through honesty than deception. I find it difficult to wear many faces."

She looked him up and down. "Yes. It's impossible to hide a wolf in silks, I would imagine."

He tossed his dark head back, and let out a laugh like thunder. "You and I will get along, little sultana. And here I was thinking you were meek and quiet."

"I *am* quiet." She folded her hands in front of her. "But that is not a weakness."

She felt the physical weight of his gaze on her. If he thought he would understand a drakon Beastkin just by looking, then he would be very disappointed. There were a hundred layers to her person; each more intricate than the last.

The wind picked up and emerald leaves fell in a shower atop the crimson caravan. Sigrid grinned, safely hidden behind her golden mask. Each leaf danced and twirled before falling underneath her feet to guide her across the uneven ground. Wildewyn bid goodbye to one of its daughters, and she felt its sadness with every step.

Their travels were relatively uneventful. She slept under the stars with Camilla at her side. Her "husband" stayed with his advisors and the beautiful woman. She saw him only in the mornings when he tried to order her into the box, and she defied him.

Instead of growing angry, the sultan appeared to grow even more interested in her with every quietly murmured "no."

On the last day in Wildewyn, she glanced up at Raheem, her constant shadow and now walking companion. "Does anyone ever say 'no' to the sultan?"

Her guard thought for a few moments, his brows furrowing before he shook his head. "I can't think of anyone who would dare disagree with his orders."

"What would happen if they did?"

"Likely death. He does not abide by fools in his sultanate."

She followed the train of Bymerians up to where her ruby clothed husband rode at the forefront. "Then why am I still alive?"

"That is a question none of us have the answer to, but many have asked." Raheem held out a hand for her to take as they crossed a stream.

She shook her head and made her way by herself. "Beastkin touch no one but family or husbands."

"Why's that?"

"It's our way."

"Ah," Raheem replied. "That doesn't make much sense. What if someone injured you and I needed to help?"

She didn't know the answer. Some Beastkin would die rather than allow anyone, man or woman, to touch them and break their unspoken rituals. Others would allow the touch to save their own lives. Sigrid didn't know which the right response was.

Water sloshed around her ankles as she paused to think about the question. Birds chirped overhead and many of the Bymerians walked by her with questioning expressions. Raheem remained in the frigid water until he cursed and stomped out.

"Are you coming, little sultana? I will pick you up if I need to."

"I think I would allow a touch if my life hung in the balance," she finally replied. "It would not be pleasant, but I believe that is a compromise I would make."

"You took that long to figure it out?" Raheem held out a hand for her to take, yet again. "Get out of the water, Sultana. You'll freeze."

She ignored his hand, but stepped out of the stream. Her toes were a little numb. She remembered this feeling from when she was a little girl. She had bathed in icy streams, teeth chattering, lungs screaming for breath as she dove underneath the surface.

"Do you have streams like this in Bymere?" she asked.

"No. Bymere is a desert. You'll find mostly sand there, my lady."

She made a quiet, disappointed sound. She would miss the rushing waters, the green algae growing on the rocks, and the quiet melody only a river or stream could make.

"It's a beautiful land," he continued. "Everything is gold

and red as far as the eye can see. Our capital and your new home is the greatest structure ever built. You'll fall in love with the Red Palace."

She held her head high but did not respond. What could she say? That she was looking forward to seeing this monstrosity that held no semblance of familiarity?

Sigrid wanted nothing more than to turn around and climb back into the waiting arms of her sisters. It was her last moment to leave. She'd made no vows, and yet, she couldn't turn back from this responsibility.

"We're here," Raheem said, clearing his throat awkwardly.

Steeling herself, Sigrid looked up at the sheer mountain that divided their countries. It towered before them, hewn through the center, leaving a ragged, straight edge carved by the ancients long ago. Water fell from the top, cascading in wide falls, crashing at the base to form all the rivers and streams that meandered through Wildewyn.

Their one and only gift from Bymere, which perched high above them on the mountain tops plateau.

She blew out a breath. "There it is."

"The Edge of the World," Raheem replied.

Silent wings brushed against her back and Camilla landed on her metal clad shoulder. Sigrid reached up to help steady her sister, but kept her eyes on the mountains.

"How do we ascend it?"

Raheem pointed. "There is a pulley system at the top. Our men will lower it, and we will stand as they pull us up."

"Everyone?"

"Everyone."

She glanced at the large number of people the sultan had

brought with him and snorted. "I pity the men at the top."

Again, her guard appeared surprised. "Why consider them?"

"Carrying the weight of everyone is a heavy burden. And what would happen if they dropped us?" She shaded her eyes and watched as a wooden platform lowered from the top. "It doesn't seem very safe."

"It would be a quick death," he sputtered.

"For you." Her gaze heated, eyes burning with the dragon inside her. "I would survive."

Raheem rubbed a hand over his head. "You're an intimidating little thing when you want to be."

"Beastkin don't hide behind their femininity. I am beast and woman." She lifted a shoulder. "One and the same."

Camilla snapped her beak and spread her wings wide for balance.

She didn't want to get on that rickety platform. Though they both had wings, it was not a rush Sigrid ever wished to experience. Once they ascended that mountain, they would never return to their home. The thought made a shiver travel down her spine.

Raheem made a choked sound. "You really believe you're a dragon."

She turned her cold gaze to him. "Yes."

"It's not possible. There's no such thing as a Beastkin who can transform into something so large."

Camilla tilted her head back and gulped, the owl form of laughter.

"I can assure you, there is a dragon inside me," Sigrid replied, her lips curved in a smile.

"Can't all women say that?"

She snorted. "Some certainly can, but I have not met many Bymerian women. Perhaps, you are more equipped to answer that question."

"Our women are terrifying." He gave a mocking shiver. "One wrong word and they turn into screeching terrors."

"Thank you for the warning."

A sharp whistle interrupted them. The platform had arrived at the bottom, much larger than Sigrid had expected.

The sultan stared them down at the front of the caravan, his brows furrowed and anger radiating from his gaze. "Raheem!" he called out. "You were charged with watching my new wife, not speaking with her."

"One and the same, Your Majesty."

"Bring her to the platform."

Raheem reached for her arm before he remembered himself. His hand froze in the air, and he asked, "Would you like to make your way to the mountain?"

"At my husband's request," she replied.

Camilla's claws dug into her shoulders as they made their way through the ranks of Bymerians. What had seemed like a small task turned daunting. The platform was little more than boards attached with ropes. They would bounce against the stone with every yanking pull.

Her stomach turned.

The sultan sat arrogantly on his horse, one knee hooked over the pommel, elbow resting on his thigh.

He stared at her until she snapped, "What is it you want?"

"I can't look at you? I think I won the right to do that, wife."

"You may call me by my name."

83

"I like wife better." He swung down from his steed and strode towards her. He reached forward, played with the clasp of her mask for a moment, then flicked a finger against the gold. "What do you look like underneath this, I wonder? I've been patient, but as soon as we are in Bymere, I intend to find out what your face looks like."

Yet another thing to make her stomach roll. She swallowed the vomit in her throat and nodded. "It's your right as my husband."

"Does the mask hide something ugly?" he mused. "Or something more precious?"

"That is up to you."

He huffed. "We'll find out soon enough then. Get up on the platform, wife. We go first."

She made her way to the rickety platform, wincing as it creaked under her feet, and stepped close to the wall. A few others joined her, the white-haired man who had been so argumentative and the beautiful woman with painted hands. Neither glanced her way although a few others that arrived with them did.

Their eyes lingered on her clothing, the iron in her spine, and the ash-white hair spilling over her shoulders. Sigrid knew how strange she must look to them. They were equally foreign to her.

She took a deep breath and stepped closer to the edge of the platform as they were slowly lifted into the air.

"Careful," the sultan said. "We wouldn't want you to tumble to your death."

His advisors chuckled, but she didn't understand what was so funny.

Bymerians confused her. Their reactions weren't normal, at least not to her. Camilla seemed to agree, because she shook her head and took flight. Downy wings sliced through the air. She plummeted towards the earth before soaring out of sight, up to the top of the mountain.

What Sigrid would give to do the same.

The Bymerians chattered around her. The sound of their voices assaulted her ears until she wanted to throw herself from the platform. She stepped closer to the edge, staring down at the ground which quickly dropped away beneath them. She waited for someone to notice her, then realized no one was watching. Even Raheem was staring at the other nobles, amused at their antics.

The woman flicked her wrist, imitating something Sigrid couldn't guess at. Laughter burst forth again, and she finally turned her back on them.

They weren't her people. She didn't have to acknowledge their existence if she didn't want to.

Sigrid stepped forward and grasped the rope in her hand. Coarse hemp bit into her fingers and splinters dug into her bare feet. But the wind rustled her hair, tugged her braid and whipped her skirts. It reminded her that she was alive, and though they didn't know it, she was more connected to the earth than they could ever imagine.

Holding on tight, she dangled one foot over the edge and leaned just enough so that her sight wasn't filled with platforms or Bymerians. All she could see was Wildewyn falling away.

Forests and swamps filled her eyes. So impossibly green she knew even the purest of emeralds couldn't compete. She would not cry. It was not becoming of a dragon, but her breath caught at the beauty of her home. Lost forever now, but the memory branded into her soul.

Someone stepped toward her, perhaps things she planned to leap off the platform, but a sword unsheathed behind her. The ringing sound echoed with a single threatening note dancing in the air.

"Raheem," her husband's voice cracked.

"You asked me to protect her, Majesty. That is what I'm doing."

Another voice, slick and oily responded, "She might throw herself from the platform. I'm only trying to preserve this tentative peace."

She heard the unmistakable sigh from between her husband's lips. "Raheem—"

"If I may be so bold, Sultan, she has said that none may touch her but family or husband. And I don't believe she's trying to kill herself." There was a tense pause, and then Raheem sheathed his blade. "I think she's saying goodbye."

Throughout the entire ordeal, Sigrid remained silent, staring out at her homeland. She couldn't turn, because they might see the red rims of her eyes, or the fat droplets of tears she refused to let fall.

It wasn't just the home. It wasn't just the land. It was the memories that came with it and the pain of leaving it all behind.

A flash of silver caught her eye, then another of gold. And Sigrid held her breath as twin falcons dipped in the air. Sunlight danced upon the embellished tips of their feathers, and she knew her sisters had come.

An owl circled them. Camilla's haunting cry served as their last goodbye.

NADIR

THEY ARRIVED IN THE TRADER'S CAMP LATE THAT NIGHT. EXHAUSTION wore at Nadir, but he had learned from his brother long ago that an army marched until their king showed weakness. He held his spine straight, stared forward as if he had no care in the world. He'd fall into bed soon.

The strange woman he'd acquired didn't seem to be fatigued at all. She hardly reacted to anything although it was difficult to tell with that strange mask on her face. It never changed expression and made her seem more animal than human.

Perhaps, that was the point.

By the time they stumbled into camp, their tents were already erected. Brightly colored, they stood out from the desert and heralded his first sign of home. If he had been able to, Nadir would have cracked a smile.

Instead, he remained as stoic as his advisors. He made certain they sent each man to their tents, waved Abdul away and promised to speak with him in the morning, and then made his way towards his own large, red tent.

Crimson fabric always marked where the king was. He brushed aside the tent flap, bare feet sinking into the thick carpet. Sighing, he cracked his neck.

"Husband," a quiet voice whispered, curling out of the depths of rugs and fur. "I've been waiting for you."

He wished that his wife's voice calmed him. Instead, the hairs on his arms raised. "Saafiya."

"You might sound more excited to see me."

She rose from the corner, all lithe limbs and smooth skin. She walked around the center brazier, firelight playing over her body. Though she had removed her traveling attire, she was still dressed as a queen.

A skirt of orange silk spilled from her hips, golden suns stitched in lines to the ground. The top bared her midriff, just as lovely as the rest of her. A matching top accentuated her curves and the heavy necklace covering her chest.

She'd taken her hair down, as she knew he preferred. The dark weight swung at her hips as she sensually strode towards him.

"I have missed you, husband."

"We both know that's a lie."

"You've been making decisions without me," she said with a pout. "I thought we were a wonderful team, you and I."

"You've always been an advisor before you were my wife."

"And I've been a good advisor." She stepped behind him, nudging him further into the tent. "Come. Let me wash the travel stains from your body. You will feel like a new man after a bath."

Nadir let her push him. He'd always been terrible at denying her. She was so lovely, and he admired her so, that it was difficult to think when she was in the room.

The fire crackled and warm hands smoothed across his shoulders. She pressed against his aching muscles as she pulled his shirt over his head. His back spasmed under her caresses and she let out a disappointed tut.

"You know better than to push yourself. You are sultan now, not some soldier on the field."

"I am sultan; therefore, I must push myself."

"That's your brother talking." She leaned down and pressed her lips against his ear. "Not you."

Nadir knew what she was doing, and he didn't like it. The warm glow of firelight bouncing off crimson walls lulled him into a state of relaxation. She would use it to get what she wanted.

"What do you want, Saafiya?" he asked.

"I want to take care of my husband."

"Stop lying. I'm too tired to argue with you tonight."

Her hands clenched on his shoulders. "Why must it always be an argument? I don't complain when you bring your concubines to bed. Neither do I care when you make a scene with women at our dinner table or any gathering. I've been a good wife."

"The best wife," he agreed. "And yet, you always want something when you are kind. What is it this time?"

"I've been your only wife."

And there it was. He knew it had something to do with the golden trinket he'd brought back from Wildewyn, but Nadir thought she would wait to attack him about a second marriage.

He brought a hand to his face and scrubbed the day-old scruff growing there. "It's done."

"You should have spoken with me first."

"I didn't realize I needed your permission to marry again."

Her voice turned to a hiss. "You can marry any Bymerian woman you want. I will parade them in front of you if it's a second wife you desire. But I will not suffer the insult of living with a second wife from Wildewyn who claims to be an *animal*."

"Enough."

Claws dug into his shoulders. "She is beneath you, beneath Bymere. You know better than to welcome a snake into the castle. Look at what happened to your brother."

"*Enough!*" He lurched to his feet, chest heaving in anger. "Get out."

"Husband—"

"Out, Saafiya. Before I do something I regret."

Her padding footsteps were his only warning she had left. The fire burned on, crackling and reminding him that there were other things in this world than a meddling wife old enough to be his mother.

What had he become?

In the flames, he saw his brother's face. Hakim had always been the handsome sibling. Better suited to be king, to the kingdom, to everything that Nadir now held in his careless hands. What would Hakim have done?

The tent flap shifted again, a shadow slipping into his temporary home.

"What is it?" he growled.

"I thought to check on you. Saafiya didn't appear happy when she left."

"She tried to meddle."

"Did you expect anything less?" Raheem chuckled, but sat on the other side of the flame. It took a considerable amount of effort to fold himself onto the floor. "She's always meddled."

"I have no patience for her."

"You don't? That's a surprise. You usually do."

He supposed his friend was right, although he didn't know what had changed. Perhaps the travel had worn on him more than he thought. Nadir shook his head again, rubbing his face hard to try to dispel the exhaustion.

"What news of the girl?" he asked.

"The little sultana? Not much."

"You spoke with her on the journey."

"Not as often as you'd think." Raheem reached forward and plucked a stick out of the fire. He poked at the embers before clearing his throat. "She doesn't like to be touched."

"History?"

"Tradition, it seems. Says only her family may lay a hand on her, and that whomever touched her without permission would be put to death."

Nadir nodded. "I'll let the men know, just in case. Anything else?"

"She's got a spine of steel on her. I'd expect most women to be nervous or afraid in a situation like this. She's taken out of her home, everything she knows is gone, and she's only got an owl as a friend. But she doesn't seem affected by it at all."

Nadir grunted. "That's what makes me nervous."

"How so?"

Because she was impossible that's why. Every inch of her was like a marble statue come to life. She was too cold, strange, exquisite in a way that seemed foreign and haunting. He shook his head to clear the odd thoughts.

"She doesn't seem real."

"No, she doesn't at all." Raheem leaned back on an elbow, the burning stick clutched in one hand. Smoke curled from the tip. "I wonder what she looks like underneath that mask."

"I hope she's beautiful."

"I couldn't imagine anything else, although I bet it's a strange kind of beauty. Like looking at a reflection in moonlight."

"When did you become a poet?" Nadir asked, but he knew what his friend meant by those words. She was unpredictable, and it made him uncomfortable.

"The moment I saw her."

Nadir threw a cushion at him. "That's my wife."

"On paper. Besides, you didn't want her. A poor guard can dream, can't he?"

"I ought to cut out your tongue for that."

"You'd be doing the world a favor."

Nadir grinned for the first time in what felt like ages. This was what he missed from visiting the war camps before his brother died and the world went to shit. The comradery, the feeling of belonging no matter who was talking, the way each man ribbed each other even though he hadn't been able to understand it at such a young age. It was a rare gift in a world full of politicians and scheming wives.

His childhood dreams were always of a life simpler than this. A single wife who waited for him at home, a small house on the edge of an oasis. A life with no one to tell him what to do or who to be.

Nadir flopped down onto the rugs and stared up at the patterned ceiling. "I should know what she looks like."

"What do you mean?"

He waved a hand in the air. "Her face. What kind of man marries a woman without knowing what her face looks like?"

"First impressions are everything, I suppose. What do you think of her now?"

"She's stubborn."

Raheem chuckled. "And?"

"She's beautiful."

"I see I'm the only poet in the room. Is beauty and stubbornness the only thing you can recognize in another person?"

It was certainly the first thing he recognized. Nadir tried to remember the first moment he saw her. Pawing through memories of beautiful masked women, he realized he couldn't remember the exact moment.

"What did she look like to you when she walked into the room?"

"Like a winter storm," Raheem replied. "All those women were snowflakes, parading into the king's white hall. But there's more to her than snow or sleet. That woman is the entire storm, and the devastation left behind. She's got ice in her veins, that one."

He remembered now. They had parted like a wave, and she had advanced towards him as if she would pull a blade and slide it between his ribs.

"There's more to her than ice," Nadir replied. "When she looked me in the eyes, I felt hatred. The depth of which I've never seen in another person."

"I don't know if she's capable of hatred."

"She defies me at every turn," Nadir spat. "No matter what I tell her to do, the answer is always no."

Raheem paused for a second, and the fire filled the silence until his friend took a deep breath. "She walked the entire journey barefoot."

"What?" Nadir sat up, stunned. "She what?"

"Barefoot as the day she was born. I've seen nothing like it. I asked her multiple times to put her shoes back on, but she never did. I snuck up behind her as she was preparing for bed and watched her put her feet in a cold stream. They were bleeding and raw, but she never complained once. I don't think she even noticed the pain."

"Why would she do such a foolish thing?" Something in his chest ached at the thought of her suffering.

"I asked halfway through the trip when I thought I saw her stumble. She refused any help, told me she wouldn't put her shoes back on, and then mentioned something that still troubles me." Raheem sat up as well, his gaze finding Nadir's. "She said if this was her last goodbye, then feeling the earth under her feet was worth a little pain."

He shook his head. "That makes little sense."

"That's what I said. And yet, she remained barefoot."

"She will put those shoes on the moment we begin our journey again." His voice snapped in the air, anger surging in his veins again. He didn't care if he had to pin her to the ground and tie the shoes onto her feet himself. She would wear them.

"I don't think that'll be a problem." Raheem rolled to his feet. "She put them back on the moment we touched Bymerian soil."

Nadir didn't know how to respond. He clenched his jaw as his friend made his way out of the tent.

He slumped back into the rugs, staring up at the ceiling of his tent. She put the shoes back on? What insult was this to his people? To his homeland?

One side of him stung that she had endured such pain, and he hadn't noticed. But he hadn't really given her a single thought on their journey. He had been too busy with the success of what felt like a raid.

Yet, it wasn't. She hadn't let it become that. Instead, she had turned it around. Every step of the way felt like it was her choice. To lower herself. To agree to this marriage. It wasn't a trade for peace; it was simply her plan all along.

His mind warred between anger and disgust at himself for what he had done. Nadir rarely felt guilt, especially for something such as this. It was for his kingdom. Every choice he made was for his people, and yet...

This somehow felt selfish.

An image flashed before his eyes. Bloodied feet and a cold woman standing up to her ankles in frigid water. She hadn't reacted at all to the cold. He only remembered because he had glanced back to see both her and Raheem standing at odds.

She was so still in the rushing water, and he had thought she was defying his guard just as she did him. But now he wondered if she only appreciated a moment of reprieve.

Why hadn't she put on shoes if she was in pain?

He rolled onto his side, willing sleep to come. The carpet was soft against his body, cushioning him from the sand that would shape to his weight as the night went on. But he couldn't banish the image from his mind.

Cursing every god he could think of, Nadir shoved the soft rugs out of his way, stumbled to his feet, and burst from the tent. He startled a guard standing nearby who struggled to stand at attention.

"Where is she?" he growled.

"Your Majesty?"

"The beast woman, where is she?"

The guard pointed to a tent far away. Dark blue fabric blended into the night sky and dark, shadowed sand. "They put her in that one, Sultan."

So far away from him? Saafiya had a hand in that, and he would see her reprimanded. Then, he would tell the rest of his people not to touch his new wife. She didn't like to be touched by anyone other than himself and family.

Why did that make his chest swell with pride?

He stomped towards her tent, not knowing what he was going to say to her. That she should wear shoes from now on? She'd already taken care of that. That she took little care of herself? Obviously, but he hadn't seen the extent of her injuries.

He would assess the situation himself, and then decide whether he should feel guilty. Then it was his own decision, not Raheem's.

Satisfied with his plan, he shoved aside the tent flap and strode into her tent.

Female voices silenced, and Nadir paused when he saw the dark woman crouching next to his wife, holding a golden mask in her hands. Sigrid flinched away the moment the tent flap stirred. He hadn't seen even the slightest hint of her face. Instead, an owl mask stared back at him with impossibly dark eyes as the other woman crouched over Sigrid in a protective pose.

He frowned. "I remember you."

The owl shifted, her hand sinking into the folds of her dress. Would she try to draw a weapon on him? Was this the Earthen folk's plan this entire time?

Sigrid lifted a pale, slender hand outlined by the single torch and touched it to the dark woman's arm. "What do you want, Sultan?"

"My personal guard told me an interesting story regarding you, and I wanted to see if it was true." He pointed at the other woman. "I'll deal with you later. You're not supposed to be here."

"You may treat your own subjects however you wish, but you'll not speak to mine with such a tone."

"Subjects?" he scoffed. "You are nothing more than a pawn for whatever country you're traded to."

Her spine stiffened, and she released her hold on the owl woman's arm. "Camilla, give us a few moments please."

"My lady—"

"Now, Camilla. I will be fine."

He watched as Camilla passed the dragon mask to her mistress. Nadir didn't appreciate the glare the owl woman gave him as she slipped by him into the night. Strange that he could still make out what her expression was underneath the cold metal. He would have to figure out how she managed to stowaway with his people when she would clearly stand out. Even the men lifting them into Bymere hadn't seen her. Was it possible she turned into some kind of bird? Or perhaps a lizard that his new wife had tucked underneath her clothes.

The tent flap sealed them into the plain space. The accommodation disappointed him. His wife should lay in splendor. Instead, the tent was filled with a thin layer of rugs, a single brazier, and only one room. She should have multiple rooms, a guard out front, a bathing area...the list went on and on.

He tucked his hands behind his back, uncomfortable. She still hadn't looked at him. The firelight filtered through her hair until a halo made her profile glow with a flaming crown.

The dragon mask rested against her thighs, staring into his soul with an empty gaze. He noticed the metal corset on a rug nearby and swallowed hard as he realized every layer of her armor was off. He was seeing her as he might in his own country.

As a woman and nothing else.

"What do you have to say, Sultan?" she asked. "It's been a long journey, and we both need rest."

Nadir cleared his throat. "Shoes."

Silence rang louder than a shout. She tilted her head slightly to the side, but still not enough that he could see her face. "Surely, there is more than that?"

"Excuse me?"

"You must have more to say than a single word, Sultan of Bymere."

"You traveled without them." Was he stammering? Nadir shook himself. This woman rattled him, and he refused to allow her any more control over the situation.

He strode forward, his legs eating up the space until she held up a single, graceful hand once again.

"What are you doing?"

"You said that family could see your face. Am I not considered family?"

She hesitated, and when she spoke her voice was quieter than before. "I've never shown my face to any man. You must excuse me if I admit my discomfort."

"I've seen many faces in my life."

"As have I. But few have seen mine."

Nadir knew he should understand her hesitation, but he couldn't. It wasn't a monumental shift in his world. A face was a face. Hers certainly wouldn't rock the foundation of his earth. Yet, exposing hers seemed to threaten the foundation of hers.

He stepped closer. "It's my right, is it not?"

"It is."

"Then you'll forgive me, wife, when I insist."

"And if I'm not ready?"

He lifted a shoulder she couldn't see. "Will you ever be?"

Nadir already knew the answer. She would hide from him the rest of her life if she could. That was how the Beastkin had obviously lived their life in Wildewyn, although he still didn't know how much merit he put in their abilities to change. She could be a master magician for all he knew.

She squared her shoulders, shook her hair over her shoulder, and nodded. "You're right. If I had my way, you would never see my face at all. But that is not the way of our lives, and as such, you should see what fate has given you in a wife."

"Second wife," he corrected.

"Second wife," she repeated.

He stepped closer to her, his eyes fixed straight ahead and hands clasped behind his back. He allowed himself a moment to wonder what she would think of that revelation. The Earthen folk were monogamous. Marriages were sacred to them, and they only had one husband or wife for their entire life.

His people were not the same. They had multiple marriages, divorced, and freely found love wherever it lay. Would she be insulted to be a second wife? Would she be angered or jealous?

Taking a deep breath, he glanced down at the woman kneeling beside him.

He couldn't quite see her entire face, presented only with her profile as she stared straight ahead, so he leaned enough to see the rest of her face. She was...young. So much younger than he thought she would be with her usual stiff posture and clipped tones.

White blonde curls escaped her braid, falling in tendrils around her long face. She wasn't a stunning beauty by any means. He'd expect a heart-shaped face with lush lips and winged eyebrows. Instead, she was a sturdy woman whose face reflected that.

A square jaw revealed a clear stubborn streak. Her upper lip was too thin to match her lower, but that was perhaps the pursed expression as she held herself still for his perusal. A long thin nose met with strong brows above the icy eyes he'd already grown accustomed to.

The firelight played across her pronounced cheekbones and strong features. She wasn't a vision, and would never be renowned for it, but she was a safe kind of strength. In looking at her, he could see why many would allow her to rule them. She was beautiful in the way a storm was. Moments of singular energy combined to create something effortlessly powerful.

Unarmored, kneeling beside him, he could almost pretend that she was a normal wife on their first night together. Her pale blue dress wasn't fitted like a bridal gown should be. It hung from her frame, pooling around her in a puddle made of linen fabric.

A muscle in her jaw ticked, and he realized he didn't know what to say. What did a man who had forced a woman to reveal a secret, even something so superficial as a face, say? She wasn't a mythical creature, she was *normal*. Just a woman who he'd made uncomfortable.

He cleared his throat, rearranged his hands behind his back, and again, nothing came to him. Words eluded every inch of his mind until he was convinced he'd forgotten how to speak.

Nadir glanced back down at her. She stared up at him, shadows casting half her face in darkness. Their gazes tangled.

What did a man say to a woman clearly made of mountains? She was a wild thing he had somehow been gifted, but now freed from her cage. She held the fury of storms, the power of lightning, within her gaze.

She seared him to the bone.

"My name is Nadir," he whispered.

Blowing out a breath, he shook his head, spun on his heel, and left the tent. Not more words passed between them and he was certain she stared after him. He refused to be embarrassed by his actions or even attempt to explain what his reasoning had been.

Nadir hadn't even looked at her feet. She could have been walking on stubs for all he had found out, but he hadn't been able to move under her icy gaze. She'd frozen him, a puppet for her to play with, a statue for her collection.

Angrily, he brushed aside his own tent flap and resolved to stay there for the night. He would deal with her in the morning, and all the strange emotions that plagued him.

SIGRID

THE SUN DIPPED LOW ON THE HORIZON, ITS RAYS FILTERING through the cracks in the tent walls. Sigrid stared at the pinpricks of light, still kneeling on the rugs where she had been last night. There was much to think about, and her mind wouldn't let her sleep.

Camilla rolled onto her hands and knees in the corner. "Are you awake?"

"Yes."

"Do you wish to get dressed?"

"The midnight gown, please."

"What time is it?" Her sister rubbed sleep from her eyes and rummaged through the trunks some Bymerians had placed inside the tent for the night.

"Nearly noon."

"And they're all just getting up?" Camilla paused, her eyes wide and her jaw dropped. "Isn't there work to do?"

"Not for them."

She had waited to hear the camp wake up. Hours upon hours, even after the sun had risen high into the sky. Sigrid tracked it through the stitches in the tent and yet she didn't hear a single sound until the sun nearly reached its peak.

"Lazy, too," Camilla grumbled. "It's almost nighttime already, and they're all still abed! I've seen little good from these Bymerians."

Sigrid agreed. The memory of her new husband was burned into the back of her eyes. He'd stared at her, his stoic expression mirroring her own.

What had he been thinking? There had been a flicker in his gaze. Surprise, she thought, and something else that made her thoroughly uncomfortable.

Sigrid knew she wasn't as beautiful as some of her sisters. They were blessed with smooth skin, full lips, bodies made from the dreams of men. She had always been a harder sort, the kind of creature that survived a famine or war.

She would never hold a claim to delicacy, and the dragon part of her soul wore that knowledge with pride.

But, would he?

Camilla pulled out a swath of dark fabric, silver stars stitched into the bodice. "Armor as well?"

"Yes."

"It'll be hot."

"Discomfort is fleeting." And she wanted them to see her in armor. They might not understand the meaning behind it. They didn't seem to understand anything, but she hoped subconsciously they would realize she prepared for battle.

She stood, knees aching, and held still while Camilla stripped her and placed the new dress on her body. This one was heavier, but the folds of the skirt hid the twin slits up the thighs. Should she need to protect herself, Sigrid knew she could move without tangling herself in heavy fabric.

"Do you suspect an attack?" Camilla asked, her voice pitched low.

"After last night, I don't know what to think."

The sultan was a strange man. He barged into her tent like he owned it. And in a way, she understood that he did.

The Beastkin were always given a semblance of privacy. Even the king would not enter their quarters without permission. All that leniency would change here. She should have guessed it, but had hoped that respect would travel with her.

Nadir.

What a strange name for a man who clearly didn't know who he was. He had stared at the wall a little too long before looking at her. She was the one who was uncomfortable, bared before a man she'd never said more than a few words to. And yet, he was just as nervous. Shouldn't a sultan be used to making others uneasy? Shouldn't he disregard their feelings for the greater good?

He made her question everything she knew about her upbringing and her own people. Sigrid didn't like it.

The tent flap fluttered in the wind. "My lady? The sultan is asking for your presence."

Camilla tugged the last strap at Sigrid's back hard.

She grimaced but called out, "I'll be ready in a moment. Thank you, Raheem."

"Raheem?" Camilla hissed, pitching her voice low so he wouldn't hear their words. "You know their names now?"

"A personal guard."

"The monolith who followed your every step during the travels." She nodded. "I saw him. The king didn't want you to step too far out of line."

"Sultan."

"They're all the same. Royal blood runs true no matter what name they call themselves." Camilla snapped one last piece into place, then ran a hand down the fabric to the ground. "You're presentable. Lift the corner of the tent for me? I'll try to spy on the guards."

"Don't get caught."

Sigrid knelt and scooped handfuls of sand away from the tent edge while her sister shifted forms. The silver owl stepped close to peer underneath the edge then wiggled free. She'd have stories to tell tonight, and it was a small bit of relief that Sigrid wasn't alone.

"My lady." The tent flap shook again. "The sultan is not a patient man."

Sigrid shook out the sand in her skirts and affixed the mask to her face. She'd hate the grains by the end of this journey, she was certain of it. Every speck dug into her skin wherever it had the chance. She wanted a bath.

Raheem must have heard her footsteps, because he pulled back the flap and allowed her to step into the blast of hot air. The sun pressed down on the land. The far outskirts shimmered in the heat. Sweat pooled between her shoulder blades and dripped down her back.

Her sister had been right. She should have worn something lighter, but she couldn't change now.

Sigrid was a drakon Beastkin. She would suffer the heat

with grace.

Raheem looked her up and down, then smirked. "A strange choice of outfit for a desert, my lady. I can stall the sultan if you'd like to change?"

"I've no need."

"Are you sure?" He gestured towards the Bymerians, each wearing less and less clothing. "It would not be surprising. Most people aren't awake at this time. On days like this, we do our work at night."

Her eyes had never been assaulted with so much flesh. Sigrid bit her tongue to keep from gasping. Apparently, all the shirts in the camp had burned to a crisp because not a single person was wearing one. Some had even forgone pants and wore nothing more than a wrapped loincloth that left far too much revealed.

She didn't know what to say. They all really were tanned over their entire bodies.

Raheem chuckled. "Your wide eyes speak for you, little sultana. You must be more careful with other people."

"I don't know what you're talking about."

"Certainly, you don't." He shook his head. "Are you sure you don't want to change?"

"No, Raheem. What use does my husband have for me?"

He held out his hand in the direction she should walk. She appreciated that he didn't try to touch her. The man was learning faster than most.

She trudged through the sand toward a garish, red tent. The sultan would insist on having the most vibrantly colored fabric. Wasn't it dangerous to be a red target in the center of so much white sand? No one could mistake where the sultan was, and very few guards stood at the entrance. It didn't appear there were even men circling it.

These people clearly didn't care for the safety of their ruler. Her lips curled in a sneer.

The guards shifted to allow her passage, their eyes lingering on her heavy dress and the metal affixed to her face. Perhaps they, too, thought she was incapable of handling the heat. They even glanced at Raheem as if it were his fault.

She wasn't a delicate flower. She wouldn't wilt or faint just because it was a little warm.

Heat built in the back of her eyes as the dragon part of her soul unfurled and stretched. It flourished in the heat, even adding more of its own to the mix until her body was as hot as the air.

Somehow, that made bearing the temperature a little easier, though she was likely adding her own heat to the tent interior.

The sultan's advisors splayed out across silken rugs. She recognized a few although others had remained silent through the entire ordeal of buying flesh. The sultan himself lay in the far corner. A pale-skinned beauty waved a fan made of feathers longer than her arm and the henna-marked female advisor sprawled at his side.

This was the first wife then. Intriguing that he would marry someone who also had a say in the success of the country. Didn't he know it wasn't good to mix politics with pleasure?

He lifted a hand and the woman holding the fan paused, reached behind them, and poured water into a small goblet.

He was waited on hand and foot, she realized with a flash of temper. These people were already overheated and tired themselves. Yet, they were forced to stand so that he might be fanned with air?

The heat deep inside her body flared again, sending pulses of warmth radiating outward.

"Wife," the sultan called. He gestured at her with the goblet when the other woman stirred. "So glad you could join us."

"Your guards said you wished to see me."

"My advisors still think you were sent to kill me. An assassination attempt upon my life would be a breach of the peace treaty, and a declaration of war. Did you know that?"

She traced her teeth with her tongue, desperately holding onto her temper. "I'm aware."

"And do you know what we do with assassins in Bymere?"

"I know what we do to them in Wildewyn." She curled her hands into fists.

"We cut off their hands, feet, and nose then bid them crawl out into the desert until they perish."

He thought to intimidate her? She demurely folded her hands in front of her, ducked her head and curtsied. "Your Majesty is kind. In Wildewyn, we feed them to the wolves."

The woman at his side chuckled. "Husband, she doesn't just spit fire. She has claws!"

Laughter bubbled throughout the tent. Sigrid held herself still with pride, knowing that they were trying to get a rise out of her. They might laugh all they wished. She would not give them the reaction they were hoping for.

Nadir watched her with a hooded gaze. His foot twitched, but he did not otherwise give any reaction. They stared at each other across the tent, a battle of wills impossible to detect.

He quirked a brow. "You're brave for a woman so far from

home. My advisors and I know little about your people. Perhaps you care to enlighten us with what has given you such courage?"

"The Beastkin are secretive. We do not regale audiences with the tales of our people."

"You do now." He bared his teeth in a mockery of a grin. "At least tell us one secret, wife."

She wanted to tell him that every one of her women was far stronger than any of his men. That her people were born of earth and steel. That they would never bow to a boy king and his people who had proven themselves unworthy of standing before her.

The dragon unfurled its wings in her mind's eye and let out a growl that rumbled through her chest. "We are all trained from a very young age to fight," she gritted through her teeth.

"Warrior women," he repeated with a nod.

The white-haired advisor sat up and leaned forward. "It *was* your people who killed all our men."

"They should not have attacked a wedding," she hissed.

Nadir slashed a hand through the air and stood. "I wish to see this prowess. You think you can fight, and that you are better than my trained warriors?"

She refused to give him a response for such an insulting question.

The white-haired advisor chuckled and gestured towards the tent entrance. "Well? If you can fight so well, if you've been trained your entire life, why don't you show us?"

"How should I show you?" she asked while staring at Nadir. "Would you like me to fight some of your soldiers? I've already done that."

"Not that we've seen." The advisor rolled to his feet and strode to his sultan's side. "What do you say, Your Majesty? It's far too hot to work. Why don't we see what your new bride is capable of? Perhaps we've been lucky enough to find you yet another personal guard."

"Abdul," he growled, "tread carefully."

"It's an easy enough task. If the girl thinks she's so well-trained, let her prove it. Her struggles will entertain the entire camp, and no one will hurt her. At least not permanently."

She watched the sultan struggle to decide. He was under their thumb, she realized. Even the slightest suggestion that was obviously a bad idea was one that he would consider.

The woman rose and slid her hands across his shoulders. "Come, Sultan. We're all bored, and you want to see what she can do. Don't you?"

Sigrid had heard of such creatures before. In children's tales, they were the monsters who came out of the shadows, whispering in someone's ear, tempting them to do terrible things. In reality, they were people with poor judgment and power.

Surprisingly, the sultan looked at her for confirmation. "What say you, wife?"

Her heart stopped, shock making even the dragon retreat in her mind as she stared at him. He asked her advice? The mere inquiry seemed so out of character that it stilled her tongue until she managed to say, "Do you wish me to fight?"

The power back in his hands, he appeared lost. She saw him for what he was now. Just a boy with too much power, tugged in all directions by advisors who were far too wicked.

Sigrid cleared her throat. "A demonstration wouldn't

hurt."

The stain on his cheeks meant he understood what she had done. She'd taken the decision away from him and forced him. Still, it was easier for her to swallow an order if she was the one who was giving it.

"Good girl," Abdul, the white-haired advisor said with a chuckle. "Shall we go outside?"

Raheem cleared his throat, a warning for her to move before someone touched her. Sigrid slid outside back into the heat. The last remnants of night filled the air, dew and sweat sticking to her skin. This would not make any fight easy, but she would endure.

The echoing hoot of an owl lifted into the air. Sigrid couldn't see her sister, but knew that Camilla was nearby if the worst happened.

They made their way to the center of the tents where a small circle was outlined. She didn't know its use although the ground was trampled by hooved animals she had yet to see. For now, it would suffice as a training ground.

Abdul lifted his voice, shouting for all to hear that there would be a demonstration by the Beastkin woman, who claimed to be the best fighter in all the lands.

She'd never said that. Sigrid shook her head and stood at the edge of the circle with her hands clasped in front of her and head bowed. There was little for her to say. They would gather as many men as they could, and she would wait until the sun set if that was what they wished.

A drop of sweat rolled down her neck and disappeared into her dress. The heat was stifling, but she refused to remove any of her armor. Not yet. This would be a show for them all to remember. To realize just how powerful the Beastkin were.

It was never her intention to frighten them. She wanted acceptance and understanding, but her patience was already running thin. They had disgraced her by giving her a tent clearly meant for slaves. They treated her as little better than the sand beneath their feet.

They would now learn just how dangerous a drakon Beastkin was, and they would never forget it.

Raheem stood beside her, flexing his hands. "Are you sure about this, Sultana?"

"I am."

"What if they touch you? I thought this was something terrible for your people. Something worth killing yourself over."

She shook her head. "I'm not worried about that." Because she hadn't been entirely truthful with him. Some Beastkin would kill themselves, others would simply kill the offending person.

Abdul strode into the center of the circle with a man at his side. Before she could step forward, Raheem held a hand in her way. She glanced up into his worried gaze.

He wrangled a small smile out of her with that small bit of kindness. "They won't touch me, Raheem. They won't have the chance."

Perhaps she stunned him because his arm dropped, and he stepped back with a dumbfounded expression on his face. They were easy to read, these Bymerians. They hid not a single emotion. Everything played out on their faces for all to see.

It was unnerving. Weren't they worried that someone would see their inner thoughts?

The man they brought forward was too young, and Sigrid knew he would not be a challenge. There wasn't even hair on his upper lip yet, and his feet fidgeted in the sand as he waited for her.

A topknot of dark hair swayed in the breeze. He was finely made although a little too feminine for her tastes. Pretty, not handsome, but perhaps he would turn into something more. Dark slashes of eyebrows winged back from his dark, brown eyes. A sturdy nose coupled with a weak jaw made him appear far younger than he might have been.

Sigrid sucked her teeth and shook her head. "This is the warrior you bring forward?"

Abdul lifted a brow and mockingly bowed. "We cannot risk hurting the new sultana."

It was another insult, thinly veiled behind the ego of a young boy who likely didn't want to fight. The irony was not lost upon Sigrid.

"What weapon do you choose, son of Bymere?" she asked the boy.

He startled back at the sound of her voice. Already he was giving her too much ground. "I fight with the traditional blade, Sultana."

She didn't know what it was, but that was good enough. Blades were something she was familiar with. They trained with them for fun in the courtyards of Wildewyn. She'd struck many a child with the flat of her blade. Perhaps she could teach this youngling a lesson he would remember.

Nodding, she turned and strode towards Raheem. "A sword?"

He arched a brow. "A wooden training sword is smarter."

"Give me a metal one. Let him fight with the real thing."

She watched the posture change of the surrounding men who could hear her. Raheem cleared his throat and shook his head. "It's far too dangerous to fight with actual swords, Sultana. We cannot risk harm coming to you."

"You wanted a demonstration, did you not?" She raised her voice, glancing over her shoulder at Abdul. The sun reflected off her metal chestplate and sent a beam of light to heat his torso.

He acknowledged her challenge with the gritting of his teeth and an angry grimace. "If that's what the sultana wants, then by all means. We shall fight with a blade."

Someone strode forward and handed the boy a curved sword she'd never seen before. It would be unusual to fight against something like that. Her own sword would catch on it if she allowed him too much leeway. Interesting choice, and perhaps something she would try later.

A piercing cry fell from the sky along with a bundle of fabric. Sigrid lifted her hand and caught the thin rapier her sister had carried from their tent. The silver owl blended in with the sky, nearly impossible to distinguish from the streamers of white clouds.

Murmurs whispered on the wind. The men didn't like the surprise, thinking her a witch or perhaps a magician of the storm. What else could she do if weapons appeared out of thin air?

Strange beings. They would rather believe in the impossible than what was right in front of them.

Sigrid handed the bundle to Raheem. "Unwrap it."

"I'm not your apprentice."

"And I'm not asking you to be. A warrior does not touch her sword until it is bared for all to see. Unwrap it."

The personal guard accepted their differences far easier than the rest of his people. Though he was clearly embarrassed, he still took the time to pull the fabric away from her sword and bare the white metal for all to see.

Helvete had been with her for a very long time. It was her first sword, forged with the heat of her own mother's breath. The blade was impossibly white, decorated with runes to imbue her with strength, honor, and courage. Lapis lazuli stones decorated the hilt that wrapped around her hand like it was melting into her skin.

She closed her eyes. "Ancestors, guide my hands. I ask your souls to flow through me, to stem the battle rage, and to train instead of harm."

Raheem opened his mouth as if he wanted to say something, but snapped it shut when she shook her head. Now was not the time to ask questions. She would answer them in her own time if she wished to.

She slid her hand to the pommel of the sword and lifted it up. A man beside her hid a chuckle, and she heard snippets of conversation as she turned.

"What is she going to do with that twig?"

"A ritual for a sword? She knows she's just going to stick it into someone right?"

"Obviously hasn't fought before."

The words washed over her, but did not penetrate through her concentration. Even training was a taste of what battle was really like. They should understand this, but perhaps they had never fought in a battle either.

The boy waited for her in the center with his curved blade touching the ground. His throat bobbled as she made her way towards him, his eyes flicking everywhere but her.

"You're afraid of me," she said. "That's good. You should always be afraid of your enemy no matter what they look like."

"I'm not afraid of you." His answering growl made the crowd burst into laughter.

"You are," she corrected. Sigrid swept her skirts to the side with her free hand and lifted her blade. "And if you are not, then you are a fool. First blood?"

His lip twitched, and he nodded.

Abdul let out a whoop which apparently meant it was time for the fight to begin. The boy lurched forward, clumsy on his feet and trying to use his weight to gain advantage.

Perhaps that worked with the boys when he trained, but he didn't appear large to her. Sigrid had fought against Wildewyn men her entire life. They were larger than life, giants among men, and only grew bigger as they aged.

She sidestepped the boy's quick attack and let him stumble to the other side of the circle.

Head cocked to the side, she pointed at him with her sword. "Never make the first move. Survey your enemy, and let them see your eyes before you try to fight them."

He huffed out an angry breath and charged forward again.

Sigrid didn't want to crush the poor boy's ego too soon. She let him get close enough to feel the heat of her body before she ducked low and swept her leg out to the side. The pivot was graceful, and she admired the silken flow of her dress as it arced around her. She even gave the boy her back for a heartbeat, but he couldn't stop his own forward momentum.

He fell to a knee, then scrambled back to his feet. Chest heaving, he stared at her with so much anger in his gaze that she knew he wouldn't change his tactics. Was this how Bymere taught their sons to battle? With rage clouding their minds?

When he charged her again, she let him meet her sword to sword. Her biceps flexed, and she held him in place, close enough to stare at her eyes, far enough away that he would never touch her.

"Fool," she growled. "Your heart has no place in battle. Fight with your head."

The anger melted from his gaze and, again, she saw his fear.

"Good." Sigrid tilted her blade, slid to the side, and let him fall forward. "Perhaps now you understand."

She was finished with this child. He would not learn as she wanted him to, not with so many Bymerian thoughts filling his head. Later, she would voice her concerns to Raheem.

Spinning on her heel, she let Helvette rush through the air and slice through the boy's arm. To his credit, he did not cry out. But the bloom of red blood clearly marked her victory.

He threw his sword to the ground and stomped away.

Sigrid shook her head. The boy wouldn't learn if he couldn't take defeat. There were always small defeats on every battlefield. One needed to learn how to recover from those so that life was not lost.

"Good show," Abdul called out. "You can fight our children well."

"Your children are nothing but that. If you wish to insult me, advisor, then perhaps you should find me an appointment worthy of battle."

They had apparently already thought of that. She fought for the rest of the day. Sand blasted in the air from her feet, from their hands, spraying up and catching in the sunlight which steadily set.

Every opponent grew increasingly difficult. Her muscles ached, her back flamed, and her vision skewed. Water, she needed water.

Sigrid lifted her blade and deflected yet another sword that arced down towards her. She could admire the man's leap into the air, it made him far stronger than he actually was. A shame that he left his belly open to her attack.

Careful, she reminded herself. *Don't gut him just because you are tired.*

The man had no idea how close he'd come to death. He slapped a hand to the red welt that beaded up just enough to mark her victory.

Exhausted, overheated, and shaking, she lifted her blade again and waited for the next person to attack. If they wished to do this for the rest of the day, then so be it. Her pride wouldn't allow her to stop. Not when she was so far from home.

Heat unfurled in her chest. She wanted to change so badly, to feel scales replace flesh and show them all what a drakon could really do. The edges of her mask seared her flesh. It heated to control the beast inside her, numbing the desire until it was little more than a festering wound on her soul.

Soon. Soon she would allow her true self to fly free, but not tonight.

A female voice lifted into the sky. "I grow bored, husband. She's showing off, and perhaps she's made herself clear. It's a shame she'll never use it again. Fighting is useless for women.

We were made for more delicate pursuits."

Heavy brocade stuck to Sigrid's chest underneath the metal armored plate. Her skirts were heavy with sand that scratched her legs. Her hair stuck to the back of her neck, sweat slicking her face underneath the mask.

But she still did not agree. She was made of steel and stone. She was not made for delicate things. She was made to feel skulls crack beneath her fists, for mountains to break underneath her claws, and to shake the sky with a roar like thunder.

Nadir strode into her line of vision. He crossed his arms and stared into her eyes. Could he read her thoughts? Did he understand that she wouldn't stop until she had made every man in this tented village bleed?

"One last opponent," he finally said.

"Who?" she snarled.

He grasped the hem of his shirt and pulled it over his head. "Me."

Her gaze caught on the slick muscles that flexed on his chest. Had he always been this large? She'd thought him a smaller man. A boy really. But he was more than that.

Powerful pectoral muscles bulged, a groove tracing down his sternum and fanning out over pronounced abs. Twin lines arced over his hips, following the valleys of strength down to powerful legs that moved towards her.

He inclined his head, shaking out his broad shoulders and strong arms. "No swords, Sultana. In the castle we do not fight with weapons."

"You want to fight me hand to hand?" She shook her head. "It's not a good idea to get so close to a Beastkin, even one who is tired."

"I'm the only one who can do it. Isn't that right? You won't allow anyone but me to touch you." Heat sparked in his gaze as he said the words.

It was unwelcome, and he had no right to even think such thoughts in her presence. But he wasn't wrong.

"Sultana," Raheem interrupted. "Shall I take your sword?"

She could get this fight over with before it even started. A part of her wanted to lift the blade and swipe a line across his chest. Such a mark would likely scar him, and the thought was tempting. She could leave him with a memory of her for the rest of his life.

Her hand shook as she handed the sword to Raheem. Helvete would feast more in her lifetime. She did not need the blood of a sultan today.

"First blood has been the tournament so far." She sighed. "What shall we say between you and me?"

"I see no reason to change it. First blood, wife."

A feral part of her rejoiced in the chance to wound him. "You're daring, husband. You ask to fight a dragon."

"I ask to fight a woman who thinks she is a dragon." He circled her. "I believe you are just a woman who wants to be stronger than she is."

"Have I not defeated your entire army?" Sigrid didn't let him get behind her. She didn't trust this boy king who was far more than he appeared to be.

"This isn't my army. This is a base camp, fodder for any Wildewyn soldiers who make it over the Edge of the World."

"You sacrifice your men so easily? Should they not be the front line to protect you and your people?"

"I don't care if your armies make it over the cliffs. You still have to make it through *my* desert." A spark simmered in his gaze. Fire she both recognized and found entirely foreign at the same time. "What of you, little sultana? Do you think you can survive my desert?"

"You wish to make me fight for hours, and then send me to the sands?" She narrowed her eyes. "You cannot punish me just yet. I've not stolen from you, husband."

"I think you already have."

He lunged forward, hands still at his side but clearly waiting for her reaction. It had been a long time since she wrestled with any of her sisters. Sigrid had fought with the blade and with arrows. Being close to anyone awoke the dragon side of her, and she had a hard time controlling the beast once it lifted its head.

She ducked and brought a fist toward his ribs. A swift blow would put him in his place.

But her knuckles didn't touch him. Instead, he slapped her hand away and reached for her neck.

Sigrid twisted away at the last second, bending to her knees and spinning away. Sand sprayed from her side like gold coins showering from a treasury.

"You know how to wrestle?" he asked with a chuckle. He jogged a few steps from her, placing his hands on his hips with a wide grin on his face. "You grow more interesting by the day, wife."

Her thighs shook. Exhaustion made her vision slip to the side, and gods, she was tired. All this heat overwhelmed even the fires inside her belly. She needed to rest, but she refused to allow him to win.

She growled, the low sound vibrating her ribs. "Get it over with."

"Are you feeling your hours of battle already? I'm not tired at all."

"You think to torture me with your words? If you are as good a warrior as you claim to be, then you should be able to end this swiftly."

"I can end it any time I want."

Sigrid made a quiet sound, a needy sound that desired both battle and for this to be over with. "Then fight me, husband. Show me just how strong you really are."

That spark grew in his eyes again. She concentrated on it, the flames that burned in his gaze. Was it desire? Men were usually easy to read, but she couldn't pinpoint what this sultan wanted from her. Those flames were too dangerous to be desire.

What did he have planned for her?

He rushed her, locking his arms around her shoulders, flipping her back to his chest, and dragging her against his front. Heat flushed her cheeks, not just from the sudden touch but from her own reaction. The smooth skin of his forearm slid across her neck, tightening slowly, like a python threading around her throat. She could feel each of his heaving breaths, and Sigrid suddenly realized she'd never been this close to a man before.

She flexed her stomach, brought her legs up, and scissor-kicked away from him. Though his hold was strong, he didn't expect her to react so quickly. His arms loosened for the briefest moment, but it was enough for her to twist around.

Mask met chest, and he snarled in pain.

"That metal is *hot*."

Sigrid didn't give him the satisfaction of a reply. She could have quipped how she was a dragon, and what exactly did he expect? It was too much of an opening if she argued with him again.

She wiggled her arms free, hands scrabbling for purchase before he yanked them back to her sides. She wouldn't draw blood with claws so it seemed.

Kicking out her leg, she wrapped it around his knee and jerked forward. They both fell, landing heavy on the ground and knocking the breath from her lungs. Sand whipped in her face, a dust storm of glassy shards. Rolling away from him, she shook her head and tried to get onto her hands and knees.

Her eyes. Her eyes were burning.

Nadir slapped a hand on the back of her thigh, tugging her back to his side by the fabric of her skirts.

"Bymerians know better than to wear so much clothing during battle," he growled. "It's too easy for someone to grab."

"Earthen folk know it can also be useful," she replied.

He rolled her onto her back, trying to straddle her. She let him, sliding a leg free from the folds of her skirts that he had assumed was pinned between his legs. Sigrid swung the free leg up and over his chest, slamming him hard against the ground where they locked each other in place. Her legs trembled as he struggled, but he stilled as she squeezed her legs painfully tight.

Nadir huffed out an angry breath. "Where did that come from? Did you grow another limb, wife?"

"Wouldn't you like to know?" She flexed, forcing him to lay flat and allowing her to roll on top of him.

He grabbed onto both her legs which had slid free from the

hidden slices in her skirts. Dark skin met pale, and she paused to lock eyes with him.

His yellow gaze burned.

"I've been trying to get you like this for a while now," he said with a chuckle. "Good to know all I had to do was make you angry enough to fight."

"Stop it."

"Why?"

"We have an audience."

"Wouldn't be the first time." He flinched to the side, avoiding the strike of her fist which pounded into the sand. "Easy there, Sultana. You wouldn't want to hurt this pretty face, would you?"

Nadir tossed her off him when she lifted a fist again. Sigrid rolled onto her side, anger flooding through her veins like a living thing. He was embarrassing her, choosing to make a spectacle when all his men were watching.

She remained in the sand as he staggered to his feet. A sardonic grin spread across his face, and he opened his arms wide. "Come on then. Are you finished already? I thought you had more fight in you."

His men laughed, even those who sported wounds from her blade.

She was done with this battle. With these people. With this land. Everything in it made her someone she didn't like. Sigrid wanted to go home where the air was cool, where water gurgled from deep inside the earth, and green leaves fell like snow.

Snow. She wanted to feel cold snow on her skin again.

An owl shrieked from the skies, and she swallowed past

her swollen tongue. Camilla was right. A Beastkin woman never gave up. No matter how tired she was.

Sigrid pushed herself up, tremors shaking through both arms.

The sudden worry marring her new husband's face was a little late. Perhaps he thought she was some immortal being who couldn't feel tired. Let him see she was a woman, and that a woman was going to win this battle once and for all.

"Enough," she growled. "This ends now."

"Still fighting?" Nadir lifted a brow, but reached a hand forward. Sweat glistened on his chest and she wanted nothing more than to claw through those pectorals until they were seeped in red. "Then I'll end it."

Sigrid rolled her neck, and let everything still inside her mind. She would not fight with anger or rage. She was a calm pool filled with silent water, iced over by a passing storm that disappeared in the distance.

His footsteps thudded against the sand. He raced towards her with a sudden burst of power that flung sand in every direction.

Sigrid twisted and snagged his shoulder as he passed. But the sultan had thought of the same tactic it seemed, because he hooked a hand around the horns of her mask. He head-butted her—a foolish thing to do—and she drew her nails from his shoulder across his chest.

The metallic scent of blood filled the air. Sigrid gasped and stumbled backward while he fell to a knee.

Bright lines of blood stretched across his skin. A small bead welled up, then trailed down the high peaks of muscle to pool in the valleys on his stomach.

"Congratulations, wife," he said. His head tilted down, staring at the sand instead of her. "You have won."

He knelt before her, and she didn't know how to respond. A sultan never took a knee to a woman. His army would wonder what he was doing. His advisors would know this was a foolish decision. So she allowed her body to sag and sink into the sand in front of him.

"Congratulations, husband," she repeated, out of breath and exhaustion sparking black at the edges of her vision. "You have won."

Nadir looked up, and she tilted her head back so that he could see the bright bead of blood leaking out of the bottom of her mask. It was a cheap win. Her mask had struck her nose, but it was still a win.

"It seems we have both won," he muttered. The crowd around them burst into laughter again, cheers lifting into the sky.

"Or lost." Sigrid pressed her fists into the ground and slowly stood.

She did not look back as she made her way to the tent where he'd hidden her. Her body ached more than her pride, but she felt as though this was a turning point that she might never come back from.

NADIR

WHAT KIND OF WOMAN FOUGHT LIKE THAT? NADIR HAD SEEN nothing like it before. She moved with grace even when defending herself with a sword. Every single one of his men fell to her blade until he stepped in.

His heart beat faster at the mere thought. He had been the only one capable of taming the icy woman. She had to be meant for him. Why else would he be the only one to bring her to her knees?

He sat in his tent, alone for the first time in a few nights. His new wife was recovering in her tent, apparently. The fight had taken a lot out of her.

The last time he had tried to see her, her maid servant had nearly tossed him out of the tent. Still, silence made him nervous. Women were supposed to talk. They never stopped making sounds, from words, to tapping fingers, to rustling cloth. But everything was eerily still inside his second wife's tent.

It made him uneasy.

His own tent was filled with boisterous noise. People walking by laughed on the way to their own tents. The fire spat sparks that sizzled when they hit the sand around the pit. Even his own breathing was loud to his ears.

How was she so silent all the time? He couldn't be as quiet if he tried.

The front tent flap opened, swishing in a smooth movement.

"Sultan?" The deep voice belonged to Abdul, though he wished it was anyone other than his opinionated advisor. "A word, please."

"Go away, Abdul."

"Nadir."

He didn't appreciate the chastising tone. Abdul always stepped a little too far when dealing with his sultan, but Nadir couldn't very well throw him out. The sultanate made their kingdom successful. No land could be ruled by a single king.

Footsteps sounded next to Nadir's head where he lay sprawled out on crimson rugs. They were far more comfortable than the nest of pillows they made for his bed. He didn't even know where they got the pillows, or who carried them this entire trip. All he knew was that they were there.

Should he know that? His new wife seemed to think less of him for not knowing the details of his kingdom. She spat words at him like they were daggers. Shockingly, he felt the wounds far more than he wanted to admit.

"Sultan," Abdul repeated. He knelt next to Nadir's side and sighed. "I don't like seeing you like this, boy."

"Why do you care?"

"I raised you like my own son when your brother died. I have seen you through many changes in your life, but I have never seen you act like this before. I worry about you. The entire sultanate worries about you."

"I have done nothing different." Nadir could hear the petulant tone of his own voice.

He didn't like thinking he had changed so quickly, either. But Raheem had stayed quiet, and the personal guard was the only person he trusted with his life. The others always had an ulterior motive. It made trusting their concerns more than a little difficult.

Abdul cleared his throat. "This girl... You know she is a means to an end, yes?"

"What are you prattling on about?" Nadir tilted his head so he could meet his advisor's gaze. The older man winced at the anger banked in Nadir's yellow eyes. "If you have something to say, spit it out."

"You're growing too attached to this little Wildewyn girl. She's the only way we could fix that little raid of yours. We aren't ready for war. Not yet. Marrying her gives us the time necessary to build and train our army. Nothing more, nothing less."

"Yes, yes." Nadir heard more about this army than anything else in the recent years.

It was a good idea to move on Wildewyn. They were too different, and dangerous, to remain so close to Bymere's borders. They had murdered his brother, assassinated the king. Those assaults could not be ignored.

He agreed with all of this. But he wasn't certain about the girl. There were so many questions he wanted to ask her. So many truths she might utter that would help them in the long run.

"She's a remarkable warrior," he said, clearing his throat. "Perhaps we should have her help train our men."

Abdul scoffed. "Earthen folk training our warriors? No, we will not stoop so low. Besides, she wouldn't stand a chance against our assassins."

"It seems as though she's already proven herself."

"The little war band you put together were only those willing to break ranks. And the border men she fought yesterday in that little tussle are hardly considered warriors. They're on the border for a reason. She wouldn't stand a chance against our hardened army. We have no need of her."

Nadir shrugged. "Seems foolish to ignore a chance to learn their ways."

"My boy." Abdul reached forward and grabbed his hand. Worn callouses scraped against his own, and Nadir remembered that Abdul was as much a warrior as those on the battlefield. "I hate to see you lose yourself over a wench."

"A what?"

"Women are a pleasant distraction from the real world. Trust me, I know." The worn lines around Abdul's eyes crinkled. "I remember what it was like to be so young. To find the glory hidden within the arms of a woman is a right you have well earned. But I want you to remember you don't have to like her. You can enjoy her, give her a good life as we promised her king, but I want you to put her in a box when we return to the Red Palace. Hide her away, so she cannot turn you away from us."

Nadir jerked, sitting up straight and staring down his

advisor. "Are you suggesting that I am allowing her to control me in some way?"

"I have observed differences in the way you—"

"Perhaps you observed wrong."

Abdul bristled, his shoulders straightening and eyes narrowing. "I helped raise you. Don't take that tone with me. You forget just how much I know about you, and just how much I can tell the people. Or, perhaps, your wives."

The coppery taste of blood flooded Nadir's mouth. He'd bitten down so hard that his gums were bleeding.

His advisor overstepped his bounds, and he wanted nothing more than to fly at the man in a rage. No one in the kingdom had any right to tell their sultan when he was doing something wrong, or when his actions were questionable. He was a sultan! He could do what he wanted whenever he wanted.

But Abdul was right about a few things. The girl was getting into his head, and he didn't have the time to suffer such an affliction. There were many plans in motion, most that he'd worked on with Abdul himself. Sigrid was a distraction to all these, and of course, his advisor was right. Abdul *had* raised him, advised him, and nurtured him all these years. He'd never been wrong before.

He jerked his chin, indicating his advisor could leave.

Abdul sighed and stood back up. His back was suspiciously hunched. Nadir remembered no weakness in the man. He'd been standing perfectly straight yesterday, while his second wife fought off a veritable army. But perhaps he was being too harsh on an aging man who had done much for him.

Pinching the bridge of his nose, he gritted through his

teeth, "I'll take your words into consideration, advisor."

Abdul walked toward the exit, then paused at the entrance to the tent. "I understand your fascination with her, Nadir. She's a butterfly we have captured in a jar. Wanting to see all the colors of her wings is natural. You should explore her, learn what you wish to learn from her, but then put her back in her cage. Don't forget that butterflies die in the desert."

The tent flap whispered shut behind him as he left, and Nadir felt the sound all the way to his soul.

Memories haunted the old man's steps. Before his brother had died, Hakim had kept a wall of butterflies. Each one pinned with its wings outstretched and affixed in place. They were infinitely delicate. Nadir had once touched a wing and watched it crumble beneath his finger.

Butterfly? He couldn't see Sigrid as anything like that. She had too much of the earth in her. Where butterflies were made of air, she was made of stone and brick. He couldn't pin her to a wall as an ornament.

He worried that was how his people saw her. And he understood why. The golden mask made her less human and more mysterious, like a performer. The billowing fabric she wore hid so much of her body it was easy for rumors to claim she wasn't human at all. That she was made of air and that there was nothing at all underneath the mask.

Nadir scrubbed his face. These rumors had to stop.

He was standing before he knew he moved. His feet sifted through the sands and carried him out of the tent without his awareness.

Moonlight turned the desert purple and blue. Rolling dunes shifted every day as the winds pushed them back and forth. It was the first thing he'd fallen in love with here. Every inch of the sand was constantly changing. He'd never met the same desert twice.

Tents dotted the dunes as far as his eyes could see, but he sought only one. A simple, sturdy tent on the edge of the camp where his second wife remained secluded.

"This will do just fine," she had called through the tent when he ordered her to step out. "I've no need of fineries. A sturdy tent and a fire will suffice."

And then he'd been ordered to leave again. Like a commoner. Like a slave she kept at her beck and call.

He had to admit it, he felt a little like a slave to her whims. She captivated his attentions, no matter how much he tried to wipe her from his mind.

Nadir stalked back to her tent, arms swinging at his side. He wore sleep clothes, an embarrassing outfit for a sultan. A tunic knotted at his waist, a simple sash tucked underneath that sufficed as makeshift pants. The gauzy, white fabric left little to the mind's eye, but he'd never felt self-conscious until he met her. She covered herself so much, it made him feel like a heathen to stand in front of her.

He cleared his throat when he made it to her temporary home. "Wife? I'd have words with you."

No one responded to his call.

Nadir frowned. "Wife?"

When no response came, he pushed forward into the tent. No fire crackled to banish the dark shadows. The only light came from the single hole at the top of the tent where the moon's rays filtered through.

Silence struck his ears like a hand clapped over them. He'd

never experienced such a quiet that terrified him so much.

Something stirred in the far corner. He might not have noticed it at all if he wasn't staring straight at it. Something was breathing there. The tiniest movements clearly meant that whoever it was, was trying to hide from him.

"I know you are not my wife," he murmured as he stepped forward. "I've no wish to harm you. But if you have taken her, or harmed her in any way, then I will make sure you feel pain unimaginable."

"I was unaware you cared for my mistress so much." The voice was familiar. Sigrid's little handmaiden turned, her eyes flashing bright in the darkness. "Or perhaps you're more interested in keeping something you consider your property."

"Don't twist my words. Where is she?"

"Nowhere and everywhere." The woman shrugged. "She battles the beast tonight, and will not return until she has succeeded."

"What does that mean?" he growled. "All you Earthen folk talk in riddles. Be forthcoming with your words."

"It is as I said. She must fight this battle alone."

"And where did she go?"

"No one knows." The woman shook herself and stood, a long cloak settled around her shoulders to keep her warm. "It is different for each Beastkin, but Sigrid has always wandered."

"She'll get lost this far in the desert."

"It's impossible for a dragon to lose her way. They can see the world from the sky if they wish. She will find us. Keeping her family and her country safe is the most important thing to her."

He shook his head and sat on a wooden stool. It was a

sturdy thing, made of wood and metal. They'd never have a piece of furniture like this in Bymere. Trees were far too precious to cut down.

The woman met his gaze with wide, owl-like eyes. He could feel her stare like a touch as she looked him up and down. What would she see in him? A boy king as so many others did? Or something more?

She eased down onto a trunk opposite of him. "I tell you this secret only because I want her to be happy, and you need to understand our ways. You will swear yourself to secrecy. Yes?"

He hadn't the faintest idea of what she might be about to tell him. Nadir waved a hand and nodded. "Consider it so sworn."

"There are two kinds of Beastkin," she hesitantly started, as if she didn't trust him. "One that is melded seamlessly with the beast. They are one and the same. Person and animal, interlocked together as a single person. This is the best option for Beastkin, and most are such as this.

"But there are also Beastkin who will always fight against their animal. They cannot meld, because a predator always wishes to fight and to kill. These are the Beastkin who must go to battle with themselves, because they will be a danger to us all if they allow themselves to connect too much with their animal side."

It explained why she was so reserved, but some pieces weren't making sense. He shook his head. "Why wouldn't they want to connect with the animal? It seems far more dangerous for them to renounce their true nature."

"Predators want to hunt. They don't think as we do, and

that is dangerous for everyone. If they connect entirely with the animal, their fear is that they will no longer have the human's emotions that allow them to decide not to kill. They don't want to become monsters."

He frowned. "Why wouldn't she be able to control herself? That seems foolish. She's still a person, and if the non-predatory animals are fine, why shouldn't the others be as well?"

The handmaiden shifted, her face twisting in discomfort. "That's not a question I can answer, Sultan. The last remaining dragon was Sigrid's mother. She had not finished her training before her mother died. There is no one else alive who can answer that question."

A disturbing thought. It also reminded him of how little he knew of this strange creature he married. Nadir frowned and shook his head.

"What else do I not know?"

"There are a thousand lifetimes of information the Beastkin know. None of which I can tell you without her permission."

"How do I get her permission?"

The woman lifted a dark brow. "Perhaps you should ask her yourself? You are her husband after all."

"In name only." He shrugged when she flinched back. "Do you think I didn't notice there was no ceremony when others seemed prepared for one? I know the war band interrupted a wedding. We signed a peace treaty and a single sheet of paper. This isn't a traditional marriage."

"Not by our standards."

"Nor by mine."

The moonlight filtered over her mask, silver edges meeting textured hair tied back in braids. She must be a pretty little thing. Too secretive for his liking. However, perhaps he would have been too if he were in her situation.

Everything in this tent was too simple for these Wildewyn women. They both deserved to be surrounded by beautiful things. Gemstones, silk, mosaics that took hundreds of years to put together. None of which he could give them until they made it back to the Red Palace.

Instead, all he could offer was to sit across from her in the dark. He dug his toes into the sand and watched her do the same.

"We leave on the morrow."

"Where are we going?" she asked.

"The Red Palace. It's my home and the capital of Bymere."

"She won't like it." Her brow furrowed. "I don't think she'll want to go at all."

"She doesn't have a choice." Nadir stood, cracking his neck from side to side. "If she has not returned by morning, we will leave without her."

The owl maid shrugged. "A dragon finds its family no matter where they are."

Something ached in his chest. He couldn't decide if it was a twist of pity for a woman who found herself caged within a life she didn't want, or a twinge of disappointment in remembrance of what he had lost.

The death of his brother took away the last living person who could call him blood. Nadir longed for someone to feel the same way as his brother had about him. They were more than just siblings. They felt the same emotions. They laughed at the same jokes. Though their lives took different paths, he always knew someone loved him.

If he were honest with himself, he feared he'd never feel that way again.

He nodded and stood. "Then I hope to see you both tomorrow. Part of my...personal guard will meet us in the morning with horses. It will make traveling easier."

"I suspect it will."

The woman settled back in her dark corner, and he wondered what kind of life they were used to. She didn't complain about the simple tent, nor did she ask for a fire to warm her back. Instead, she curled up in the sand without a word and closed her eyes.

Nadir left her alone, a single thought burning in his mind as he left. These Beastkin women were strange, and far more dangerous than he gave them credit for.

SIGRID

SIGRID LISTENED FOR THE SOUNDS OF AN ATTACK. SOMETHING hadn't settled in her chest ever since she returned from wandering the sands, the dragon safely tucked back in its cage. She'd felt the angry chuffing of the beast and forced herself to meditate far away from distractions. The dragon could never be free, not when Sigrid didn't know what it would do.

When she returned, there was change riding on the wind

As the sun rose on the horizon, the first wave of men entered their tented camp. They brought with them a handful of horses, each more glorious than the last.

Most of the advisors were given dun-colored beasts. Their tan bodies twitched as each man jumped into the saddle, their hands gripping long waves of dark mane.

The sultan reached out for a chestnut beast. It was so tall, even Sigrid would have to tilt her head to look it in the eye. She watched it lash out at every man who tried to touch it, until Nadir pressed a palm to its nose. Immediately, the great beast calmed and stilled under its master's touch.

One horse was white as snow, and perfectly clean. Its long mane fluttered in the breeze like a banner crying out for peace, but its hooves struck the ground like hammers. This was given to the first wife. She sat astride—her crimson gown pooling down its sides like blood—and gave Sigrid a look that clearly stated she knew her place.

The first wife would always remain the most important. Her tent was more lavish. Her horse cried out for attention. Such was the way of the Bymerians.

Sigrid could care less. She didn't want attention as she looked for her opportunity to discover their hidden knowledge. The Council wanted her to watch these people, find out their secrets, and return to them with the head of a king.

She would do that and more with pleasure. They didn't seem to care at all whether the king survived. He was constantly alone, and his guards were lazy. Even his advisors forgot he existed.

Nothing was more confusing than the way these people chose to live.

Camilla had laid out a midnight gown for the journey, deep blue like the deepest pools in the Wildewyn forests. Tiny stars were hand-stitched in silver all over the bodice, falling like shooting stars into the heavy skirts. Her golden mask flared around her face like the sun.

A young man approached her, reins of a black stallion in his hand. "Sultana, if it pleases you."

Horses never pleased her. They didn't like sensing the predator inside her, and rarely reacted the way they should. But this creature was different than the others. She saw rage in his eyes when he looked at her, not fear.

Sigrid turned her gaze to the boy who led him. His head was covered by a dark red scarf, revealing nothing other than a sliver of tanned skin and bright blue eyes. Odd for someone from Bymere to have those colors.

Cocking her head to the side, she narrowed her eyes. There was something familiar about the boy. Something hidden in his gaze that wasn't Bymerian at all.

"Are you from here?" she asked.

"Yes, Sultana."

"Where are your parents from?"

He lifted that cold gaze and met hers head on. "From here, Sultana."

Anger shook his voice. He had a right to be. No one wanted to be accused of having mixed blood, and he'd likely heard such accusations his entire life. But she knew eyes like that, and hadn't thought they could be housed inside a man.

Sigrid reached out and caught the filmy sleeve of his shirt. She pitched her voice low and asked, "What are you known by?"

His gaze flicked side to side. "Sparrow, Your Grace."

A nickname or some kind, he likely wouldn't give her an exact answer. And he shouldn't in this place where they thought all Beastkin had been hunted.

Sigrid was overwhelmed with a surge of purpose. There were people here who needed her. A kind she recognized and found a part of herself inside. *Beastkin.* They weren't entirely gone in Bymere after all.

"I thought we could only be female," she whispered.

"I thought we could only be male," he echoed. He was so

young, his voice cracked on the words.

"Are there others?"

"More than the royals know." His gaze slanted to the side, watching a few guards walk past to reach their horses. "I cannot say more here, Sultana."

"You can find me at the palace?"

"I can."

"Then do so." She released her hold on his sleeve and narrowed her gaze on the mount. "He'll do. Until we meet again, brother."

The boy trembled, bowed, and then left the horse with her as if he didn't know which one would bite. Perhaps he was the only one in the camp with sense.

Sigrid flattened her hand and reached out to the horse. "I understand you have no interest in allowing me to ride you. I have no desire, nor need, to tire you with my weight. But we both must endure."

The black beast leaned forward, sniffed her palms, then touched a velvet soft nose to her hand. When it lipped at her fingers, clearly trying to bite her, she pulled back with a laugh.

"I've always admired creatures with spirit. You'll do."

She rounded him and placed her hands on the simple saddle. Sigrid was used to leather pieces with designs carved into the edges. Bymerians rode with little more than a blanket on the backs of their horses. Though it was beautifully designed with spirals of red and gold fabric, it would do little to ease her bottom on the long journey.

No matter, she supposed. What was a little more pain?

Sigrid swung herself onto the horse's back and caught the reins when it side-stepped. "Easy," she muttered. "We've got a long way to go just yet."

Camilla called out above her, the haunting owl cry her only warning before taloned feet clutched her shoulder.

"Where have you been? I have news," she said. A single downy feather landed on her lap.

Her sister didn't answer. Instead, she stared off into the distance where a dust storm was forming.

The last thing they needed was to ride through a storm. Sigrid already had sand in every crevice of her body, and with no bathing room in sight. She didn't want to think what discomforts a sandstorm would bring.

But then, she realized the sand cloud wasn't caused by the wind. She narrowed her eyes and felt anger burn a hole in her chest.

"This is not a personal guard," Sigrid growled. "This is an army."

Camilla sat on her shoulder, and then lifted her wings in agreement. They had spoken quickly this morning when Sigrid returned. She had heard of Nadir's sudden entrance to the tent, and what Camilla had explained to make him leave.

Trading information was not something unheard of between enemies, but she didn't like him knowing any more about her kind than he needed to. The Beastkin women were sacred to Wildewyn. Bymerians should remain in the dark about all they were capable of.

"Cursed man," she gritted through her teeth, yanking the reins to spin her horse around. "He cannot lie to me for long before he'll feel the lash of my tongue."

Before she could get far, another horse stepped in front of hers. The black stallion gave a cry and reared up slightly before settling beneath her.

Sigrid glowered at Raheem. "What are you doing?"

"Stopping you from making a poor decision."

"Explain that to me." She pointed at the angry storm cloud made by hundreds of hooves. "Give me one good reason why that exists, and I won't ask him."

"I can't do that."

She jerked the reins. "Then I will hear those words from his lips as well."

"Why are you so angry?" Raheem reached forward and yanked the reins out of her hands. "He's not going to change that army just because you raise your voice. Excuse me if I overstep my bounds, Sultana, but he'll answer to kindness far better than anger."

She stared at him, trying to figure out why he was helping her. What did he mean that the sultan would respond better to kindness? Everyone did. That didn't mean he deserved kind words when he was acting the fool.

"That army is clearly meant for my homeland, for my family," she growled. "Give me one good reason why I shouldn't try to stop it?"

"There are hundreds of ways to stop a war. The least effective is yelling. The most effective is understanding your enemy."

She stared at the strange man in front of her and saw him through new eyes. Raheem was not just a personal guard. He wasn't a man who had spent his entire life fighting and doing nothing else.

Small scars spider-webbed away from his eyes, she realized. Not the natural wrinkles brought about by laughter and happiness. Those were scars etched into his skin from some kind of wound, explosion, or simple accident. And beneath those scars was a man who knew how the world worked and who tried to help other people understand it as well.

"Are you a politician?" she asked.

"No."

"Were you an advisor?"

"No."

"Have you any ties to Bymere other than being born here?"

"Not a single one." A shadow passed through his gaze. Sadness, the kind she recognized from a bone-deep ache that festered in her own soul.

"Then why are you helping me? Why do you care what I do?"

Raheem straightened, releasing his hold on her reins. Perhaps he understood she wasn't going to race off to scream at her fool of a husband. Or perhaps he was letting her make the choice to be a fool, or not.

She stayed where she was.

His dark eyes searched hers for some explanation as to why she remained at his side. Then, he cleared his throat.

"Did you know Bymerians do believe in Beastkin? It's not that we haven't seen your kind; it's that we choose to ignore the obvious. There used to be shifters like you in these deserts. We hunted them down until they disappeared forever."

She'd heard rumors before, but never anything so certain. Her heart ached for those souls wandering the deserts, lost from their brethren, never able to join their families in the halls of the dead.

"It's a sad fate for one of our kind."

"I know more than most." He folded his hands in his laps, reins dangling loose and hanging in loops down the dun horse's neck. "My wife was one of the last Beastkin surviving in Bymere."

Sigrid's stomach flipped over, and she tasted bitter bile on her tongue. "What happened to her?"

"She died."

"How?"

"The sultan's father hunted her down and murdered her as she ran. The soldier threw a spear from a great distance, a nearly impossible throw, that somehow caught her between the shoulder blades. She was pinned to the ground for days before I returned with a hunting party. No one dared touch her body for fear the sultan's troops would return and kill them too."

"That's terrible." Anger burned so hot in her blood the stallion sidestepped. She needed to control her anger. The waves of heat rolling off her were dangerous to everyone. "Why are you telling me this? I already dislike your sultan."

"For that reason precisely." Raheem squared his shoulders. "All that changed when the sultan's older brother began to make decisions for Bymere. And it's changed even more with the current sultan. This land is changing for the good, but you cannot fix it in a day. He's doing his best, little sultana. He's changing the old ways inch by inch."

"He's changing them? Or his advisors are?" She lifted a brow.

"His advisors may seem as though they play him like a puppet, but make no mistake. The sultan has a mind of his own and a plan for this country that will make it great once more. You are in a unique position to help him do exactly that."

"How?" The storm grew ever closer. "He barely speaks to me."

"He's shy." Raheem tilted his head back and let out a booming laugh. "A strange consideration perhaps for a sultan, but he is just a boy. You are just a girl. You may need to make the first step. He's never had to be nice to a woman before."

"Perhaps he should learn."

"Perhaps you should teach him." A bright smile split Raheem's face. "I found the best advice I've ever received was from my wife. You women are far more capable than we give you credit for."

Her mask lifted slightly as she smiled beneath it. The man was quickly becoming one of her favorites, and that was an honor very few laid claim to.

Camilla brushed her wings upon Sigrid's shoulders, a sign that her faithful friend agreed. Raheem was astute in a way very few men were. He understood their people, their sex, and gave them the respect they deserved. She hadn't thought to see such treatment here.

Every precious thought was dashed to the ground as the white-haired advisor rode up on his stallion.

"Sultana." The sardonic grin on his face made the words seem like a mockery. "We cannot allow you to see the way to the Red Palace, I'm sure you understand."

She stared at the red cloth he held in his hands and forced her tongue to still. She didn't understand, but for reasons he couldn't comprehend. She could turn into a dragon and lift herself into the skies. All of Bymere would be laid out like a map at her feet. If she wanted to know where the Red Palace was, then she would find it easily enough.

But they still didn't believe she was a dragon. They thought she was little more than a pretty bauble the king kept around who knew how to lie through her teeth. No matter what tricks she showed them, they wouldn't believe a single word she said until she transformed in front of them.

A part of her wanted to. She wanted to feel her skin stretch and her claws grow. But she hadn't transformed since she was a little girl. Sigrid was a veritable security blanket for Wildewyn, when she didn't even know if she could become that dragon again.

Or what she would look like.

Abdul nudged his horse closer and gave her mask a severe glance. "I must ask you to remove the mask, Sultana."

"Why?"

"It will make it too easy for the blindfold to slip."

"Will you personally kill every man who looks upon my face other than my husband?" She narrowed her gaze on him. "I will know if you do not. It's worse to leave them alive."

He rolled his eyes. "You Earthen folk are so dramatic. Fine, we'll tie it around the mask. But if it slips, you must put it back in place. As I am respecting your ways, you shall respect ours."

Sigrid gave a nod and allowed him to tie the blindfold around her head, noting he was careful not to graze her with his fingertips. The black stallion huffed an angry breath, side-stepping to get away from the dun which attempted to nip his hind-quarters. Did they think to kill her? A horse accident would certainly suffice to snap her neck.

"Watch her, Raheem," Abdul said with stern tones. "The sultan himself has ordered she not be able to trace her steps back to the Red Palace."

When the sound of hooves disappeared, Sigrid shifted her hold on the reins. "Wake me when we arrive, guard."

Raheem chuckled. "Guard, is it? And I thought we were on a first name basis, Sultana."

"Not quite. If you allow a man to blindfold me and place me in danger of falling off my horse, then you are certainly not a very good personal guard."

"Would you like me to tie you to the horse?"

"There's no need."

Sigrid had ridden as a child, even slept on horseback when she was a wild little thing in the forests of Wildewyn. Of course, the horse had always been one of her kind, but horses were remarkably intelligent creatures.

She already felt a strange connection to the beast she rode. The stallion didn't want to be here either. She felt the twitching hide and understood the depth of his anger. He wanted to run free, to ride to the horizon and leave behind this life of servitude.

"Ride free," she murmured, letting the wind take her words to the horse's ears. "Ride true."

She let her eyes fall shut and drifted off into a deep, dreamless sleep.

"SULTANA."

The voice drifted through her conscious. It took very little to snap her awake, although she kept her body in the same position as before. Her posture did not change; her head did not lift. She listened for the sounds around her.

Armor creaked against the sides of horses. Hooves pawed at the ground, not moving, but standing still. A single rider approached, his horse oddly smooth in its gait. She heard fabric rustling as the man on the horse shifted his weight upon approach.

He was close enough that she could feel the heat of his leg against hers, and then he brushed against her, thigh to thigh.

Sigrid lifted her head, reached up, and whipped off the blindfold. It floated through the air like a banner of war as she glared at the man who dared touch her.

Nadir sat next to her, his burnished skin glistening with sweat in the sunlight. "So," he said, "you were serious that no man other than me may touch you."

"I don't lie."

"Just testing you. I think you might have killed me if I were anyone else."

"I wouldn't have done them the honor. I'd have cut off the part that touched me, and told the man to consider himself lucky."

"Losing a leg might be worth touching you." He grinned so brilliantly that it rivaled the sun. "Oh, don't narrow those eyes at me. I can imagine what kind of expression you're making. You should learn to take compliments better."

"It's not a compliment when you're being sarcastic."

"Who's to say I am?"

She rolled her eyes and gritted her teeth. There were more important things to do than indulge a spoiled king who had little to do other than bother her. Where was Camilla?

Shifting her weight, Sigrid noted the owl woman had burrowed herself underneath her skirts. It was likely cooler there than sitting in the sun.

Sweat made the back of Sigrid's dress cling to her skin. Her hands were shaking with the need to submerge herself in water, something to cleanse and cool her body. She'd even jump into a muddy pit if it relieved the unbearable heat for a few moments.

When Nadir didn't move away, she turned a cool gaze toward him. "Why are you here?"

"I want to witness your reaction firsthand when you see my palace for the first time."

A child wanted to see someone find pleasure in what he had recently received. She touched a tongue to the hot metal and reminded herself that ladies did not roll their eyes. "Then show me, Sultan. Where exactly is this palace?"

He pointed directly ahead of them. "Watch the sand dunes. All will be revealed in but a moment."

She kept her eyes on the horizon and did not have to wait long until they crested the nearest peak. The Red Palace sat on the horizon.

White sandstone jutted out of the dunes, pristine and so clean it was almost impossible to tell where shadows lay. The palace nestled between the jutting monoliths. Red stone carefully placed to create an entire city hovering above the sands.

High towers lifted into the sky, bulbous tips strange and unusual to her gaze. The sun reflected on the glass domes sprinkled throughout the city. Palm trees could barely be seen this far away, but her sharp drakon eyes caught on the only green she'd seen in weeks.

It was beautiful, in a way she'd never imagined. Stairs led from the desert up into the palace. Tiny figures made their way to the top, baskets on their head likely laden with food.

She couldn't understand the reason for living so high above the desert. Everything was infinitely more difficult to obtain that far away from their resources. It was too small to have enough crops or cattle to sustain. What if a war was fought at their doorstep? They would be dead in weeks.

Nadir's voice broke through her thoughts. "Is it not the most glorious building you've seen before?"

"It's not functional."

His mouth gaped open. He turned to stare at her for a moment before his brows drew down in anger. "It's a modern marvel. Such a palace has never been built before, and never will be built again."

"Because it is impossible to defend."

"There is no war in Bymere."

"There may be someday," she accused. "Placing yourself and your people in such a dangerous position is foolish and irresponsible."

A muscle ticked in his jaw. "No Bymerian would ever start a war on our sacred grounds."

"What makes it sacred? Because it is your home? Or because it houses the king?" Sigrid let loose a bitter laugh. "Kings are dispensable. Their people love to see them fall, because it reminds them that even royalty can bleed."

She turned her masked face towards him, hoping her eyes were devoid of all emotion. What she saw in his gaze chilled her.

It wasn't anger or disgust at her words that clouded his gaze. The bone deep sadness that filled his eyes nearly overwhelmed her. She'd never seen people who wore their emotions so close to the surface as the Bymerians.

Nadir inclined his head. "You forget, Sultana, that I'm closely acquainted with the darkness in people's hearts. They love to see a king die, and they rejoice when a new king takes the throne. No one mourns royalty for more than a few days. We are figureheads for an entire country, not a person. You should remember that *you* are now one of *us*. A sultana is just as easily forgotten as a king."

He jerked the reins in his hand hard and charged away from her. He lifted a hand into the air, letting out a whooping cry that sounded like the shriek of an eagle.

The entire army which had escorted them echoed his call. The soldiers around her kicked their horses into motion. Wind buffeted her back as they raced from her. Sand kicked up into her eyes, but she kept her gaze solidly on their spines.

Her horse shifted beneath her, but she held him firmly in place and allowed the army to sift away from her like sand from an hourglass.

"Sultana?" Raheem's ever-present voice questioned. "We must join them."

"Just one more moment," she whispered. Sigrid wanted to watch as every single soldier raced home, so she could see all the holes in their safety. It made her stomach sick to see how many there were.

"What are you waiting for?" he asked.

"I wanted to see how safe we truly are."

"And what do your Beastkin eyes see?"

"Everything," she whispered. "And none of it good."

"The people will look at you as a trophy he has won." Raheem reached for her reins and nudged them both into motion, careful not to touch her. "They will not see you as a person. I will keep them from touching you, but it would have been easier with the army around us."

Camilla noisily made her way out of Sigrid's skirts. Sigrid reached back and helped her owl sister onto her shoulder.

Raheem's expression at the owl's aggressive frown made Sigrid chuckle. "It will not only be you helping to keep me clear of all those who may be too friendly. Let them look. And if they dare touch, it will surprise me."

They reached the stairs, and she felt the heavy sigh of her horse. It was a long way up, though not nearly as far as the Edge of the World. She reached down and laid a comforting hand on her mount's neck.

"Nearly there," she whispered for his ears only. "And then we shall see what these Bymerians are capable of."

Sigrid listened to hoof beats striking the hard, white sandstone steps and stilled her mind. She had no idea what these people would do when they saw her. So far, the Bymerians she knew were volatile people who remained skeptical and at least marginally respectful. But these were peasants, those who had no say in the government, those who still believed in the old ways.

Someone was bound to recognize her. The Beastkin were a legend that few still believed in, but that everyone knew. Even if she was emulating her own kind, they would still find her terrifying.

It felt like only a few heartbeats before they were at the top of the stairs. The stallion's sides heaved and its coat glistened with sweat. He seemed to recognize where they were. His complaints eased, even though he was clearly exhausted.

The army charged through the streets, knocking people out of the way and racing towards the Red Palace which towered over the city. The banner of soldiers continued up the small hills, led by their sultan who was little more than a small figure in the distance.

She shook her head disdainfully. He didn't even pause to speak to his people after being gone for such a long time. Instead, he ran from them.

"I'll warn you again, Sultana," Raheem said, clearing his throat. "These people do not know you."

"Let them come."

Crowds lined each side of the street. Red brick buildings listed to the sides, warped awkwardly as if the ground had moved underneath them after being built. Rough, hemp cords stretched high overhead, clothing hung from its length. The wind billowed through silk and fine chiffon, and she wondered if there were any peasants in Bymere. Hundreds of colors dotted the air along with the people who now stood staring at her.

These were sturdy folk. Sigrid had seen such lined faces before. A man stood holding onto a fork she knew stirred laundry. Another man in brilliant aquamarine carried a basket of eggs. His wife reached for his arm, adorned in similar colors, with a woven basket of fruit balanced atop her head.

All were silent as they stared at the newcomer who had invaded their lands. Sigrid nudged her horse forward. She kept her posture stiff and her head held high. They would not think for a second that this mysterious woman from Wildewyn was uncomfortable in their midst.

A woman dressed in crimson fabric whispered, "Who is that?"

The woman next to her, a mirrored image of the first, covered her hand with a giggle. "Did the sultan bring back a prize?"

"Why does it wear a mask?" An unseen voice shouted from within the crowd.

Sigrid flinched as someone finally recognized her. "Beastkin!"

The gasping crowd shrank away from her. Suddenly, voices lifted in the hundreds, too many to understand, but she picked out a few of the complaints.

"Beastkin are not allowed in the city!"

"Kill her *now*. Before she kills us!"

"We don't want your kind here, witch!"

Such calls would never have been uttered in Wildewyn. They still valued the magic that brewed inside the breasts of the Beastkin women. Her soul ached at how far these people had been led astray.

Was it not useful to speak with the cattle that pulled your plow? Did they not wish to sing notes no human voice could ever reach? Were they so heartless that they didn't see the beautiful things the Beastkin could bring? Not to mention the culture, the visions, the assistance…

She heard the whistle in the wind long before the rock struck her mask. It was a sizeable stone and might have left an open wound if it had caught her in the face.

The turbulent chatter froze as her head whipped back from

the force of the throw. Sigrid lifted a hand slowly and touched a hand to her mask.

"Sultana," Raheem growled. "I shall kill the man who dared."

She held up her other hand, relaxed and calm. The rock wasn't something she could concern herself with. She took the time to feel the edges of the mask, making certain her face wasn't showing and that the strap would still hold. There were some mistakes these people couldn't come back from. Seeing her face was one of them.

Sighing in relief, she turned towards Raheem and shook her head. "It is but a rock."

"If we allow them to throw one, then more will follow," he growled. "We should cut off the hand of the man who dared."

"Your sultan didn't tell them who I am. They think I am a prisoner of war, at best. A pet, at worst. I don't blame them for their fear."

"Sultana—"

"Raheem," she interrupted. "You won't change my mind on this."

He appeared torn. His hand rested on the pommel of his sword, and his eyes continually flicked to the crowd waiting for what he should do. Finally, he sighed and relaxed his shoulders. "They dented your mask."

She shrugged. "It's soft metal."

Taking a deep breath, Sigrid made her decision. She had known this may be a trial she would have to endure. Of course, a part of her had hoped they would be more understanding than this. But drakon were hardy beasts, and if the villagers wished to throw stones, then she would bear their misplaced hatred as proof the Beastkin were harmless creatures.

Or most of them, at least. She wasn't certain she could say a drakon was harmless.

She swung her leg over the horse and set both feet firm on the ground. She tucked her fingers under Camilla's claws and settled her atop the saddle. The owl's eyes were luminous and sad.

"Raheem, I have no wish for such glorious creatures to be harmed because of me. Keep them ahead of us."

"I'm staying behind you. I don't want them to turn into an angry mob and attack."

"Then stay behind me if you wish, but do not interfere." She looked up again and felt a sting from the pity she recognized in his gaze. "I must do this."

"I have no doubt that I cannot change your mind." He made a fist and pressed it against his heart. "I wish I could take the pain for you."

It was a kind statement, and a surprising one coming from a Bymerian. She felt a small bit of pity for this man who did not understand her ways. "A drakon doesn't feel pain."

Sigrid turned on her heel, midnight skirts flaring around her in a dark arc. Those closest to her gasped. They stared at her mask as if it were the face of a demon. Perhaps, it was to them. She'd never taken the time to truly understand why the Bymerians feared the Beastkin.

She set her gaze on the last tail of the army as it disappeared inside the Red Palace. She could see in the distance that the gates stood open, waiting for the sultan's newest prize. It would take a while for her to get there if they waited for her to walk through the streets.

Good. She would arrive tired, dirty, and likely battered from the fear of his own people. If that didn't knock sense into his head, she didn't know what would.

The first step was relatively easy. People gasped as she moved, marveled at how human she looked, wondered at the mask and the way she covered her body. But they allowed her to step forward nearly five paces before the second rock was thrown.

This one grazed the top of her head. She felt the wind shifting through her hair, but no pain. The third struck her in the chest. The air chuffed from her lungs, and she paused for a second before walking forward.

"We don't need your kind here!" A woman shouted, her caramel colored skin darkened in anger.

"We already rid our lands of your tainted blood," a man snarled from the shadows. Sigrid noted the goblet clutched in his hand, ale leaking over the edge and flowing onto the stone.

Another man lurched forward, reaching for her arm. He was a big man, scars smattered across his face from war or brawls, she couldn't tell. His hand never reached her. Raheem's sword gleamed in the sunlight.

The people around her seemed to recognize him. They all gasped, confusion warping their expressions.

Raheem's deep voice resounded through the street. "You may throw all you like, but you'll not a lay a hand on her."

"By who's orders?" the man grumbled.

Sigrid interrupted her guard long before he could speak. The deep chuff began in her chest, too loud for a woman to ever make. The rumble was that of a mountain groaning during an earthquake. The shifting crack of stone against rock. An earthen sound so foreign to these people that they knew exactly who made the sound.

The man stepped away from her with his hands held up.

She resumed her journey through the crowd and endured the stones, the fruit, the roughage that were thrown in her path and at her body. Three more people managed to strike her mask. It held in place, a testament to how wonderfully made it was.

She sent a silent prayer to the heavens, thanking her sisters for their wondrous abilities to create incredible masks that held even in the worst situations.

Through the torment, she noted the faces of each person. They were marred by fear and anger, but she knew the people beneath those emotions.

The woman who tossed a bucket of dirty water at her feet was a seamstress. The pins in her skirts and measuring tape wrapped around her neck meant she knew her work, and the tiny scars on her thumbs meant she'd taken her time to learn the craft.

The man who threw the most recent rock was a farmer. His front was considerably lighter than the back of him, suggesting he spent more time bent over in the fields than upright. Sigrid had seen people like him before and knew that he wasn't educated enough to understand change could be good.

A small child threw a rotten tomato at her, striking her hip. The juice soaked through to her skin as she noted the dirt smudging his face. He didn't have a home, that one. Not a single person to take him in, to explain why throwing refuse at a stranger was wrong.

Her heart broke for them even as red rage boiled deep in

her veins. The drakon wanted to rear up, to fly into the sky, and rain fire down upon their heads. They couldn't possibly understand what she was capable of, but they would.

Sigrid let fire play in her mind's eye for a few moments until she saw the crowd jostling ahead of her. Trouble. Perhaps, these were people who hadn't heard Raheem's declaration. Regardless, she balled her fists in preparation for a skirmish.

Just as she reached them, a small child was shoved from the crowd. An accident, no one would put their child in harm's way like that, but she tumbled forward all the same.

Without thinking, Sigrid lunged forward and caught the tiny girl in her hands just before her head struck the ground.

All sound stilled, and then there was only silence.

The little girl was a tiny thing, made of mostly bones and awkward limbs. A vibrant green scarf hid her dark hair. Her face was thin, but obviously pretty. Almond-shaped eyes, so brown they looked like a forest of trees, met Sigrid's icy gaze without fear.

She hadn't touched a person other than her sister's in her entire life. Sigrid's chest burned with the knowledge that this was wrong, but her heart answered with another heat. She had *missed* this. Being able to touch someone, to save them, and she'd never realized it was something she desired so much.

The little girl lifted a hand and touched it to the mashed metal of Sigrid's mask. "I like your mask."

Her voice was that of a sparrow's. Light, airy, delicate. This was a creature who had no right to be in an angry crowd of people. She should be sitting in a tower, looking out over her domain and composing her next song.

Sigrid smiled and her mask lifted slightly, touching the

girl's palm again. "Is it not frightening?"

"A little."

"You don't seem scared."

"I am a little." The girl chewed her lip. "But you caught me."

"Be careful in crowds like this. Next time, you might meet a horse instead of a Beastkin."

Sigrid gently placed the little girl back onto her feet, making sure she was settled before stepping back. A woman behind them in the crowd pressed a hand to her mouth. The little girl's mother? They looked alike, but Sigrid wasn't very good at telling the Bymerians apart yet.

Her gaze tilted down as the little girl got onto her knees. Furrowing her brow, Sigrid watched in confusion until she realized the pose was one of prayer.

Of worship.

"No." Her arms snapped forward and jerked the child to her feet. The answering wave of movement forward from the crowd did not go unnoticed, but Sigrid smoothed her hands along the girl's shoulders and smiled. "Beastkin never bow to another woman. We are equal, you and I. We curtsy if we wish to show respect, but only at the same time. Like so."

Sigrid showed the little girl the grand, sweeping motion of a curtsy.

The little one was smart. She mimicked the movement almost perfectly and gave Sigrid a wild grin as she joined in on the movements.

"You're odd," the little girl said, her voice loud and innocent.

Raheem cleared his throat. "Shall I take her hands, Sultana?

It is the punishment for touching you, after all."

The woman in the crowd let out a whimper that Sigrid felt in her soul. The entirety of the mob listed back at the word "sultana." So, no one had told them that a new queen was arriving with their sultan. Her instincts had been correct.

Sigrid sighed, straightened, and shook her head. "No, honored guard. She is but a little one, and does not know the ways of Beastkin. I will take the punishment on myself. It was my choice to not let her fall."

"How so, Sultana?"

She glanced up and saw the bite of anger in his gaze. He was proving a point to the crowd. A clear message that Sigrid was not a monster, and that she would be respected.

"I'm not going to cut my own hands off. For such an innocent touch, I believe three days of fasting is plenty." She looked back at the little girl and curtsied again. "Feel no guilt, bright soul. It was an honor to save you, and I would do it again if you stumbled."

"You should eat, Sultana." The girl stared at her feet, suddenly afraid. "The sultan will be very angry at me if you don't."

The rage in her veins was different this time. This was an anger that ran through the very foundation of mountains and deep in forest streams. The drakon inside her saw a youngling that needed mothering, a protector, a matriarch.

She gritted her teeth and reached forward. One finger slid under the chin of the child. A chill settled on Sigrid's shoulder at the blatant disrespect for her own traditions.

"I do not regret my previous touch, nor this one. If the sultan is angry, then let him be angry at me. My shoulders are strong. They can bear his rage, if I wish it."

The worry did not abate from the girl's gaze, but her shoulders sank. "Thank you, Sultana."

Sigrid let her hand fall and turned away from the little girl. The crowd parted like a wave in front of her. The fear was still in their eyes, but something like respect was there as well.

Saving a child did wonders for the opinions of the masses. She'd seen it done before, and was pleased to see that Bymerians and Earthen Folk were one and the same when it came to children.

The future was far more important than the past.

When it became clear there would be no more rocks or fruit thrown, Raheem nudged his horse forward and rode at her side.

"You knew that would happen, didn't you?" he murmured.

"I am not a soothsayer. I had my hopes, but I certainly did not know it would happen."

"Why?"

She glanced up. "Why what?"

Raheem shook his head, leaning an elbow on his knee and staring down at her. "Why take the risk if you didn't know it was a sure thing?"

"Risks are meant to be taken. These people would always see me as a monster if they didn't have a chance to glimpse the person underneath the mask." She set her gaze toward the castle. "Your sultan is correct in one thing. The people don't want to see royalty as anything other than a figurehead. Not unless they are given a reason to believe there is a person underneath all that finery."

She remained silent for the rest of the long walk. Each step felt like glass had wiggled its way into her shoes, but she refused to show the pain. Her back ached, sweat trickled down her spine, mere little things that were mind over matter.

Finally, they reached the open gates that stood five men high. Guards stood at the entrance, leather armor reflecting the sun in her eyes. Their hands rest on the gem encrusted hilts of their blades and they stood at attention. But their gazes flicked to her in surprise.

Raheem dismounted and urged her forward with a gesturing hand. Talons landed on her shoulder, gently squeezing to give comfort more than for stability. The Red Palace loomed over everything like a monolith of old. She shook her head, but made her way through the second gate and into a hall clearly meant for the sultan and his advisors.

Red and gold mosaics covered the floor. The hall was bisected by a pool of sapphire water where emerald lily pads floated. Two tiers of seats lined the edges, creating a clear arrow that led all the way to a dais where the throne overpowered the steps leading to it. Crimson fabric hung from the ceiling, spilling down the steps in a train that was almost embarrassingly ostentatious.

The sultan already sat upon his throne, one leg carelessly tossed over the throne. He gestured at the splendor around them and asked, "Well, wife? Is it not the grandest building you've ever seen?"

She did not respond. Her heart was weary, her soul aching, and she wanted to lie down more than anything else in the world.

He frowned at her. "You've nothing to say? I find it hard

to believe you are speechless."

"I am tired," she finally replied. "And I don't have the energy to play your games."

The sultan's jaw dropped open for a moment before he gave a hesitant nod. "Then Raheem will escort you to the women's chambers. May your rest be peaceful, wife."

"And yours."

Sigrid barely noticed the journey, took little more than a few steps into the chambers where Raheem had led before Camilla transformed and grabbed her shoulder.

"Sister?"

"Sleep," she mumbled. "I need nothing more than sleep."

She allowed Camilla to guide her to a comfortable pile of rugs and pillow, her last thought a desperate lance of fear, wondering if they'd fallen into a pit of vipers.

NADIR

NADIR STARED DOWN AT THE PAPERS IN FRONT OF HIM, HOPING his eyes would find some detail he'd missed in the maps of Bymere. He had seen these maps a hundred times in his life, perhaps more. Every time he sat at this desk, there was more of the same.

He knew the uppermost part of Misthall was falling into ruin. Even though it was in the capital, there was nothing he could do for its people. They were unruly, disliked having a sultan, and refused to play any of the tariffs the throne ordered from them. They even attacked the soldiers he sent to coerce them into following their Bymerian duty.

Falldell was a mystery even to him. The assassins that came out of that deserted land were legendary, but no one knew how they were trained. The men rarely spoke. Their women were deadlier than any feminine creature had a right to be, and no one knew the exact number of people who lived in that part of his kingdom.

Glasslyn was by far the most profitable. They were the fodder to his army, but also the people who harvested most of their food, raised the cattle, and paid more dearly than any other group of people. He wanted to focus on those lands. To provide them with much-needed assistance so the entire country would prosper.

His advisors disagreed. They wanted him to focus on Misthall. Peasants weren't worth the energy of the sultan, they said. Leave them to continue their work, no need to give them any hopes of their lives bettering just because the sultan thought to send them a little extra water this month.

A voice in Nadir's head screamed that wasn't right. That the people who kept his kingdom afloat might not be of royal blood, but they should at least receive incentive for their hard work.

He felt the throne was a prison. He couldn't do anything he wanted to do without his advisors whispering in his ear that there were more important things to focus on. They'd already considered all the options for his kingdom, they spoke while he was with his concubines, out riding, any time he wasn't around them.

If he were a more argumentative man, he might have put a stop to it. But they were more family than advisors. They'd *raised* him. They had a right to tell him their opinions…didn't they?

A resounding knock interrupted him. Clearing his mind of such troubled thoughts, Nadir called out, "Enter!"

The doors eased open and Raheem squeezed his large bulk through the horseshoe frame.

Arches decorated his castle, each more intricate than the

last. Contrary to the name, the Red Palace was not entirely red. Each wing had its own color, meant to inspire certain emotions in the people who walked the halls. This wing, the sultan's private wing, was emerald green.

He hadn't thought about how much it mimicked the colors of Wildewyn until he'd returned. Now, Nadir saw the forest in every carved mosaic on his wall. The forest and its women haunted his every step.

Raheem knelt, one knee on the floor and the other raised. Pressing his fists together, he said, "It's an honor, Sultan."

Nadir grinned. "I thought we did away with tradition when it was just the two of us?"

"Some conversations call for traditions."

"Oh, gods." Nadir pushed the stacks of maps away from him. "What do you want now?"

"It's your wife, Nadir."

"I know. She's been meddling again."

Saafiya had a way of taking the entire happiness of the kingdom and turning it sour, starting with the women closest to her. The concubines were now in an uproar. They didn't want something so dangerous as a Beastkin in their private quarters, let alone the dark-skinned woman who was only there sometimes and moved in the shadows like a wraith.

Raheem's lips twitched. "Not that wife, Sultan."

"Nadir," he corrected. He tapped his chin with the sextant in his hand. "The second wife?"

"Yes, Sultan."

"What is she doing?"

"Nothing, Sultan."

"Then that is a good thing," Nadir replied. He reached for

a map and pulled it closer. "Come back when she is doing something. That will be a more entertaining conversation."

"Nadir." Raheem's voice deepened, sounding almost disappointed. "You have a new wife. We've been back in the capital for two weeks, and you've not said a single word to her."

"Does she seem unhappy with that?"

"Well, no—"

"Has it ever occurred to you she might want to be left alone?" Nadir's voice shook with anger, and he didn't know why.

He was doing the right thing by respecting her solitude. She didn't want to be here anymore than he wanted to take a second wife. He certainly had no need of one, Saafiya kept him busy enough. Let the Beastkin woman make his palace her home, and soon he would make her another palace. One where he could hide her away and forget that they had forced him to marry a compelling woman who drifted through his waking dreams.

"Then I failed you in this, and I apologize for that, Sultan." Raheem stood, his wide chest puffed out in anger that Nadir couldn't explain. "I know you weren't raised like a normal boy, but I thought I'd had enough influence to teach you better. The girl doesn't have a single friend within these halls. The concubines are afraid of her. The people are terrified of what she can do. All she has is that silent owl that follows her like a shadow."

"And what am I supposed to do about that?" Nadir tossed the sextant onto the table with a disgusted sound. "She chooses solitude, and she should. I took her from her home without permission, we violated this woman and I refuse to make that worse. I've heard it all from Saafiya. Sigrid sits in her room, praying or meditating. She won't talk to the others, which isn't particularly helpful when forming friendships. And she didn't eat for the first week she was here."

"Are you believing the lies Saafiya tells?"

"She lies," Nadir agreed, "but there's always truth in them. That's why people believe her so easily."

Raheem spat on the floor. It was the ultimate insult to give when another person spoke of a viper. Nadir had seen the movement done often regarding his first wife. "You think she fasted because she was...what? Protesting being here?"

"I assume so."

"She touched a child that fell in front of her in the streets. Instead of having me remove the girl's hands, as is her tradition, she took the punishment herself. You didn't introduce her to your people, so they greeted her with stones and rotten food. They ruined the mask she wore beyond repair and likely gave her a bloody nose. *I taught you better than that.*"

Nadir felt as though someone had punched him in the stomach. Yet again, he'd been wrong about this little captive who was now his wife. He leaned back and pinched his nose. "Find them."

"Who?"

"The ones who threw the stones. Find them and kill them."

"You can't fix everything by killing the people you disagree with." Raheem stepped forward and placed his hands on the desk. "She doesn't want anyone to kill them."

"I want someone to kill them. That's an order, Raheem."

"She won't forgive you for it. You weren't there with her. She didn't flinch or react when they threw stones. She even told me that the mask wasn't important when it was damaged by a stone, but their fear of her was. She took a risk so your people would understand she isn't some monster who will murder their children in their sleep."

"Why would she even care?"

"That's a question I hoped you could answer." Raheem pushed himself away from the desk, taking a few steps back. "And one I assumed you would want answered."

"I can't very well ask her."

"Why not?" Raheem spread his arms wide. "She's your wife now, bound to answer all your questions. You could learn about her kind, bring their ways into Bymere, and make this a better kingdom for it."

Nadir arched a brow. "Do you really think the advisors would even entertain that thought?"

"*You* are sultan! This kingdom is yours, not theirs. I've made that clear many times, boy, and I've been waiting to see you take it back."

Nadir's stomach lurched at the thought. He wasn't Hakim. His brother could have done so much good in this kingdom and had planned to.

A completely united kingdom had always been Hakim's dream. He wanted to work with Wildewyn, to make their countries stronger by joining them in a way that had never done before. It was the first of many plans his advisors claimed "foolish." Wildewyn would always want to be the dominant country. Their ways were too different, their people too strange. Bymere could not unite with a place that differed from them so.

He sighed and scrubbed a hand over his face. "We've had this conversation many times before, Raheem. It's impossible to do. Every sultan needs advisors to teach him the ways of the kingdom."

"For a time. But then a sultan must stand on his own two feet."

"How does this relate to my silent wife?" he spat.

"She can help you, Sultan. Give her a chance. The girl wants nothing more than to prove her worth. To prove herself to *you* although I don't know why."

"Perhaps, I have swayed her with my good looks," Nadir said with a scoff. Of any woman he'd ever met, she was the last to covet physical appearance. She hid hers and valued others even less than her own.

His knee bounced. Since when did his knee ever bounce? He was always in control of his emotions, or he liked to think so. Nadir slapped a hand down on the offending leg and growled.

"Fine. There is a hearing of complaints at high noon today. Invite her. No—" he corrected himself "—don't give her an option. Order her to be there, and we'll see how well she responds to the people."

"Are you testing her?" Raheem chuckled. "She seems to do well with those."

"We'll see."

His guard left without complaint, and Nadir wondered what about the Beastkin woman had everyone so obsessed.

She wasn't a beauty. Her clothing was strange, and though the mask was certainly compelling, it didn't mean she was any more intriguing than Bymerian women. In fact, he would argue that she wasn't beautiful at all by their standards.

She didn't speak, so it wasn't her words or thoughts. What

was it? She held herself with a certain mystery that made people fall over their feet trying to understand her. He knew first hand she was little more than a locked box he would never figure out how to open.

But damn, if he still didn't want to try.

He scrubbed a hand over his face again. Raheem's interruption had come at a good time. He would have been late to hearing his people's complaints, and that likely wouldn't have ended well. The advisors would scold him again for the hundredth time this day. They constantly chided him for not living up to their standards. He'd long ago stopped trying.

Nadir took the hour to scrub his mind clean of women and his body free of sweat. The heat was ungodly this year. Perhaps, it would teach his second wife that Bymere was a dangerous land not to be trifled with.

Or make her hate it even more. Either way likely worked in his favor. She wouldn't try to run although she'd shown no intent to do so.

Donning the royal crimson robes, he pulled his hair back with a leather thong. Ten rings decorated his fingers, weighing his hands down every time he moved. A heavy necklace dripping with rubies hung from his throat.

He glimpsed himself in the mirror and grimaced. They made him look little more than a pretty bauble.

"A distinct show of wealth makes people remember who you are," his advisors always said.

He thought it made him look foolish.

Still, Nadir made his way to the chamber where his citizens could air their grievances, and he would pretend to address their complaints. The ruby room contained towering, cathedral ceilings and horseshoe arches. Silk hung from the ceiling, the long tails dipping in four pools set in the marble floor like blood seeping into the azure waters below.

A crowd of people already waited for him. They stared up at the throne with a mixture of apprehension and hope. Too bad they'd likely be disappointed with him. He tended to inspire that emotion far more than any other.

Nadir made sure he didn't make eye contact with anyone as he strode up the stairs. He nodded to his advisors and sat on his golden throne. It was smaller than the one in the entrance, but the other intimidated visitors. This one, so his advisors said, made him easier to address.

He thought anyone seated on a throne was unapproachable.

Gods, they were all staring at him. This was his least favorite part. It felt like every single person in his kingdom was looking at him with hope in their eyes, and he didn't know how to help them. He wasn't his brother. He wasn't trained to be king, and so he relied on others to tell him what was the right choice, what to do, how to be.

"Sultan." The quiet voice was the burbling of a forest stream, washing away the gritty sand that abraded his mind. "Thank you for inviting me."

He glanced over at Sigrid seated by his right hand. He hadn't even noticed her. "I thought it time for you to meet our people."

"I already have." Her eyes sparkled. "But I would like to meet them again."

Gods, she was a dangerous woman. That mask revealed nothing of her thoughts, not like the Bymerians. If she were

Saafiya, he would be able to read her every thought in her face.

She was a still pool of water, and all he saw was his own reflection.

"Sultan?" she inquired again. "Shall we begin? Your people have been waiting for you."

He let loose a small breath and turned away from her. Abdul stood, made his way down the stairs, and gestured for the first person to approach the throne.

After that, it was all very much the same.

The people always had the same complaints. It was a neighbor who was stealing from them, a cheating wife, a man trying to break an engagement for a younger, prettier version of the peasant woman who he'd already been caught kissing.

Nadir found it all petty. There were more important things in the world to worry about than whether a cow had gone missing. His eyes usually glazed over as his mind wandered, but this time he realized that his second wife was very much engaged in what his people were saying.

She leaned forward during the stories, listening to them in rapt attention. She inclined her head when someone said something truthful, tapped her fingers when a person was lying, and shifted her weight closer to him when she wanted him to give the peasant what they had asked for.

It was all very fascinating. Nadir watched her reactions to gauge how he should respond, instead of listening to his people. He was treated to the sight of her eyes crinkling at the edges and her mask lifting ever so slightly. In a smile? What did it look like when she smiled without the mask?

"Sultan." Abdul's voice rang through the hall. "Perhaps you would like to listen to the complaint again. The advisors do not agree with your decision."

He knew for a fact the advisors had not convened with each other. They rarely did, but spoke as if they were one mind. He turned and saw them all staring at him with varying degrees of disapproving expressions.

What had the peasant asked for?

Clearing his mind of the strange woman beside him, he turned to the peasant. "Repeat your story."

The man was little more than a beggar. His clothing was moth-eaten at the edges, his skin darkened by the sun so much that it cracked. He wrung a hat in his hands until it was crushed beyond repair.

The man cleared his throat. "I was saying, Your Majesty, that the poor in your city would greatly appreciate your help. Some of us look for work, but there's not much to be had. We sleep on the streets, and the sands are hot. We don't ask for work to be given to us, but perhaps a safe place for us to rest our heads."

Abdul shook his head. "It's not something the sultan can entertain. That coin could go elsewhere."

Nadir might have left it at that, but his second wife placed her hand atop his. Stunned, he met her gaze beneath the cold mask. "I see no reason why you shouldn't help your people. Showing kindness to the weakest of your people is the mark of a good king."

"You are in a sultanate now, girl," Abdul called out, and the advisors laughed. Some people in the crowd did as well. Those who were clothed in silks.

Sigrid ignored them all, capturing his gaze. "It's a small price to help so many people. Give them a place to sleep and bathe. Being clean will make them more likely to find work. Send food to them every few weeks if you have the heart, and perhaps they will return the favor once they have money to feed their families."

He was stunned. No one had ever suggested such a thing, but it made sense. Why wasn't he focusing more on these people? It was a small request, and there was plenty of money in the royal coffers.

"Find a house on the outskirts of town," he said. "Whichever one best suits your needs. Return when you've found it, and I'll dedicate it as a house for those who need it. As my wife has said, we can offer food bi-weekly, although I cannot promise what kind."

"Whatever is left over from the palace?" she suggested.

"A remarkable idea, Sultana." And because he knew it would anger his advisors, he lifted her hand to his lips and kissed her fingertips. Her eyes widened.

Abdul waved the man away and stalked up the steps. "Sultan—"

"We'll speak of this later, Abdul," Nadir interrupted. "For now, there are more people who have questions."

When was the last time he'd felt so worthy of the throne? Nadir couldn't remember, but it had been longer than he could remember.

The happiness on that single man's face was enough to make Nadir sit straighter. Every bit of him suddenly felt like a sultan. He'd done something that would improve Bymere. A house like that wasn't that much of an expense. Likely, they wouldn't feel it in the slightest. And there wouldn't be that many people in his land that needed such a home. His advisors would have seen that issue and fixed it long ago if there were many in need of a home.

Sigrid moved to withdraw her hand, but he held it firmly beneath his own. Her touch strengthened him, her ideas made him wiser, and damned if he was letting her go just yet. What other ideas did she have in her head?

He was bursting with thoughts of his own. A lifetime of dreams beaten down by advisors who had their own plans for the kingdom. What would she think of his plans to siphon water through the ground into their kingdom? Of his desire to teach more people to farm and work the land like those in Glasslyn? How he wanted to make apprenticeships more accessible and create more artisans in the country?

"Perhaps, we should listen to this man," Abdul said, gesturing to the newest citizen kneeling on the floor. "His complaints were of trouble at the border."

"Which border?"

"Wildewyn, Sultan," the man replied. "Many people are uncomfortable with the new sultana hailing from our most hated enemy."

"We are bridging the gap between the two countries." Nadir scoffed, but Sigrid's hand spasmed beneath his own. "There is much to learn from our enemies. We now keep them close."

"A Beastkin woman has no right to sit upon a sacred throne. We request a formal petition that she abdicate."

"No." Nadir shrugged. The request was ridiculous, and his people had no right to question his judgement so publicly. The man was lucky he didn't behead him for such insolence. "She remains where I have placed her. Your complaints are noted, however. I can promise I will not marry another from Wildewyn."

A few chuckles resounded, but he knew trouble brewed the moment the man lifted his head. There was darkness in his eyes and a plan that Nadir hadn't thought possible.

"Then it is you who must abdicate the throne."

Time seemed to slow. The man pulled a wicked dagger from within his robes and lunged up the stairs. Nadir was so shocked that someone would dare pull a blade on him that he didn't react. Let the man plunge it through his breast. Perhaps Bymere would be better without him.

His guards had failed him. They hadn't seen the man enter with a weapon. They jolted, but were far too late.

It was Sigrid who met the man just before the dagger touched Nadir's skin. She gripped his wrist in a brutal hold, twisting his hand back sharply. The man gave a shout of pain just before the chamber rang with the crunch of bone.

The attacker howled in pain, only to be cut short as Sigrid twisted the man's arm and drew the blade still in his grasp across his throat. Screams turned to gurgles as blood slowly poured down the man's chest.

She let him fall to the ground where the pool of blood began to drip down each golden step.

A warrior goddess stood before him, looking out at the crowd of people who stared back in silent shock. She wasn't even breathing hard after killing a man so quickly no one had had time to blink. She did not speak, nor make a single sound. Instead, this Beastkin woman allowed the crowd to look at her and understand that their fear was warranted.

This had all gone wrong. She was supposed to be here so

his people *wouldn't* be frightened of her. They were supposed to feel her compassion, and she had been doing so well.

Now a man lay dead at his feet and she'd protected a sultan his own people obviously did not want. Such a shame. They might have made something good of this.

Her head cocked to the side, and she spun on her heel. "Down!"

Another? Already? How had they created such an impressive assassination attempt without a single person seeing them?

Nadir didn't duck. Instead, he watched his wife move with impossible grace. Her skirts flared around her like that of a blue waterlily. She had no weapons. They'd taken those from her before she entered the room, but she still reached directly for the sword slicing toward his throat.

She caught it in her palm, let loose an animalistic snarl, and wrenched it from the man's hold. It was the only sound she made as she whirled the sword in the air and plunged it into the man's chest, twisting savagely. He fell to his knees, holding onto the hilt of his own blade, then slumped to the ground.

What an impressive creation he had in front of him. Both dead bodies reflected in the gleaming metal corset she always wore, and now he understood why. This beautiful, deadly creature always suspected someone to attack her. She didn't just wear armor.

She wore death like a well-worn cloak.

Her icy eyes found his. "Are you alive?"

"Not a speck of blood on me."

"Good." Her own blood dripped from her fingers, splattering on the floor and mixing with that of his attackers.

"You may regret stopping them."

Sigrid shook her head. "No, husband. If anyone will kill you, it will be me."

She was a feral, savage thing, and he didn't know what to do with her. One part of him wanted to lock her up for daring to suggest that, even after saving him. The other part wanted to crush her to his chest, rip off that damned mask, and find out what her lips tasted like.

"Husband, are you all right?" Saafiya's voice was worried and fearful.

"I'm fine. Not a blade touched me, thanks to my Beastkin woman."

Nadir saw Sigrid flinch at the words and wondered what he'd said wrong. He'd called her by title, though perhaps that was insulting. He would have to ask her what was wrong with calling her by what she was.

"Such a creature is dangerous," Abdul hissed as he raced up the steps. "Guards, take care of these bodies and discover who allowed them in."

"Creature?" He pointed at the assassins. "Hardly likely. They appear Bymerian to me."

"I wasn't speaking of them. We'll deal with that later, but having such an animal next to our king isn't safe. Perhaps, we should reconsider allowing her in the throne room during public functions."

"She saved my life, Abdul." Nadir rose out of his throne, not caring that there were bodies at his feet. "It's more than our own guards did."

"I am certain if you had allowed them the time—"

"A sword would have sliced through my throat in only a

few seconds more. Are you suggesting the guards you hired have capabilities exceeding natural human speed?"

Abdul stared at him as if he'd grown another head. And perhaps he had. Nadir's blood sang with the power she had given him. Free thought, even for a boy king who didn't deserve his throne.

He wanted to peel back every layer of his kingdom and force his people to see the way he did. That there was more to this land than just sand and dust. His advisors didn't need to agree with him, just as Raheem had told him for many years. He could do what *he* wanted without their dreaded approval. The final vote rested on his shoulders.

Sigrid stepped away from him, her hand resting on her stomach. "Do not fight on my behalf, Sultan. I believe I will retire to my room."

"Why would you?" He laughed, gesturing at the fools behind him who were supposed to protect their sultan. "You've done more than my entire guard in just a few moments. I shall hire you as my personal shield, wife. At least I know you will keep me alive."

"I grow weary, husband." Her voice didn't sound right.

Nadir tilted his head to the side, watching her strange movements. Had she ever put her hand on her stomach like that? It was an odd posture for a woman who usually stood board straight.

"What is wrong?" he asked.

"Nothing, Your Majesty. I just—" She paused. Her hand lifted to ghost over the opposite arm, coming away with a small dart fletched with vivid yellow feathers. She squinted and shook her head. "What is this?"

He'd seen it once before, though he wished he could wipe the memory from his mind. *Poison.* The same kind which had flowed through his brother's veins and rotted him from the inside out. Twelve endless nights of pain flickered through his memory as his wife dropped to one knee on the stairs.

Sigrid let out a rattling gasp, then a guttural groan that was both inhuman and terrifying. He'd only heard the sound once before in his life.

A woman near the front of the crowd gasped. She pressed a hand against her mouth, hennaed swirls standing out in stark relief against her suddenly pale skin.

"Out!" Nadir roared. "Everyone out of this hall immediately!"

The peasants didn't need to be told twice. They raced out the door until only his advisors remained in the crimson room.

Sigrid coughed. Her mask muffled the sound, but he remembered it all too well. He'd only been eight years old when his brother died, yet the memories would plague him for a lifetime.

She twisted and lost her balance. He raced forward as she rolled down the stairs, landing hard on her elbow and side. Nadir knelt next to her and pressed a hand against her shoulder.

"I've seen this poison before," he began, not knowing how to tell her that death would take her slowly.

Sigrid shook her head and pressed a hand against her chest. "My sister."

"What? There is no time to bring you back to Wildewyn."

Again, she shook her head. "My sister. Make everyone leave."

It was bad luck to break a last wish. He glared over his shoulder at the cluster of advisors standing close enough to listen, but never close enough to help. "Leave."

Saafiya stepped forward, crimson veil hiding her face. "My husband—"

"I said, leave." Nadir didn't have it in him to shout, not now. But perhaps the low, angry tones of his voice were more effective than blustering anger.

His advisors stepped away, one quiet movement at a time until they too disappeared beyond a horseshoe archway, then all was still in the throne room.

Nadir turned back towards his second wife and sighed. It was a shame she would die. He'd quite liked her and thought admiration might grow into something more if he had the time to allow it. She was a mysterious creature with thoughts that astounded him. What could they have built if she hadn't been poisoned trying to save him?

Taloned feet skidded across the floor. Nadir's heart jumped in his chest, and he flinched back at the silver owl that silently appeared beside them. Feathers melted away, and her flesh warped into that of the dark-skinned woman he'd seen before.

Eyes wide, Nadir breathed, "So, you are a Beastkin as well."

"Sisters are always Beastkin. We're all family." She didn't even look at him as she knelt next to Sigrid and pressed a hand to her forehead. "What happened?"

"Poison," he tried to say, only to be interrupted by Sigrid.

"Ravenweed," Sigrid croaked. "Burn it away."

She knew the name of it? "How?" he asked. "How is it possible you know what this poison is without being privy to its making?"

The dark-skinned woman hissed. "Ravenweed is a common poison. It's a cruel death, but it's easily recognizable. It always makes the tongue taste mint."

Yes, he remembered that. Hakim had complained for days about the maddening flavor that plagued him. They'd all thought it was the herbs the healers brought. They'd certainly tried a considerable amount, but no one had ever thought it was the ravenweed itself.

He was helpless against this poison that haunted his steps. Nadir knew he wasn't a good man, but he never thought he would be so hated that someone would kill everyone he held dear.

"Fire," the woman was saying. "She needs to cleanse herself in fire."

"She's not dead yet. I won't order a funeral pyre until she is."

"Fool! She needs to transform, and there must be a safe place for her. The dragon has never controlled her before, a most perilous and uncontrollable creature will break loose the moment she changes. She will be dangerous and must be contained."

He felt his stomach drop to his feet. "There's a cure?"

"For Beastkin," the woman corrected. She stroked a hand over Sigrid's forehead, then traced her fingers over his wife's eyelids, closing them. "For her. The dragon can heal many wounds, even those which are mortal."

He shouldn't feel so relieved that there was little he could have done for his brother. But for this beautiful, powerful woman who had given him even a moment of feeling as though he was worthy…*there was a cure.*

Nadir decided in that instant he would do everything he could to keep her alive. She might be his enemy and they may hate each other on the morrow, but she deserved to live.

"I know of a safe place," he said.

"Hidden from prying eyes?"

"Hidden from everything."

When she nodded, he launched into movement. Nadir scooped his wife up into his arms and spun on his heels. The room he was thinking of lay deep underneath the palace where a previous sultan had once held parties. Royalty from all over Bymere would flock to this giant cavern.

He'd played there as a child for most of his life. It was a quiet, safe place for a little boy who felt so different and alone.

"I'll come with you," Camilla grunted as she stayed close to his heels.

"No, you won't."

"With all due respect, *Sultan*," she spat his title as though it left a bad taste in her mouth. "You hold my dearest sister in your arms. I will not leave her alone with you when it is her life on the line."

"You lost your importance the moment you allowed her to marry me."

"How dare you even suggest such a thing?" Her voice vibrated with rage, and the distinct sound of feathers rustled as she changed.

Nadir grinned, oddly comforted that his wife had such a fierce protector of her own. "Remind me to bring more Beastkin to my palace. You're a refreshing change."

An owl gave a battle cry. He almost flinched when her

wings brushed the top of his head, but refused to give her the satisfaction. These women were cold and angry all at the same time. He feared he'd never understand them.

Nadir ran through the vacant halls of his palace. Was it always so silent? He liked to think the palace was a calm place, but now he realized it was lonely and hushed as a tomb. He remembered the concubines running through these halls, chased by his older brother who always liked to cause a scene. Hakim hadn't cared what others thought of him. When had Nadir started?

His wife shifted in his arms, a faint groan slipping between her lips.

"Only a few moments now," he reassured her, skidding to a halt in front of the secret door. "You'll be able to change, and then I'll have saved at least one person from this poison."

He could almost feel his brother's spirit standing beside him. Nadir nudged a stone with his foot and the small passage crunched open. Turning sideways, he slid through the opening, and then closed it from the other side before the owl could find her way through.

This was a conversation for a man and his wife. Or perhaps, more accurately, his dragon.

A spiral staircase led deep into the heart of the mountain. Bymere was an arid country but underneath the sand lay abundant caverns.

The walls had a thin trough where oil leaking from the ceiling landed. It was an old trick by a very intelligent sultan who had not wanted even his servants to see this hidden place. When his people emptied their braziers for clean, new oil, it all ended up here.

Nadir leaned back against a wall and shifted Sigrid in his arms until he could reach into his pocket and pull out a small flint. He always carried it. A man never knew when a fire might be necessary. A few strikes and a spark set the line of oil aflame.

He chased after it with a dragon in his arms, knowing there were only more flames in his future. Not a single shiver of fear chilled his blood. In a strange way, he felt as though he'd been waiting his entire life for this moment.

The spiral wall disappeared on his left side, and he burst forth into the wide-open cavern that had once entertained hundreds of Bymerians. He raced down the long hall, fire blooming to life in rivers all the way to the center where it turned into a grand ring around a makeshift throne.

He gently set Sigrid down in the center of the room where burning oil burst outward in lines that fashioned a giant star.

Her chest heaved as she struggled to suck in a breath.

"Easy, second wife," he teased. "You'll feel better in a moment. Your sister said this would cure you, and I don't take kindly to liars."

The metal of her mask was hot against his fingers. He ran them along the edges and found the clasps that held it onto her head. Nadir let out a slow breath, then twisted the locks and pulled the golden prison away from her lovely face.

Nadir realized with sudden shock it was only the second time he'd seen her face. He hadn't realized how lovely she was. The strong features, the tangled braids of her hair, even the stubborn set of her jaw reminded him of a fierce warrior. Her smooth, alabaster skin took him aback even as her kohl-ringed eyes opened and met his gaze.

"No," she whispered. "Not you."

It wasn't disgust in those eyes or even hatred. It was fear in her eyes. Fear for *him,* and it rocked him to the core.

He smoothed a hand over her slick forehead and smiled. "This felt like a husbandly duty."

A tear built in the corner of her right eye then slid free to drip over his finger and sink into her hair. Such a shame that this woman could only feel so powerfully when she was in pain. Did she think she would kill him?

"I—" Her tongue was already too thick in her mouth to speak. That would come and go if he remembered his brother's torment correctly. But when she could speak, there would be so much pain she would become incoherent.

"Hush. Your sister said changing would help you, and I won't watch you die. Let the dragon free, Sigrid."

Her icy gaze warmed, reflected yellow in the firelight, then her eyes rolled back in her head. For a moment, he thought she might be seizing as his brother had done, but then those eyes focused back on him, and he knew it wasn't Sigrid meeting his gaze.

Her pupils had elongated into tiny reptilian slits. She surveyed him and then dismissed his presence. Flicking her gaze towards the braziers alight with flames, she let out a wheezing hiss and slowly rolled onto her stomach.

Nadir rose from his crouch and backed away. He didn't know how long it would take for her to transform, but the last thing he needed was to be caught in the midst of it.

She tried to push herself up onto hands and knees, only to crash back to the floor. Whimpering, she crawled on her forearms, dragging her legs behind her. He set his teeth and clenched his fists, restraining from helping her.

This was something she needed to do herself, he understood that. It was a battle she would fight and win. A woman who could catch a sword in her hand rather than allow it to touch his skin could endure this.

Sigrid reached for a brazier. Her fingers hooked at the edges of the searing metal, and the sound of sizzling flesh filled the chamber. She pressed her weight against its side which must have been too much for the ancient structure. It crumbled under her weight and sent a wave of oil across the floor.

Nadir jumped back. The fire raced toward him until he had to run farther from her side. Spinning to check on her, he let out a shout as the fire spread across the oil and consumed her.

What had he done? A dragon could survive but he didn't know enough about Beastkin to hazard a guess whether it would harm *her*. Her human form seemed just as delicate as any other.

Her body disappeared under the swarm of flames that rose ever higher into the air. A muscle under his eye ticked. He couldn't walk through the fire to get her, not like this, but maybe—

A low rumble echoed through the chamber. Deep and aching, it filled his chest with an answering call as sudden movement burst from where she had fallen. In an instant, she was no longer a woman at all. Instead, a graceful long neck lifted from the ground.

Alabaster skin gave way to opalescent scales that stretched across the entire expanse of her new body. A long, spiked tail waved behind her, thin and graceful. She was easily the length of ten men, if not longer. She rested upon what had been her arms, but were now ephemeral wings. Taloned tips clicked on the floor as she shifted and turned her great head to look at him.

Icy eyes, just as he had expected. The vivid blue gaze locked onto his. Small sets of horns stretched back from her head, like a crown made of bone and precious stone. She opened her mouth, revealing rows of sharp teeth, and hissed.

He thought he would feel disgust seeing this creature that should not exist. He thought she would make him want to run or perhaps even vomit.

Instead, all he felt was a sudden sense of elation that filled his chest until he might sing with it.

"You're beautiful," he said.

Again, she hissed, and that tail swiped across the braziers, knocking them down and spreading more flames across the entire chamber. He narrowed his gaze on her and lifted a hand.

"Now, Sigrid. That's no way to behave."

The grumbled response wasn't one he would expect from his wife. He watched the dragon's restless movements and realized that there wasn't a piece of Sigrid left in this giant being. It was in pain, frightened, and had no memory of where it was.

He stepped forward, hoping that if he could get her to *look* at him that he might help her to remember.

The movement must have startled her. She scrabbled, her wings dragged against the ground, her mouth open in a near constant hiss as she backed away from him and pressed her wings against the ground. She reared on her legs and heaved back, slapping the air and pushing him back with a gust of wind.

"I'm trying to help you," he soothed.

She wanted none of his help. Nadir didn't notice her tail

until it was too late. She swiped it across the floor and caught him about the middle. She flung him across the chamber like a rag doll. Nadir landed hard on top of a brazier. His back cracked ominously, and he rolled onto the floor panting. Pain lanced through his legs but he pushed through the pain and stood.

Fire and rage spurred him on. He spun on his heels and lifted his arms.

"Fine. If it's a fight you want, then it's a fight you'll get."

And for the first time in nearly fifteen years, Nadir did exactly what he'd promised his brother he would never do again.

He let go.

SIGRID

WHERE WAS SHE?

She couldn't clear her head, couldn't remember where she was, how she came to be here, *who* she was. What had happened? She knew she was a person. There were important memories in her head, but she couldn't get to them.

Flames lifted in her face, startling her. It smelled like oil and burning flesh. Why? Had she hurt someone? She never wanted to hurt anyone, but she didn't know how to stop sometimes and...

Metal rattled against stone. She spun, her tail clumsy behind her and arms reaching up to the sky. No, they *were* wings. She didn't remember that being part of her body. But she didn't remember these glimmering scales either.

A man shouted behind her. A man?

She knew he was a man, and that was more than what she had known only a few minutes before. She twisted her head, turning to stare at him with one eye. He lifted his arms wide, and she recognized him.

Captor. Husband. Sultan.

Her name was Sigrid of Wildewyn. She was a drakon and Beastkin woman who had been traded to a Bymerian king in a bid for peace.

She knew who she was.

Tossing her head back in victory, she let out a chuffing call of elation. She was a *person* with memories and thoughts. She wasn't just a dragon. She was far more than that.

Another creature cried out. The man? Her husband. Had she hurt him? She hadn't wanted to do that, but the poison running through her veins was so painful, so strong, she lost control.

Her breath caught in her lungs. She lowered her wings to the ground and tried to make herself look small. It wasn't an easy feat; dragons weren't easy to hide which was why she hadn't changed in such a long time but it felt so good to be in her true form once again.

Both woman and dragon were now linked. It felt as though she had aged, died, and been born anew in a skin she didn't recognize but that felt like home.

The call cried out again, and she looked for the man in the corner where she'd flung him. She tried to convey an apology in her gaze but couldn't find him. Instead, her eyes struck a burgundy wall of scales that pillared high into the air.

Flat plates of scales covered his chest, marching up his long neck like his own personal army. They stopped underneath his chin, hitting the blunt jaw marred by long teeth that poked out of his mouth even when it was closed. Twin horns spiraled back from his head. Yellow eyes stared back at her, familiar and yet different at the same time.

He was larger than her, not by much but enough that she felt a twinge of fear. Leathery wings fluttered as he reared back and let out a roar that shook the ceiling. Stalactites fell in great swaths, cracking against the ground and shaking the floor.

She ducked down, pressing her head low and moving it slowly from side to side. She recognized the wild look in his gaze. He didn't know who he was yet, stuck in the single moment of euphoria. He wasn't just a man. He was a drakon.

But how was it possible?

She'd thought the sparrow boy was an anomaly, or perhaps a woman masquerading as a man. But this was proof that Beastkin existed here. That they weren't only female. That everything she'd been taught was a lie.

His front wings struck the ground, black talons close to her head. She let out a hiss of warning, but he didn't attack her. Instead, Nadir lowered his scaled head and ran the length of his chin along the top of her skull.

Her mind spun with questions which she couldn't ask them in this form. Letting go of all the pain and fear, she allowed the dragon to drift back into the depths of her mind. A single transformation would no longer suffice now that she knew what a blessing it was to be in her true form. But she would explore this new part of herself later.

Scales melted away into fabric until she knelt on the floor in front of him, panting. Her pale, blue gown suddenly felt like a lie. How could she dress like this when she knew what lingered underneath her skin?

The beast in front of her let out a series of gulping coughs that rocked through her body. She looked up at him and saw confusion in his eyes. He shook his head back and forth, rocking as if he didn't know how to join her in his human skin.

Panic set in, his slit pupils dilated. His chest rose and fell as he fought for air, and he stepped away from her.

She held her hands up in the air and followed him. "Easy," she lulled. "It will be all right. Husband, come here."

He shook his head again.

"Nadir," she tried. He froze at the sound of his own name, his head tilting to stare at her with one golden eye. "Let me touch you."

If those were the magic words with him, then she would use them more often. He stilled, hunched on the floor like a great beast of old. She suddenly understood why so many people were afraid of dragons. Why the old tales considered them monsters that pillaged and burned.

He could kill her so easily. But then again, she had tried to kill him while in her own dragon skin.

Sigrid strode toward him, placing one foot in front of the other. She made sure she stayed in sight, not wanting to make any movements that would frighten him. Only when she was a few feet away did she reach out and gently place her hand against his leathery wing.

The shaking membrane was soft and warm. She slid her hand along what she could touch and marveled at how it felt so much like the animal skin tents they had slept in. She skated her fingers over the large ridges of scales, each the size of a dinner plate and far more utilitarian than her own had appeared.

"Easy, husband. Relax and let the change wash over you. It's harder to turn back into a human, I know. But this is the form in which we can speak and reason. The dragon is good for war and for pleasure, but never for politics."

He huffed out a breath, then another. Under her calming hands he stilled and then she felt him relax.

Scales disappeared under her hands until all that remained was a man kneeling at her feet.

She didn't understand the magic that made them. Their clothes did not rip or disappear in their transformation, but remained whole when they wished to return to their human state. Beastkin had tried to explain the strangeness of their magic for centuries. Eventually, they all agreed that they could not explain it.

There were some things in life worth leaving a mystery, if only to know unexplainable things remained in this world.

She waited for him to look at her. Silence filled the air until he took a deep, steadying breath. Nadir pressed his fists onto the floor until his knuckles turned white, then finally, he looked up at her with yellow eyes.

Now she understood. Those eyes had always seemed impossible, and now she knew they truly were. They were not some defect of birth but that of a Beastkin who had long ago accepted his beast as part of himself.

"It's not possible," she whispered.

Yet, an impossible man knelt before her.

"And now you know," he said, slowly rising to his feet.

She let out an aching sound that hovered between a sob and a sigh. Reaching forward, she smacked him so hard that his head rocked to the side. His eyes widened and then narrowed when she slid her hand smoothly over the opposite side, turned him back to her, and pressed her lips to his.

Sigrid had thought perhaps he would feel rough, like the

sand of his home. Or that his lips would burn with the heat of the sun that had plagued their journey. But he didn't.

Cool lips touched hers, soothing a ragged wound in her soul she hadn't known existed before she came to this place. He remained still for a moment, perhaps shocked at her change of heart, but then he swept her up in his arms and pressed her close to his chest.

His heart thundered against hers. She wrapped her arms around his neck, anchoring him close even though he already pressed her against every inch of him.

They explored each other for a moment in time. She tasted salt and sand on his tongue, but even more. The bitterness of a man who had been alone for a very long time.

When she pulled back to take a deep breath, she gasped, "Where have you been?"

He shook his head, speechless.

"Why didn't you tell me?" she asked, leaning back far enough to trace her fingertips over his face. "I thought I was alone. I thought I was the last."

"I thought the same."

"Did you know? When you came for me in Wildewyn, did you know? Why did you wait so long to tell me?"

He smiled, and she felt as though the sun had peeked through a crack in the walls she'd built around her heart. "I didn't know. I thought your king was lying, or he knew some secret about me. It was impossible."

"I didn't know there were any others. We have always been told that the only Beastkin are female."

"The only Beastkin here are male, although there used to be females. They've all been hunted."

"Are the royals here Beastkin?" She felt pride swell in her chest. "How many know?"

"None. None other than my brother knew, and now...you."

She smoothed her hands over his shoulders, feeling as though she couldn't stop touching him. He was a miracle, everything she'd always prayed for and more. She wasn't alone.

She wasn't the only dragon.

Sigrid gasped. "We can create more like us. We don't have to be the only dragons. *We* can bring our people back. Do you know what this means, Nadir? We don't have to be the only ones anymore."

A shadow passed over his face, and he released his hold on her. He stepped back, shaking his head. "No. No, we can't do that."

"Why not? It's our right. You are Sultan of all Bymere. We can make this place a home for our people."

"They aren't my people, Sigrid. They're yours."

She felt as though he'd stabbed a lance through her chest. "What?"

Nadir pressed his hands to his eyes and shook his head firmly. "I should never have done this. I promised my brother I wouldn't do it again, and he's likely rolling in his grave."

"No." She stepped forward. "This is who we are. This is *what* we are. You don't get to deny that."

"I've denied this —" he swept a hand between them — "my entire life."

"Why? For what reason? You are a dragon, a Beastkin *man*. I've seen nothing like you before. Why hide that?"

"Beastkin are hunted in Bymere." He stepped away from her, pressing a hand against his chest. "I cannot be anything other than a human man. A sultan is not Beastkin."

"Who told you that? Who said a Beastkin cannot rule?"

"*Both* our kingdoms," he barked.

Silence again filled the space between them. And she knew he was right.

Even Wildewyn would never have let one of her kind take the throne. That would make even the most hardened of politicians laugh. A Beastkin ruling humans? Why would an animal be allowed to make decisions for man?

She shook her head, refusing to focus on such darkness. "You're already sultan. No one can take that away from you."

"They can, and they would. My brother knew they would hunt me down. He trained me, helped me learn to control the beast no matter what, and I have hidden it from everyone for a very long time. You will not ruin this for me."

He was afraid, she realized. Of what his people would think, what they would do. She didn't know how to change his mind on this. They would accept him if they loved him.

But they didn't. And that made things even more difficult.

She huffed out an angry breath. "What do you want to do? Live your life in hiding, forever?"

"That plan has served me well thus far."

"I won't do it."

"You don't have to. You're already the masked Beastkin who has frightened my people and now survived the very poison that killed the man who should have been sultan." He raked his hands through his hair, angrily pulling out the tie that bound it all at the nape of his neck. "What am I going to tell them? We all know Wildewyn is to blame for the murder of my brother, and now you survive the poison. This will look bad."

"Look bad?" Sigrid repeated. "Their sultana survived and stopped an assassination attempt on their sultan. They should rejoice."

"That's not how it is in Bymere."

"Then you're all *wrong*." Her shout echoed in the chamber and fell back upon them like rain.

Nadir's lips twisted in a half-smile that was both sad and pitying. "Things don't always work the way we want them to, wife. They'll try to crucify you for this."

"Let them try." A dragon-like rumble made her voice shake as she spoke.

"We can never let them see the dragons."

"Give me one good reason why we shouldn't let your people see them."

"They will revolt against us. It's not just fear, Sigrid. It's the same reason why your king let no one see you. They cannot know what we are capable of, or they will hunt us down like the animals we are. We may destroy an entire village, but an army against one of us will quickly end in our blood."

Her mind caught on a single word in this speech. She stepped away from him, once, twice, three times until she stopped and wrapped her arms around her waist. "You think we're animals?"

"No," he shook his head, "I think we're monsters."

"How do you live with yourself if that's what you think of

our people?" She let out an angry gasp that sounded too close to a sob for her own comfort.

"I ask myself that question every day."

He turned away from her and walked toward the spiral staircase she barely remembered. When he reached the opening, he paused and glanced over his shoulder. "The bottom right stone will open the passage. I trust you to behave yourself around my people, and we'll not talk again about revealing what we are."

"You're making a mistake, Sultan," she spat. "We should be proud of what we are."

"I make my choices for my people."

"Is that why you let your advisors walk all over you? Is that why you've hidden in a drunken stupor while your people suffer, your city is left defenseless, and your army grows weaker by the minute?"

It was a low blow, and she knew it. Already she felt the promise of her future slipping away. She wanted to grasp onto the moment when she realized she was not alone and hold it to her breast for all eternity. But he wouldn't let her.

He nodded. "It's better for them to live a life like this, than to know a monster sits on their throne."

He disappeared into the shadows of the stairwell and Sigrid slumped to the floor.

Pale, blue fabric pooled around her like the petals of a lily pulled off the stem, piece by piece. She let out a ragged sob that echoed until it sounded like a thousand women crying out in pain and sadness. And perhaps it was. Every ancestor, every drakon woman who had thought themselves the only one and found peace in the existence of their single daughter, now knew that their lives were wasted.

And that no matter what, their future always ended alone.

SIGRID SAT IN HER SMALL BEDROOM, TRYING TO FIND SOME

semblance of privacy. Giggles drifted on the slight breeze.

She missed her sisters more than she wanted her next breath.

Everything reminded her of them. The sound of women moving in the night. The way they each poured tea for another before they sipped their own. She wanted desperately to be accepted by them, but also knew it wasn't her place.

Saafiya made that very clear. They were the first wife's maids, and if Sigrid wished to have her own, then they would find her some. These women were devoted only to the first wife's happiness.

Sigrid knew better than to intervene in such relationships. And so, she remained in the section of the hall which was allotted to her.

The room was small, but comfortable. Curtains made of blue silk hung from every corner. The bed was marked by four posts anchored to the ceiling. Gilded leaves were carved onto each metal post and tiny strands of gold chips danced between them. Every shade of blue silk humanly possible was flung from edge to edge.

Likely it was a room fit for a sultana. She wouldn't know. Regardless, Sigrid wished for cold marble floors and the tomb-like silence of her home.

Someone had set a small table in the far corner at her request. They'd looked at her as though she was insane for even asking. Atop the small table, she'd set three candles, a small stone from Wildewyn, and an incense holder where she burned the small sticks each night.

They didn't understand her rituals. Some of the concubines and courtiers complained nonstop. The incense smelled. The candles set off shadows that frightened them. And what was the strange woman doing, anyway? Was she cursing them?

Sigrid shook her head and leaned forward to blow out the candles. She should have left them lit—and would have at home—but one wrong move and the entire concubine hall would go up in flames.

That was the last thing she needed to happen.

The sound of soft footsteps reached her ear. She glanced over her shoulder at Camilla who mockingly bowed. They'd found it easier to say she was a maid from Wildewyn, and that explained why she disappeared so often. If she acted the part of a lady's maid, no one questioned where she was.

"My lady."

"Sister." Sigrid shook her head and reached out her hands.

The simple gesture was all Camilla needed to race forward and flop onto the cushions at her feet. "You are feeling well?"

"Better than before."

"The poison is gone then." Camilla rolled onto her belly and plucked at the strings of a nearby pillow. "I told him it would work."

"You took a risk."

"*He* took a risk. I should have been the one with you."

"I fear what I would have done." Sigrid sighed. "It's been too long since I allowed the drakon to take control. Neither of us knew where we were, or even who we were."

"Loved ones can always help the beasts remember. We aren't animals, Sigrid. The beast and us are one and the same. I wish you would accept that."

"I'm nearly there."

She remembered the freedom of being the dragon. There was so much power in that body. So many reasons to feel as though she were free. The beast knew how to keep itself safe, but more than that it seemed to understand a part of Sigrid that she had never seen before.

It knew she wanted to soar through the skies just to hide from other people. She wanted to be alone as no one else on land could ever be alone.

Gods, how she wanted to fly. Could she? Her wings had felt strong, her body lithe, and the moment she beat at the air with her arms, she knew she could have lifted herself from the ground.

It didn't feel possible to lift such a large animal into the air, but she knew deep in her belly it could happen. She could have burst free from that underground chamber and launched herself into the sky. Then she could have flown away, across the sea, far from this place until she found a new land where Beastkin could say what they were, be who they were, without fear.

Camilla touched a hand to her knee. "Sigrid? Where did you go?"

"My thoughts are troubled."

"The sultan again?"

"He has no wish to let anyone know what we are." Sigrid was careful with her words, choosing each one so that anyone listening to their conversation would think she was speaking of her sisters. "It feels as though I'm betraying our people just by agreeing to his terms."

"Then perhaps you don't need to." A spark of mischief lit in Camilla's eyes. "There is more than one with whom you could speak."

The sparrow boy.

"Have you found him?" Sigrid asked excitedly, then lowered her voice to a whisper. "Are there more?"

"Many more."

Camilla's mask lifted in a grin, and Sigrid felt a door open in her future. One she could enter but never exit from again. She blew out a breath. "When can we meet them?"

"They said I could bring you any time, although it will be a little more difficult now that I cannot fly. They are far from here, out in the deserts."

"Why so far?"

"The city is a dangerous place for them. We would need at least three days."

"Three days?" Sigrid repeated. "I don't know if I can disappear for that long. I'll have to tell the sultan a story. Perhaps a religious walk we must do? Something he would believe and that he won't insist on coming with us."

"Why do you even need his permission? You're the sultana." Camilla tapped her fingers against her mask, a bad habit she'd had since they were children. "You shouldn't have to ask for permission."

"And yet, even here I am a caged pet." She tried to think of any plan that might work and found herself lost. "He won't let me go without a guard."

"Why does he care? If he didn't want to..." Camilla paused then rolled her eyes. "You know what I mean. All that talk for nothing, and he still protects you as if you cannot do it yourself."

She wanted to meet these men desperately. What more could they tell her? Did they know what had happened to divide their people between countries? Men and women alike?

Her mind spun with unanswered questions that were infinitely important.

Camilla tapped her mask again. When Sigrid didn't look at her, she reached up and tapped Sigrid's mask.

"What is it?" Sigrid huffed.

"A little sparrow told me there's a balcony nearby."

She narrowed her eyes. "A sparrow?"

"Rather small and insignificant, but an intriguing little beast to say the least." Camilla's gaze glimmered as it did when she knew something exciting was about to happen. "Perhaps you want to speak with this sparrow as well?"

The boy had taken a great risk in coming here. Sigrid pushed to her feet and smoothed a hand down the silver bodice of her icy gown. Bells were sewn into the bottom of the bodice, and they chimed as she moved.

"Shall we investigate this balcony? I would very much like to look across Bymere and see the city from up high."

Shadows danced in the corner as one of the concubines moved. Sigrid couldn't tell for sure if the woman had been listening to their conversation, but she wouldn't be surprised. It seemed the sultan's first wife had her finger on every pulse that existed within these walls. Sigrid had yet to figure out what the woman did with her information.

Camilla linked their arms and dragged Sigrid through the concubine hall. It was a beautiful place. The center hall was three steps down from the level which led to each woman's room. Twin pools lined the hall with waterlilies growing from the depths. She'd seen no one taking care of the flowers. They seemed to grow as if by magic.

The hall itself was made of yellow marble. Intricate carvings and statues filled every nook and cranny. It was a blessing for the women to be gifted such beautiful artistic works, she'd been told. Women could appreciate the finer touches of mankind.

It made Sigrid want to vomit. They held these women like little birds in golden cages, only taking them out to sing every now and then.

However, the concubines seemed quite happy with their lives. A cluster of them walked in the opposite direction of Sigrid and Camilla, giggling and falling over each other on their way to one of their rooms.

Pretty things. Each one was a delicate flower. A rose bloomed in one corner, the fabric of her pale pink dress dancing as she moved. A tiger lily lifted a graceful hand to pour water for another, the orange fabric fluttering in the slight breeze.

Sigrid nodded to them all as they walked by, hiding her emotions behind her mask. They were weak little women, but she admired their beauty all the same.

Camilla tugged her away from the hall and down through the servants' quarters where none of the women were supposed to go. They weren't allowed to be alone with men. Unless, of course, they were also a servant.

"Hurry," Camilla urged. "I don't want anyone finding us. They'll ask questions, and we don't have time."

Sigrid lifted her skirts and raced after her sister. "I have to wear these dresses, you know that."

"Not all the time!"

"If the sultan orders my presence, I cannot show up in men's pants and a training shirt."

"Why not? He's already seen you at your worst." Camilla glanced over her shoulder with a saucy grin on her face. "Or maybe not your worst. I've also seen you swimming."

"Run faster, owl. I suddenly desire roast bird."

They tried to hold hands over their mouths to muffle their laughter, but Sigrid was almost certain at least one man saw them. She tossed caution to the wind. Let the sultan find out she had gone down into the servants' quarters. What would he do? She was enjoying his palace and all of the hidden secrets in its halls. Surely, he wouldn't be angry at her for that.

Camilla skidded to a halt in front of a door and pressed a finger to her lips. "Wait, let me make sure he's still there."

"You aren't my personal guard, by the gods." Sigrid pushed by her and opened the door.

The balcony had an impressive view of the desert, but not of the city. Perhaps, this was why it was in the servants' quarters. A bucket sat in one corner, likely waiting for someone to take and clean, but it was the view that caught her eye.

The sun was low on the horizon. Sand caught its rays and turned the entire desert to gold. Rolling sand dunes gently sprayed in the wind, and the entirety of the view was framed by giant, black mountains far in the distance. The Edge of the

World could be seen even from here.

A shadow peeled away from the wall, and the blue-eyed boy she remembered stepped forward.

"Sultana."

"So, it is you," she said, smiling and reaching out for his hand. "I'm glad you made it here."

He stared at her hand in horror. "My lady, are the rumors not true? It's said to touch the sultana is to lose a hand."

Sigrid understood why he would think so, but it hurt her heart to know he feared her. She shook her head and swallowed all her own fear that rose in response.

"It's true for any human. The rules of the Beastkin are clear. None but family may touch a Beastkin woman, the punishment is removing whatever touched their skin. None but family may see a Beastkin woman's face, the punishment for that is death." She took a deep breath, reached up, and unhooked the clasps of her mask.

It was a dangerous thing to do, but as matriarch of the Wildewyn Beastkin, it was up to her to make the right choice. Their people needed to understand that Beastkin were united, even across countries.

She pulled the mask away from her face and held it out to Camilla who stared at her with wide eyes. Only one other male had ever seen the last remaining drakon female's face. She squared her shoulders in pride and met the boy's gaze.

He paled. "My lady, I don't wish to die."

"And so you shall not." She reached forward again and caught his hand. "You are *family*. Don't you understand? All Beastkin are family in some way, shape, or form. It's an honor to meet you, because I can see you without the mask. You are a blessing to me and to my people. We have been alone for so long."

Tears built in his eyes. The boy stared at her with wonder, his eyes flicking to the side where Camilla removed her mask as well.

"I didn't think it was possible to find people like you," he finally choked. "We thought all our women had died, hunted down by the Bymerians. Our numbers have dwindled for centuries until we finally ran away to the desert."

"Then it's good we found each other." She released his hand, feeling overwhelmed by the sudden touch. Sigrid didn't know how to be this woman who was comfortable with other people. She would try. It was the right thing to do. Unfortunately, it would take time.

"The leader of our people would like to meet you," the boy said.

She waved a hand in the air. "Yes, we will speak soon. What is your name?"

"My name, Sultana?"

"Yes." She smiled at the surprise in his voice. "I wish to know *your* name first, and then his."

"I am Altair." He stared up at her with wide eyes. "Why do you wish to know my name?"

"So I know what to call you." And because she wanted to know the name of the angel who had taken the first step in bringing their people together. "And the name of your leader?"

"He is known as Jabbar. He sent me to ask when you will come."

Sigrid tried to think of the lie she would tell Nadir, but couldn't come up with anything believable when her head was filled with such magic. There were *Beastkin in Bymere,* and they knew who she was. They wanted to meet, to talk, perhaps even to unite their people. Her soul sang with the possibilities.

"Tell him I will send a message soon. I must find a way to sneak away from the palace without anyone knowing where I have gone, but I eagerly await meeting him."

"Shall I tell him the truth?" Altair glanced at her mask. "I have not told him what kind of Beastkin you are. I didn't know if it would be an insult. Our ways are very different."

Bless the boy and his foresight. She hadn't thought at all what the Beastkin men would do if they knew a drakon was in their midst. Having such a powerful creature was both good and bad. If they wished to rise up against the sultan...

It was too much to think of. She didn't know what she would do. The man wasn't good for his country. He wasn't taking the steps she wanted him to take, but he also wasn't evil.

And he was a drakon as well. She couldn't allow them to risk his life.

Sigrid shook her head. "No, don't tell him yet. If he insists, say I wanted to tell him what I was myself. That it's better to know in person."

"He'll hazard a guess at that."

"But he won't guess a drakon." No one would. They had been dead for hundreds of years other than her own single line hidden away in Wildewyn.

And that of the sultan.

"Go now," Sigrid said. "It's not safe for you to be here, and I won't risk your life. Camilla will find you again when I know how to reach your people."

"Be safe, Sultana."

She watched him change into a sparrow at the blink of an eye and dive off the edge of the balcony. Her chest ached at seeing him go.

There was much her people didn't understand or know. They couldn't have possibly guessed at what she would find here in Bymere. This was a country full of secrets hidden deep within the sands.

"Shall I fetch Raheem?" Camilla asked.

"Why?"

"You'll want to ply the sultan with sweets and alcohol to get anywhere," her sister grumbled. "That man will not let you out of the palace without a guard. And we can't take a guard where we're going."

"I know that. I don't intend on walking though."

Camilla stepped in front of her, holding up the golden dragon mask. "Just how do you intend to greet these men?"

The mask settled over her face once again. The cold metal felt like a prison the moment it touched her cheeks.

Sigrid reached for Camilla's mask and did the same for her sister. "As a drakon."

NADIR

NADIR STOOD IN HIS GREAT HALL, STARING AT THE THRONE.
What would his brother have said about all this madness? A
Beastkin woman as sultana, a dragon as sultan. A secret neither
of them could ever share with the people of Bymere.

Madness, that's what he would have said. He'd said time
and time again, if Nadir insisted on remaining a Beastkin then
he would have to control it. Merge the man and the monster,
learn how to be the stronger side of the coin, and never flip it
over unless he absolutely had to.

Hakim had always feared the dragon. Even when Nadir
was just a boy, and the dragon was just a whelp, his brother had
looked at him with pity and sadness.

To be Beastkin in Bymere was a curse. Whoever found him
in his other form would kill him on sight if they could.

His brother had been right. There were too many people
who despised him. Too many vipers in the sands who wanted
to strike at his ankles.

Nadir didn't want to think what his first wife would do if she found out. She hated Beastkin nearly more than he did. Every inch of her was afraid of them. Likely because she couldn't explain them.

He understood that fear. He'd been afraid of himself long before he understood he could control the dragon, and that it was as much a part of him as anything else. But explaining that to someone who couldn't change into an animal would be impossible. Saafiya couldn't understand him, so he didn't even try.

He'd been careful his entire life to never have a child. The advisors thought it likely that he couldn't have them. He'd heard their whispers behind his back, wondering why there wasn't an heir. Saafiya had a child from her first marriage, the boy nearly the same age as Nadir, so it wasn't that she wasn't capable.

Let them spread whatever dark rumors they wanted to. He wouldn't curse another to this life in the shadows.

"Husband?"

He stiffened at the voice, squeezing his hands hard behind his back. "I requested that no one enter."

"I didn't ask for permission." Her amused tones eased the tension in his neck.

Sigrid. How did she always find him when he was at his worst? He turned and found her striding toward him.

Her graceful steps hardly shifted the fabric of her gown. Icy blue today. Tiny bells sang at her waist with every slight movement. She was beautiful, like the babbling brook in the forest he'd seen only once in Wildewyn.

What a woman he'd captured.

Bowing low, he said, "Wife, you're looking particularly beautiful today."

"Flattery will get you nowhere."

"And what can I do for you?" He gestured at the horseshoe arches revealing the sinking sun. "It's not yet time for dinner."

"I thought perhaps you would be interested in escaping with me for a few hours this evening? Surely, the sultanate can survive without you for one night."

"It's a dangerous request. My advisors will plot yet another assassination attempt."

"You could kill them instead."

How he wished he could. Nadir lifted a hand and ran it through his hair. "The advisors come from all areas of Bymere. They are more representative of this kingdom than I am. It is through their mouths that my people speak. To kill one, or send one home, is an act of civil war."

"Even if they try to kill you?"

"Even then."

She arched a brow, mask shifting with her movement. "They must do much better than last time to get through me."

"Yes, I suspect they know that."

The memory was one he couldn't easily forget. She was a far better warrior than his men although he was proud to know he'd bested her. Nadir rested easy knowing that if he had to, he could subdue her.

A heated part of his mind also enjoyed the knowledge that his dragon was larger. He couldn't have guessed that if he wished. The male sand lizards that basked in the sunbeams around the palace were always smaller than their mates. It made little sense that dragon males were larger, and yet he was.

He furrowed his brow. "How old are you?"

"Nineteen summers."

So he was older than her. Only by one summer, but enough. Perhaps, that was the reason for the size difference.

He sighed. "Where do you want to take me, wife? We'll need a guard if we're exploring the city. The people still don't know what to think of the masked woman married to their sultan. You know they are calling you the Undying?"

"Are they?" She shrugged. "They aren't wrong."

"I think it's meant to be an insult."

"Or a warning." Her skirts swished as she made her way to him. "I've been advised to spend more time with you. That perhaps we will find common ground together."

"Ah." Nadir nodded. "You've been talking to Raheem."

"How did you know?"

"He's said the same thing to me." He gave her a sardonic grin. "I just didn't act on it."

She tilted her masked face to the side. "Why's that?"

"I didn't want to put you in a difficult situation. After all, I stole you from your home, forced you to marry me, and then kept a secret from you." Nadir lifted a hand and pinched his fingers together. "A small secret."

"Ah, of course. Just that tiny little secret." She nodded. "Well, that's all behind us now. And I would very much like to know you, husband."

"Because of the secret?"

"The tiny secret," she agreed.

When was the last time he'd bantered with someone like this? His soul felt light, knowing she was teasing him with her words. She swayed side to side, as she had done when calming his dragon, and he realized she was playing him.

He let her continue pulling his strings, knowing he was falling into a dangerous web. What could it hurt?

She was, after all, his wife.

"What do you have in mind, wife?"

Her mask lifted when she grinned. "Camilla has been exploring your great sands, and she found a place where no man has been. It's near here, easily reached by horse, and we would be safe to spend an evening together as we truly are."

"No," he replied. "We're not doing that again."

"Why not? One time wasn't enough, husband. Not for me."

"It has to be. We will not do that again, ever."

She stepped closer, took a deep breath, and nodded. "All right. Then please enjoy your dinner and don't mind when I'm not there."

"Why?" He already knew the answer, but he wanted to hear it from her lips. "Why won't you be at dinner?"

"I'm going to this place with or without you. I thought perhaps you would like to watch over me."

He scrubbed a hand over his face and let out a frustrated growl. This damned woman would be the death of him. "I forbid it."

"You cannot forbid a drakon from anything."

"I'll put guards at your door."

"If you want them to see a drakon tonight, then by all means, please do so." She lifted a shoulder. "It matters little to me."

And once again, she'd tricked him.

He couldn't afford his people seeing her. They couldn't know the rumors were true. Let them think up whatever myths they wished about the Beastkin. Stories were innocent; facts were dangerous.

Nadir curled his hands into fists, nails digging into his palms to remind himself that controlling his dragon had always been easy. He knew how to control his baser urges. And yet, she antagonized his inner beast as never before.

"Fine," he growled. "We'll visit this place your maidservant has found. But we will not change."

"If we're there already, we might as well enjoy it."

"Someone might *see* us, Sigrid."

"And would that really be the end of the world?" She tapped a finger to her mask. "If I remove this, then I know we will not be disturbed. I'd rather a man see my dragon than my face. He'll survive the dragon far easier."

Nadir took a step closer to her. "Why is that? No one has yet explained what strange ritual your Beastkin women follow that if someone sees their face, they must die."

"Only family may behold what our human bodies look like."

"But why?"

Her eyes narrowed, and he was certain the mask tilted slightly to the left as if she were lifting a brow. "I don't know."

"How can you not know? It's a harsh punishment." He stepped closer again.

"It's how it's always been."

Nadir was close enough now he could feel the heat emanating from her body. Leaning down, he pressed his lips against her ear and whispered, "Do you always follow ancient rules?"

Her shoulders shivered. "They were created for a reason."

"Sure." He leaned back and held his arms out at his sides. "To be broken."

The mask lifted. Nadir was certain that meant she was giving him a disapproving look, but it mattered little. She'd learn his ways soon enough. She was a Sultana of Bymere. Rules had no merit to her anymore.

He strode from the great hall with a lightness in his steps he hadn't felt in a while.

"Nadir?" She called out. "Sultan? Where are you going?"

"You said you wished to travel, wife. I find I don't hunger for the dinner our cooks will prepare tonight. Let us see what the desert has to offer us."

Her footsteps echoed on the cold sandstone as she raced after him. It felt as though they had done this many times. He ordered his guards to ready their horses, held out an arm for her to take, and they strode through the palace.

She fit on his arm the way he had always expected a wife would fit. Her hand was cool and relaxed. She held her head high, the way a sultana should, but she was also thoroughly different. An exotic wildflower somehow blooming in the desert.

Nadir nodded to a few red-clothed advisors who walked past them, ignoring how they ducked their heads to whisper in shock.

"How are you finding the palace?" he asked.

"It's well enough."

"Well enough? It's the gem of Bymere, the most impressive building ever built. And you find it well enough?" He exaggerated his words, hoping to make her laugh, or at least get some kind of reaction.

She lifted a shoulder, but mirth danced in her eyes. "There are a few things I would change that could improve it."

"Like what?" Nadir guided her around a group of concubines who giggled as they saw him. They wore filmy clothes in every shade of red that billowed as they moved. One hid behind her hand the moment her eyes fell on Sigrid, her words lost behind feminine bodies.

He'd heard they weren't accepting her well, but hadn't thought it was quite that bad. Nadir found it strange simply because he'd seen many women added to the harem who'd done well. The women welcomed new additions with open arms. They were kind, considerate, and helped any newcomer ease into the life of a royal concubine.

Why weren't they doing it with Sigrid?

She shook her head, the mask lifting with her smile. "That is not something anyone can change, husband."

"And why not? I'm sultan. I can order them to like you if you wish."

"Sincerity is something I value above all else, and their friendship must be earned. A new sultana is difficult to accept. Especially one from a country many despise."

"Ah." He squeezed her hand. "They remain loyal to their original mistress, I understand. I'll have words with Saafiya."

"I'll say it again, Nadir. Don't get involved. Their lack of regard is partially my fault, and there is nothing you can do."

He thought of what Raheem had told him. That there were more to the lives of women than men could understand. In this, he would take Sigrid's request seriously. There was no need to meddle as long as his second wife remained comfortable here.

"Then what is it you would change?" he asked. "I'm eager

to hear the list you've compiled."

They made their way down crimson halls teeming with people, and she advised him on every hole that made this place dangerous to live. He allowed her to speak and tried to stifle any amused expression that might have crossed his face. Passion burned deep in her soul when it came to any potential attack.

It was strange to see a woman know so much about the subject. They usually disliked any talk that might suggest the kingdom wasn't doing as well as it could. At least, that had always been his impression. Even his concubines wanted to talk more about pretty things, how he could improve their living quarters, what more baubles they would enjoy.

But this woman wished to talk of war. Her usually still, flat voice became animated. She gestured to the slatted windows and explained why they were an intelligent choice but lacking in their abilities to protect should the enemy come with arrows.

He saw his home in a new light. Not unsafe, as she would have liked him to think, but that there were such clear differences between their countries. What she thought was a weakness, he saw as strength.

The windows weren't easy for arrows to fly through; they were a safety measure. They could see enemies coming. The Bymerian soldiers would hide inside, wait for shadows to cross over the windows, and then they would attack through the slats.

But he told her none of this. Let her think them defenseless, that they foolishly didn't protect their home. She wouldn't get far if she ever betrayed him.

They left the safety of the Red Palace and mounted their

horses of blood and shadow. He noticed his wife give the black stallion an appreciative glance.

"You like Zalaam?" he asked.

"Is that his name?"

He nodded.

"What does it mean?"

"Darkness." He hadn't been a particularly original name-giver in his youth. The stallion had served him well for many a year before the retired warhorse was given a chance to sire more foals that would serve the sultan. He rode one of the great, black beast's children now.

A smile spread across his face when she leaned down and brushed her hands along the horse's neck. The wind carried her voice as she repeated the Bymerian word.

So, the Beastkin could learn after all.

"Hup," he cried out, urging his horse into movement. He heard his wife's answering call and the tell-tale crack of a whip. It didn't take her long to catch up with him.

They charged through the city as if a dust devil were on their tail. People fled from the streets, staring in awe as the sultan and his new sultana fled out into the whirling dervish of the sands.

Hair blasted away from his face, wind whipping the long tail behind him until the tie loosened and fell free. Long locks fell around his shoulders, but he didn't tie them back again. Nadir was free from the tangled web of the Red Palace. Here in the desert, he was nothing more than a man.

For once, the beast and him were entirely synced. They both felt the sting of sand striking their face, the wind underneath their arms that could not fly, and the heaving breath of the horse underneath them.

The black stallion appeared at his side, its head creeping forward and then inching ahead of his chestnut mare. For a moment, Nadir was stunned. He hadn't seen the stallion ride that well since he was a boy although the beast was nowhere near old.

Her braid snapped and caught him on the arm like a whip. Shocked, he faltered just enough for her to sneak ahead of him. She rode like she'd been born on a horse. Her body molded to every long stride of the stallion.

She glanced over her shoulder, and he swore the mask laughed at him.

Setting his jaw, he lifted onto his feet and spurred his horse to race ever faster. They tore across the desert, neck and neck, and he couldn't remember the last time he felt so alive. Dust billowed from their horse's footsteps. The snaking trail they left behind looked like the long tail of a dragon.

Eventually, she pulled back on the reins and slowed their ragged tear. Both horses were breathing hard, but neither appeared worse for wear. In fact, there was a gleam in the black stallion's eyes he hadn't seen in a long time. The old boy had enjoyed stretching his legs.

Sunlight reflected off his new wife's golden mask. The bright ray nearly blinded him, but he only had eyes for her. She rode atop the horse without a hair out of place, even as the wind blew against her. No ragged breathing made her sit uncomfortably. Her posture was impeccable, and her hair smooth. Even her dress didn't have a single mark of sweat.

He'd seen nothing like her in his life. What kind of creature could ride a horse full tilt through the desert and not show a single second of it?

"This is the place," she said, interrupting his thoughts.

Nadir glanced around. The wind had built up sand dunes on either side, creating a bowl in the desert that was large enough for his entire castle to fit in. He hadn't noticed their steep descent, but then again, he'd been staring at her.

The sunset streaked the sky with pinks, oranges, and bright fuchsias. Streams of clouds stretched overhead, enough that they could likely hide behind them if they so wished. And all around them, the rolling hills of golden sand billowed in the slight breeze.

He exhaled. "It is a good enough place. Your maidservant has an eye for hidden places such as this, I take it?"

"She's not my maidservant."

"Ah, yes. Your sister."

Sigrid nodded, passing the reins back and forth between her hands. "Have you ever flown before?"

"When I was younger."

"I've never flown anywhere," she murmured. "I don't know if it's even possible for my wings to lift such a massive body."

"*You can fly.*" The passion in his voice startled even him. Nadir cleared his throat and swung down from the back of his horse to hide his discomfort. "I'll teach you, if you'd like."

"I wouldn't even know where to begin." Her masked face lifted, staring off into the desert. "It seems like something our kind would learn as children."

There were no words to explain away her worries. He wasn't certain he could even do what she wanted, but he also knew how important it was for a dragon to fly. Hadn't he desired the same thing for his entire life?

Nadir strode over to the side of her horse and lifted a hand for her to take. "Come along, Sultana. It's long past time you learned how to fly."

She reached up, hooked her fingers beneath the edges of her mask, and lifted the gold free. Waning sunlight played across the high peaks of her cheekbones. Her alabaster skin glowed like some mythical creature who lured him farther and farther into the water.

The cool slide of her hand in his startled him.

"Shouldn't you be warm?" he asked, helping her from the stallion's back.

"I am." But she looked at him with a question in her gaze.

"You don't feel it."

Her lips parted in a breath. "That's because you're far warmer than me, Sultan."

And perhaps he was. A dragon burned in his chest, knowing freedom was only a few moments away.

This was a drug he would have to be careful with. The dragon had always been caged, beaten, abused so badly that it would never consider trying to overwhelm him. It knew there was no chance of it breaking free from the chains with which he'd bound it.

But now? The dragon's mate had arrived on wings made of moonlight, and she sang a siren song of freedom, cool air, and starlight. Both he and the dragon desperately wanted to follow her to the edges of the earth and beyond.

"Nadir?" she asked.

"What is it, Sigrid?" Something about her hesitation made him stare into her icy eyes. There was something in those depths he recognized, and yet couldn't name. A heat, a welcoming embrace, an acceptance he'd only seen a few times in his existence.

"Thank you," she answered.

She dropped his hand and stepped away from him. Each movement sent a thousand grains of sand tumbling toward him.

Sigrid tilted her face to the sky, and her smile rivaled that of the setting sun. She opened her arms wide, took a deep breath, and changed. Nadir saw the exact moment she released her hold onto the human form when the air shimmered with magic and tightened with the electric power of Beastkin.

She shifted effortlessly into a creature made of diamond and opal. Stretching her long neck, she let loose a haunting call that sounded like the low strum of a violin.

He couldn't deny the command in her voice. The dragon inside him heard the cry of its mate and thundered to the forefront of his mind. Nadir shattered, shredded, ripped apart, and then became something new.

His scaled body was powerful. Muscles flexed, shifting underneath the leathery skin. He too lifted his head and let loose a bellow that shook the ground they stood upon.

Everything about this body felt *good*. This was the form he was meant to be in. The horns on his head were perfect for war. His claws dug into the sand, relishing the scrape of earth beneath them. The fire in his belly churned until he could stand it no more.

He turned from her, opened his mouth, and let loose a roar that rode on an inferno. His breath was fire. His call was magic.

The dune in front of him crystallized in the heat. Each

granule melted into something that glistened like diamonds before them. *Glass.* He'd created glass with little more than a breath that didn't even empty the air from his lungs.

Rearing back, he stared at his creation with heaving lungs. A nudge at his side made him turn, and there she was. This beautiful creature staring at him with pale, blue eyes full of compassion and understanding.

She brushed against his side and made her way to the molten glass dune. Sigrid hunched over the heat, digging her wings in and dragging her chest through it as she tried to reach the highest peak. He knew what she was feeling, what she was doing. The heat was a balm to their aching soul.

Glass stuck to her wings, glistening as she lifted them to catch the last bit of the dying light. Her tail lashed back and forth, the triangle at the end creating a pattern in the sand.

And gods, she was beautiful. He couldn't stop looking at her, filling his eyes with the impossibility of her.

How long had he felt alone in this world? How long had it been since he'd been able to be himself without fear someone would look at him with disgust?

To think, he'd been convinced she lied. That there couldn't possibly be another person cursed to be a dragon, not when he already lived in this hell. He'd been so convinced that the Earthen folk lied that he hadn't even entertained that *this* could be possible.

She arched her neck, stretching up to the sky with her wings spread wide. Rainbows danced on the surface, and he wondered if she could learn to fly. The membranes looked so thin, nearly transparent. He worried she would tumble from the sky if the slightest thing touched them.

But then he reminded himself that he too could fly, and that she would never fall far from his grasp.

Stretching his own wings wide, he gave a few experimental beats. It had been a long time since he'd attempted this. The last time, he had been nothing more than a child. Just a boy wanting to impress his older brother, not realizing that Hakim was terrified of the beast his little brother could turn into.

Wind caught on his wings, stretching them to their fullest and it felt right. Everything about this felt as it should. He tried harder, pushing his body to the limits and pushed his back legs into the sand, lifting off the ground. Up and up he went until the tip of his tail was the only thing left touching the ground.

Excited, he looked at Sigrid and continued to laboriously hold himself in place. She had to see this. To see that it was possible. If he could fly, so much larger than she, then she could lift herself from the ground.

She watched him with narrowed eyes. Determination was perhaps her best quality, he decided, as she flapped her wings. She struggled, wavered for a moment, then slowly lifted into the air.

He swelled with pride and he felt yet another roar building in his chest. Was this connection what his brother had talked about all those years ago? Hakim had always been searching for a sultana who would make his heart sing, his soul take wing, and all the stars in the sky dim in comparison to her beauty.

Nadir had laughed at him then. He said such a woman didn't exist, and in a way, he'd been right. Such a woman didn't exist. Only a beast.

She shot up into the air, higher and higher until she slid between the clouds and disappeared from his sight. Concerned, he followed her. Red rays of light streaked his scales, turning the burgundy to ruby red.

Cold clouds soothed the heat in his chest. They brushed his skin like the hands of a lover before he pushed through the wisps and was nearly blinded by the sun.

He held himself still in the air, wings beating as he searched for her.

This place looked like a different land. The clouds rolled, mimicking the ocean but capped in white and so still he felt like he could hear for the first time. No birds flew this high. No people talked or animals brayed. This undiscovered place now was home to only him and Sigrid.

A soft, songlike call from behind made him crane his neck. She glided on a ribbon of wind and gently sailed past him. Graceful, even though she'd been frightened to even attempt this.

Her tail caught him at the shoulder, trailing along the length of his neck and then slipping off his blunt chin. Gods, she knew what she did to him, and it didn't bother her in the slightest. An icy blue eye caught his attention. Laughter bubbled in its depths.

Had he ever seen her laugh? Truly laugh. The kind that came from deep within a person and exploded so forcefully they wouldn't try to stop it?

He didn't think he ever had. And he'd hazard a guess that she couldn't remember the last time she'd done it. He wanted to see her laugh. He wanted to see her face when she did a good many things, and there wasn't enough time in their lives for him to explore every emotion inside her.

A pity, but he planned to try.

They flew for hours above the clouds until there was no more sunlight to heat their skin. Then, they were guided by the silver light of the moon and the stars twinkling above them. He couldn't remember a time when he'd been this happy. Not since his brother had died, at least.

Eventually, he noticed her breathing change. She didn't want to land, not quite yet, but he decided for them knowing she grew tired. It was possible to hurt herself like this. And he wouldn't see her harmed.

He powerfully opened and closed his wings, nudging clouds out of the way so that he could see where they were. He stopped every few minutes, checking their location, until he finally found the bowl in the sand where her maidservant had declared it safe.

Landing on his back feet, he buffeted the sands and let his wings strike the ground hard. He was exhausted, but still turned to watch her land clumsily. A bellowing chortle escaped his mouth. It wasn't a sound he'd ever made before, but he found that he quite liked it.

The second time changing back to his form was easier. This was how he remembered it as a child. There wasn't any feeling of being locked in as a dragon, just the quiet shift from scale to flesh.

He stood in the center of the bowl, now much deeper than before from their powerful wing beats, and stepped closer to Sigrid.

She crouched in the moonlight, looking like a creature out of some mysterious myth. Her neck extended the closer he got. A welcoming invite for him to touch her, he hoped, because that was what he did.

Nadir slid his hand along the flat of her cheek to the ring of tiny horns that made up her crown. They were white as bone and just as hard. He let his hand wander until he couldn't reach any further forward, marveling at her design.

"You're beautiful," he said.

She dropped her head until her chin rested on the sand, and then she melted back to the woman he was enamored with.

This creature from Wildewyn had more than captured his attention by now. The glimmering icy dress gave its own song even as she remained crouched in the sand at his feet. The white locks of her hair shone blue in the moonlight. She looked very much like a djinn, suddenly appearing to grant him three wishes.

Nadir gulped. "Was it everything you hoped for, wife?"

"And more." She looked up then, and he was gutted by the appreciation in her gaze. "Thank you."

Would he ever get used to seeing her face? It was such a rarity, and he wanted to see it more often. The longer he knew her, the more her beauty glowed from within. "Good."

He reached out a hand for her to take and pride bloomed in his chest again when she took it without hesitation. They were moving forward. She didn't hesitate to touch him anymore, had even initiated it in the great hall. Now that they were alone together, her eyes met his without defiance or anger.

He led her out of the bowl to their horses. He'd glimpsed them while in the clouds and had to still his own animalistic hunger. Even as a dragon, they looked like they would be a delicious meal. The mere thought sent gooseflesh rising all over his skin. He wasn't an animal. He was a man.

He could control the beast.

"Nadir?" she whispered.

"Yes, wife?"

"We were safe here. No one saw us, and no one bothered us. I know it's not something you'd like to do often, but I am just finding this part of myself." She paused, gaze skating away from his. "I should like to return, with my sister if possible, and no guards."

His gut reaction was no. He didn't want her to be anywhere far from the palace without a guard. Though Bymere was relatively safe, there were plenty who would attack him through a defenseless wife.

But she wasn't Saafiya. She was trained in the art of war, and she knew far more than any female he'd ever met before.

He nodded. "The first time you see anything that looks dangerous, you return to me."

"I promise, husband."

Nadir took that promise to heart. She would keep herself safe and hidden, or he would destroy all of Bymere to find her.

SIGRID

SIGRID RAN THROUGH A HUNDRED DIFFERENT SCENARIOS IN HER head every day, each more detailed than the last, to get out of the Red Palace and into the sands. But no matter how hard she tried, there was always one person who found her out. Namely, the first wife who seemed determined that Sigrid would remain in her room and not touch anything.

Although Sigrid understood her dislike, there was something more than a general disdain for Beastkin. It was almost as if Saafiya was afraid of her. The warrior capabilities of the Wildewyn Beastkin were renowned throughout the realms, and yet it didn't seem that this was the first wife's concern.

Eventually, Sigrid could take it no more. She had to sort this out, for her own peace of mind and to ensure Saafiya wouldn't interfere. She didn't care if the woman wanted to hate her for a reason unexplained. But she couldn't stop Sigrid from seeing the other Beastkin.

She stood outside the first wife's personal chambers and took a deep breath, adjusting the mask on her face once more. It was a nervous tick. She logically knew that no one could see her face and that the mask had never fallen off before. Still, she worried that she would turn too fast. The entire piece might fall off, and then she would have to kill the first wife.

Old traditions were brutal. Best to avoid them at all costs.

Camilla wanted to come. She said that the concubines should see that there was at least one person willing to support Sigrid. Her sister bristled at the mere idea that people disliked her because one person decided they shouldn't.

Sigrid said her sister's dedication was unwarranted in this case. She had little desire to make the first wife feel as though she were being attacked. The purpose of this meeting was to understand where the woman was coming from. Nothing more, nothing less.

She lifted her hand and knocked on the door. The solid wood thudded under her fist, echoing through the chamber beyond.

A muffled voice, too far away to understand the words, responded. Footsteps strode toward the door, and then it opened to reveal a sun-darkened face surrounded by dark hair that fell like a waterfall to the concubine's waist. She wore a bright and sunny smile that promptly fell away when she realized who was at their door.

"The sultana is not taking visitors," the woman whispered, then began to shut the door.

"I wish to talk," Sigrid insisted.

She might have put her foot in the door jamb if she hadn't heard Saafiya's voice call out, "Who is it?"

"The second wife, Sultana." The concubine kept the door cracked only a small bit so that Sigrid couldn't see into the room.

The silence afterward was the still silence of a tomb. Sigrid waited with her hands clasped at her waist. They would see no reaction in her body. She simply wouldn't allow it. And none of them knew her well enough to recognize the slightest movement of her mask as she chewed her lip.

"She may enter," Saafiya responded.

Steeling herself for what felt like a battle, Saafiya stepped into the inner sanctum of the first wife.

She'd always wondered what kind of place this woman would live in. Saafiya seemed the type of person who would enjoy opulence. The glamorous interior proved her correct.

The room was an oasis in the middle of the desert. Palm trees created shady havens in the corners, planted directly into a floor made of polished white marble. Twin pools outlined the room. The thin channels teemed with golden fish that flicked their tails and swam away as she crossed a thin bridge over the pond.

Red curtains hung from the keyhole windows. The room was high enough in the palace that there was a lovely cross breeze that shifted the curtains with each movement. A high ceiling rose into what Sigrid suspected was one of the domes. An artist had painstakingly painted a giant mandala with gold paint that glimmered overhead.

She'd never seen such splendor in a single room, and it appeared that was the entire point. Saafiya lazed on a small bench next to the pool, her gown nearly touching the water. The red fabric was hand-stitched with gold embroidery that glimmered in the light. Her handmaidens fanned her with a giant palm leaf though her skin still glimmered with a slight sheen of sweat. Just enough to make her look as though she, too, were made of gold.

"Why have you come?" she asked, her words acidic. "I didn't summon you here, second wife."

Sigrid wanted to ask why the woman insisted on calling her that. It was almost as if she thought it were an insult. That because Saafiya had been here first, that she was more important.

Perhaps to the people of Bymere, she was. But Sigrid now held a secret of the sultan that no one else knew. And that secret gave her strength.

Sigrid cleared her throat. "I've been here for a few months now and have yet to have the pleasure of your company. I thought, perhaps, we might speak."

"I've no wish to speak with—" Saafiya caught herself, pausing on a word that Sigrid knew would cut to the core. "With you. I've no wish to speak with you."

"You don't like Beastkin." It was blunt, but obviously the truth.

The first wife sighed. "No, I do not."

"I'm sorry to hear that. I understand we must make you uncomfortable. Bymere does not welcome my kind as easily as Wildewyn."

Saafiya sat up, the crimson fabric of her gown pooling around her like blood. Her top was cut at the ribs, revealing natural, caramel skin that was not darkened by the sun. Ebony hair flowed over her shoulder. It reflected the light in blues and greens and a few strands of white ribboning through the river of her hair.

The first wife shook her head and a razor-sharp grin spread across her face. "We've welcomed none of your kind before. Humans should not live with animals. It goes against our nature. As you can see, there's no easy way for any of us to be comfortable with you here."

"We don't consider ourselves animals. Why should you?"

"Let me educate you, because you know nothing about our land or the dangers of your kind. You barged into my private quarters. Now you will listen." Saafiya flicked her fingers, and a concubine ran for a chair.

Sigrid sat in the offered seat, her thighs tense, ready to leap to her feet if need be. She didn't trust this woman enough to take a drink from her hand.

"Please," Sigrid said, echoing the first wife's gesture. "Continue."

A spark seared in Saafiya's gaze. "My husband should have told you this when you first arrived. Bymere doesn't have a kind history with Beastkin, and it was only through blood that we beat them back into the hovels where they now remain. Let no one else fool you. The Beastkin still exist in our realm, and we will continue to hunt them until our dying breath."

So, the first wife knew that there were still some lingering Beastkin. Many people in the palace had claimed Sigrid was the only Beastkin in Bymere. Did she know her own husband was one of these "beasts" as she liked to call them?

Saafiya continued. "Bymere has long been a warring kingdom. Each part used to have their own leaders, tribal like your homeland. Misthall, Falldell, Glasslyn, each with its own sultan and each believing they alone knew how to unite the kingdoms. The Beastkin came to our kingdom only when the kingdoms united. But then again, they've always been an opportunistic race.

"Soon they tried to raise their own leaders. They wanted rights, they wanted to be seen as people. And when we refused, they started a war." Saafiya shook her head. "It was the bloodiest time in Bymerian history."

A few concubines joined Sigrid. They sat down around her as if she wasn't there. In looking at them, Sigrid realized just how young they were. The first wife had filled the sultan's home with concubines who were nearly children. Saafiya had made herself a matriarch without the title.

"We tried to fight them," Saafiya's voice shook with anger. "For years, we tried. I was a little girl when a lion attacked our village. We thought at first it had simply wandered out of the desert. Its ribs were showing, and surely it was starving. But then we realized there was a smarter mind inside the beast who tore through our guards like they were nothing more than flowers in a garden. I watched my brother die a horrible death. All because these creatures weren't controlled as they should have been."

And just like that, Sigrid understood where her hatred came from. Losing a family member, and one so close, must have made Saafiya into the woman she was now.

Sigrid leaned forward in the chair, her hands tucked into her skirts. "I'm Beastkin, and I can tell you that we do not think like animals while in our other forms. Though he was not thinking like a lion, it sounds as if that Beastkin was truly starving. Perhaps he had gone mad—"

Saafiya shook her head and interrupted. "The animal

attacked our village because it wanted to. Not because it was starving or any other excuse that you'll make up for it. The beast *killed* fifteen of our men and didn't swallow a single one. If this animal was starving, I might have forgiven the deaths. But it wasn't. It killed fifteen men and left them there to rot in the sun."

Sigrid didn't have a response or an explanation for the Beastkin's actions. It wasn't like their kind to be so brutal. But there must have been a reason.

"I can see your thoughts behind those strange eyes," Saafiya murmured. "He wasn't doing it for any reason other than he wanted to. Men and beasts are similar in that way."

"It's not like any Beastkin I know to do such a thing."

"These are not the Beastkin you know. Regardless, there's a monster inside you that always wants to claw its way out. People reason. Animals attack."

Stunned and speechless, Sigrid watched Saafiya stand. She shooed the concubines away, some grumbling that they wanted to listen to their mistress's conversation with the Beastkin.

"It's like watching a dog be scolded," one whispered.

Their words stung. Sigrid squeezed her fists and remained silent while they insulted her as if she wasn't in the room. Perhaps she wasn't in their eyes. Perhaps they fundamentally thought she couldn't understand them.

Finally, it was just Saafiya and Sigrid next to each other. Saafiya stood to the side, her eyes staring past Sigrid.

"So, you see," the first wife said. "I have good reason to hate your kind."

"One rogue Beastkin doesn't justify a hatred for an entire people."

"Have you forgotten the war? The centuries of fighting, the beasts who attacked us at every corner. Do you know how many stories there are of farmers slaughtering their cattle for food and having it turn back into a person?" Saafiya shivered. "Your kind hide wherever they can. It's unnatural, and it needs to end."

"Perhaps it is you who is unnatural."

Saafiya lifted her shoulder with grace. "The victor of this new war will determine who is natural and who will be run out of these sands. I don't intend it to be my kind."

A fire burned in her chest, spreading to her fingertips, and sending out a wave of heat. Saafiya flinched as it reached her, and Sigrid could almost hear the dangerous sizzle of hair.

Sigrid let out a slow breath. "I don't take kindly to threats."

"And yet you seem comfortable giving them." The first wife pointed toward the door. "You may leave my private chambers now. I've given you the reasons why I dislike you. I owe you nothing else."

"I didn't come here asking for friendship."

"Then why did you come?" Saafiya met her gaze as Sigrid stood. They were similar height, both tall enough to be intimidating.

"To understand."

When the first wife's eyes widened in surprise, Sigrid dropped into a low curtsy then left. She had no reason to linger within the opulent chamber any further. She was not welcome, and beyond that, she was making the other woman uncomfortable.

With such a past, she wasn't surprised Saafiya wanted them all gone. Still, it wasn't fair that she had judged an entire race of people because of what the Bymerians had done. She would have to talk with Jabbar about this history, learn if he had been there, and discover the Beastkin's side of the tale.

If Sigrid had learned anything in her short life, it was that there were many sides to a story. Some more favorable than others.

She made her way as quickly as possible to her own, smaller chamber. They had no privacy, and yet she still grabbed Camilla's arm and yanked her into a corner.

"Can you get a message to Jabbar?"

Camilla's dark eyes widened. "Do you wish to meet him already? I thought you hadn't figured out how yet."

"I haven't. This is about something entirely different. I spoke with Saafiya, and she shared some troubling stories of the Bymerian Beastkin."

"You believed that witch?"

"She wasn't lying, Camilla." Sigrid felt a shiver trace down her spine. "She wanted me to know the truth, and now I need to understand their side."

"He hasn't even met you yet," her sister whispered. "It's unlikely he'll share any truths with you."

"Then how else are we going to find out what happened?"

Camilla tapped her mask. "There must be a library here?"

"Do you think they would record the truth as we do?"

"I think there's always something to be learned, regardless of who writes it. We can read between the lines and draw our own conclusions."

Sigrid found it odd that Camilla wouldn't want to directly ask those who had lived it. She narrowed her eyes. "Why don't you want to ask the Beastkin men?"

"I-I..." Camilla stammered, then sighed. "Because I'm not sure we can trust them yet. With our safety, yes. But that they'll tell us the truth? I wouldn't bet on it."

"Why?"

"I think they want something from us. I just don't know what yet."

They were used to that story. Someone always wanted something from the Beastkin women of Wildewyn. Whether it was protection, reassurance, or just a beautiful bauble, no one ever wanted the Beastkin around as a friend or confidante. Not even their own kind, so it seemed.

She blew out a breath and nodded. "To the library then."

"Shall we ask one of the guards?"

"I don't think they're allowed to speak with us." As soon as she said it, she knew the words would merely antagonize her sister.

Camilla immediately spun and made her way toward the nearest guard in a doorway. The man stared straight ahead, ignoring the tiny dark woman in a mask. She crossed her arms over her chest and stared up at him until his fingers give the slightest twitch.

"What are you doing?" she asked with the slightest chuckle. Had she laughed in public? When was the last time she'd done that out of her sister's sight?

"I'm staring at him until he breaks."

"I think they're well-trained." The man stood up a little straighter at her words.

"Oh, he'll break. Eventually, he will be uncomfortable that an animal is staring up at him, wanting something, but I won't tell him until he asks. I can stand here all day."

Sigrid sighed and seated herself across the hall on a bench. She didn't need to stare at the man, Camilla could do that on her own. Instead, she closed her eyes and tried to process all that Saafiya had told her.

Were the Beastkin here so feral? Perhaps, it was a bad idea to be visiting them if that were so. It hurt her heart to even think so. These men were *her people*. They could change form into animals that were glorious and wondrous. Surely, they had to share at least a few traits with herself and her sisters.

Regardless, it was important that she speak with them. They had to know something about this world that she wasn't privy to. That even Nadir wasn't privy to.

It felt important that she meet them. If they were dangerous, then so be it. So was she. Sigrid and Camilla were warriors by their own right and had yet to find someone with strength to compare to theirs.

The journey may be difficult, but the end would justify the means. She was certain.

"Ah, ha!" Camilla shouted, her words bouncing off the walls. "You moved!"

The guard gave a long, suffering sigh and relented. "What is it that you want, Beastkin?"

"Where's the library?"

"The what?"

"The library." Camila opened and closed her hands as if they were a book. "You know. Reading."

He glanced at Sigrid with a helpless expression.

Slowly standing, she dusted off her skirts and said, "We wish to review the historical records of the kingdom."

He grunted, then pointed down the hall. "The door with

the red curtain."

"They all have red curtains."

"The bigger one," he said with a snarl. The guard lifted his arms and gestured above his head. "You can't miss it."

Camilla looked at her. Sigrid shrugged. "Leave the poor man alone. I'm sure we'll find it easy enough with his directions."

He gave her a dubious look. The man was underestimating them if he thought they would have a difficult time finding a room with a door as large as he made it sound. Or perhaps he was lying to them. She had no way of knowing.

Camilla took her arm, and they walked down the halls side by side. A couple passing by, both dressed in the crimson colors of the sultanate, looked them up and down. They whispered words she couldn't quite hear. Likely nothing good.

It took a long time to find the library with no small amount of searching. But eventually, they made it to the opposite side of the palace where a large keyhole door was covered with sheets of red silk.

They quietly slipped inside. A library was a sacred place in Wildewyn. The tomes hidden inside held the history of the world. Everyone knew to tread carefully in such a place.

A few people wandered through the tall stacks, but Sigrid was surprised to see that the massive library of Bymere was mostly empty. Instead, the only people here seemed to be the librarians themselves.

One such man rushed toward them, wringing his hands. He was small, more round than stocky, and shorter than her by more than a full head. He wore gold silk wrapped around his body and tossed over one shoulder. Tassels swung behind him as he walked.

"Sultana," he gasped, swallowing hard and looking everywhere but her mask. "It's an honor for you to grace this hall."

"I wish to view historical references of my kind."

He blew out a long, slow breath. "Why? If you'll pardon my asking, Sultana, it's an unusual request."

"How so?"

"They aren't kind renderings of your people," he hesitantly replied. "I shouldn't wish to insult you."

She smiled beneath the mask, the movement lifting the metal ever so slightly. "Then fear not, Wordkeeper. It would be my honor to read the recordings of Bymerians. Regardless of what is said in such holy relics."

He stared up at her with wide eyes and mouth agape. "Wordkeeper?"

"In Wildewyn, books are the most precious of treasures. We honor those who keep them safe and well. Wordkeeper is the title for those who dedicate their lives to the written craft."

"Wordkeeper," he repeated. "I quite like that."

Sigrid inclined her head. "As do I."

The librarian shifted side to side before nodding. "Come with me then. The section on Beastkin is small, but I'm certain you'll find something of interest between the pages."

She was certain of that as well. The Bymerians were an intriguing lot, and the hatred for Beastkin ran deep in their veins. Sigrid already knew she would find that it also ran deep in their history.

They traversed between the tall walls of shelves that were meticulously taken care of. She admired their dedication to preserving the old vellum and new papyrus. The straight spines showed a level of care that proved their appreciation for history. Perhaps, even as much as the Earthen folk.

The librarian cleared his throat, and she turned her attention back to the man who led them through the stacks. "They suit your fancy?"

"More than I can say. You have an impressive collection. I believe it rivals even Wildewyn's famed Greenmire Castle, and the libraries there are renowned throughout both kingdoms."

He let out a soft snort. "They aren't, Sultana. We've always known that our libraries were far more impressive. But what can you expect from people who live close to nature?" He shivered. "All that dirt and earth is bad for the pages. Who knows how many insects might chew through them, and then there's no replacing those tomes."

"Not unless you have multiple copies. There are many monks in Wildewyn who spend their lives transcribing tales into new books in case of fire or...insects."

Sigrid was glad for the mask that hid her grin. The man stammered for a moment, clearly uncomfortable and without words. She'd put him on the spot, however, and that was cruel. Sigrid took pity on him and gestured toward the nearest shelf.

"Is this where I will find the stories of Beastkin?"

"It is, Sultana."

"Thank you, Wordkeeper. Your direction was invaluable. If we have further questions, we will seek you out."

His cheeks burned bright red. "Sultana, I mean no disrespect, but we allow no one to touch the books other than the librarians like myself."

"We honor books more than people. I assure you, we will

handle each book with utmost care."

He couldn't say no to a sultana although she could see he wanted to. His mouth opened and closed multiple times before he finally let out another huff and crossed his arms over his chest. "Fine then. There are gloves in that box, but make sure that you take care with them. Otherwise, I'll have words with the sultan."

Sigrid inclined her head and reached into the box placed at chest height on one of the shelves. She grabbed two pairs of the soft leather gloves and handed one to Camilla. When the man stomped off, Camilla let out a quiet laugh.

"I thought he would reach for the nearest book and hit you over the head with it," her sister giggled.

"He wouldn't dare."

"And what does he mean by threatening to speak with the sultan? So many people throw that around. Do you think they realize it's not threatening in the slightest? Their leader has done nothing to make me frightened of him."

"They seem to think he's frightening," Sigrid mused. She selected two green volumes. The color spoke to her. "Read this one?"

Camilla took it without glancing at the title. "Sigrid, think for a moment with me. Is there something about the sultan that we don't know? A reason they all belittle his name like he's the worst person in the kingdom?"

"Because he is. The sultan is the only person who seems to order people's deaths, and with that panel of advisors, I think this is a much more bloodthirsty regime than we are used to." Sigrid searched for a place to sit, only to sigh when she realized there was none. There had to be a table somewhere. "I wouldn't let it bother you."

"It doesn't bother me at all. I just think it's strange that they throw his name around without his knowledge. Does the sultan know that they paint him as a warlord who will chase children down in their sleep while murdering their parents?"

Sigrid tossed her head back and let out a barking laugh. "They don't make him out to be that. You're delaying your reading."

"It's not my favorite pastime, now is it?"

"Camilla."

Her sister pointed behind them. "There's a table over there if that's what you're looking for."

"Ah, perfect. Are you coming with me, or are you going to stand in the middle of the stacks looking for the next book to hand me?"

Camilla perked up immediately. "Is that an option?"

"No."

Sigrid made her way to the table and nodded to the librarian who stood on the other side. The man looked her up and down, turned white as a lily, and immediately closed his tome. He tucked it under his arm and walked away swiftly.

When would these people get used to her? Probably never. However, she hoped that at some point they would see her as a person, not as an animal.

Homesickness burned in her stomach. She had dearly loved traveling to the library with her sisters and losing themselves between the pages. They had traded stories like jewels. Each more precious than the last, and a gem that each sister could carry with them for the rest of their lives.

She missed them. They would have seen this library as a

haven. And not a single one of them would ever have let her think for a moment that she was less of a person because a librarian wanted nothing to do with her.

Sigrid ran her gloved hand over the bindings of the book. The supple leather was well-oiled and carefully woven so that not a single page would fall out. It looked almost as though it had been created yesterday. The Beastkin were so despised here that it would be odd for them to take care of these particular tomes so well.

Wrinkling her brow, she gently opened the cover and set it against the table. Sigrid dove into the pages, and the world melted away. She didn't care that Camilla might not be reading, or that the librarians likely stared at her, or that the sultan might stride in at any moment and demand that she stop.

All she cared about were the scrawled words written in black ink.

The author was, oddly enough, a farmer. He dictated the story to a scribe. A Beastkin had attacked their village. The farmer said it looked like a serpent, but longer than two men with venomous fangs and a hiss that turned men to stone.

A basilisk, she thought, although their kind had long since died. Humans didn't like snakes that could kill them with a single bite. Even in Wildewyn they'd been hunted to extinction.

The beast had slithered into the farmer's small hovel and killed his wife and three daughters. In return, the entire village had hunted the creature down. They had lost six men, but finally they had severed its head.

When its form shifted back to that of a human, they realized it was a woman they all recognized. She'd lived in a neighboring village and had been caught in a battle between two families.

The story ended there, but she could see that some words had been struck from the page. Sigrid leaned closer and could barely make out the lingering ink that made the hairs on her arms raise.

The farmer continued in his story to say that he'd been young when he saw her, but that they hadn't treated her "well" in the exchange between families. She'd been promised to him in marriage. He'd bedded her before their vows, then tossed her aside when he found out what she was. He claimed Beastkin weren't meant to marry humans, and he had done nothing wrong.

But she'd hunted him down, regardless.

Another story told of a bear that attacked a merchant as he traveled to Misthall. It hadn't hurt the man, but had stolen all his wares. They'd hunted it down and shot an arrow through its neck. The body and all the merchant's things tumbled down a large hill.

By the time they found the body, now a man, they'd also found two emaciated children who needed the food their father had stolen. The merchant, being the good Bymerian that he was, had taken the food back and left the children in the desert.

Story after story filled the pages with Bymerians who were too frightened of the Beastkin to ever stop and speak with them. True, some of them were the Beastkin's fault. Some of them were a shared fault, and others were filled with such cruelty that tears burned her eyes.

Camilla reached forward and pulled the book from her hands. "Come now, you'll get tears on the pages."

"They couldn't see past their own hatred," she whispered,

looking up to catch her sister's gaze. "They've spent centuries hating each other so much that they've picked each other apart."

"No. They've picked our people apart." Camilla gently closed the book. "And don't think that it's just here, Sigrid. Even in Wildewyn, they've taken advantage of our people. Locked us away, made us little more than gilded pets they keep in cages. You know it isn't right. You've known it for a long time."

She had. It made her heart hurt and her stomach clench just knowing that everywhere she went, her people were suffering. "What are we going to do?" she asked.

"Endure. As we always have."

Sigrid let Camilla take her arm and pull her away from the pages of heartbreak and pain. But she couldn't shake the images from her mind, no matter how hard she tried.

NADIR

NADIR SMOOTHED A HAND DOWN HIS GOLD SHERWANI. THE
formal outfit was perhaps a little more than necessary, but he
wanted to make a good impression. His people needed to see
that he was serious about this new wife. If that required formal
attire, then so be it.

The sherwani fit snug across his chest, ruby-encrusted
buttons glimmering in rows down to his knees where it ended.
The silk fabric was carefully embroidered with gold swirls,
made by only the most talented of artisans. He stuck a finger
down the high collar. It made it hard to breathe sometimes, or
perhaps that was his own nerves.

Underneath the sherwani he wore traditional churidars.
The trousers were loose around the hips and thighs, but tight
on his ankles where they met his bare feet. Shoes were the last
thing he worried about right now.

He reached out and grabbed a dupatta. The crimson scarf
would look appropriate wrapped over his shoulder. Nadir

fussed with it until an amused voice interrupted him.

"You're all dressed up for the occasion," Raheem said with a chuckle.

"Should a sultan not dress up for the Osaos festival?"

"You never have before."

Nadir turned to see his guard leaning against the door jam, ankles crossed and arms firmly across his chest. "I have."

"When was the last time you took part in any festival? And you can't claim that waving from the balcony is taking part. It's not."

He sighed. "I've been busy these past few years."

"Doing what exactly? I thought your advisors did all the menial work so that you could focus on more important things."

"Such as preparing myself for festivals."

Raheem tossed his head back and laughed. "Have they just begun working? Or are you trying to make yourself a little more presentable for your new bride?"

"Hush."

Nadir turned around so that Raheem wouldn't see the smile on his face. Of course he was trying to impress his new bride. What else was there in his life other than this mysterious woman who made him feel like a man for the first time? Not a monster, not a secret wrapped in flesh, but a man who wanted desperately to be liked.

Or loved?

He banished the thought immediately. Though he hadn't enjoyed his new wife's treasures, there was no reason to be thinking like that. He wasn't the animal inside. She would come to him on her own terms, or not at all.

"Is she preparing herself?" he asked.

"It was a fight. She didn't want to wear the traditional gown, and isn't happy that the concubines have attacked her with henna. She said there was too much of a chance for them to touch her."

"Did any?" Nadir felt a spear of worry slice through his chest.

"No, of course not. They were carefully instructed to take care. Though they weren't pleased with the notion."

He didn't doubt that. The concubines loved festivals. They helped each other get ready, hennaed their skin, wove flowers through their hair, and draped the finest fabric over their shoulders. Everyone in Bymere would celebrate the festival on this day, and he suddenly felt all the more connected with the kingdom.

The joy of this holiday beat through his soul as if the entirety of Bymere lived inside him. Perhaps this was what being sultan meant. Perhaps this was how he was supposed to feel every day.

"When will she be ready?" he asked.

"She's ready now, and will leave with the rest of the concubines."

"She should come out with me." Nadir knew it wasn't tradition, but some part of him wanted her to walk at his side. Let his people see that she was his new wife. That he was *proud* of his Beastkin wife, regardless of their history.

They could work towards a better tomorrow if they simply exposed his people to her more and more. Already, stories of her kindness flew through the city. The more stories like that, the better. And he would have them be true stories above fable.

"Sultan," Raheem scolded. "You can only change so much. Let her walk with the other women, mask and all."

"She won't take the damned thing off?"

"Not unless you want her to murder people along the way." Raheem grinned. "She's a feral little thing, but I quite like her."

That made two of them.

Nadir smoothed a hand over the dupatta once more, making sure the pleats laid flat against his chest. "I'm glad you like her. At least one person in the palace does. Are we ready?"

"Don't let her hear you say that. She'll turn on you like a dog and nip at your fingers." Raheem clacked his teeth, but straightened. "They're waiting on your command."

A thought formed in his head. A dangerous thought, one that would likely get him scolded for hours by his advisors, but one that would make him happy. He cleared his throat. "What do you think of Sigrid performing the ceremony with me?"

"That might cause the women to faint. She also doesn't know how."

"I can walk her through it."

Raheem shrugged. "It doesn't bother me. She's the new sultana, if it were anyone else then your people wouldn't blink. Let her try it and see how they react."

"They won't like a Beastkin at my side."

"They already don't like that." Raheem gestured for Nadir to follow him into the hall, likely rushing them. Nadir was usually late; his people were used to that. But some festivals required a little more respect.

He followed his guard from his personal quarters and made his way through the halls to the entrance of the castle. The sun shone down on them as it traversed the sky. They were only a few hours from sundown when all the bonfires would light to celebrate another year passed.

The concubines waited for him in the gardens. The land there overflowed with greenery that spilled over the ledge and reached for the crowds that stared up in anticipation. Vines flowed like waves, and poppies bloomed in abundance here. Red flowers of every species, some even he couldn't name, scattered on either side of a path that led to a circular clearing in the center. Two pillars stood side by side. On each sat a matching golden bowl.

He joined the women at the front where Saafiya and Sigrid stood. Nadir paused between them, casting his gaze to Sigrid who held her arms at her side with fists clenched.

"Comfortable?" he asked.

"You know I'm not."

Nadir bit his lower lip to control his grin. The dress she wore was certainly very different than the concealing gowns she usually wore. At the very least, the concubines had allowed her to wear blue.

Her lehenga, a long pleated skirt, was the color of midnight. So dark it was nearly black, the bottom hem had been embroidered with tiny silver stars. A matching choli covered her top, the low-cut neckline revealing she was much curvier than he had thought. An odhani scarf draped over her shoulder, covering most of her body in a way he'd thought would have made her comfortable.

They'd braided silver strands into her hair until she looked like she was the walking embodiment of the night sky. She was a pretty, wild thing standing amid roses.

All his concubines were beautiful flowers, while she was a thunderstorm.

"Husband," Saafiya greeted him, her voice radiating warmth. "All of Bymere is ready to greet you."

"Have they been waiting long?"

"It no longer matters. You're here now, and look how proud they are to see you." She waved her hand, and he saw what she saw.

Thousands of people, all who lived in the Red Palace and more from the villages beyond, all standing to see the ceremony of Osaos performed by the sultan and sultana. He saw smiling faces, women with their hands pressed to their chests, men with their arms around their children's shoulders. So many people, reminding him why he was here.

Nadir was the Sultan of Bymere, and these people needed him. They might have had his brother—a sultan worthy of them—but they had still accepted the younger brother with open arms. It was an honor he wore with pride.

"They seem ready," he replied. "Shall we begin the celebration?"

Saafiya smiled and held out her hand for him to take. The ceremony was always performed with the sultan and his first wife, unless he chose another. The entirety of Bymere would ring with rumors, how their sultan favored another. And perhaps they would say he was spoiling Sigrid, but he didn't care what anyone else thought.

Nadir bowed low to his first wife, showing her the respect she deserved, but he held out his hand for Sigrid to take.

Her eyes widened beneath the mask. "Sultan?"

"Husband," he corrected. Still low in a bow, he glanced up.

"Take my hand, Sigrid."

Saafiya hissed out a long breath. "Nadir, they are all looking. I am the first wife. It is my duty to walk with you and bring about the new year."

"It is the sultan and the sultan's wife's duty," he replied. "This year, Sigrid shall walk with me. Perhaps next year, I will choose you."

Saafiya bit her tongue, but he knew there was a viper resting beneath her sullen gaze. They would have words later. She wouldn't want to shame their family in front of the crowds, but already a few of the concubines whispered about the injustice.

All the while, he kept his gaze locked on Sigrid's.

He barely heard her whisper, "I don't know what to do."

"Let me guide you. I'll hold your hand, and tell you what to do at every moment. You won't shame us, Sigrid. I won't let you."

She hesitated for the briefest moment before reaching out and taking his hand.

Her fingers sliding into his brought about a surge of. The dragon inside him stretched its wings wide and roared.

Nadir guided her down the path. "Slow," he murmured. "We walk slowly to let them gaze upon us."

"I don't like people staring at me."

"They already do, my wife. Let them do so without hiding their eyes."

Lush, emerald leaves framed their bodies, touching their hips with cool fronds. The path was littered with white lily petals. It softened their steps, cold between his toes.

He let out a quiet chuckle.

"Are you laughing at me?" Sigrid asked. "Have I already done something I'm not supposed to?"

"Look down."

He waited for her to see his bare feet and listened carefully for the quiet huff of laughter beneath her mask. "You seem to be lacking shoes, Sultan."

"I was apparently in a rush to get here."

"How fortuitous," she replied.

His brows drew down, and he glanced over at her. "Strange words coming from you, wife. Why would you say that?"

Her gaze flicked down.

Nadir turned his attention back to their feet, and on their next step she revealed her own bare toes. It seemed he wasn't the only one who rushed out of his room to get to the ceremony.

He grinned. "I do believe you're lacking shoes as well."

"At least we match."

And gods if that didn't make him happy. The grin remained on his face as they reached the twin pedestals. He stopped her before their people and lifted their hands.

There was a stillness in the air as the Bymerian people stared up, unsure how to respond. They were meant to cheer. The sultan was showing them his bride, the woman he was proudest of, the most beautiful in the kingdom. A slow clap started before the rest of the crowd joined in.

Though the cheers weren't as loud as they might have been, they were there.

He glanced down at her. "See? I told you they would accept you."

"I don't think it's acceptance if you force them." But her

mask raised at the edge, and he knew she was smiling.

Nadir kept their hands lifted and guided her to the first bowl. Clear water filled it to the brim, and a long white cloth was laid underneath it on the pedestal. He pointed toward the bowl of water.

"Dip your hands in."

She followed his orders without question, and he reveled in the moment. It was likely the only time she would actually listen to him. Nadir knew when to savor something rare.

The water reflected light around her fingers. She held them still until the ripples disappeared, then quietly asked, "Now what do I do?"

"Wash my face clean."

"From what?" Her eyes narrowed. "And why?"

"It's a ritual Sigrid. It's not something I'm making up. Just follow our ways, please."

"You didn't have to choose me, you know." She pulled her hands from the water. "Your first wife was horribly insulted by your choice."

"Yet, it was mine to make. And I chose you."

Nadir didn't miss the way her eyes widened, or the appreciative look she gave him. Good. She should feel proud that he had chosen her. That meant she was settling into his home better than he had originally thought, and he wanted her to be happy here.

It was a strange feeling, caring about another person. Nadir had spent his entire life being waited upon, hand and foot. He expected others to bow when he walked into the room, and that they treat him with the level of respect that no other would receive. He didn't care when his concubines were insulted or when his wife was angry. They would eventually come around, because they had to.

But with this moonlight creature, he found himself wanting to make her happy. He wanted to see those rare smiles and know that she fit into his home. He didn't know how to interpret the thoughts, but found they were easier to bear than he had ever imagined.

Sigrid reached forward and touched his face. Her fingertips glided across his cheekbones, and he let his eyes slowly close. The mask hid her expression, as much as he wanted to see her face in this moment. He would simply enjoy feeling her touch him like this for the first time.

She cupped his cheeks in both her hands, gently moving her palms down over his jaw. Her hands were strong. He felt calluses scrape over the scruff of his beard, hard-earned roughness that spoke volumes about who she was. A warrior, not simply a bride.

His heart began to pound. The rhythmic thumping rang in his ears until he could hardly focus on anything other than her warm touch that heated him to the core.

Her hands left his face and the musical sound of dripping water reached his ears. Then she returned, cold water slick on her palms. She smoothed her hands across his forehead. Two fingers danced down his nose, and he forgot how to breathe.

"Done," she whispered, her fingers sliding off his jaw.

Did he know how to speak? Were there words in his head other than ones that would stop the ceremony and rush her back to his private quarters?

Nadir cleared his throat but did not open his eyes. "The white cloth. Pick it up."

"It's underneath the basin?"

He hummed deep in his throat, a sound of agreement.

The sound of shifting fabric reached his ears then stilled. "What do I do with it now?"

"Pat my face dry, wife," he said with a chuckle.

Silk touched his jaw, smoothing across his face. He thought she would continue to pliantly play her role until she pinched his nose with sharp fingernails beneath the cloth. Flinching back, he opened his eyes wide to see the mischief dancing in hers.

Laughter rose up from the crowd, and he realized that he had moved enough for them to see. He flicked his gaze to them. A woman pressed a hand to her mouth, hiding a grin. A man looked down at his wife and murmured a joke that made her jab him between the ribs. They didn't mind that she had blatantly assaulted their sultan. Perhaps, they could accept her after all.

"Is this really a ritual or you making me pamper you?" she asked.

He growled at her, baring his teeth in a mocking grin. "Behave."

"No promises."

Nadir reached for her hands and just barely stilled his rolling eyes. She was going to be the death of him, but she was exactly what the palace had needed. In her own quiet way, she brought happiness and laughter to a usually still ceremony.

When had he heard the Bymerians laugh like that? Nadir could count the times on one hand. They were a solemn folk who followed rituals when necessary, and reserved their laughter for celebrations. Rituals were respected and honored in silence.

Yet, she had managed to make them laugh. And not just find mirth in her teasing, but remember other times they had laughed. He had to take that as a good sign. That perhaps they could accept a Beastkin as their own. If they could do that, then they would certainly be able to accept him.

Nadir knew he was being a coward. By forcing her to reveal herself first, he was only prolonging the inevitable, while throwing her to the wolves. But his fear was stitched into the fabric of his being.

Sigrid slipped her hand into his, lifting it up. "Is there more?"

"Yes." He lifted their hands higher, then gently led her to the other pedestal. "Just a bit more."

The bowl on the second pedestal held a very small amount of red powder. They only used the powder in ceremonies and on days like today, the beginning of a new year. He stood on side of the pedestal and moved Sigrid until she stood on the other.

She investigated the bowl, and he swore he saw her frown. "What is this?"

"We call it crimson."

"That's a color."

"And a name." He nodded to the white fabric in her hand. "Put that down for now."

She set it gently next to the bowl on the pedestal. Pride bloomed in his chest when he saw her smooth her fingertips down the hand-stitched edge. She took care of the cloth as a Bymerian woman would have. Though she didn't know their customs, she was a natural at honoring their traditions.

"Carefully dip your hands into the bowl, just so your palms and fingers are covered," he advised.

There was no hesitance to her movements. If he were a betting man, Nadir would have said it seemed as though she trusted him.

Sigrid pressed her hands slowly into the powder. Not a single puff lifted into the air, a sign that their year would be good. The omens all pointed towards success and happiness thus far. He hoped that they were correct.

When her hand was coated, he nodded. "Now place both hands in the center of the fabric."

"Won't that ruin it?"

"That's the idea."

She moved to the side as he rounded the other edge of the pedestal. Nadir pressed his own hands into the cool powder, remembering all the times he'd seen his own family do this. His father and his mother, and on one occasion his brother with Saafiya who had been promised to him. This was what sultans did. This was what helped his people find peace in the new year.

"Circle the pedestal as I did." He stood in front of her and pressed his hands down on the silk. Avoiding marring the fabric again, he used his forearms to pull the tail and shift clean space for them to continue. Traditionally, she should be doing it, but he didn't mind performing this part when she didn't know how.

Thankfully, Sigrid was a quick study. She moved the cloth after pressing her hands to the fabric the second time, and each time after that.

Round and round they passed until their handprints filled

the entire strip of cloth. Her hands were smaller than his, though not by much. Nadir allowed himself a moment to marvel at that oddity before he stopped walking.

She froze and lifted her gaze to his.

"Pick up the cloth," he said.

True to her nature, she seemed to understand without asking that she needed to keep the cloth clean. She used her forearms to scoop it from the pedestal, then lifted it up into her arms. The tails almost touched the ground.

He took a deep breath, the sight of her stealing into his lungs and making it difficult to breathe. She lifted the cloth the same way his mother had. Even Saafiya didn't mind pressing a few fingertips into the stitched edge. But not Sigrid.

"Repeat after me. As best you can will suffice." His voice was a mere croak, and he awkwardly cleared his throat.

For a moment he thought she would hesitate, but she nodded.

He couldn't think about that just now. They had a ceremony to finish, and she had done well thus far. Nadir switched to the old Bymerian language, one very few spoke as it was far more difficult than the common tongue. His accent thick, he said the words on a low growl.

"As this cloth symbolizes our union, let it symbolize a healthy year for this land, happiness for its people, and prosperity for the kingdom."

She repeated the words. Her accent was wrong, and she stumbled over a few of the more difficult sounds, but all in all, she did well.

Nadir grinned. "As the favored of the sultan, I say now that he is favored by me. With this ceremony I honor him, his people, and our marriage. I continue to pledge my love, my happiness, and my life to him. Let all us do the same." At the last second, he added in a line that had never been said before. "I am beast, I am woman, and I vow to protect him with my life."

Her voice echoed in the hall. As the last sound dropped from her lips, the crowd cheered so loud the very foundation of the castle shook.

Sigrid's arms trembled, and she looked up at him with wide eyes. "What did you make me say?"

"It's part of the ceremony."

"What did you make me say, Nadir?"

A concubine came forward and pulled the fabric from her arms. Sigrid remained frozen in place until Nadir linked their red fingers together. He tugged her into his arms, careful not to get a handprint on her dress.

"That you may be a beast, but you would protect me with your life."

Her eyes narrowed. She searched his gaze for something, and seemed to find the answer in their depths. "Then you only told them the truth."

His heart surged and his soul took flight. The dragon inside him wanted to burst free, to fly with her into the clouds and to truly make her his mate. That was all that he desired and yet, it was not something he could have. Not when so many people were staring at him.

What would the Bymerians think if they knew that two dragons ruled their people? They would have an uprising, or worse, a civil war. He would ruin his family name, disgrace his bloodline... There was too much at stake to ever allow himself

269

the freedom to be true in front of the crowds.

Instead, he lifted a hand and pressed it against her mask. The red powder stained the metal, marking her as his.

"Is that part of the ritual?" she asked with a slight laugh.

"No," he replied, chuckling as well.

Another raucous cry burst from the crowd, a few pointing at the handprint on her mask and nudging others.

Sigrid did not disappoint. She lifted a hand and ever so gently pressed it against his cheek. She left her own mark on him. Nadir would wear it with pride.

He tucked her under his arm and turned to his people with an arm raised. They cheered again, and he felt hope for the first time in many years.

"Now we really do match," she whispered.

"In more ways than I could ever say, wife." Nadir didn't know what this feeling in his chest was. He felt like he was being pulled apart, while a heavy weight pressed down on him. Regardless, he felt the happiest and, strangely, the saddest he'd ever been in his life.

SIGRID

"USE THE CLOTH TO COVER YOUR FACE," CAMILLA WHISPERED, holding up a black sheet of fabric. "We can't risk anyone recognizing our masks."

"It's too much of a risk."

"They will know who you are immediately. Do you want to go or not?"

Her sister was right, but Sigrid's deeply ingrained values made her hesitate. To take off the mask and walk through a crowd without the shield of metal made her insides twist. A wrapping of cloth was flimsy. Anyone could pull it off her face, and then what would she do?

She'd have to choose between following the old ways or her heart.

They whispered in her small room. Pillows were strewn all around them, and two matching sets were lined up to look like bodies with blankets over them. Everything was ready for them to slip out of the palace. No one would notice they were gone until it was far too late.

Sigrid had told the sultan that they were going to go to the sands tomorrow. It gave them two nights and a day to get back to the red palace and pretend that nothing was amiss. Plenty of time to speak with these mysterious male Beastkin who had hidden themselves from the known world.

She looked down at the strange clothes Camilla had given her. The male leggings were billowy, large, and loose around her thighs but tight at her ankles. The top was much tighter and made entirely of interlocking sections of fabric that looked a little like a mummy wrapped for burial.

It all made her very uncomfortable. Her sister had an easier time with the threat of showing skin.

Sigrid blew out a breath and snatched the cloth from Camilla. "Fine, but you will need to make sure no one gets close to us until we're out of the city."

"No one will," her sister said with a laugh.

Camilla had painted her face and body as she would have for a ceremony with their sisters. White circles and runes decorated one side of her body. Some depicted wings, others were swirls of the wind, and one circle around her eye was homage to the beast inside her.

Her sister was from a different part of Wildewyn, but had been sent as a friend for Sigrid. Their mothers had been childhood friends, and it only made sense that they would be as well.

Sometimes, Sigrid wondered what she would have been like without the beloved influence of her sister. Camilla was everything that Sigrid was not. She was outgoing, made friends easily, laughed often. All the things that Sigrid wanted to be, but couldn't get past the barrier in her mind.

They'd always wanted to visit Camilla's homeland. Woodcrest was home to very few, and most who lived there were of ancient bloodlines. Camilla could trace her line back to the original owl shifter.

Sigrid knew nothing about where her family came from. Only that they existed, and that she was the last. Or so she thought.

She stretched the black cloth over her face, wrapping it a few times and securing it with a pin in her hair. "How are we getting out of the palace?"

"You're comfortable with heights now, aren't you?"

Sigrid had told her everything that had happened above the clouds, leaving out a few details she kept for herself. There had been a few moments when she forgot everything other than the fact that another dragon existed, and that he was glorious when the sun played on his scales.

"Yes?" she asked. "Why are you asking?"

Camilla leaned over the mounds of pillows and opened the window. "We're going across the rooftops."

"We can't do that! Someone will see us."

"Not this late at night. And besides, what will they see? Two servants playing on the roof at night are hardly something to call the guards about."

"With our faces covered?" Sigrid pointed at her own. "They'll think we're robbers or assassins and shoot us down."

"Then you'll turn into a dragon and we can finally go home."

She had a point. Even Sigrid wouldn't allow someone to attack them. A part of her itched to reveal her true self to the

Bymerians. They were so lost in their own prejudices that they still thought her a monster, even as they struggled to believe that she told the truth.

A sultana was untouchable. They couldn't kill her as they would with any other Beastkin, not without fear of what the sultan would do. But they also didn't have to accept her.

Either way, this would be the ultimate way to show them what she was truly capable of.

"Fine," she said with a heaving sigh. "Let's go."

Camilla slipped out the window, her toes gripping onto the edge of the building, and held out a hand for Sigrid to take.

She glanced back at the room one more time, trying to see it through the eyes of a concubine. They would believe for a while that Camilla and Sigrid were sleeping in. By the time they checked late in the day, Nadir would make an excuse for where they were. It wasn't the perfect plan by any means. But it should work.

Telling herself not to be silly, she leaned out the window and took Camilla's waiting hand. Strong and sure, her friend pulled her out and they both turned to press their backs against the building.

"Are you ready?" Camilla asked.

"Just don't tell me how far the drop is."

"About three building heights."

"Camilla!" Sigrid rolled her eyes and felt sweat pool in the center of her palms. "That's not helpful."

"At least I'm not making you do this alone. I could fly the entire way, but we must get you out of the city. Everyone will notice a dragon flying above the Red Palace. Why couldn't you be something sensible? Like an eagle?"

"Would you just shut up and jump?"

Camilla flashed her a grin then leapt away from the Red Palace. She landed on her shoulder and rolled onto the roof of the nearest building. Graceful as always, she stayed in a crouch and waved for Sigrid to do the same.

Gritting her teeth, she launched herself off the building. The weightlessness made her stomach jump into her throat. Arms pin-wheeling, she waited until the last second before she tilted her body, and tucked her shoulder upon striking the ground.

She rolled onto a crouch, lungs heaving, and looked up into Camilla's waiting grin. "I don't like that."

"I think you do." Her sister burst into a full tilt run, racing across the rooftops with feet as light as her owl wings.

Shaking her head, Sigrid followed. They used to do this when they were children, albeit it wasn't across the tops of buildings. Camilla would dare her to do the most ridiculous things, and Sigrid always had a hard time saying no. They raced through the forest, leaping over fallen trunks, darting up trees, and swinging from branches.

Now, they used those skills for something much bigger than that.

She did her best to stay silent. Bymerian roofs were made of clay plates, and each step felt like thunder. But no one stopped them as they leapt from home to home until they crouched at the edge of the city. They looked down the small cliff edge.

"Now it's time to fly," Camilla breathed.

"Someone could still see us."

"It's nearly midnight, Sigrid. No one is going to see you,

and if they do, they'll explain it away as a dream. Let's *go*."

Camilla burst into feathers and dove off the edge of the building. Her silver wings glistened in the moonlight. She didn't look back at all, just made her way through the desert. If Sigrid didn't make her decision soon, then she would lose yet another chance to meet these strange creatures.

She exhaled, frustrated, and scrubbed a hand over the cloth covering her face. What was the harm? Who cared if she made the sultan angry? He should be more welcoming of their people, that was the entire point of her existence.

She couldn't give herself too much time to think about it, or she would never transform. Sigrid turned to look back at the city. Not a single light was on in the windows of the homes. She held her breath, opened her arms, and fell backwards off the side of the building into oblivion.

The dragon was quick to awaken. Her clothes and flesh disappeared for scale and sinew that twisted easily in the air and beat strong wings.

Her back feet trailed in the sand as her arms struggled to keep her aloft. Glimmering streams of tiny sandstorms swirled to life in her wake. Sigrid burst up into the air, though she kept herself from letting out a roar of accomplishment.

She could *fly*.

A tiny owl flew in front of her, and Sigrid gained on her so quickly it was as if Camilla hadn't had a head start at all. Sigrid angled herself higher than her friend and neatly snagged her out of the air with a back foot.

She felt the peck of a beak, just a tiny feeling of something tapping against her scales, and her belly rolled with a chortle. Was that what it felt like when something attacked her? No wonder both Wildewyn and Bymere had wanted only one dragon to exist. Nothing could harm her in this form.

Camilla changed in her hand, holding onto the long claws and angrily shouting, "Just keep going straight, you overbearing witch!"

It would be faster this way, Sigrid wanted to tell her. But the other part was that she'd seen Camilla fly so many times. Her sister could know what it felt like to not be able to fly while Sigrid was truly free.

They glided over the desert for hours before she felt Camilla tap on her foot. Sigrid craned her long neck to see Camilla was pointing down.

There, so hidden that Sigrid would never have noticed it, was an abandoned kingdom. Blocky buildings surely used to make up a castle, but sand had blown over most of the structure. Only a few towers could still be seen, even from above, and the rest had been swallowed by the desert.

Sigrid circled a few times to see what the Beastkin men would do. A few stepped out of the buildings, climbed atop what used to be the roofs and waved up at her.

What did they think? They'd been alone for such a long time, thinking that they were the only ones to exist, hunted and afraid. Now, they knew that not only did others exist, but that a dragon was still alive.

What would they do if they knew their sultan was one of their own?

Pushing grim thoughts away, she took herself lower. Buffeting the sands with her wings, she gently set Camilla down and waited until her friend had raced away before landing hard on her hind feet.

She chuffed out a breath, choosing to remain a dragon for the time being. Let them see what she was. Let them understand that she was not a woman to be trifled with and that if she wished, she could destroy everything they built.

A leopard raced towards her, sand flying in all directions as he skidded to a halt. The whites of his eyes were showing as he met her gaze and froze. A long line of fur rose upon his spine.

The sparrow boy was close on the beast's tail. He waved both his hands in the air as if he needed to let her know not to attack. She could recognize her own people. She'd recognized him easily enough.

A crowd followed them both. Men and animals spread across the sands in pitifully small numbers. She hoped this wasn't it, but had a sinking feeling that it might be.

Thirty men, she counted. Not many at all.

There was a bear in their ranks, loping towards her and shaking his head. A lion followed him, and twin golden eagles circled above her. The rest were in their human form. They were in varied groups. Red hair, blonde hair, black skin, and a person who was entirely white as snow.

He led the group, the long length of his hair tied in a high peak. His pink eyes caught hers, and she marveled at the realization that at least one Beastkin was entirely albino.

He stopped in front of her and held his hands out at his sides. "Sigrid of Wildewyn, I assume?"

She inclined her head in a slow nod.

"Welcome to Falldell, where the sultan's assassins are trained and the remaining Beastkin of Bymere hide."

So, this was where the acclaimed assassins hailed from. Sigrid had so many questions racing through her mind that she didn't know where to begin. She'd have to be human for that, although the drakon inside her had other plans.

Rearing up, she stretched her wings wide and let out a guttural call. She wanted them all to see one more time how dangerous she was. How much she could harm them and that every movement up until this point had indeed been a threat. She wouldn't hesitate to kill any of them, and she hadn't seen a single one who could threaten her.

Landing hard on her forearms, the drakon finally allowed her scales to disappear until all that remained was a woman kneeling in the sand. Sigrid pressed her fists into the ground and took a deep breath.

There was only one thing left to do, and that was to speak with the men before her.

She slowly stood, unwrapping her headscarf as she went. Camilla stood to the side and followed her actions. A few of the men stepped back when they saw their faces. Some of them stepped forward, but Sigrid eyed the albino man.

He appeared to be surprised, but not overly. This man had seen a female Beastkin before.

"You are Jabbar?" she asked.

"I am."

"And you lead the male Beastkin of Bymere?"

"I lead all Beastkin of Bymere." He pressed a hand to his chest. "There are no females left in our lands. And if there are, then they have already been lost to us."

She looked him over with a critical gaze. He wore a simple leather jerkin, loose pants similar to her own, both the color of sand. He'd been hiding for a very long time, she assumed. Even their clothing blended into the place where they lived.

He was a handsome man. His face was shaped like those in Wildewyn, bold and stocky with hard edges and deep planes. Pink eyes reflected a familiar determination. Strange how she saw so much of Wildewyn in this man.

"It sounds as though you have already accepted defeat, Jabbar of Bymere." She waited for an angry response, but did not receive one. He was a still pool and had clearly been trained just as she had.

"I ask your definition of defeat, drakon. Is defeat when we have all died? Or is it when the few remaining live out their lives in safety?"

She didn't have an answer to that question. Her heart said defeat was only when they all lay dying on a battlefield, incapable of fighting for a moment longer. But her head said these men deserved to live out their lives without fear of being hunted.

This man was perhaps smarter than she gave him credit for. She nodded, "A wise choice then."

"It's the only place we've found safe enough."

"Do all assassins coming out of Falldell have a drop of Beastkin blood in them?"

"Perhaps some do, though most are entirely human. They would be hunted just as we are."

"A shame." She looked at the small crowd of men and smiled. "Bymere would benefit from Beastkin warriors. I've found their soldiers lacking."

An appreciative laugh lifted from the crowd, and she noted that the leopard shifted back into a man. He was a lithe creature, caramel skin stretching over an abundance of muscles. A beautiful beast, both as an animal and as a man.

Camilla watched him with rapt attention, and Sigrid wondered how long it would take for the man to fall in love with her. She had a way with beasts. He didn't stand a chance.

Jabbar visibly relaxed in front of her, although she didn't know what she'd done to ease his tension. He swept into a low bow. "It's an honor to host one of your house. Shall we call you sultana?"

Gods, the word made her uncomfortable. She shook her head. "*Sister* will do just fine."

"Then it is with a welcome heart we bring you to our home. One cannot be too careful when someone is arriving from the Red Palace. Our people were hunted by an order from within those walls."

"I wish to hear the entire story." Even though it already made her heart crack in her chest.

Was it Nadir who had ordered his own people to be hunted until their numbers were this small? How could he have done such a thing? She understood that he felt no connection with them. It would be hard when he hadn't been raised within the ranks of their people. But some part of him had to feel guilty. Taking the lives of other Beastkin was equal to killing a part of themselves.

The crowd of men parted like a wave when Jabbar motioned for her to follow him. Camilla joined her and together they walked towards the single opening that led into the buried city. Twin carved elephants marked what used to be the gates of this ancient city. One of them had a crack running down the center of its face. Considering she could touch one's eye, these must have been monoliths buried beneath the sand.

"What is this place?" she asked.

Jabbar walked ahead of her and lifted his arms. "This was once the home to thousands of Beastkin."

"Is it not dangerous to remain in the place where you once lived?"

"No one would ever think that we would come back here. This is where it all started." He pressed a pale hand to a wall, trailing his fingers along the cracked sandstone. "Blood once coated these walls. Fallen heroes and those who fought for our right to remain alive. It seems only right that we fill the halls with the remaining souls of the Beastkin."

"There are many still in Wildewyn."

"And do they live in fear of death?"

Sigrid could almost feel the cold rush of anger that passed through every man that followed them. The city path disappeared underneath the sands before them, but she could feel their rage sinking deep into the earth.

They were more connected to each other here. She could almost feel their heartbeats, the age old anger and rage that had nowhere else to go. It was a heady feeling, knowing that so many men waited here while her own people had no idea they existed.

Jabbar stooped through a window and gestured for them to follow him.

"No," she replied. "They don't live in fear that they will die, but they are caged. Our people are split into three groups, and then split even further to remain with the royal Earthen folk who provide for us. Our lives are comfortable, but we are still valued pets more than we are people."

She crouched to get through the window and followed him down a dimly lit hall. Fire reached for her as she walked down the passage. Sconces were the only thing that cast light, but thankfully her eyes saw far more than a usual human.

Camilla made a noise beside her and pointed down a hall where a small cluster of men leaned against the wall. They were sick. Sigrid could smell the cloying bitterness of illness that wafted from the room and made her cough.

"Living in the desert is difficult," Jabbar called out. "There are many things here that make it hard on our people."

"I can see that. If it's so hard to live here, why do you remain?"

"This is our home. Where else would we go?"

"To Wildewyn. We would take you in. It would have eased the minds of many to know that there were Beastkin men here."

Jabbar set his shoulder against a door stuck in place by the sand and shoved it open. They walked into a small room where a fire crackled happily in the center. Smoke stains blackened the ceiling and streaked the walls, but it was large enough to house the lot of them.

Some of the men following them flopped onto the piles of sands in the corners. Others pulled rugs closer to the fire and crouched there. It seemed as though they might have their own hierarchy. Those with higher ranks were allowed close to the flames. Those without, remained in the shadows.

She frowned. Beastkin took care of each other. They should be alternating people around the fire, allowing the ill to be there longer.

These people were her own, but not. A warning sounded in her mind as the drakon inside her reared up again. Something was wrong. This wasn't the Beastkin she knew and loved.

Jabbar gestured at a rug closest to the flames. "For our honored guests."

Sigrid made her way to the fireplace and sat, but she kept her posture stiff and her hands carefully loose on her knees. She didn't know if she could trust these men who were clearly influenced by Bymere. These weren't her people, although she longed for them to be just like the women she'd left in Wildewyn.

"We cannot go to Wildewyn," Jabbar began. "How would we get past the guards? There is an entire army between us and the Edge of the World. Not to mention the descent. Few of our people can fly."

"Can you?" The words blurted off her tongue before she could catch them. "I have yet to know what you are, Jabbar of Bymere."

"Hardly as impressive as you." He stood in front of the fireplace, close enough that she could have touched him if she wished. Placing an arm on its cracked mantle, he blew out a breath. "But, there are not many ancients among us anymore. It's good to know I'm not alone."

"You're not drakon," she replied.

"No, but we are not creatures who roam this earth." A bitter smile crossed his face, and he shoved himself away from the mantle. "My beast is a thunderbird. I roam the skies just as you. The clouds obey my beck and call, thunder and lightning at the tips of my wings."

She nodded in recognition of the hidden words underneath the explanation. "Then you have not flown in a very long time."

"My wings have been clipped in this war."

Sigrid understood the root of his anger. They all longed to

be free. To fly through the skies as they were meant to do, to allow those to see them as beasts of legend. No human should be afraid of a dragon or a thunderbird. They should revere them and ask for their assistance when needed.

She stared down at her clenched fists. "How long have you been hiding?"

"My entire life. My father was the first to bring men to this abandoned place. He kept us safe as long as he could, but we lost him a few years ago in yet another battle. I have continued his work. Bringing all Beastkin men I can find to a haven in the sands."

"Are there more of you?"

"Hundreds. All spread out over Bymere. It is a fraction of what we once were, but it's more than the Bymerians know of. Some move here when they can, under the cover of night and with our protection. Others remain in their homes."

"Homes?" She couldn't imagine what they must go through, knowing that they had to hide every aspect of themselves from those who loved them. Her heart suddenly ached. She did know what that was like. She was married to such a man.

"Beastkin men can still marry, hide the affliction their child inherits, and continue to deny that we exist at all." Jabbar's fists closed, but he still gestured at the leopard man. "Malik leads them here if their safety is threatened."

She looked over to the man he had gestured to. He was stronger than the others, broad in the shoulders and stood with a warrior's stance.

"You've killed humans?" she asked.

"Many."

"In protection of our people?"

"Sometimes."

She didn't like the hard edge to his voice, and recognized the tang of bloodlust. Not that she blamed them. Sigrid knew what it was like to wish to break the chains that captured her. She'd wanted it her entire life, but was held back by the ancient songs in her veins. Wildewyn Beastkin knew what the loss of life meant.

It seemed the Bymerian Beastkin did not share the same thoughts.

"We cannot kill humans," she implored. "It will only continue this ancient battle, and there is no place for fighting. We can work together now. I am sultana. Certainly, there is some change I can assist with."

"That's why I wished to bring you here." Jabbar caught her gaze and held it. She saw anger in their cold depths, but also a sadness that she felt echoed in her own soul. "Our people are dying. They are hungry, afraid, sick. There's nothing more I can do for them. But you are *sultana*."

"What would you have me do?"

"War."

The word made her flinch back. "War with whom?"

"Bymere. Be true to who you are. Let them see that Beastkin are not just cattle and fowl. That we are strong beasts that could rend them with tooth and claw. Let them understand that a sultana sits on the throne who could destroy the entire capital. And then let us fight for the rights we desire."

"What will war accomplish?" Firelight danced over their faces marred with years of anger and rage. "Death cannot beget anything but more death."

"That's where you're wrong. We have seen what these Bymerians can do. We've felt their swords running through our bodies and the sting of their whips on our backs for centuries. The Beastkin will no longer take this treatment without returning it in kind."

Jabbar knelt in front of her, and she realized that they had somehow made her the hope of all their people. His hands reached for hers. She didn't flinch when he lifted her fingers and pressed them to his cheeks.

"Sultana," he murmured. "You will lead our people to war, and you will help us win."

"I am not a weapon for you to wield."

"I don't ask to wield your great power, dragoness. I ask for you to wield it yourself. Become the warrior goddess we have prayed for and bring about the age of Beastkin."

She couldn't be that person. She couldn't return to her husband knowing that she was going to betray him.

The Bymerians were a strange folk, but they didn't deserve to die. Her mind flicked through all the faces she'd seen in her travels. The little girl on the street who had shown her kindness. Raheem, who had helped her connect with her husband in a way she hadn't thought possible. Even the loyalties of the concubines to the first wife who still refused to speak with her.

Sigrid was about to shake her head, to tell him that his plan was impossible, when a racket from the hall made all the men stiffen and turn towards the door.

A boy burst through, chest heaving and sweat slicking his dark skin. "Jabbar! There are more, they come from the sands!"

The albino man immediately stood, yanking Sigrid up with him. "Now you will see," he said. "You will see how they arrive."

He did not release her hand as he raced back through the dark halls. She found herself dragged along with him, terrified of what she was about to see. Would this change the entire foundation of the world as she understood it? Were these men really as mistreated as Jabbar made them sound?

He didn't pause to help her through the window, only yanked so hard she nearly fell before he thrust her in front of him and pointed through the elephant gates.

"Do you see?" Desperation laced his words. "Do you see them? *This* is why we must help them."

And she did. She saw every emaciated inch of the men shambling towards them like the undead. Beastkin raced past her to help their brothers who stumbled. Some sank to their knees when they saw their own kin. Others became even more determined to reach the doors of this place hidden underneath the sand.

What had they done to these people?

"We have to help them," Jabbar implored. "They are dying, *we* are dying, and there is nothing more I can do. You are the Sultana of all Bymere."

"Second wife."

"But still a sultana. You are not a concubine, Sigrid of Wildewyn. It is your right, your place, to help your people no matter how much it costs you."

She realized in that moment that she had forgotten her place. She was a royal now, as Nadir had said. A sultana wasn't just a woman. She was a figurehead for her people and the voice of reason in every way possible.

Forgetting this had already cost her too much.

She swallowed and pushed away from Jabbar's hold.

"Sultana—" His words trailed off as he realized she wasn't leaving. She made her way to the emaciated men and caught hold of the first one who reached her.

His ribs were like daggers against her palm, his cheeks so sunken that she likely wouldn't have recognized him were he whole. "Thank you, brother," he said, then stilled when he noticed the long tail of her golden braid.

"Sister," she corrected. "Come, let me help you."

He let her shoulder most of his weight. His feet were bleeding from the journey, bare to the elements as they were. There were holes in his shirt and pants that revealed lash marks. Each wound was swollen and yellowed with infection.

She kept herself still and did not flinch when he traced a finger down the side of her face. "Female?"

"There is much to tell you, my brother."

"But we're the only ones left."

She looked into his confused gaze and a piece inside her heart shifted. These men weren't just Bymerians, and they certainly weren't her people, but they needed her help. She couldn't leave them here alone. It didn't matter who was hunting them, or why. This would stop the moment she made her way back to the palace.

Nadir had to listen to her. He wasn't an unreasonable man. And even though he hated the beast inside himself, he had enjoyed letting it out with her. He'd watched the sunset above the clouds and she knew he'd felt pride. She'd felt the same emotion in her own chest.

He would listen to her words because he had to. There was no other option for them.

She reached Jabbar's side and handed the man off to him. The pale man held the other up without issue, and his eyes remained on her, waiting for a sign.

"I will speak with the sultan," she said. Her eyes found Camilla. "Stay here with them. Help if you can."

Jabbar shook his head. "It won't do any good to speak with the sultan. He follows in his brother's footsteps where hatred walked."

"He won't have a choice but to listen to me." And with that said, she let her human form melt away and a drakon shot from the abandoned palace and into the night sky.

NADIR

NADIR STOOD IN THE CENTER OF HIS PRIVATE QUARTERS, HANDS limp at his side, wondering what he had done for the world to punish him so thoroughly. He was a good man. He'd done everything that his brother had requested and more. The ancient rituals were followed, his kingdom prospered. And yet, he still felt as though he wasn't doing enough.

Didn't his advisors tell him every day that his name would go down in history as a benevolent king? Didn't his people lay red poppies at his feet when he walked through the city? What more could he want?

He didn't have an answer for that. An empty hole had opened in his chest, and he didn't know how to fill it. Or what to fill it with.

His private quarters were filled with opulence. The walls were painted with molten gold, reflecting hazy images like a mirror. Red curtains hung from the ceiling to surround his bed. A mound of red silk pillows and dark crimson rugs piled high for his comfort. A dark oak desk in the corner was drowning beneath papers and maps.

Two pools graced the corners opposite his bed. One with aquatic plants and fish swimming in the depths, the other home to a stone woman who poured water from a vase. The sound of burbling water, rare in Bymere, lulled him to sleep.

The most beautiful and most expensive items in all the kingdom decorated his walls. And yet, this entire place felt like a prison.

The doors to his chambers opened. The telltale swish of fabric heralded the arrival of his advisor and wife.

Nadir tried to hide the reaction that shook his shoulders. "Saafiya, has the second wife arrived from her travels?"

"Is that all you have to say to me, husband? I remember a time when we were much closer. Now you spend your time worrying about another woman."

He sent a silent prayer for assistance to the gods, then turned.

Red fabric hung from her shoulders, sliding across her curves and parting to reveal caramel skin with each movement. She was stunning no matter how much she aged. Golden chains arched from her nose to ear, capped her shoulders, and slid between her breasts to anchor at her navel.

Not even a few months ago, he would have fallen to his knees to worship her. She was goddess made flesh, a creature that even the most ancient of beings would wish to sample.

Now, he couldn't tell if he wanted to savor her or identify her most poisonous part.

"Leave," he said firmly. "I have no need of you tonight."

"You always have need of me. You just don't know it yet."

She sauntered towards him, all hips and flashing skin, and he could remember the time when he had fallen completely and utterly in love with her. She had been his entire childhood fantasy, given to him on a golden platter.

Saafiya walked her fingers across his shoulders. "You've been lost, Sultan. I've seen you wandering the halls at night. You aren't yourself."

He shrugged her off. "My mind has been busy. And rightfully so. A kingdom is difficult to run."

"You have your advisors. We're here to lessen this burden."

"And yet, the ultimate responsibility falls upon my shoulders. I'm the Sultan of Bymere."

He wanted her to remember that. He wanted all of them to remember since it was clear they thought the kingdom was at their feet simply because they had his ear.

She smiled. "Of course it does, my husband."

Gods, how he hated that tone. She'd used it when he was just a child as well, and only when she wanted something from him. If only Raheem were here to scare the witch way.

"I have much to think about tonight," he advised. "I don't have time to entertain you."

"Rest easy, Sultan. I'm not here to distract you." She laid herself across the red silk pillows of his bed and dragged one of the gauzy curtains over her legs. "You may continue thinking."

"You shouldn't be here, Saafiya."

"And why not? You're my husband, too. Or have you forgotten that?"

"I have not forgotten." How could he? She was everywhere he looked, regardless of her physical presence. Saafiya had made a mark on the Red Palace that would last for years.

The carvings on every column, the flowers laid out in the halls, even the stained-glass windows were her doing. She'd taken a male's kingdom and made it better. For all that he didn't like her meddling, he would admit that this place had become a home.

Saafiya rolled onto her side, framing her hip with her hand. "I don't mean to alarm you, husband, but your new wife isn't fitting in all that well."

"I thought you weren't going to distract me."

"Don't you want to think about your wives as well? She is a dangerous new addition to our home, and I would hate for her to catch you unaware."

"Unaware?" he scoffed. "She's not particularly hard to track. The woman doesn't lie. I've asked her many an uncomfortable question, and she has always answered without hesitation."

"And yet, she is already sowing seeds of disgust among your people. They aren't comfortable with an animal ruling them. And they never will be."

He turned on his heel and stalked to his desk. His hands curled into fists, and he reminded himself that she was only telling the truth. Saafiya meant no harm from the words. She said what she believed, what the entirety of his kingdom believed, and he had to live with that.

Still, it stung more than it would have months ago.

Nadir sat down at his desk and cradled his head in his hands. "What would you have me do, Saafiya?"

"Teach her our ways. Show her that there is more than just remaining rigid as a board. Women are supposed to be like the rivers our home lacks. We are supple, we react to change, and we remind all others that there is beauty left in the world."

"Does she not do that?" He certainly thought she did. It wasn't the flowing beauty of Bymerian women, although he'd always appreciated them for their fluidity. Sigrid was like a mountain. She could not be moved, but there was a beauty that made others flock to her.

Saafiya snorted. "No, husband. She does exactly the opposite of that. It's making the concubines uncomfortable."

"Everything makes the concubines uncomfortable."

"Nadir," she scolded, leveling him with a look. "They're just as important to you as your wives."

"I never said they weren't. However, even you can admit that they've been less than welcoming to our newest addition. I'd suggest that they may be following in *your* footsteps."

He lifted his head and had the satisfying victory of seeing her stiffen. Saafiya never gave him enough credit. For all that Nadir had fallen under her spell, he'd seen it the entire time. She didn't have him on puppet strings as firmly as she thought.

"I see no reason to reach out a friendly hand to someone who hasn't done the same for me," she replied with a sniff.

"I don't think Sigrid is the kind of person to reach out to anyone."

"She has to you."

She had. It was something Nadir was infinitely proud of. Sigrid was a strange anomaly and she had somehow chosen *him* to confide in, to trust, to show the most hidden part of herself that he could have used to his own advantage.

But why? He didn't have an answer, although he fully intended to ask her. She'd suddenly trusted him because he had proven to be the same as her. He hoped she wasn't so foolish that she would trust any person simply because they were Beastkin as well.

Saafiya lifted an arm. Gold bangles jangled down her wrist, and she pushed them up again, only to let them fall. She repeated it, allowing the strange music to fill the room. "Why is that, you think?" she asked.

"Why is what, Saafiya?"

"She's opened up to you, of all people, and won't even speak to the other women."

"Of all people?" he repeated, slightly insulted. "Why is it surprising that she should wish to speak with her husband?"

"Because she was an unwilling wife." Saafiya's gaze met his, and he saw something he'd never seen in her gaze before. Understanding. "Hasn't it occurred to you that she might be playing you?"

"She isn't capable of that kind of deceit," he scoffed. A worm of doubt wiggled in his chest. Could she? Sigrid didn't seem like the kind of creature who could look at a man and lie outright to his face. But she had professed to being willing to do anything for her people, had even asked him to reveal that he too was a Beastkin.

Could she have been playing him this entire time? Did she have it in her?

Saafiya slithered off the edge of the bed and strode towards him on long legs. "My dear, every woman is capable of deceit. We are poisonous creatures at heart, and lies come naturally to us. Find me a woman who doesn't lie, and I shall proclaim her an angel."

She walked around his desk. The filmy material hanging

off her shoulders trailed along the wooden edge as she reached for him. Her fingers toyed with the curls of his hair, then dragged him closer to her.

"Haven't you given it thought, husband? Your new wife is alone here. No other Earthen folk grace these halls other than her silent maidservant. It stands to reason that she might try to grasp at whatever power we allow her."

Nadir took a deep, calming breath. "She has power, Saafiya. She is the Sultana of Bymere."

"She is an animal." Saafiya's voice burned with acidic hatred. "She's sultana by name only, but that does not make her a ruler, nor will it make our people follow her. It hurts my heart to even think that you cannot see the darkness she is breeding here in Bymere."

"What darkness?" He pulled away from her hand and stood abruptly. "What has she done that is so terrifying to you? She's kept to herself, she rarely speaks with our people, how could she possibly be doing anything dangerous?"

"Mark my words, *boy king*, she intends to incite an uprising and we must stop her."

"I don't worry about any darkness she might spread," he quietly replied. "I worry about what is already festering inside of you."

He felt immense pleasure when she gasped and stepped away from him. Saafiya narrowed her eyes. "You know I always have the kingdom's best interests at heart."

"I know you always have your own interests at the forefront."

"Every decision I make is for the betterment of our kingdom. How dare you suggest anything other than that," she hissed. Saafiya lifted a hand as if she might strike him, then lowered it when she saw his answering frown. "I should have known you weren't man enough to make the right choices."

"The right choice is to leave her be, Saafiya."

She glared. "You know nothing. You are a child seated on a throne that was never meant for you and have become spoiled. Count yourself lucky that an entire panel of advisors helps you make decisions that have allowed this country prosper."

Anger burned hot in his chest. How dare she? She waltzed into his private quarters, uninvited, then insulted him like this? Certainly, he hadn't been an entirely active sultan, but he'd made good suggestions that they continually shot down. His entire sultanate was afraid of change. That ended now.

"Tread carefully, wife," he growled. "You might walk into quicksand."

"Am I supposed to be frightened of you, husband? Shall you strike me down where I stand? Then do it." She stood before him proud with her chin lifted. "Show Bymere what the sultan does with people who follow the ancient traditions, who know the value of old Bymere. Let them see what their sultan does with his revered first wife when she tries to protect them from a monster in their midst."

His hands shook with the desire to do just that. Saafiya had overstepped so many bounds that he didn't know where to begin in her punishment. What would his brother have suggested he do? Likely, hang her by the toes. But that would also suggest to his people that he was siding with the Beastkin. If he didn't punish her, then Sigrid's life might get infinitely worse.

Nadir didn't know what to do or how to react. Instead of making a choice, he hesitated.

She laughed. "That's what I thought. It's a good thing I've made the decision for you, dear husband. Otherwise, nothing would get done in this kingdom."

He froze at her words. "What have you done?"

She sashayed away from him, her hips swinging in tune to the trickling sounds of water. "What you have been afraid to do since she arrived here."

"Any harm upon her is an act of war," he reminded her.

"War with Wildewyn is imminent. It's just a matter of who starts it."

It took a moment for the words to hit him.

"What did you do?" he growled.

"She said she was a warrior. Let her try and fight her way back into the city then. If she makes it, then she can stay. I won't bother her any further, husband. If she doesn't—" Saafiya lifted a shoulder in a careless shrug "—then she was lying about more than just her abilities."

Every thought disappeared from his head. His body moved without thought or reason, even as anger flowed through his veins until he feared the dragon would burst free. He'd never been this close to losing control, even when Hakim died. The poison had been an unknown assailant, until later when they discovered what had killed him.

Saafiya knew what she had done. She had willingly attacked another sultana, his own wife, and then acted as though it hadn't happened? Or that it didn't matter?

Nadir only awoke from his anger-hazed madness for a moment when he walked his first wife back against the wall. He was so much larger than her, but he'd never realized it, because she overpowered a room with her personality. Looming over her, his nostrils flared in anger, he realized that even now she didn't think he would hurt her.

She stared back at him with just as much rage in her eyes, her fists balled. "Your people will never trust an animal seated on the throne, and they will not suffer a weak sultan."

"If she dies, then so do you."

"You wouldn't dare."

He slipped away from her and out the doors of his private chambers. Once in the public halls, he shouted, "A sultan has no need for a wife, Saafiya. It's by choice that I keep you!"

And then he was running. Every footstep thudded against the sandstone floors, and he prayed to every god that he wouldn't be too late. She was a warrior. He'd seen her fight before. Surely, she could keep back a few assassins.

He didn't know how many Saafiya had sent. She wasn't a foolish woman by any means.

Racing by a group of his guards, he shouted for them to get his horse. He took the long way to the courtyard only to stop by the armory where he snatched a scimitar that had recently been sharpened. The blade gleamed in the afternoon sunlight.

"Sultan!" Raheem ran toward him from the back of the palace. "Are we under attack?"

"Of a sort." He searched for a chestplate in the piles of armor laying around. Why weren't they prepared for war? If Wildewyn attacked now, not a single man would be ready. A chestplate lay underneath a blanket on a bench, and he yanked it free. "Saafiya has sent assassins to attack Sigrid upon her return."

"The girl can handle them."

He looked up and met Raheem's gaze. "She intends to kill her."

The big man swallowed. Raheem knew how dire this situation was. He'd seen Sigrid fight, but he also knew how devious Saafiya could be. She wouldn't have sent anyone but the best.

He might lose his wife.

"I'll come with you," Raheem replied.

"In anything else, I would ask to go alone, but today... Bring armor, Raheem. We may need it."

"You wish to fight against your own assassins?" Raheem asked, but didn't pause in his movements. His own armor, too large to be worn by anyone else, set on a stand where it waited. Well-oiled and supple, he pulled it on with ease.

"I won't hesitate if that's what it takes."

He grew restless waiting. Every second was one that he wasted in catching up with the men. There was a chance that he might stop them, order them to return on penalty of death, and then he could meet Sigrid himself.

Why had the blasted woman chosen today to go into the deserts? He should never have agreed to let her go.

"Let's go," he growled, spinning on his heel and running to the courtyard where two horses waited. His faithful companion must have known Nadir would need a second man.

"What did Saafiya tell you?" Raheem asked, swinging a leg over his horse.

"Only that an animal should not sit on a throne, and if she could battle her way into the city then she could stay here."

The words had struck home. What would any of them do

if they realized that Nadir was also Beastkin? They'd take the throne, that was for certain, but he didn't know what his own people would do. Some would likely feel the same disgust as Saafiya. Others might not. No one had ever asked the people of Bymere how they felt about the Beastkin. The royals had simply made the decision for them.

"Then we go this way." Raheem wheeled his horse in the opposite direction from the front gates.

"If we hurry, we might catch them!"

"We'll never catch up with them. But we can come up from behind and stop her from murdering them all. Think ahead, Nadir. I'm not worried about her safety. The girl has a dragon heart." Raheem paused at an alleyway entrance, staring at Nadir as if he'd lost his mind. "She'll kill them all."

How easy it was to forget his second wife wasn't a damsel in distress. She could take care of herself. It was his own men he had to worry about. They waited for her at the front of the city, where everyone would watch as she was attacked.

So that was Saafiya's plan all along. Kill his second wife if possible, or turn the entire populace of Bymere against her.

Cursing, he dug his heels into his horse's side and fled down the alley towards the back entrance to the Red Palace. Their horses needed to be swift and agile to make it in time. He prayed they remained steady and true.

Every breath seemed as though he had already lost her. They didn't hesitate for any of the people in the streets. Some jumped out of the way long before they were in danger. Others shouted at them and were knocked to the side.

Let his people think whatever they wanted. It was Nadir's job to keep them safe, then that included his wayward wife who insisted upon her own freedom. He should have known better than to allow her that. Freedom was the root of all issues. Those who had it were careless with it. Those who didn't, desired it above all else and would do anything to get it.

They burst through the back entrance to his home and hooves struck sand. His heart thundered in his chest in time with the roar of his dragon who wanted to break free. Let them see what happened when they threatened a dragon's mate.

And she was his mate.

She was the only remaining female dragon in the world. His animal side had already claimed her as his, and they'd only met twice. It was cruel to take away that which he had only just found.

Breathing hard, he rounded the mountain they'd built the palace on and bent low over his horse's neck when he saw the gates were already open and that Sigrid had arrived.

Raheem shouted, "tread carefully, boy," from behind him.

He intended to tread as carelessly as he wanted to. His own men were attacking his wife.

The blurred smudge of bodies moved. Swords lifted into the air, sun reflecting off the blades until they were nearly blinding. A few of the assassins were lying on the ground, staining the golden sands red with blood. Were they dead? He didn't care, but knew that he should. The peasants wouldn't like seeing one of their own lying on the sands.

The remaining assassins circled her. Ten men with full armor and scimitars at the ready. Even for her, this would be a difficult battle. Sigrid had proven to be talented one on one, but she'd never shown how she fought outnumbered.

She wore a strange outfit he'd never seen before. Men's

clothing and lacking a golden mask. Instead, she wore little more than a cloth wrapped around her face.

What was she playing at? And where was her maidservant?

"Halt!" he shouted, thundering up behind them. "On whose orders have you attacked the sultana?"

Only one of the assassins glanced his way. "On *your* orders, Sultan."

His face flushed hot in anger. So this was how Saafiya had managed to order them away.

Nadir didn't waste his time in looking at Sigrid. He knew she would be angry, but he'd make it very clear that none of this was his order.

"Then you were told wrong, soldier. The punishment for attacking the sultana, as has been made very clear, is a fate worse than death. She is under the protection of my house as well as the house of Wildewyn. No one is to touch her but myself and her sister, who remains safe as my ward."

"We were told you'd say that. Got the papers you signed, Sultan. We know this animal has you under her spell, and that the only way to break it is to sever her head from her body."

Spell? What lies had Saafiya been spreading?

Sigrid let out a choked cough. "If you truly think I am capable of magic, assassin, then by all means. Attack me. See just how far you get."

"You're unarmed, Sultana," the soldier replied. "We don't wish to make this more difficult than it has to be. Many Bymerian women have given their lives for the betterment of the country. Kneel, and allow us to give you an honorable death."

"Death by ten swords, or ten deaths?" She tilted her head to the side. "We'll see how this ends."

Nadir nudged his horse closer, only pausing when an assassin turned on him. "Sigrid. You cannot kill them."

"And why not? I find it hard to listen when you signed papers stating that my life should end."

"I did no such thing."

The soldier who'd spoken before cleared his throat. "It says no animal should sit on the throne. We agree with you, Sultan, and it's best to make it known now so that all of Bymere knows where you stand. We won't allow this Beastkin to think she can rule our beloved lands."

The words cut him to the core. Of course, his soldiers felt that way. But his people? Surely, they didn't speak for the populace of Bymere. They couldn't. Bymerians weren't so cold that they would forsake the most natural of their own kind.

Sigrid let out a growl and lunged forward. They hadn't expected her quick movements. In truth, neither had Nadir. The first assassin she touched hesitated for the briefest moment which allowed her to grab onto his sword and twist it from his grip. She dragged the sharp edge along his throat and he dropped to the ground without a sound.

Stunned silence followed her movement, until the assassins let out an angry shout. This would not be a battle that tested her metal. They did not attack one by one to allow her a breath. Instead, they all moved at the same time with their swords raised.

Nadir cried out in anger and let his feet fall from the stirrups, ready to leap into the fray, but then paused along with all the others to stare in shock.

Nine swords arced above her and met as one in a circle, slicing towards her head. She lifted her stolen sword and crouched in the center, holding every single one away from her. The assassin's arms shook, each man pressing down as hard as they could. Metal screeched as one sword slid along hers. Sparks showered in the air.

She snarled, an animal trapped in a cage, and then swung her sword up. The powerful movement sent each assassin stumbling away from her. What kind of strength did this woman have? She'd held nine men away from her without showing strain.

Sigrid swung her leg out and caught a man in the thigh. He was already stumbling, and at her movement he fell. One knee in the sand, he knelt as she swung her sword and cleaved his head from his body.

Nadir watched it fly and realized how wrong he'd been. Not one of them were going to touch her. Raheem was right.

They were all going to die.

"Stop her," Raheem shouted, "or the kingdom will never accept her!"

Nadir jumped from the stallion's back and ran into the fray. He caught one of the assassin's swords. Planting a foot directly in the man's chest, he kicked him so far back that Raheem could grab him. The big man slapped both hands on the sides of the assassin's head, and he dropped like a stone.

"Sigrid!" he called out. She didn't listen to him in the slightest. Her sword lifted again, blood slicked and dripping. "Enough!"

Another man fell, this one missing an arm and clutching the bleeding stump desperately to his chest. Nadir's ears rang with shouts of battle, all in front of his home.

He paused, looked up at the palace, and realized nearly the entire populace of Misthall was watching them. They stared down from every window, standing in the streets and peering through the gates. They saw their sultana attack their own men, and anger reflected in their gazes.

There was nothing he could do to fix this. All he could do was stop her from killing more people.

"Wife!" Desperately, he dropped his sword and ran toward her. There was only one way he knew how to stop this, and already he thought of how to beg her forgiveness. She was a proud woman. She'd likely wish to kill him for what he planned to do.

Nadir waited for the moment she attacked the next man before he reached forward and caught the tail end of the cloth binding her face. He ripped it away, letting the black fabric flutter in the wind. It floated to the sand, along with her choked cry, then sudden silence as she stopped and stared out into the desert.

The assassin she'd been fighting stared back at her in shock.

A chuffing cough echoed from her throat, the dragon trying its best to be free. An answering call escaped from his own lips. He hoped no one heard it but her.

Carefully, he stepped up behind her and wrapped his arms around her trembling frame, holding her face away from the city. "Enough, wife," he whispered, pressing the side of his head against hers. "It's over."

"I am not an animal."

"You are Beastkin, and so much more than just a creature sitting on a throne."

"You signed the papers," she exhaled.

Nadir's heart cracked. "I will be more diligent when my advisors hand me paperwork to sign. I've not been a good sultan, Sigrid. You're helping me become a better one."

Another tremble wracked her body, and he knew it was because another man stared at her face.

The assassin rocked back, his sword drooping to touch the sand. "She's very young," the man said.

Nadir met his gaze. "Yes, she is."

"She doesn't look like an animal under that mask. We all thought—" he cleared his throat. "She's just a girl."

Raheem walked up behind him and sighed. "It's a shame you won't be able to tell anyone that."

Nadir frowned, but didn't have enough time to ask what his friend was doing before Raheem palmed the man's head and snapped it to the side. He let the assassin fall to the ground, then pressed a meaty fist to his chest.

"Sultana," Raheem said, his tones revered and quiet. "It was a pleasure to cast my eyes upon your form before my death."

"Not you, Raheem," Sigrid choked, her voice thick with tears. "I would never ask that of you."

"And what is the punishment for seeing your face?"

"Death."

"What punishment would you take for me?"

Her body rock forward, but he forced her to remain securely pressed against his chest. He couldn't risk her racing to his friend and allowing any more people to see her face. Already, rumbles of anger and discontent lifted from the crowds behind them. He needed to hide her. He needed her to be safe.

Sigrid shook with a sob. "No punishment is too lenient for you. I would not see your kindness leave this world so early."

"And for them?" Raheem gestured to the crowds. "What punishment is too great for them?"

"Don't ask me that. Not now."

"Why? What has happened?" A shadow passed over Raheem's face, and suddenly he became someone Nadir did not recognize. His eyes narrowed, his jaw tightened, and he became far more frightening than Nadir had ever seen him be before. "What have you seen?"

"I've seen what Bymerians do to my people. I cannot stand by and watch it again."

Nadir squeezed her tighter. "This was a mistake, Sigrid. This is not how Bymere treats Beastkin. There are none left here. It's old prejudice that can be changed."

"Can it?" She twisted in his arms and stared up at him with a rage that echoed in his own chest. "There are Beastkin *here*. Men, like you, who have been hunted, mistreated, hated for their entire lives. They want to *live*. They want to *love*. They wish for normal lives, and you sit on that throne and do *nothing*."

He released her as her skin started to burn. "You don't know of what you speak."

"You don't know your own kingdom, Sultan. Your people see us as nothing more than animals they can exploit, beat, and kill. I won't stand by and watch it any longer. I can't do it."

Nadir looked past her. Raheem stepped forward and placed a hand on her shoulder. The big man sighed and said, "You've met Jabbar."

"Who are you talking about?" Nadir snapped. "What is

this information I don't know?"

Raheem's fingers tightened on Sigrid's shoulder, and Nadir realized it was the first time his guard had ever touched her. His gaze narrowed on the touch as his dragon growled deep inside him. "Sultan, there is much that goes on in this kingdom that you do not know. The royals have hunted Beastkin for centuries. I did not tell you because you have only followed in your brother's footsteps. I've asked you to change, and you haven't. Not until she came, and even then, it wasn't enough."

Sigrid twisted to look up at Raheem. "You knew?"

"I wondered how long it would take them to find you."

"I have to help them."

"As I expected."

Nadir shook his head, his mind racing with new found knowledge but not knowing what to do with it. "Beastkin? In Bymere?"

"Choose now, husband." Sigrid's eyes swam with tears. "Help our people. Tell Bymerians to accept our kind. Show them what we can really do. *Who we are.*"

"No." He stepped away from her. How could he do that? Bymere was his kingdom, his family's kingdom, his *brother's* kingdom. He might be Beastkin by blood, but that didn't change his responsibilities. This was his homeland, and he couldn't abandon them or subject them to Beastkin running free. It was dangerous.

Two dragons without chains could decimate the world.

"I'll ask again." Her voice shook. "Choose between enslaving the Beastkin and hunting them for centuries more, or giving them the freedom they've asked for."

"It's not that easy, Sigrid—"

"Make your choice!" Her voice lifted in a shout that all his people would have heard. She softened, reaching out a hand for him. "Nadir. We have to change, or we will all die."

"Is that really a bad thing? We shouldn't be like this, Sigrid. This is not how humans are meant to live. Animals live inside us. Creatures with immense power that we must keep in cages for the safety of all others."

"Don't project your self-hatred on everyone else. There are so many people here who could love them."

He thought of Saafiya, his guards, the rumbling crowd behind her and couldn't see how that future was possible. He looked at her as a goddess, a woman who saw a future made of gold and sunlight. But it was an impossible future and a war that would only end in blood.

Nadir shook his head again and stepped back once more. "Come home with me, Sigrid. This future you speak of is a great folly. We cannot save everyone, but we can live a comfortable life together."

"In hiding."

"Living in hiding is better than dying young."

"I would rather die than deny what I am." Her eyes burned silver and gold. Nadir reached for her, knowing that this could end poorly. But she darted away from him and raced forward until all his people could see her face.

Sigrid lifted her arms and shouted, "People of Bymere, see this face! I am Sigrid of Wildewyn, Beastkin woman, and last of the dragon bloodline. Hear me when I say this. Beastkin are coming home. We will fight for our freedom, for our rights, and for you to recognize us as citizens of Bymere. We are not *animals.* We are men, women, and children who will make the skies thunder with our war cry. Accept us, or prepare for war."

A cry lifted from the crowd, a group of men he recognized from the war barracks. "We will fight you, and we will win! No animal should sit on the throne."

Sigrid smiled without happiness. "You underestimate us, warrior. Now see what you will battle."

"No!" Nadir cried out, but he couldn't reach her side in time.

Sigrid burst into her dragon form. He'd forgotten how large she was, easily filling the space in front of the great hall, larger than some of the buildings. She reared up and let out a roar that shook the ground. Slats of roof tile nearby fell from the homes and shattered on the ground.

The crowd turned into a mob, fleeing from the first sight of a living dragon in hundreds of years. Sigrid took to the air and circled the Red Palace. She stretched out her neck and breathed fire in billowing sheets that never touched the city, but warned all within it that a dragon would battle them.

Nadir fell to his knees in the sand and watched as his people experienced true fear for the first time in centuries. He'd lost. He'd lost everything, and now all he had was a throne that would soon drip with blood.

The silver dragon circled back to him and landed hard in the sand. She stared at him with an icy gaze, and he knew she would never forgive him for this. Numb and silent, he stared as Raheem walk over to her and set a hand on her side.

"I'll go with you, Sultana. It's long past time this happened," he said.

"Even you?" Nadir called out. "Even you will abandon

me?"

"You've made your choice, Sultan. The Bymerian people will need a sultan who can lead them in this time of war and strife. Your advisors will help you as they see fit." Raheem paused and glanced over his shoulder. "I still hold hope that you will not be the man your brother was, but the dragon boy I've always hoped you would be."

Sigrid reached forward and wrapped a clawed hand around Raheem's waist. She reared back and blew sand over Nadir as they fled into the desert. She took a piece of his pride with her.

Worse, she took his heart as well.

SIGRID

SIGRID PLUMMETED FROM THE SKIES, LANDING HARD IN THE sand and rolling to keep Raheem from being harmed. She skidded to a halt on the outskirts of the abandoned kingdom where the Beastkin hid. Her chest heaved in silent sobs, because a dragon could not cry. There were no tears to slide down her cheeks, only flames that burned in her chest with anger and disappointment.

How could he say those things? How could he renounce his own people so easily, without even a modicum of guilt?

She'd thought he was better than that, and the folly was entirely her fault. A few adventures in the sands, enjoying their shifted forms in every way that they could, didn't mean that he would change his mind about the people he knew and loved. He'd made it clear how he felt about Beastkin, and in her foolishness she'd thought she could change him.

A hand slid along her leathery leg.

"Sigrid, let me down." She released her hold on Raheem

and allowed him to move off her body and into the sand. He knelt next to her head, nearly as large as he was, and placed a hand on her brow. "I know it wasn't easy for you, Sultana, but it was the right thing to do."

She shook her head miserably. Nadir had offered her a future with a husband, a family, a draconic future that while hidden, was still a chance to continue her line. Now what was she to do? Teach only her daughters that they were still the last? Pass down throughout history this loneliness that slowly poisoned her?

Raheem continued smoothing his hand over her skull. "I know it wasn't easy for you. There were opportunities there, and believe me, I love him just as much as you do. Nadir has a way about him that makes people want to love him. He's never seen it, but I knew he could become a sultan like no other.

"It's a shame he cannot see the future the way you and I can. He doesn't see Beastkin and humans living side by side, but he's never had a chance to see what that could look like. He only knows people who are afraid. And fear is a dangerous emotion that cannot be controlled no matter how hard we try.

"I still have hope that someday he will understand what we are fighting for. *Why* we are fighting for it. I dream of a day when eagles soar overhead, hunting with humans even while a dragon scours the land, protecting the city from any invaders. I saw that it could work between human and Beastkin. I married one. And those years with her by my side were the happiest I have ever been."

Sigrid huffed out a breath, rolling to press her leathery wings to the ground. She could do this. If there was a chance that others existed like Raheem, those who would accept her people with open arms, then it was worth the fight. It had to be.

He smiled at her. "Good, now get up when you can. Jabbar and his people don't want to see your sadness. They want to see your strength. As much as you never wanted this, you've become a Sultana of Bymere. Just of a different sort of Bymerian."

She didn't want to be a sultana or a leader, but that was the way her life had led. Even the Beastkin had named her matriarch long before she was grown. Her mother had been a leader, and now Sigrid would follow in her footsteps.

Scales melted away, and she stayed crouched so that Raheem couldn't see her face. She could feel tears leaking from her eyes, and she didn't want him to see her weakness. Not yet. Soon she would control the tears, but until then, she would stare at the ground and will them out of existence.

This was not the end of her. A man did not control her happiness, her thoughts, or her desires. She was the master of her own fate.

Raheem reached for her, but it wasn't a hand he offered. Instead, a black cloth fell in front of her vision. "I picked it up off the sands. I thought, perhaps, you might want it."

Determination filled her with a strength she had forgotten. "No," Sigrid replied. "I don't need that anymore."

She would never hide her face behind that golden mask again. No matter how many people tried to put the symbolic cage on her, Sigrid wanted them to see her face. She wanted them to know exactly who led the Beastkin army, and that she was willing to do whatever it took for their freedom. Even reveal herself and forsake the old ways.

"That's a big choice," Raheem said, but let the cloth drop

to the ground. "You said seeing a Beastkin woman's face is punishable by death. What will the others think when they see you like this?"

"Then they will know something terrible has happened. All Beastkin are my family, they may see my face without repercussion. It is everyone else who must see me and all that I am capable of. The Beastkin will know that now is the time for war."

Even though she desired to keep them all safe, Sigrid knew what this meant. She had revealed herself to the entirety of Bymere. Not because she wanted them to die, but because she wanted them to remember her.

Now, it was time for all Beastkin to do the same. Men and women had to stand together to free themselves. In Bymere and in Wildewyn.

A plan formed in her mind. Crazy, perhaps, but one that would make a statement neither country could back away from. She would put them all to the test.

"Come," she said, standing up and walking toward the twin elephants. "There is much to talk about with the Beastkin of Bymere."

Raheem followed her through the sand, a silent shadow who surveyed their surroundings for a potential attack. She didn't have to tell him that his own skin might be at risk. Raheem was the strange one here.

She stooped through the window and waited for him to fit his bulk into the long hall, then followed the lit sconces on the wall to a larger chamber. Jabbar had not taken her here before. It opened into what had once been the great hall, ceiling high and dark. Cobwebs covered the wall sconces here, for the only light was from a large bonfire in the center.

"Jabbar of Bymere, I have returned," she called out.

They were gathered in the center around the heat. Some attended the new Beastkin who had arrived. They were laying closer to the fire than the others, a sight she was pleased by. Camilla crouched near a man, laying sheets of soaking wet fabric on his back where whip marks bled freely.

The albino man stood at the far corner of the great hall and made his way toward her. "We did not expect you so soon."

"I was attacked."

Jabbar frowned. His hands closed into fists. "They dared attack the sultana? They've lost their senses."

"The sultan ordered it." Unknowingly, irresponsibly, but it was his signature on the paperwork. And the knowledge still stung. She'd given him too much credit, he was still capable of creating because he refused to think things through.

"I'm not surprised. The man is more beast than any of us here." He gestured at the crowd of men and animals. "He sees only what he wants to see, not what is in front of his face."

Raheem emerged from the shadows behind her. "Now that's not fair, Jabbar. I remember a time when you could hardly see anything in front of your face. The boy is young, and there are many who surround him that are far more dangerous."

She tensed, wondering how the Beastkin would react. They were sensitive at a time like this, and she hadn't entered their enclave in a way that would ease Raheem's presence. If she were honest with herself, she was feeling a little prickly toward him herself. There was a dangerous edge to her anger. It wanted to tear down any human who stood in her way, no matter who they were.

But instead of their anger or disgust, Jabbar and his men smiled at Raheem. The albino leader strode forward and grasped forearms with her personal guard. "Well, I'll be. I never thought to see your face around here again."

"It seems no matter how far I try to run, I always end up with a Beastkin woman on my arm."

They laughed together, and warmth bloomed in her chest. Not anger, but something that rivaled its heat. There was a comradery between these men that she hadn't seen before. Not between human and Beastkin.

Even in Wildewyn, there was a certain fear when dealing with humans. Both sides were uncomfortable with the other. Earthen folk revered them, wanted to keep them safe from all harm, and use them only if necessary. But by doing so, her people were still imprisoned.

"Jabbar," she said, "there is much I need to discuss with you."

"So, you've decided to help us after all?" He turned and crossed his arms over his chest. "I'll be truthful and admit when you said you were going to the sultan, I was disappointed."

"I imagine you were. It was foolish of me to think that he would change his mind so easily, simply because of what I know."

"And what is it that you know?'"

She shook her head. "Some things must remain between husband and wife. I'll thank you to keep it that way."

She didn't want to admit that Nadir was also Beastkin. In some ways, it made his betrayal all the worse. That was a wound which would fester in her own soul, and no one else's.

Camilla made her way to Sigrid's side, a cautious smile on

her face and worry in her eyes. "Sister?"

Tears sprang to her eyes. She wanted to tell Camilla everything that happened, but couldn't. Not while all the others were staring at her and waiting for whatever she would do next.

Instead, she nodded firmly. Her sister wouldn't push. They knew each other like they knew their own soul. Tonight, she would cry in Camilla's arms. Now, she would tell these Beastkin her foolish plan and take them away from this place forever.

Squaring her shoulders, Sigrid made her way to the center of the room. The bonfire burned hot at her back, and her dragon unfurled its wings in her breast. Together. They would lead these people together as they should have since she was born.

"Beastkin of Bymere," she began. "Friends and new family. Today was the first day in a war that we have started. I've seen your suffering. I've seen the hatred and fear in the eyes of humans. And I watched as they attacked me and not a single person tried to stop them. I asked the sultan to take pity on us, and he refused."

Murmurs lifted into the air. They had a right to be angry. Nadir was their sultan just as much as he was anyone else's. And their leader had forsaken them.

Sigrid cleared her throat to gather their attention. "I say you to now, you do not need a sultan. Standing before you is a *sultana*, and I wish nothing more than to see you safe, comfortable, and loved by your family and friends. There should be no more hunts of our kind. We should not break our backs to sow their fields with food they do not share. I ask you now to unite and follow me.

"It will not be an easy path to walk. I don't blame any of

you if you turn away from this future. Many of us will die in a war against the humans. Those that survive will carry these memories into our old age. But we will carve a path to safety for all who come after us.

"I am the last of the dragons, and I will carry you to safety if I must. But I will not stand by and watch this any longer. Beastkin, I ask you now to take back what is yours. I ask you to take back not just Bymere, but Wildewyn and every square inch of land which should have been ours from the start."

They cheered for her, and she felt the dragon in her chest hum. She wanted to shift, to tell all the others to shift with her and race away from this terrible place. But not yet. The people might follow her, but she needed their leader to believe in it as well.

Sigrid found Jabbar in the crowd. His arms were crossed over his broad chest, his loose-fitting torn shirt revealing pale skin underneath it. He was whiter than snow, and his pink eyes saw too much. He wanted to know more, but he was also reserved.

She understood that they hadn't been treated well by anyone. And here she was, another foreigner trying to tell them how to save themselves. Again, and again, the Beastkin were tossed between people and they didn't want to trust.

Jabbar had to support her for all these people to follow. That was the only way she would take this step.

She held out a hand for him and called out, "Jabbar, will you walk by my side? I am young, and not from this place. I don't know your customs, your rights, your stories. A sultana is no one without someone like you to help guide her."

"You want me to be an advisor?" he asked, lifting a

pale brow.

"I want you to be more than that. Beastkin will never be ruled by a single person who makes all the decisions for us. I ask that you stand by my side and rule our people. Choose another, choose three. However, many people you deem fit to join your side, and we will work through our issues together. I will do the same with Raheem, Camilla, and those I choose once we arrive in Wildewyn."

The crowd quieted. It seemed for a moment that everyone was holding their breath to hear what he had to say. Jabbar quietly picked his way through the men. Each step closer felt like a victory, although she had no way of knowing what he would say or if he would even agree to her insane plan.

Finally, he reached her side. He sniffed loudly and asked, "Wildewyn?"

"We know there is no safe place in Bymere where Beastkin will not be hunted. Wildewyn is far safer."

"You keep your Beastkin in glorified cages." He gestured to Camilla who stood off to the side. "Your sister has told us the tales, and we have no desire to be caged. Even if it comes with food and a bed."

"I'm not asking for that. The Beastkin in Wildewyn came down from the mountains, and our old homeland is waiting for us. I don't want you or any other Beastkin to be in a gilded cage. I want us to be free."

Jabbar furrowed his brows. "Then what you are proposing, Sultana?"

"There's an army waiting for us in Wildewyn. All we have to do is go get it."

And with those words, she knew she had him. Jabbar met

her gaze with the same fire he had when he first saw her as a dragon. No longer were the Beastkin weak or outnumbered. There were many people waiting for her return in Wildewyn, and they were trained warriors like herself and Camilla.

Now, they would return not only as lost sisters, but bringing with them the hope of a people. A new start. A new life.

He turned to his men and lifted his arms, calling out, "Men! We're going to Wildewyn!"

MANY DAYS LATER, THE MEN WERE READY TO LEAVE. THEY STOOD in a crowd outside the place where they had been safe for so many years, then said their goodbyes to their home. Sigrid stood next to Camilla at a respectful distance.

"Are you sure you want to do this?" Camilla quietly asked. "You've made a lot of promises to them."

"Ones that should have been made a long time ago. They deserve more than this life."

"So do we." Camilla reached out and linked her fingers with Sigrid. "But the journey will be long, and hard."

"All journeys are. We've managed quite well traversing across the countries, finding ourselves sultana and maidservant, finding Beastkin men. We've handled ourselves well and we'll continue doing that as the world changes more and more. I want to see a future where Beastkin can walk the streets knowing that they don't have to justify their existence.

Don't you?"

Camilla squeezed her hand. "Of course I do. I just want to make sure that you really want to take all this responsibility on."

"I was matriarch, then sultana, then—" Sigrid shrugged. She couldn't find the words for what she was now. There wasn't a name for a woman who led a war like this. She was queen, sultana, warrior... A hundred names and more.

"Oh, keep your head out of the clouds." Camilla jostled Sigrid with her shoulder. "You aren't some goddess now that you're the leader of a small group of male Beastkin. Hell, I could even argue you aren't the leader at all. You're just the one that Jabbar acknowledges that might have good ideas."

"Thanks for keeping me grounded."

"Any time. Don't need you getting a fat head as well as an army."

Sigrid laughed at Camilla's wink. Her sister strode toward one of the men who would likely need assistance on the trip. One of his legs had been broken in three places. Jabbar said it was a miracle he'd even made it to their hidden kingdom. Most people like him would have died in the sands along the way.

She thought he was a horse shifter, even looked like one. His legs were abnormally long for a Bymerian. He stood a good head and shoulders above the rest. Lanky and thin, he might fill out into a larger man, but she doubted it. That was a person destined to remain slim his entire life.

"Sultana?" Jabbar's voice cut through her musings. "Shall we?"

"You've split some of them up to go straight to Woodcrest, yes?" It was the homeland of all Wildewyn Beastkin, and the only place where she knew they would be safe. Camilla would lead them there. Her mother had known where to go, and Sigrid trusted her to bring them to the right place.

"The ones that are healthy enough to travel, yes. There are a few gryphons here that have agreed to carry some additional men who are only ground animals. I'll take the rest myself."

Thunderbirds were incredibly large animals. Not quite as impressive as a dragon in size, but he'd be able to carry at least five men on his back, more if he didn't tire easily.

She nodded. "Then the rest will come with Raheem and I."

"Are you certain of this? You wish to take our most wounded directly to Stoneholt, the capital of Wildewyn, and convince them to free their own Beastkin?" Jabbar shook his head. "You're mad."

"I'm determined. I know my sisters will follow me if I ask them to. It's not a matter of convincing anyone to free them. The humans don't have a choice anymore."

Each word fell from her tongue like a vow, but she wasn't sure how she felt about them. Sigrid waffled back and forth between certainty that this was the right choice and worry that she might be starting something bigger than herself. Was this the right direction for their people? Was she guiding them to a fate where they would all disappear in a few generations?

War was always a dangerous choice. She didn't know if this was what she wanted, but knew this was what her people wanted. It was worth it to fight. It had to be.

Jabbar stared at her with an appreciative gaze before he nodded as well. "Good. You'll have to carry them all yourself."

"I'm sure I'll survive the weight."

"Then I'll let them know their chariot awaits."

The longer she was around the man, the more she liked him. Jabbar had a quiet strength. He didn't have the charisma many of the leaders she'd met before had. He didn't have to talk or tell people that he was the leader. He simply was, and it made sense that he was.

She trailed after him, searching for Raheem in the crowd. He'd have to ride with the men and make sure they didn't fall off her back. It was going to be a difficult enough journey without having to compensate for their weakness.

He stood with the seven men they'd chosen to travel with her. Most were on death's door with a coughing illness that had spread through the ranks of the Beastkin men. Sigrid had never heard such sounds before. They weren't wet or croupy coughs, but dry and rattling in the men's chests.

It didn't bode well for them. But she wanted to see if the Stoneholt healers could do something for them. Perhaps they knew what this sickness was and could stop it before it spread.

She chewed on her lip and strode forward to stand by Raheem's side. "Are they ready?"

"We'll have to tie them to you, Sultana." He shrugged his shoulders, arms crossed firmly over his chest. "It's not ideal, but otherwise they'll slip off, and I won't be able to catch them. A few are birds and would have made the journey if they weren't ill. Two are large cats, and one seems to be some form of elephant."

"Some form?"

He lifted an arm and scratched his head. "Well, it's not an elephant I've ever seen before. We use them in the Bymerian army when we can train them, but this man has more tusks than a male elephant should have. And... Well,

Sultana, he's got fur."

A gasp escaped her lips. "He's a mammoth?"

"A what?"

"Native to Wildewyn, they all died out a long time ago." She searched through the crowd for the man, certain he would be large enough to pick out. "Which one is he?"

Raheem covered his mouth for a moment, then pointed to a small boy who leaned against another man. He was slight with bird-like bones and a forehead already lined from a tough life.

"He's a child," she whispered.

"Not that young actually. Well past his sixteenth summer. They didn't feed him well enough in the family who bought him for sport. Stunted his growth and kept him small so he took up less space in their household." Raheem spat on the ground. "Awful way to treat a kid."

"I can only imagine."

He wasn't that much younger than her, and yet he looked at least ten years younger. Sigrid made her way to his side and crouched.

"I'll have you ride at the front," she said. "If that's all right with you?"

"Why, Sultana?"

"You seem to be the healthiest of the group. I'll need you to help guide me through the forests." She was making it up as she went. In truth, she wanted the boy to have a good memory to start replacing the bad ones. He'd feel the incredible glory of flight if he was in the front. And he'd be the first to see the splendor of her home.

"I have good eyes."

"I'm sure you do," she replied with a soft smile.

Sigrid stepped back and looked at the men who were now her responsibility. Jabbar had given her a great gift in them. He trusted her to take care of them, to make sure that they came to no further harm, and her stomach tensed with the mere thought of it.

Footsteps crunched behind her, and sand rolled down to pile at the back of her ankles. Raheem cleared his throat. "Are you ready?"

"I believe so."

"Good, it's a long journey from here to Wildewyn."

She glanced up at him. "Are you comfortable with me carrying you in my claws again? The rest will ride on my back, but I might need you to direct me along the path."

"I will ride however you need me to, Sultana."

His blind faith burned. She swallowed hard and nodded. "Make sure they're all lashed on tight. I don't want any of them falling off."

"They will be safe. I promise."

Still nodding, Sigrid backed farther away. She forced herself to continue walking until she knew there was enough safe space between herself and the men. The transformation wouldn't touch anyone, although she knew the dragon was a fearsome creature to behold.

Letting out a breath, she lifted her face to the sun and accepted that change was coming. Though she was afraid, though she felt underprepared, these people believed in her. They needed her to be calm and to take them to safety.

She could do this.

The dragon surrounded her in warmth and strength. Scales

shimmered to life all down her form. She grew larger and larger, the stretching sensation no longer uncomfortable but welcome.

When it was done, she lifted her long neck and saw the world as a much smaller place. She couldn't cry in this form, couldn't express her emotions other than anger or rage. Sigrid stretched her wings wide and stretched them up into the air. She gave a few test flaps before selling back down, wings pressed against the ground, the claws at her knuckles digging into the ground.

Raheem stood a few paces away, waiting for her to look up and nod. He started moving the men one by one to her back. They were heavy, but not impossible to carry.

She stayed still and silent until the last man was tied onto her.

Raheem patted her side. "That's the last one. How do you want to pick me up?"

She looked up into the sky then back at him.

"Ah," he said with a cough. "First time for everything, I suppose. Go ahead."

There wasn't any chance she could lift herself into the air with him and all the others as well. She needed a running start.

Sigrid raced on all fours, the movements awkward but effective. Galloping across the sands, she gained enough speed until she could leap into the sky and pound the air with her great wings. They lifted into the sky and the men on her back gave a shout. She could smell their fear, but it only made her all the more determined. They wouldn't ever feel fear again if she had anything to do with it.

Circling the abandoned kingdom, she found Raheem on

the sands below. He was a small dot already, but not so small that she couldn't see him.

Sigrid swooped down and grabbed him with her back foot, then lifted to the clouds once more. Together, they would travel to freedom.

But the wind under her wings felt bitter cold. Sigrid tilted her long neck to stare back at the sands unfolding behind her, and her heart hardened beneath ice.

NADIR

NADIR'S ARMS BURNED, HIS THIGHS ACHED, AND HIS LUNGS struggled for air, but it still wasn't enough. He couldn't focus, couldn't think. He only knew that his mate was far from his reach now, and there was nothing he could do about it.

Another heaving breath rocked through him, and he couldn't control it. He couldn't even control *himself*.

He'd never lost control. Not once in his life, even when his brother died. Yet, this little Wildewyn girl had unraveled his self-control and now he was crouched in the hidden cavern under his palace trying to breathe. Why couldn't he breathe?

A cough rocked through him, the sound guttural and all too familiar. The dragon tried to claw its way out of his throat, and heat rose in his chest. He was burning up from the inside out, but he couldn't let the monster free. The dragon would burst out of the castle and search for her to the ends of the earth. It would burn villages along the way, regardless of Bymerian or Wildewyn homes. It would destroy everything in its path to make it to her side.

He struck the ground with a fist, tearing open his knuckles. He would not let it out. No matter how much he wanted to follow her, she'd made her choice. She had chosen to live in Wildewyn. She had chosen to support the Beastkin who had attacked his people for centuries.

Sigrid had renounced everything they had built with little thought other than to beg him to come with her.

Go with her? Was she mad? This was his kingdom! His people, his home, his blood, they all resided here within these walls.

And he knew it wasn't some misplaced respect or guilt that kept him here. She'd made him feel more tied to this land than he'd ever felt before. It wasn't his fault that he had a taste of what being sultan was truly like. That blame was entirely on her.

He coughed again, smoke billowing through his lungs and pouring from his nostrils. The dragon disagreed with him. It wanted to prove that Nadir was lying to himself, that life was better with her at his side regardless of where they were.

He couldn't let the monster win.

The cave echoed with the distinct crack of boots meeting stone. A familiar voice met his ears. "What are you doing down here, boy?"

"Not now, Abdul," he growled, turning away so his advisor wouldn't see the feral eyes and smoke coming out of his nose. "I'll return to the advisors soon. Allow me a few moments."

The footsteps approached instead of leaving.

"Abdul, what did I tell you?"

But he was beyond caring. He remained crouched on all fours. Let his advisor see what he truly was. If the man dared to claim that Nadir was a Beastkin as well, all others would laugh at him. They wouldn't believe him no matter how hard he tried to spread the rumor.

Abdul knelt in front of Nadir, tucked a finger under his chin, and lifted his face.

It wasn't horror that Nadir saw in his advisor's eyes, but pity. "Ah, so that's the way of it then."

"Are you not shocked?" he growled. "Your revered sultan is one of the hated beasts himself."

"I'm not," Abdul replied. "I've always known what you were, boy, although I couldn't tell you for fear of what you'd do with that knowledge. Some secrets are passed through families, and though you wouldn't believe it, I fought at your father's side in many a battle. I was there the day you were born."

"My mother didn't care to tell me that story. She said it was too painful to ever let loose from her lips."

"That's because she wasn't your mother, Nadir."

The words rocked through him. For a moment, even the dragon stilled inside him. Not his mother? Of course, the sultana had been his mother. Why else would they have kept him in the palace? Raised him with Hakim as an equal?

He shook his head. "What blasphemy are you speaking of?"

"The revered sultana was not your mother. Beastkin blood is passed through the mother's line, and if you paid attention in your schooling, you would have questioned this much sooner. Your brother certainly did." Abdul released Nadir's chin and stood. He held out a hand. "Come with me, son. Let me tell you your story so that you might understand your own history."

Nadir didn't want to know. He wanted to remain the son of the Sultan and Sultana of Bymere, the youngest boy that was little more than a miracle when his mother hadn't been able to conceive after Hakim.

If that wasn't his tale, then who was he?

His hand lifted of its own accord, and he allowed Abdul to pull him to his feet. The advisor led the way to a stone bench that was mostly whole and pointed to its twin a few feet from him. "Sit, Nadir."

He sat without question.

"Your father was an honorable man. He loved his sultana with all his being, a rarity when he could have had as many wives as he wanted. But he kept only one wife and was happy with that until he found a concubine in the deserts. We'd been fighting for a long time. The Beastkin were attacking villages across Bymere, and we didn't know how to stop them.

"Then, out of nowhere, a woman walked out of the desert. She was the most beautiful creature any of us had ever seen. Small, dark-haired, dark-eyed, she seemed like something out of a story. None of us stopped her when she walked right up to your father and asked for his help."

Abdul shrugged and lifted his hands. "What man could have resisted her? Your father laughed and asked what she wanted from the Sultan of Bymere. We thought she would ask for gold, but instead she asked for a child.

"I thought your father was going to swallow his tongue. It was the first time I've ever seen him speechless, and we were all certain he'd turn her away. He loved the sultana more than life. But then...he agreed. He followed her into the desert and told us all to wait for a few days. If he didn't return, then we were to leave him.

"He returned. Healthy, whole, but changed in a way I couldn't understand. Something had happened in the desert that made him a different man." Abdul ran a hand over his silver-haired head. "And not in a good way. We retreated to the Red Palace and pulled all our forces out of the deserts. It was the first and only reprieve in killing the Beastkin."

Nadir could guess where this tale was going. But he wanted to hear it from Abdul, not make assumptions. "How long did the fighting stop?"

"Nine months."

"Of course." Nadir slumped forward, resting his head in his hands. "Keep going."

"I can stop if you wish, Your Majesty."

"*Keep going.*"

Abdul cleared his throat. "I thought it odd, but none of us had counted the months of peace. We simply enjoyed being with our families for the short amount of time. I didn't expect to be personally called by the sultan, but a messenger arrived in the middle of the night announcing that I'd been summoned.

"We didn't go to the palace. Instead, the messenger brought me across the sands where I met with the sultan. He sat on his horse, staring down at a hut, and told me to stay until I heard a baby crying. Someone would put the baby in front of the door, and I was to take it to the palace.

"I knew then, where we were. I picked you up as a babe, and I saw those strange eyes. Yellow eyes, as no person has ever had before. I knew what you were then, even when I brought you back to the palace and met with the sultan in private.

335

"The sultana took you in her arms the first moment I arrived and looked at you with so much love in her eyes. Never doubt that your family wanted you, Nadir. You might not have been the sultana's by blood, but she always thought of you as her son. We all vowed that night that we would never tell anyone but your direct family. Hakim knew of it the first moment he saw you. But that boy was always good at keeping secrets."

Nadir stared at the ground between his feet and tried to keep the vomit behind his teeth. When he swallowed hard, he said between gritted teeth, "You've known all this time?"

"Long enough that I knew it would be a bad idea for you to keep that girl around."

"Girl?" Nadir shook his head. "None of this was her fault."

"Nadir, that is where you are wrong. A farmer arrived a few hours ago. He'd been passing through to his village when he saw her at an abandoned castle a few days ride from here. It took a while for him to get here, but he recognized one man that none of us will ever forget. Jabbar the White."

The air turned chilly at the name. Jabbar the White was known throughout the kingdom as a murderous, cold-hearted man. He'd killed hundreds of humans in the wars. His favored method was barehanded, because he liked to see his victim's eyes as he killed them.

Sigrid was with him? She had chosen to side with the most dangerous man Bymere had ever fought?

Nadir looked up. "It can't be possible."

"Though I don't like to make any excuses for the girl, she doesn't know who he is. The librarians said she was looking through some of the books related to Beastkin, but not one that included him within its pages. She would have no way of knowing what he wants, or what he has done."

He lost his breath again. Sigrid was in more danger than he could ever have imagined. That butcher had his claws in her, and Nadir was sitting underground.

"I have to find her." He gasped. "I have to bring her back here to safety."

"You will do no such thing. You are needed here, in the Red Palace, where your people can see you, speak with you, air their grievances."

"Anyone can sit on that throne and listen to them complain, Abdul. It's not a difficult job to tell one farmer to shut his mouth and the other to stop letting his cows into the wrong pasture. I need to bring her back."

Abdul sighed. "I'm not asking you to do that, Nadir. I'm telling you that your people have seen a dragon today. Not you, but a dragon that frightened them all the same. They cannot see you fly away from the Red Palace, in your human form or in your dragon form. They need you to be strong for them."

Nadir felt the responsibilities of his station press down on his shoulder. His advisor was right. He needed to calm the populace of the Red Palace so they didn't panic. His people needed to understand that they were safe no matter what Beastkin took to the skies.

But his mind wandered to Sigrid, who had no idea that a murderous bastard had taken her away from him. She wouldn't fall in love with the albino butcher. She couldn't.

They were made for each other, that much he knew now. Regardless of their dragon souls that called out for their mate, he knew her soul echoed his. Human or dragon, they were bound.

Why couldn't he have gone with her?

Abdul stood and strode to Nadir's side. Gently, his advisor placed a hand on his shoulder. "Regardless of what you are, you've been a good sultan. You've listened to those of us who have kept you in line. You've learned as much as possible, and accepted your failings. You've hidden this dangerous part of yourself that could have destroyed all of Bymere. Your parents would be proud of you, my boy."

"They were." He hadn't known either of his parents knew about his affliction. Hakim had been the first person to find him during a change. Nadir had been hunched over, coughing, fire billowing out of his lips with every exhalation.

Perhaps, he should have known then how strange it was that Hakim hadn't flinched. His brother had merely pulled up a chair and watched, elbows braced on his knees. He'd waited until Nadir calmed down enough before he reached forward and put a hand to his shoulder.

"You are cursed, brother," he had said. "And it is not a curse I can break. But know that I will always fight by your side and help you control this monster inside you. I vow it."

And he had. Until his last dying breath, Hakim had made certain that his younger brother knew what it felt like to be loved. His last words, weak and flimsy, made it very clear what Nadir had to do.

"Keep hiding," Hakim had croaked through cracked lips and a face so sunken it already looked like he'd been claimed by death. "They can never know what you really are."

Nadir took a deep breath and nodded. "What now then? She's gone, and I don't know what to do with myself."

"You'll continue being Sultan of Bymere. You'll speak with your people and ease their worries. Let them know you are not afraid of a dragon, and that we have the means to battle her if she returns. They will listen to you, my boy. You've proven to be an attentive sultan these past few months." Abdul paused, then cleared his throat. "Another thing I might thank the Beastkin for. I didn't like her methods, but she certainly woke you up."

"She's a remarkable woman," he replied. Then shook his advisors hand off his shoulder and stood. "A speech? Now?"

"They're already gathered, uncalled for, but they're still here. They've been crying out your name for the better part of the morning. You might have heard them if you weren't down here." Abdul bowed. "The kingdom needs you, Sultan."

The words bloomed with pride in his chest, though it was a bittersweet ache. Pride and guilt warred side by side until he couldn't figure out who he was.

The Sultan of Bymere who stood by his people until the bitter end? Or the man he was slowly becoming with Sigrid at his side?

Nadir couldn't tell. She had placed ideas in his head that made it difficult to think, let alone decide. She'd helped him with that. All the thoughts in his head stilled when she made her way into the room. Like his mind was a sweltering desert, all the air wavering with heat, until she strode out of the sands like a mirage and doused him with cool air and babbling brooks.

Romantic, but the truth.

"Then let us speak with the people of Bymere," he said.

Together, they ascended the stairs and stepped out into the

339

castle. Sunlight blinded him immediately, and he lifted a hand to block the light. Why did it feel like he was stepping backward? All the things Sigrid had said burned a hole in his mind and he still felt as though something was missing.

Shaking his head, he strode ahead of Abdul and made his way to the garden where he knew his people were gathered. That was where they always gathered, for ceremonies, for serious declaration, and for war.

They waited for him beyond the small cliff. Thousands of people, all packed shoulder to shoulder, their voices stilling the moment they saw their sultan striding toward them.

The last time he stood here had been beside her. Nadir picked his way through the garden, imagining that he stepped in the same footsteps as before. He could still remember the way she'd stood, proud and straight. The way the air sang through the threads of her hair and brought with it her icy scent.

His stomach clenched. Would he see her again? Likely not, and if he did, it wouldn't be a friendly meeting. Jabbar the White had sunk his claws into her.

Sigrid was effectively lost to him, and he hadn't even realized she was running. Could he have done something different? He hadn't kidnapped her. Neither of them wanted the marriage, and he'd been respectful. Hell, more than respectful. Any man had a right to claim what was his, but the thought never crossed his mind. She would have put up a glorious fight, but he knew he would have won in a battle between them.

And yet…it had never crossed his mind to even consider forcing her. He hadn't even wooed her, not really. She didn't want that.

He tilted his head up and let the slight breeze play across his sweaty forehead. The masses of Bymere waited for him to speak, to condemn the woman who lived in his heart like a living, breathing embodiment of the future he could never have.

"My people," he called out. The wind ripped his voice away and carried it across the crowd like a whip striking at the air. "Today will go down in history as the first time a dragon returned to the sands."

A rumble started. His people whispered to each other, the hushed sound quickly becoming a combined shout into the air.

Nadir lifted a hand, and they stilled. "I'm here to tell you there is nothing to fear."

But there was. There was so much to fear when the Beastkin were mobilized and Jabbar the White had a dragon in his pocket. A thunderbird and a dragon could do so much damage to the city he loved.

"We will stand together as we always have. Our armies are prepared. Our soldiers capable of taking down a winged beast." He swallowed and forced the words out of his mouth. "I will fight by their sides if need be. I vow to be more than just your sultan, but your protector as well. If the Beastkin wish to rise and take Bymere, then they will have to go through me first."

The cheer that blasted through the air rushed toward him. Nadir soaked in their approval and their confidence in him, knowing that he would need it very soon. The winds of change were coming for Bymere, and he didn't know if that were a good or bad thing.

Before his facial expression changed, he turned and strode back through the palace. Let them revel in the knowledge that their sultan would stay with them.

Abdul jogged after him. "You did well, they'll want more than just a few words though. Turn around, give them a plan."

"I don't have a plan, Abdul."

"The advisors have spent the past few hours and we—" Abdul ran into Nadir's back when he stopped in the hallway.

"I have no plan," Nadir growled. "I'm not interested in listening to the advisors' thoughts on this. Leave me alone, Abdul, in silence. I will consider the current situation and call the advisors to me when I'm prepared to advise *you* on how we will proceed."

His advisor's jaw dropped open, and he did not follow as Nadir walked away. Even putting his advisors in their place was a bittersweet victory when he didn't have her to celebrate with.

SIGRID

COOL AIR SLID BENEATH SIGRID'S SCALES AND CARESSED HER SKIN.
Emerald green leaves stretched as far as her eye could see.
Clouds brushed over her wings and chilled her heated skin.
This was what she had missed, and Wildewyn had been
waiting for her.

If it were possible for the lush forests to be even more
beautiful than before, they were. Autumn would soon be here,
and those leaves would turn to red and gold. The entire forest
would look as though it were set on fire. Sigrid let out a long
sigh.

Why didn't it feel like home anymore?

Her heart ached, overwhelmed with the beauty of her
homeland and knowledge that she could never see it the same
way. Love made it difficult for her to breathe as the emotion
rose over her head like a great wave. Love for her people, for
her country, and for a place so far away that she could no longer
feel its warmth.

Raheem shifted in her back foot and shouted, "We must be close!"

They were. Greenmire castle was just over the mountain in front of them. It wouldn't be long before she saw the place where she had been imprisoned for nearly her entire life. How would she see now that she'd left?

Sigrid was bringing an army with her, although they didn't know that and it wasn't a large one. Would her sisters agree to leave the castle? Or would they insist on staying where it was safe and comfortable?

She hoped not. They were in a cage, although some of them might not view it as that. But she wouldn't force them. No one would force the Beastkin to do anything they didn't want to again.

Wings spread wide, she glided on a large updraft of air. The membranes strained to hold all of them up, and she oddly felt as though they were bruised. She glanced down and saw purple and black splotches blooming on the pale white stretch of her wing. Perhaps the weight of all these men had been too much for her after all.

But it was almost over, and then she would be back in her sisters' arms. They would enfold her in their warmth and love. Healing her from the inside out.

An updraft helped her surge over the white peak of the mountain and down into the valley where Greenmire castle stood. It was a beautiful building, made entirely of white marble. Spires lifted into the air from the seven towers circling the main part of the castle which stretched high into the air. Stained glass windows, taller than seven men, could be seen even from their height.

Sigrid's heightened sight helped her pick out the tiny, ant-like people wandering through the gardens and through the courtyard. The first person saw her, pointing up and letting out a scream that echoed through her mind and body.

They'd seen her, and now she couldn't turn around. Determination fueled her. Sigrid tucked her wings to her sides and plummeted from the sky toward the largest courtyard in the castle. She landed hard, huffing out a breath and curling her back foot inward to keep Raheem from harm.

Screams erupted from every direction. Women in elaborate dresses ran from the scene, while noblemen in embroidered doublets shouted for the guards. The silver-armored soldiers arrived quickly. Their helms gleamed in the sunlight, the hammered edge of their chestplates looking nearly as sharp as the spears they held in their hands.

She slowly backed away from them, hissing out an angry breath. Their plan was for her to stay in the dragon form as long as possible. She'd told them it wasn't likely that she would be able to stay in that form for long, but the men were still strapped to her back. If she changed, they would plummet to the ground and they were already injured.

The soldiers stood shoulder to shoulder, lifted their spears, and slowly advanced. She'd seen them fight like this before, and knew it was a death sentence for any caught in the trap they were creating.

She hissed again and released her hold on Raheem. He would have to be her voice for the time being, at least until they could untie the men who relied on her dragon form. Then she could shift, and they would all understand.

To his credit, the Bymerian rolled out from underneath her

and strode underneath her raised wing as if he'd done it a hundred times.

Raheem lifted his hands into the air. "Stop! We mean you no harm."

"Arriving on the back of a dragon suggests otherwise." The general? Sigrid recognized his voice but couldn't see his face under the helm. Alexandre wasn't supposed to be here. He should be guarding the border, not here in the castle.

"It was the fastest and safest way to get here. Put down your weapons, and we can talk."

"I'll not have a Bymerian ordering my men about."

Raheem kept his hands lifted and stopped next to Sigrid's head.

She eyed the soldier nearest to her, far too close for comfort. Her lip curled and the snarl that rumbled from her throat was thoroughly terrifying. She'd have been more pleased with herself if it didn't cause the rest of the soldiers to step forward in unison.

"I wouldn't do that if I were you," Raheem said with a chuckle. "She's a dragon, gentleman. Large enough to knock all of you to the ground if she wanted, so why don't you take a deep breath and back away."

"Forward!" Alexandre shouted.

Soon, she would feel the bite of spears. Sigrid lashed out with her tail, knocking the deadly barb at the end against the metal tips of the spears nearest to her. They clanged against her scales and the soldiers let out a shout.

Just as she thought they would attack and she would have to do something to protect the men on her back, a familiar voice shouted, "Halt!"

Sigrid lifted her head high to see Hallmar as he rushed down the palace steps. The royal blue doublet on his chest made his dark hair reflect blue. A large, jewel encrusted mantle draped over his shoulders. He looked a little older than she remembered. The gray hair at his temples had spread and he walked with a limping gait that was new.

What had happened while she was gone?

She let out a huffing breath and waved her tail again. Gently pushing the soldiers away, she gave them her back. Raheem still stared at them, so she folded her wing around him and pulled him to her side. He needed to take the men off her back so that she could speak with her king.

"Sigrid," he scolded. "We're not out of the fire yet."

Silly man, didn't he realize she *was* the fire?

Her insistent urging finally broke him. He gave a grumble and reached up to untie the first man. Once they all slid from her back, she quickly melted back to her own form. Her clothes were loose fitting and clearly made for men, hair tumbling down her back in a tangle of loose curls and old braids. She wasn't exactly presentable to the king, but it would have to do.

Exhaustion hit her like a stone wall. She stumbled and fell to a knee, her lungs heaving as she tried to drag in enough air. Bruises covered her arms which were puffy and swollen. She shouldn't have pushed herself quite so much apparently.

"Sigrid," Hallmar's voice rang with warmth. "You've returned to us."

Footsteps echoed beside her, and Raheem slid her mask across the ground. She stared down at it with new eyes. It wasn't a cage, not anymore, but a symbol of her people. Walking into the castle barefaced, enraged, and a proven dragon would help no one. They needed to listen to her words, not be lost in their own thoughts.

The mask was cold to the touch. She slid it back into place, hooking it into her braids that held it in place. Perhaps it was for the best, anyways. She would need to hide her emotions here. A task easier said than done.

She looked up from her crouched position and met his gaze. He was truly happy to see her. She could see it in his eyes, and Sigrid realized immediately that *this* was what she had been missing in Bymere. He didn't try to touch her, didn't say anything other than a few words, but she could feel his thoughts radiating from deep inside his soul.

The Bymerians might wear their emotions on their sleeves, but Earthen folk felt with their souls.

She inclined her head respectfully. "My king."

"We hadn't expected you to return so soon." He paused, hesitant in his next words. "Or alone."

"The situation in Bymere has changed. I need to speak with you in private."

"Should I be concerned?"

She slowly stood and met his gaze. "I'll let you decide this after I tell you everything that has occurred."

Hallmar looked at the ragged Bymerian men behind her. His eyes narrowed slightly, gaze landing on each individual as he pieced together her story without words. He had always been a perceptive man. She had no doubt he already knew what she was going to say.

He sighed and said, "Sigrid, what have you done?"

"I think you've already guessed."

"I have, but I hadn't expected..." He ran a white gloved

hand over his face. "Who are they?"

"Bymerians who need our help."

"We don't help Bymerians."

He was pushing her to admit what he had already guessed. Sigrid shook her head. "Not here. I need medical attention for these men, preferably healers I can trust."

"I can call the herbalist—"

"No," she interrupted. "You know what I'm asking for Hallmar. I need more than just a healer for them, but protection and understanding. Solitude and secrecy are the utmost importance to me."

Hallmar nodded and gestured for Alexandre. "Lead these men to the Beastkin quarters. No one else is to enter other than them."

The captain of the guard took his helmet off, revealing a handsome face with blond, curly locks framing it. "Your Majesty, none enter their private quarters other than women of their own kind. They won't allow these men to enter."

Sigrid cleared her throat for their attention. "Let them know that I ordered it. They will allow these men into their domain as long as they know they stand with me."

She hoped. Her sisters were suspicious at best. They had to be. Their lives were constantly at risk. Hopefully, they still trusted her enough to allow these men sanctuary. They would all need to get used to each other eventually, regardless.

Alexandre nodded his head, hesitating a moment before he left. He had a right to be reluctant. The man had never particularly liked Beastkin. She'd overheard him once say that her kind made him feel inferior. The women were easily stronger than any man in the Wildewyn army, and he didn't know how to reconcile that in his mind.

Let them be afraid. They should be.

Hallmar looked her over and sighed. "Shall we? I assume my office will suffice for what you have to say."

"Yes." She turned to Raheem. "Stay with the men, make sure my sisters know who you are, and why you are allowed to remain with the Beastkin."

"As you wish, Sultana." He bowed low, but his eyes remained on the soldiers and Hallmar. "Make sure they know I am your sword should you need it."

She wanted to tell him that she wouldn't. She could take care of herself, likely better than he could take care of her, but she was touched that he cared. Sagely, she nodded and watched them all leave. A few of the Beastkin men were helping the others walk.

"The journey was hard on them," Hallmar observed. He tucked his hands behind his back and strode towards the castle. "I suspect you have traveled very far."

"All the way from Bymere."

"And these men... they likely are not men that your husband would approve of you being around?"

"Unlikely."

"Then the situation in Bymere is worse than we ever imagined."

They walked through the giant doors and into the castle where she had spent most of her late childhood. The cool stone floors were familiar underneath her feet. Vines crept in through the carved windows and through broken glass panes. If the land wanted to join them in their homes, the Earthen folk did nothing to stop it. They merely built around it.

A giant tree stood in the center of the castle, sunlight filtering through the stained-glass roof and giving it life. Twenty people could circle its trunk with hands linked, and the legend was that it was over three thousand years old. She'd never seen anything like it in the wild.

As they passed, she touched her fingertips to her forehead in reverence. Hallmar cleared this throat, and she glanced up to see the warmth in his gaze.

"So," he said, "you have not forgotten our ways."

"It would be impossible to do so, your highness."

"I'll be honest, even I was slightly worried. Some of the Council members thought you would fall under their spell and become entirely Bymerian yourself. The desert is a natural home for someone like you."

A small part of her had loved the sand and heat. The dragon was comfortable there. No trees would press in on her large body, no branches in the way of her flight. But the more connected she was with her inner beast, the more she appreciated her own home as well.

"There is a beauty here that lives in my soul," she replied. "Wildewyn is my home and always will be. Bymere is beautiful. Its people are very different though."

They made their way down a hallway in silence. She counted the slats of light from the roof, knowing it was exactly fifteen until they reached Hallmar's personal office. He held the wooden door open for her, and she stepped into the room that had always felt like an extension of her home.

A large fireplace in the center, made of riverstones held together with earth, crackled merrily with heat. His oak desk took up an entire corner while fur-covered chairs took at the other. He'd never been a man interested in finery. Instead, he preferred comfort.

She sank into one of the chairs and sighed as the sheepskin cushioned her body. Bymerians knew how to make things comfortable with their cool silken fabric and cushions. But there was nothing like a straight back chair with sheepskin blankets.

Hallmar seated himself closer to the fire and relaxed along with her. "Well? What have you done now, my brave dragon?"

Her lips twisted into a smile. "Did you know there were male Beastkin?"

The fact that he didn't react said volumes.

Sigrid blew out a breath. "You did."

"I knew that there used to be male Beastkin, but not that they were still alive."

"You're lying to me. I can smell it." The dragon in her reared to the surface, her eyes burning with a heat so profound that she knew her eyes must have turned cold. The colors dimmed in the room.

"You're much closer to your beast now than you ever were," he mused. "I don't know if that's a good or bad thing."

"It's good. I feel more like myself than I ever have."

"And the men, these are the male Beastkin you found in Bymere? Do you expect us to welcome them into our fold as well? There will be many who dislike the idea of your population being able to grow so easily."

"I have no interest in speaking with anyone but you." She leaned forward, elbows braced on her knees. "Hallmar, they were mistreated in Bymere and it made me realize that myself and my sisters are mistreated here as well. We aren't pets. We aren't dangerous creatures you can keep locked up in cages so that we don't make you frightened of what we might do next."

He remained silent, blue eyes meeting her own. Hallmar was a master of keeping his thoughts hidden from all around him. He had to be as king.

Sigrid continued. "I'm not here to ask for your help or your acceptance. I'm taking my sisters and these men to Woodcrest. Along the way, I'm also going to stop and gather the rest of the Beastkin who have been spread across Wildewyn for too long. We are not starting a war within Wildewyn, we're not interested in fighting. I wanted you to know our plan and that we will be sending the inhabitants back to Stoneholt and Greenlea. The region of Woodcrest is effectively under Beastkin control now."

His eyes widened as she spoke. Sigrid knew this was a lot for him to take in, and likely that he would try and stop her. He wouldn't give up a portion of his kingdom without trying to fight. He wouldn't be as good of a king if he didn't.

"You want me to just...hand you the keys to your own kingdom?"

"Like I said, I'm not asking." Pity made her stomach churn. "I know this is hard for you to take in, and I don't blame you for any anger you may be feeling now. I have an army at my disposal that could tear through Wildewyn in a moment, but I have no wish to use it."

"An army? What army is this?" Hallmar spread his arms wide, nearly hitting the stone fireplace behind him. "I see no army with you, Sigrid. I see a group of wounded men who can barely stand on their own. Your sisters are locked far away from you. I could end this right now."

"You couldn't. I'm a dragon, you so easily forget, and I

could crush this castle if I wanted to." Sigrid shook her head firmly. "No, you misunderstand me. These are the weak and the wounded, the ones I wanted you to see so that you might feel some pity. The rest are already on their way to Woodcrest, I will meet them there with the rest of their kin. I'm not asking you to fight us, I'm not warning you of impending doom. I'm asking you to see who we are, what has happened to us, and understand that we are simply taking back what is ours."

"This land was never yours."

"We came from the mountains in Woodcrest. Our home is still there." She remembered it only slightly. The safe wooden cabins, the sound of birds crying overhead, the rush of the sea. Her mother reading by the fire and entertaining children with her dramatic voices. She'd only been three or four, but these memories stayed with her.

"You're making a grievous mistake, Sigrid." Hallmar met her gaze and held it, so much emotion in those depths that she could barely understand his words. "Wildewyn is already in turmoil. There's no need for this."

"What turmoil?" She pointed to his leg. "I already noticed the limp."

"There are some council members who did not react well to your union with the Bymerian sultan. Disturbing rumors have started that there is a war coming to us, and your return is not likely to help." He pressed a hand against his hip and winced. "I got into a particularly nasty discussion with the Greenlea leader who has been feeling the pressure of Bymerians on his borders."

"Discussion?" The Earthen folk were already worried then. Her return would only make them even more nervous about their future. Especially if she carved an entire region away for herself. Sigrid sighed. "I will speak with my people and see if we need the entire region. Those who are comfortable with Beastkin may remain in the same area, but they will see us in the wilds. There will be harsh punishment for any who attack us."

"It's something."

"I'm sorry it had to be like this." She reached forward and took his hand. He let out a sharp breath of surprise. "You've always been like a father to me, Hallmar. I am very grateful for all that you have done for me, but it's far past time that we broke out of these cages. I hope you will work with me and my people in the future for a mutual understanding."

He gripped her hand. "I'll be far more understanding of it than the rest of Council."

"I know."

"Are you going to cut off my hand now?" He let out a chuckle. "I'm afraid you have my sword arm, Sigrid. I'd be loath to lose it."

"Many things are changing. Some of our old traditions need to give way to new ones."

Curiosity bloomed in his eyes. "Shall I see your face someday, then?"

"Perhaps. Small steps first though." She stood. "I need to go to my people now. They will wonder what is going on."

"I'll speak with the Council. I cannot guarantee that you'll leave without some form of resistance."

"They won't have the chance."

She left his private quarters and walked down the halls of her childhood with growing apprehension. Had her sisters accepted the male Beastkin into their quarters or would she find them at each other's throats? There was no guessing how her people would react. They were volatile when surprised.

Rounding the familiar corner, she was pleased to see no one had been left in the hallway. Instead, two guards stood outside the doors with more likely lurking in the corner.

She gave them a polite nod, placed her hand on the door, and breathed out a steadying sigh. Whatever was beyond the door, she would handle it as their leader. Soon the weight of responsibility wouldn't just be on her shoulders. She could do this for a little while more.

Sigrid gave the door a shove and strode into the private quarters of the Wildewyn Beastkin.

Both sets of people stood on either side of the room. Some of the Bymerian men were seated on the floor—those who couldn't remain standing even if they tried. The others stood around them in a protective circle.

Her masked sisters clustered together on the other side, staring at the men with a mixture of shock and fear. Sigrid remembered what that felt like. The mixed emotions of a brightening future and the understanding that they had been lied to their entire lives. That there was more in the world that they hadn't even attempted to find because they hadn't the faintest clue that it was out there.

Brynhild stood at the front, her long blonde hair in a braid over her shoulder. It struck her metal chestplate every time she breathed. The cold gaze of her sister flicked to the door and returned to the men, only to slowly return back to Sigrid when she realized who had entered.

Her voice cracked on a quiet utterance. "Sigrid?"

"I've returned for you, sisters."

They raced towards her, each laughing and crying in their happiness. Ingrid, Freya, Astrid, Hilde, more people than she could count. They wrapped their arms around her and welcomed her back into their home with loving touches and shouted laughter that rose into the rafters.

This was what she had missed. Her throat tightened and tears flooded her vision as she laughed with them. There were no words for a little while, only babbled excitement as they all gathered around her.

Brynhild was the first to gather her composure, and she quickly asked, "Where is Camilla?"

"With the others."

"Others?" Her tall sister pointed to the group of men who stared at their antics in shock. "Like them?"

"There's so much I want to tell you, but we don't have time. In short, yes. There are more like them, and we need to find the rest in Bymere. It's time to take back our freedom, sisters. I've already spoken with the king. We're going to Woodcrest. We're taking over our homeland and sending the humans back here or anywhere else they need to go. Beastkin will no longer live in cages or be afraid. We're going to live together in a kingdom of our own making."

Silence met her. Brynhild straightened with pride, but Astrid and a few others curled in on themselves in fear. They weren't predatory creatures. Astrid could turn into a rock lizard, while a few of the others were fishes and seals. They didn't know what the world would hold for them if they left, and Sigrid didn't blame them in their fear.

She reached out for the few who were afraid, tugging them

into her arms. "No fear, not now. We will build a future that is ours by choosing, not held by the limits of what the Earthen folk tell us to do. I know it's not something we planned or desired. But this is our future and we must do something. We cannot live in gilded cages forever."

Brynhild nodded firmly then asked, "What happened in Bymere? You'd never have agreed to this before. You wanted us to live side by side with the humans, not separately as you're suggesting."

"They happened," she nodded at the men. Raheem answered her with a soft smile. "The Bymerians treat them like livestock at best. At worst, as monsters. These are the weakest that need healing before we begin our journey. I brought them here, so you could tend their wounds, and see to their health. I will not be treated like an animal any longer."

"There is more to your story, I can see that." Brynhild strode away from the group and knelt next to the first man. "But we will heal your people, and we will go with you. When we reached Woodcrest, I expect you to tell us everything."

The no-nonsense tone was one she had missed. There were no minced words in the way Brynhild spoke. She knew exactly what she wanted and told everyone around her.

Sigrid found it appropriate that she had knelt next to the man who was a bear shifter as well. Perhaps like called to like, even without them knowing.

She smiled and nodded. "The whole story, and likely more from the men you are helping. Be quick. I'm sure Hallmar is giving us a little time, but the Council will have to be informed eventually."

Her sisters rushed into action, each taking a man,

sometimes two helping depending on the injuries. There would likely be a few fights when they finally reached Woodcrest. There weren't enough men to go around, and many of the sisters had always wished for a husband. Now that there were no rules on who they could see or how many children they could have, there would be a learning period.

Sigrid wasn't looking forward to that. She stepped back until her knees hit a wooden bench and sank onto its surface. There were going to be many changes in all their futures, and she would have to prepare them for it.

The Bymerian Beastkin didn't understand their ways, and now they were the strangers in this land. Earthen folk customs would linger in her sisters, and herself. She didn't know which ones to keep and which ones to get rid of.

The masks? Each of her sisters wore their masks, likely hastily thrown on when the men had been sent inside. They wouldn't know what to do when they saw her remove her own mask. But these men were Beastkin. They were as good as family already.

Perhaps, she had been wrong. They might not wish to remove their masks around the men, and now they would expect that kind of behavior because Sigrid had already set the stage for it.

Could she do what she had done with Nadir? Would they feel understanding, because she cared for them? Or would they be so different from her husband that she would have to learn all over again how to change their minds?

Her head was spinning.

Raheem picked his way toward her and settled next to her on the seat. "What's going through that mind of yours?"

She gestured at her people. "They're my responsibility now."

"It is a great weight, isn't it?"

"How did you know?"

He chuckled. "I've been living close to a sultan for the better part of fifteen years. I know the look of a troubled royal when I see one. He felt the same way many times, you know. All this power resting on your shoulders, and people expect you to make the right choice. But no matter what choice you make, there will always be people who disagree with you."

"It's daunting."

"It's life. Royal or not, there will always be decisions in your life that people will disagree with you for." He looked over at her with a sad smile on his face. "Like falling in love with the sultan."

"I'm not in love with him," she denied. Thankfully, the golden mask hid the burning of her cheeks.

"You have everything you've ever wanted. Your people, your freedom, a purpose, and yet you are sitting here thinking about him."

"I'm not. I'm thinking about all the changes that are coming to our people and wondering if I can guide them in the right direction."

"And comparing your success with them to your success with Nadir. You needn't hide from me, Sultana. I've been there throughout it all. If anyone can understand your mixed emotions, it's me."

Her thoughts whirled with all the possibilities of the future. There was too much out there, too much she didn't know and couldn't predict. All of it swam around her in a sea of decisions she would need to make, threatening to drown her in fear.

"This is really happening," she whispered. "My people are all together now. They've met, they understand the doors opening for them. The Bymerians have all seen me, they know the threat we are and they won't let that go easily. The Earthen folk are losing a large portion of their kingdom and there's nothing they can do to stop it, but they won't let it go easily. Not to mention that our people still need guidance, how to create their own merged culture of both Bymerian and Earthen folk."

Raheem lifted a hand, pausing her in the rant. "You'll figure that out. One thing at a time, first get your people to their new home. Settle them in so that they are no longer hungry and cold. Then tackle each thing as it comes. Otherwise, your thoughts will overwhelm you."

He was right. She took a deep breath and forced the wild rush of her thoughts to still. Finally, she nodded. "You're right."

"I always am."

A small smile broke free at his words. Rocking to the side, she nudged his shoulder with hers. "And arrogant as well I see."

"Anything to see you smile, Sultana." He looked back at her people, nudging her back. "Besides, I think many of your worries are for naught. Look at them. Already, they are tolerating each other far better than I had ever expected."

She followed his gaze and tried to see through his eyes. The female Beastkin were taking care of the men far more gently than they would have each other. Even Brynhild was carefully wrapping gauze around the Bymerians shoulder. His dark eyes were fixed upon her, murmuring words of thanks and wonder as she cared for him.

Hopefully, this kind of behavior would continue once the newness wore off, but she wasn't so sure. She felt a connection to Nadir that she'd never had with her sisters. There was something visceral between them. Something raw and untamed that went beyond logic or reason.

It wasn't attraction. Not that she hadn't felt heat bloom in his presence before, but it was something deep in her soul. He was the other part of herself that she hadn't known was missing. Two pieces in a larger game that came together to create something so much larger than themselves.

She heard a group of people marching toward them. The sound of footsteps and the clinking of armor echoed in the hall beyond. Sigrid stood slowly. "Our time is up."

"There's more we could do for them, sister," Brynhild said, standing as well.

"Matriarch," she corrected.

They all needed to see her as they had before they left. They needed to understand that she was their leader, though she would choose more of them to help when they arrived in Woodcrest. She didn't want to lead alone, but knew in this moment she had to. One person needed to make the decisions right now, or more people would die.

Brynhild hesitated for the briefest moment, and Sigrid knew that she would be difficult when they arrived in Woodcrest. Her sister had enjoyed leading their family too much to give up that right soon.

"Brynhild," she warned. "Now is not the time."

"Matriarch." Brynhild inclined her head, but her words rang with sarcasm. "It is my honor to serve you again."

"We go now. I need seven of you who can fly to go to our other sisters living with the lords and free them as well. If you have any issues, you are to bring them to me immediately. The lords will learn what it means to feel fear if they deny me."

"They won't believe us," her sister replied. "It was always a rumor that you were a dragon, nothing more."

"They'll see me leaving." All would see her as she lifted herself above Greenmire castle. She'd make certain of it. "There are three gryphons here still, yes?" At their nods, she ordered, "Take what men you can on your backs. The others will go on foot. Transform when you must and stay to the shadows. I will meet you back in Woodcrest."

She trusted her sisters to get them all to safety. They wouldn't stand for anyone trying to stop them, not when freedom was so close to her fingertips.

"And you?" Brynhild asked as she helped the bear to stand. "What will you do?"

"I'm going to deal with the Council and make it clear that they are not allowed to follow us."

When she was done, no one would dare step foot in Woodcrest without her permission. She only hoped Hallmar could forgive her.

Her sisters gathered up the men and made their way toward a secret passage only they knew about. They'd always known that the Earthen folk may make a decision they didn't agree with, and had prepared for a flight into the night. But there had never been a reason to leave. Not until now.

Raheem stayed at her side.

"You should go," she said quietly. "This is bound to get ugly."

"I stay by your side. I don't want anyone to get hurt. As you said, that wouldn't end well for anyone."

"You're here to protect me?" She shook her head. "I don't need protecting, Raheem."

"You don't. But it's nice to know someone is there sometimes. You won't stand against them alone."

Gods, how she wished it was Nadir saying that, and not his ever-faithful guard. Why couldn't the man she married understand that? All she wanted was for him to support her, to listen, to know that she wouldn't have made this decision if it wasn't the best one for them.

She shook her head to clear it. "Have they left?"

Raheem glanced behind them and nodded. "Your sisters are rather impressive. That was faster than I would have thought possible."

"Beastkin are impressive creatures. You know that."

"I do." A shadow crossed over his gaze, and she knew he was thinking of his beloved wife. She wished she could have met this paragon of a woman. Although she might not have been a queen or anything more than a farmer's daughter, but Raheem had held her in high regard. That was enough for Sigrid to wonder at what kind of woman she had been.

The door to the Beastkin's private quarters burst open. It was the first time the Earthen folk had forced themselves into the Beastkin's home, and she would make sure it was the last.

Jacques led them, the Council member who hated her kind the most. She knew for a fact that he kept three songbirds in cages, forcing them to remain in their animal forms because he thought it was entertaining. There had never been anything she could do until now.

Now, she would remind him why he should never try to keep a woman in a cage.

Jacques brandished a finger. "Just what do you think you're doing? We are *not* giving you and your people any part of this country. Have you forgotten how we've kept you safe all these years?"

"You've kept us in cages."

"We've kept you away from people who would try to use you to their own advantage! Just how little did you listen while you were here, foolish girl?"

Sigrid's mask hid her infuriated expression. She strode forward inhumanly fast, and he wouldn't have seen her move until she was directly in front of him. She lifted a hand and slapped him so hard he fell back into the other council members.

"You will never use my people as pets again. We are taking Woodcrest whether you want it or not. Do you hear me? If you try and attack us, we will start a war that will end all wars. Our fight is with Bymere currently, but do not think for a second that I will not fight two wars at the same time."

Jacques' mouth gaped open, jaw working as he tried to mouth a retort. Coming up short, he merely looked at Hallmar and flailed a hand in her direction. "Do you see what happens when we give them freedom?"

But the king wasn't looking at the Council member. He was looking at Sigrid with a mixture of pride and sadness. "What is your choice then, Sultana? Your people are fleeing, I assume."

"They are."

"To Woodcrest?"

She nodded. "There will be a few stops along the way, but

please don't try to hide our kin from us. We'll find them, no matter where they are in Wildewyn. News will spread quickly that the Beastkin are gathering in Woodcrest. As I said, if you leave us alone, then I promise we will do the same."

"Are you so certain that you can promise that?" Hallmar crossed his arms over his chest with a gleam in his eye she recognized from the moment when he had tested Nadir. "You have started something you might not be able to control, Sigrid."

A pit formed in her belly. It frightened her to no end that he might be right. She cleared her throat. "If that is the way this ends, then so be it. At least I will know that my people are fighting for their freedom, rather than sitting in their cages."

She stepped away from them and lifted her arms at her sides. Tilting her head back, she closed her eyes and heard Raheem move toward the Council members.

"You might want to move back," he said.

"What is she doing?" Jacques asked.

"You're about to find out."

Her skin and the fabric of her clothes melted away into the dragon. The room was too small for her, but that didn't matter. She stretched her wings and rocked side to side until the stone walls cracked and then crumbled.

The Council members shouted in fear, stumbling back into the main part of the castle. She didn't care if they injured themselves. This wasn't about frightening them; this was about sending a message.

Raheem ran toward her as the floor began to give way under her feet. The stone disappeared under his feet and he leapt toward her. She caught him in a clawed foot and lifted into the air.

The place where they had kept the Beastkin for centuries now was nothing more than rubble attached to the rest of the castle. She beat her wings in the air, hovering above the wreckage, and let out a mighty roar that shook the foundation of stone. Tilting her head back, she let out a banner of fire that made the air shimmer with heat.

Through it all, Hallmar, king of Wildewyn, watched her while holding onto the castle stone. She wished she could stay with the man she might have called father. But there was more to this life than living safely within four walls

Sigrid beat her wings and soared into the sky. Woodcrest and her people awaited her return, and then they would plan their war.

NADIR

"THAT'S IT, MEN!" NADIR SHOUTED. "POSTURES STRAIGHT, EYES ON your opponent! Don't look down at your feet, you should know the footwork by now!"

Over and over he shouted until his voice started to turn hoarse. It had been like this for a week now. He helped train their forces personally. The people wanted to see that they were preparing for an attack, that they would remain safe, and he was going to show them that nothing would get through those walls.

Even if he wasn't certain of that.

"Sultan," Abdul called out behind him. "We've finished the dragon slayer."

The words sent a line of ice and fire down his spine. His hands clenched and an image flashed in his mind. Sigrid, that glorious, moonlight dragon, falling from the sky. His dragon could barely stand the image, and the man hated every second of it.

But he wasn't just a man and he wasn't just a dragon. Nadir was Sultan of Bymere, and his people had to come first. No matter how much he adored his second wife.

Tucking his hands behind his back so no one would see them shaking, he strode away from the sandy training grounds and toward his advisor. They were outside of the palace, on the sands where the sun burned hot but they were visible by all. It was the perfect place to train so everyone knew what they were doing. At least, that was what the advisors said.

Nadir only agreed to go along with their plan because he thought it was good for the men to train where they would fight. He didn't want anyone coming to the Red Palace. The crimson stones would remain untouched in this battle as a symbol of Bymere. He'd see to it himself.

They strode away from the training soldiers, sand glimmering under their feet in the heat waves.

"It's finished already?" he asked.

"The men were enthused to create a beast killer. I think you'll be impressed with what they have done."

Nadir wasn't so sure. He didn't want to see the creation that could kill not only his wife, but also himself.

They crested a sand dune, and there it was. *The dragon slayer*.

It was a simplistic design, something between a harpoon and crossbow that only a giant could have wielded. They placed wheels on either sides, and the base could be rotated. A soldier was already testing it out, leaning down to aim the deadly spear at the sky. The serrated metal tip would stick inside whatever it struck, tearing flesh if the beast tried to pull it out.

The hairs on Nadir's arms raised. He raised his eyes to the clouds for a moment and prayed his wife would not return.

"What do you think?" Abdul asked, crossing his arms over his chest. "It appears as though it would do damage. The question is whether or not we could ever hit the creature."

"It wouldn't be easy."

"All about the speed, eh?" Abdul clapped. "Men, show the sultan what this weapon can do."

The soldiers burst into action. One aimed the dragon slayer away from them, the other pulled a rope attached to a level. The bow cocked back, clicking through intervals until they all paused and shouted, "Release!"

The man holding the rope let it go, and the spear flew so quickly Nadir lost track of it until it passed over the sun. It moved faster than anything he'd ever seen before and with deadly accuracy.

He couldn't react the way he wanted to. He had to be proud of them, even with the pit in his stomach telling him to destroy the machine. That would kill her instantly if they managed to hit her with it.

"Impressive," he finally said. "I've never seen a creation like it before."

"Enough to shoot a dragon right from the sky." Abdul clapped a hand on his back. "If that witch returns, then she'll have a hard time getting close to us."

He was supposed to think this was a good thing. So, Nadir bared his teeth in a mockery of a smile and nodded. "Congratulations, advisor. I do believe this is a weapon that could kill a dragon. Now, how many of them are you building?"

The proud expression on Abdul's face faltered. "How many?"

"Yes, how many. Do you think one of these things will hit immediately? How long does it take to load the weapon? The men cannot hope to hit her on their first attempt. She's a dragon, not a bull."

A voice in his mind screamed to shut up. Let them have the contraption, they would never manage to hit her. The other, more logical side of him saw the weapon as his city's last defense not just against Sigrid.

But against himself as well.

Nadir was torn in two directions, and his heart didn't know which way to look. One side of him, the dragon side, longed for her to return. They could run away together, leave this horrible place behind and find a new land where they could live out the rest of their days. The other side knew how important it was for him to remain here, as sultan, and to continue his family line.

His mother might not have been the sultana, but the blood of a sultan ran in his veins. He had a responsibility to his people and his land.

Abdul interrupted his thoughts. "The men will work on those details. You're right, of course. Impressive, Sultan."

Nadir inclined his head, turned on his heel, and walked away.

Predictably, the advisor wasn't ready to let him go anywhere just yet. Abdul fell into step with him. "How are soldiers training?"

"Well enough."

"Should the Beastkin attack us, we will be ready."

"We don't know if they're going to attack us," Nadir

replied, trying his best not to growl the words. "They may very well retreat and never return."

"Do you think that's likely? Wherever she took them isn't going to compare to what they think is their home. They'll return, mark my words. When they do, we must be ready for them."

Nadir wasn't so sure. Sigrid was a convincing woman, and she wouldn't have left with the Beastkin if she didn't have a plan.

No one had seen a Beastkin since Sigrid left. Everyone in the kingdom was looking for them, assuming that they were lurking in the shadows. But no one had seen a single one. It made the populace nervous, considering the stories usually popped up on a regular basis. Now, they were simply…gone.

Leave it to Sigrid to make an entire race of people disappear with ease.

He stared out over the sands and replied, "She wouldn't want to attack our people unless absolutely necessary."

"There's no reason why it would be necessary. They're animals, we treated them as such."

"Watch your tongue, Abdul," he growled. Yellow eyes flicked to meet Abdul's and his vision shifted to that of what the dragon would see. "You're speaking of my wife."

He didn't need to add that Abdul also spoke of him. The way his advisor paled was enough proof to know the man had already made that connection. Though he was tolerated as a Beastkin because he'd been raised by a man Abdul respected, Nadir didn't think for a second that Abdul truly thought Nadir capable of ruling the country.

After that night in the caverns, Abdul had tried to become

closer with Nadir. Perhaps the man thought that now they shared a secret. He seemed to think even in their meetings that he could speak over Nadir.

For the time being, he would let Abdul think whatever he'd like.

Nadir had plans for his country. There were a hundred and one things he wanted to do for Bymere, and he intended to put those into practice as soon as the advisors were looking the other way. This kingdom needed someone with a firm hand.

Had his parents? He couldn't remember. His brother certainly hadn't. Hakim was more interested in making sure that everyone was happy, even if that meant that his orders were slightly contradictory. And though Nadir had worshiped his brother as a child, he now saw the faults in Hakim's edicts.

This was Sigrid's doing, and he couldn't thank her enough for it. Somehow, this cold woman had brought with her the winds of change. She'd accepted his culture while still retaining her own. It made him realize how much he was missing; how many things he could be integrating into his country that would be helpful.

Nadir straightened and squared his shoulders. "Keep a watch on the men training. Their footwork is still sloppy."

Abdul inclined his head. "Where will you be?"

"The palace."

"Ah, yes. Saafiya has been asking for you."

He knew that she had been scouring the Red Palace searching for her wayward husband. He'd been avoiding her ever since the attack, mostly because he didn't know how to face her. Rage burned deep in his chest that she would dare attack Sigrid, that *she* was the cause of his loss.

He'd never struck a woman before, but his fists curled just at the thought. She had gone too far this time. Eventually, he knew he'd have to confront her.

Today was as good as any other.

Nadir sighed and nodded. "It will be a conversation she doesn't want to have."

"She loves you, Sultan. The choice she made was the best for the kingdom and for you."

Nadir didn't agree with that assessment in the slightest. But he still inclined his head and turned on his heel to make his way back to the palace.

His advisors must have known that at some point he was going to grow up. He wasn't the boy anymore who they could tell what to do, and he would do it without question. He was growing into his manhood, or at least he hoped, in a way that would better the country.

Some of the advisors would be quick to follow this change. He did believe that a few of them loved Bymere as much as he did. Others, such as Abdul and Saafiya, were only advisors because this was their grasp at power. If they could control him, then they were as good as sultans.

Had there been advisors like this when his father ruled? Nadir tried to remember, but he didn't think that he'd ever seen them back then. There were, of course, advisors. They came from far and wide to tell his father their opinions of the outer stretches of Bymere. But there hadn't been so many living in the palace, constantly watching over their sultan.

That needed to change. And he planned on doing it as soon as possible.

Sigrid and her king were right. He was just a puppet for

those who did not have royal blood in their veins. It was time to take back his throne, no matter what they thought.

He strode through the streets with purpose. No guards followed him. They wouldn't need to. Nadir could take care of himself, but he also liked to think that his people trusted him. The trust had grown between Bymerians and their sultan in the recent months.

They understood that he would do everything he could to take care of them. That he had chosen them over his favored second wife, even if he had let her run. Nadir had heard people talking. They didn't blame him for letting such a beautiful woman live.

The men who had seen Sigrid's face very quickly spread the legends of her beauty. She'd become something like a myth in Bymere. The strange woman with a mask who hid her beauty from the world so she wouldn't blind it.

The rumors made Nadir smile. She wasn't quite the paragon they'd built her up to be, she was rather average if he were truthful, but her strength shone through all the layers of her physical body and turned her into something more like a goddess than a woman. He didn't' blame the men of Bymere for falling in love with her instantly.

A commotion from the street ahead caught his attention. Curious, Nadir stepped into an alley. He'd found out so many things lately by simply listening in on conversations. Perhaps not the most glamorous of roles he'd chosen for himself, but people were far more honest with each other than they were with their sultan.

A tiny body raced into the alley after him. The child slammed into his legs and fell backward onto her bottom.

She was little more than a slip of a girl. Dark hair tumbling down her shoulders in tight curls, unusual for a Bymerian child. Her large eyes stared up at him as horror filled their dark depths. Her caramel skin turned ashen the moment she recognized who he was.

Nadir smiled softly, not wanting to frighten her. He stooped down onto a knee and held out a hand to her. "It's all right, don't be afraid. Did you steal something? I'll pay for it if you'd like, provided you don't do it again."

She shook her head, scrambling backward on all fours.

Strange reaction. And here he'd thought all Bymerians within the Red Palace were enjoying his rule.

Nadir tried again, licking his lips. "Not stolen then? I'm a good listener, and it sounds like there's at least a few people chasing you. What did you do?"

A tear leaked from her right eye, traveling down her rounded cheek. She glanced over her shoulder at the sound of footsteps growing ever louder. "I didn't do anything."

Her whisper made little sense. He frowned. "You must have done something, little one. They're chasing you."

Another tear slid down her cheek. "I did nothing, sir. I just wanted to see the dancer from high up. I'm too small to see through all the people. I turned into a dove, like my mother taught me even though she said that I could never, ever do it in public. But the colors were so bright, I just wanted to *see*."

His heart froze in his chest. This little girl with limpid eyes and great crocodile tears was a Beastkin. He'd made it very clear that Beastkin were not welcome within his home, and that they would fight them.

No wonder she was so frightened of him. He must seem

like a demon to her.

Ice spread through his veins. She wasn't a monster, not like the advisors would say. This was a little girl, *a girl*. And they'd thought all female Bymerian Beastkin were gone. She should go to Sigrid. She should be safe with her own people. Far away from *his* reach.

Nadir blew out a slow breath and forced his outstretched hand to remain steady. "Don't worry. I'll keep you safe from them."

"No, you won't. You don't like us, any of us. You want us all to leave Bymere, that's what my mother said."

"Said? Where is she now?"

More tears rolled down the little girl's cheeks, but she forced herself to say, "Dead. They caught her in a cage, and then they took her head off. Just pulled it off like it was nothing, because she couldn't turn back into a person soon enough. I ran away, but I didn't know where to go. I ended up on the streets, and then I did something foolish to see something pretty again."

Gods, his heart was bleeding. Nadir grimaced and murmured, "That's my fault, and I'm sorry for it. I promised to take care of Bymerians, but there are more than just Bymerians here, aren't there? The crowd is getting closer, little one. I know someone who can help you. I'd like to get you to safety, but I need you to trust me. And I know there's no reason for you do to that."

She shook her head firmly.

He continued, "But I need you to trust me even for a few moments. You know what those people will do to you if they catch you. I think taking the lesser known evil would be more preferable than letting them catch you, yes?"

He wasn't certain the child was following his words. She seemed more confused than ever, so he held his breath and waited until she reached out and slipped her tiny hand in his.

"My name is A'dab," she whispered. "Mama said it means hope."

An apt name for this little sprite who made his heart hurt just by looking at her. "It's a good name," he replied. "Now, can I pick you up so we can move faster?"

At her quick nod, he swooped down and lifted her into his arms. Nadir knew this city like the back of his hand. He'd poured over the blueprint designs for his entire life, memorizing all the small alleyways and hidden entrances to buildings. The crowd would never be able to keep up with him.

Racing with the little girl in his arms, he fled through the city to the back door of the Red Palace. The shouts would forever ring in his ears.

"Find the beast!"

"A monster cannot be loose in the streets!"

Once he would have agreed with them, but this little girl wasn't a monster. She was just a little girl, without a mother, who feared for her life.

Gods, what had he started?

These were his people, too. They had to be, although they weren't Bymerians in the traditional sense. They still deserved to live without fear of death. And wasn't that what Sigrid had told him? There had to be another way. There had to be something he could do without starting a war.

Beastkin and Bymerians didn't need to fight against each other. Diplomacy had to be a viable option for the future.

SEA OF CRIMSON SILK

Yet, his gut didn't agree with his mind.

Nadir nudged open the kitchen door to the Red Palace, shoulder against the ancient wood. He ducked his head in, looking around for any servants who might talk. Thankfully, the entire place was empty. Dinner wouldn't start for another hour or so. He'd chosen his entrance perfectly.

He rubbed a hand down A'dab's back. "Stay quiet now. We don't want anyone knowing that you're here."

She nodded and went so still that he wasn't certain she was breathing. Another sign that this child had led a very difficult life. She knew how to remain so still and quiet that she almost didn't exist. He wondered how long she'd been hiding from people who wanted to kill her.

Nadir shivered and slipped into the Red Palace.

This would be the last place anyone thought to look for her. No one would ever think that the sultan himself was hiding Beastkin from the crowds. But then again, no one would ever guess that the Sultan of Bymere was a Beastkin himself.

He stayed to the shadows in the corridors, only ducking behind a tapestry once when a group of concubines passed them. Their giggles filtered through the woven fabric. A'dab lifted her head as they walked by, her eyes filled with something he could only akin to longing.

It was so easy to forget that Beastkin were children once in their life. That they were little girls who dreamed of being beautiful women who could cajole men with little more than their voices. That they were little boys who dreamed of fighting for their sultan and country, playing with wooden swords in the fields.

He ducked into his personal chambers, letting out a long

breath. She'd be safe here. Even if one of his advisors entered without his permission, they would only see her as a child he'd saved off the street, someone he had cast pity on.

They wouldn't see her as a Beastkin.

He set her on the ground carefully, kneeling on the floor with her. "I need you to wash up. Do you know how to do that?"

She gave him a look and nodded firmly. "I know how to do that."

"Any of the pools will do, the water filters away once a day. Take one of my shirts from the chest over there," he pointed, "and put it on. If anyone asks who you are, just say that you're the sultan's new child. And that if they have any other questions, they should ask me. Understood?"

A'dab nodded. "You said you could help me? That you know someone who will keep me safe?"

He did, but how was he going to get a message to Sigrid? Nadir couldn't even hazard a guess where she was now. Between all the secret places in Wildewyn and Bymere, she could be anywhere. Not once had she ever said anything about her homeland where she thought they could be safe. If anything, she'd kept information about her own land very secretive.

He saw now what a mistake that had been to let her keep those secrets.

"I'll find a way to get a message to her," he grumbled, running fingers through his hair. "There has to be a way."

"Are you talking about the golden lady?"

"Who?"

"Everyone's talking about her. That she's like a goddess

carved out of marble, and she flies through the sky on wings of moonlight."

Sigrid. She could only be talking about Sigrid. "Yes, that's exactly who I'm talking about."

"No one knows where she went. She took most of the men with her, but some of the Beastkin in the city have claimed they saw her fly over the Edge of the World with animals on her back."

She had returned to Wildewyn.

Nadir patted A'dab's head. "Thank you for that, little one. That is a good start." He'd figure this out later, but now, he had to confront his first wife. He stood up and gestured to the pool in the corner. "Clean. I'll return soon with food and water for you."

He didn't wait to see if the little girl did as he said. She seemed to be a sweet little thing, one that could easily take direction. She knew when a good thing was happening. Hopefully she would clean herself well enough that whomever saw her next would believe that she was his ward.

The halls echoed with his footsteps, and he wondered just what he was doing. Fighting a war from two fronts? He couldn't be on both sides, and he'd already made his choice very clear. But her big, dark eyes had pulled at something in his gut. He couldn't let her be killed.

Nadir nodded to a guard and strode into Saafiya's private quarters. It was as beautiful as he remembered, although he rarely entered her private domain. It was distinctly feminine in a way that made him thoroughly uncomfortable. Like he'd walked into a den of women and trespassed on sacred land.

She lounged on a large pile of silken pillows, only looking

up when he was close enough to touch her. Her concubines surrounded her, like petals that had fallen off a rose.

"Husband?" Saafiya blinked her eyes sleepily, although he knew it was a ploy to look weak. She was anything but. "I've been asking to see you. Have you finally come to me?"

"Get out," he advised the concubines.

Saafiya held up her hand. "Anything you have to say to me, husband, can be said in front of my handmaidens."

"No, it can't." He bared his teeth. "Get out."

The women were quick to stand and rush out of the room. Perhaps they felt the rush of heat that blasted off him, or perhaps they simply saw the feral look in his eyes. He wasn't a man in this moment, he was nothing more than a predator who wanted to avenge his lost mate. And though he hoped she would return, Nadir wasn't a foolish enough man to bet that he'd get Sigrid back any time soon.

Saafiya slowly rolled onto her side. A delicate gold chain hung from her neck, trailing down her exposed belly and disappearing into the silken skirt she wore.

Perhaps she had known he would come to her, today. She was smart enough to know that he didn't want to hurt a woman. So she had made herself as feminine as possible. The ploy might have worked if he couldn't see defiance glimmering in her eyes.

"They are my handmaidens. You have no right to order them around."

"They are here only because I gave them permission to be," he replied. "Now, you and I have something to speak of."

"Are we talking about the little Earthen girl again? Husband, I will not explain my decision any further. It was the best one for this country. You know how dangerous they are. Beastkin will be the end of Bymere. They are dangerous and they cannot be allowed to wander the streets. She showed her true colors, in the end, did she not? She chose her own people over ours."

He didn't want to listen to a word she had to say, but he was already having trouble controlling his dragon. The beast wanted to break free, to slip from his skin and devour the woman in one fell swoop.

Saafiya stood, silk spilling down her curves like water. She reached out and placed a hand on his shoulder, trailing her fingers over his skin without realizing how much danger she was in.

Her voice fell like a melody in the delicate room. "She chose them over *you*, my love. And I know you don't want to hear it, but those were her true colors. She doesn't feel as strongly for you as you feel for her. And I'm sorry, Nadir. I know how much you enjoyed her company, how much you valued her opinion. It's not an easy thing to lose, but I will do my best to fill that gap."

She leaned forward and pressed her lips against his. Once, long ago, he would have responded immediately with a boyish infatuation that felt at once consuming and overwhelming. But now, the feeling of her lips against his only made him feel cold.

He put a hand to her shoulder and pushed her back. "That's not what I'm here for, Saafiya."

"Then why are you here?" Her voice snapped in the air, the composure she held wrapped around her shoulders fraying like a worn shawl. "I won't allow you to lecture me about right or wrong decisions, Nadir. I did what was best for our country, what *you* couldn't do."

"No, you did exactly what you wanted, and that ends now."

"How? Are you going to punish me if I do my duty for this country? If I fulfill the role of advisor as I have for nearly your entire life? And the role of wife as well?"

"You aren't an advisor anymore." Rage filled his words until he could taste the bitter emotion. "You're no longer allowed anywhere near people who are making decisions for this country. You betrayed not only myself, but all of Bymere with what you did."

"You can't take me off the Council," she said with a laugh. "That's not something that anyone can do without the agreement of the rest. It's a vote, Nadir."

He was aware of that. It was how it had always been. The advisors would listen when he wanted to do something, they would vote, and then they would tell him no. That would no longer happen. He was sultan of this country, and they would hear his edicts.

He reached out and wrapped a coil of her hair around his finger. "No, first wife. Everything is going to change. The country will move forward without you. Your name will sink away into the ancient history books that no one reads, and soon everyone will forget that you exist. You will remain here, in your private quarters with your handmaidens, and you will only be allowed out with my permission."

Her face paled. "You can't do that."

"I can, and I will. You made me Sultan of Bymere. Now, I'm unmaking you."

A surge of victory filled his chest with pride and strength.

Sigrid would have celebrated this victory with him. He was taking back his kingdom and the first step was overthrowing this woman.

Saafiya stepped away from him, nearly tumbling back onto the pillows. "I will speak with the other advisors on this. They won't let you do this."

"What power do they have? I've broken free from the chains you wrapped around my throat when I was just a boy. If they want to argue with me, I'll have them beheaded. Be thankful that I'm not calling for the same in your case."

Nadir turned on his heel and walked away. The surge of triumph would only last so long before dread set in. He needed to go tell the other advisors of this change before his courage waned.

"Husband!" she shouted. "You're doing all this for a little girl who isn't even here. She's never coming back."

He paused at the door, glancing over his shoulder at her. "No, she isn't. And I'm not doing this for her. I'm doing this for our people, as I should have a long time ago."

He left her standing alone in her quarters and told the guards not to let her out without his permission. They stood at attention, but he saw the approval in their gaze.

Nadir was a man on a mission. He would tell the other advisors that he was finally taking the crown for himself, then he would find a way to send a message to Sigrid.

SIGRID

"TOO LONG, WE HAVE LINGERED IN THE SHADOWS!" JABBAR'S voice lifted over the crowd. He lifted his arms and the hundreds of Beastkin gathered around the ruins of Woodcrest castle cheered along with him.

They'd finally found a place they could call home. This strange, unusual ruin would be where they laid their heads to rest. Unfortunately, Sigrid could see there was much work to do.

It was a sturdy beast, but would suit them very well. She didn't remember the squat structure and style of building. It was much more utilitarian than the Earthen folk preferred now. Their buildings were always filled with carved spires and delicate pinnacles. This was mostly square with blunt towers and functional walkways.

It would make a perfect hideout for them, and a safe place to rest their head.

She stood to the side, allowing him to speak to his people

without interruption. He needed a moment to shine. Although Sigrid had been the catalyst, she recognized that she had done nothing other than give them a back to ride on.

The Bymerian people didn't need someone from Wildewyn coming in and saving them. They had been prepared to do that themselves. She just gave them a faster route.

Pale eyes wild, Jabbar punched the air with his fist. "Together, we shall prepare for war. We will return to Bymere and destroy all they tried to keep from us. If we cannot have it, then neither shall they!"

Cold ice skittered through her veins. He wasn't talking about justice or a means for peace. Was he saying this simply because he thought this was right? Or had she misunderstood Jabbar's intent?

Their people certainly had no issues with what he said. Their cheers thundered and their feet pounded the ground until she swore it shook.

Sigrid didn't want to argue with Jabbar in front of their people. That would only end poorly, especially considering the tension between the two groups. Wildewyn and Bymere needed to be a united front. They had to see each other as family, or old prejudices would sink in. She didn't know any other way to pull them out of that.

She stepped close to Jabbar and slid her hand into the crook of his elbow. "Shall we speak? Allow them to go to their work."

His arms slowly fell back at his side. The pink irises of his pupils seemed to be bleeding into the whites, she noticed. Perhaps that was the thunderbird looking back at her.

He nodded curtly, and gestured to the leopard man who was his right-hand man. Sigrid gave a subtle nod to Brynhild, and together they all walked toward a fire set off from the others. It wasn't a perfect place for council meetings, but she appreciated that the rest of the Beastkin were able to see them. They weren't ignoring the difficulties of the future. They were actively, and visibly, working on it.

Sigrid settled on a log and spread her skirts around her. The icy blue fabric somehow felt dull now that she saw so many people wearing the same. She almost missed the vivid colors of Bymere.

"What is it, Sigrid?" Jabbar asked. He reclined on the log, one leg raised with his wrist dangling from his knee. "Do you not agree with the rousing speech I just gave?"

He raised an eyebrow, and she recognized the challenge in his voice. "I don't think we should be promising our people any retribution we have no intention of following through on."

"Oh, I intend to follow through. Didn't you know you were leading a war?" He gestured toward the Beastkin who were going back to work cleaning the old castle, tilling the fields, setting up their home. "They want justice."

"Justice doesn't have to come with the price of blood."

"Of course, it does. What did you think this was? That you were going to create some kind of kingdom for us, and people were going to let you?" Jabbar shook his head. "It doesn't work like that. You have to *take* a kingdom. We're going to be attacked by both sides, and I'd rather have the advantage of surprise."

"We don't have to attack anyone." She leaned forward, clasping her hands together to hide their shaking. "Politics have been conducted for centuries. Talking *can* work."

Brynhild clasped her hands at her waist and shook her

head. "I'm afraid I don't agree with you, Sigrid. There's more than just the worry that the humans will attack us, and I stand by Jabbar on that, but it's also the knowledge that our people have been used for years. They desire retribution. They want the blood and the screams so their souls can rest."

"I refuse to believe our people are that bloodthirsty."

"We are animals at heart," Brynhild reached forward and took her hand. "Isn't there a part of you that wants to see them screaming? That wants to reach into their chest and pull out their entrails so they can feel exactly what they've done to us for so long?"

Not even a single speck of her wanted that. Sigrid held herself painfully still, forcing every muscle on her face to remain as a mask. They had no right to say these things. Beastkin were not animals, that was the message she fought for, and yet now they wanted to behave as one.

She cleared her throat. "I won't stand by this. Needless killing is a waste for both of our kingdoms. What you're asking for is a war started out of pride and greed. This isn't who we are."

Jabbar tsked. "That's your opinion, but what we seek is justice."

"It's blood and death. Nothing more than that." She didn't know how to convince them to see it her way. Humans had a right to their lives as well, all they had to do was talk with them.

Brynhild sighed and shook her head. "You asked to build a council of people, and as I see it, that's what we've built. You're outvoted Sigrid. We prepare for war."

"We haven't officially built any council."

The leopard chuckled, leaned forward, and pointed at

Jabbar. "He's the only one around here who can give orders to the Bymerians. Sorry, little sultana. We might be in your land, but the reality is that he gives the orders around here. We're not following any Earthen folk orders without his agreement."

And in that moment, Sigrid realized that she'd lost control. No one was following her blindly. They knew exactly what they were doing the moment she walked into their camp.

They saw her as their chance at freedom, the key to the chains that bound them.

Now, the beasts were free.

JABBAR AND HIS PEOPLE WERE USED TO LIVING IN RUINS. THEY had seen the crumbling stone castle and cared very little that the floors were slippery with moss and algae. They didn't care that the windows were broken and scattered glass cut their feet. Instead, they had found corners to rest their heads in.

Her sisters were exactly the opposite. They very quickly took the old castle as a challenge, and cleaning became their work. Sigrid was filled with pride to see them making this place a home. They'd heated the rooms, cleaned out the moss, and bit by bit tackled the monolithic castle.

With her sharp, dragon eyes, she could see them all moving around the gardens they were now building. One of the Bymerian men had changed into a hulking stallion and allowed the Earthen Beastkin to strap an old plow to his back. He trudged through the ancient dirt, pulling and tilling until it looked like a garden.

Behind him, birds trailed with seeds in their mouths. They each dropped one in the perfect spot, while a few badger women covered the holes efficiently. They were quick in their work, far faster than a human could do and with much less hardship on their bodies.

They could do this, she realized with pride. They could create a safe home here and live together in a way that she had never dreamed possible. There were men and women who could start a kingdom all on their own. A safe kingdom for all who shared an animal soul.

Yet, the shadow of war loomed over the castle. Beyond her sight, they built machines that would kill men easily and could be carried on the backs of all Beastkin. Elephants prepared themselves, leopards sharpened their claws.

More Beastkin joined the cause every day. The thirst for blood and battle spread through her people like a disease. They wanted retribution, justice, a sense of peace in the knowledge that no human would ever hurt them again.

Sigrid might have felt the same if she didn't have an image of her husband tumbling from the sky with banners of blood streaking behind him. It was a risk to start a war. People died every day, in great waves, but she didn't know how much more death she could stand in her life.

Chuffing out a breath, she sank lower and pressed her jaw against the edge of a wing. They were such *good* people. She'd seen more kindness in the few days here than she had in much of her life. Why couldn't they extend that past the label of Beastkin to human?

Rocks tumbled at her side, the skittering sound echoing in

the small canyon. She huffed out another breath and turned her head away from whomever was disturbing her troubled thoughts.

Raheem's voice interrupted her thoughts. "Sigrid, you cannot hide up here all day. They'll need your help soon."

She shook her massive head and turned it further away from him. Childish? Yes, absolutely. However, she didn't have time to deal with any other worries than her own. There was too much going on in her head, she wasn't sure if she could fit anything else in there.

"Sigrid," he grumbled, scrambling on the stones until he could place a hand on her scaled shoulder. "Nadir managed to get in touch with me."

Nadir? What did he want with them? Another plea for her to reconsider what she was choosing to do. He wouldn't want his people to lose their lives in this war either. She just wasn't sure she could stop it.

"It's an odd letter brought by a very old falcon," Raheem continued to say. "I thought perhaps you would like to read it. Or...listen to me read it if you're insistent on staying in this form."

She arched her neck just enough to stare at him with one great eye.

He cleared his throat. "Alright then. He apologies for the path your lives have taken, requested that I watch out for you, and that..." he paused for a moment, took a deep breath, and then said, "That he's found a Beastkin he'd like you to come and relocate."

She lost her footing on the cliff edge, lunging forward so quickly that she nearly knocked Raheem off the cliff. He cried out, but she managed to catch him in the folds of her wing. Setting him back to standing, she nudged him hard with her nose.

"It doesn't give any explanation. Only that he asks you be careful when you enter the city so that you can get the Beastkin out alive." Raheem met her gaze. "I don't know what he's trying to do, Sigrid. But perhaps this is his way of apologizing."

It wasn't much of an apology. He was asking her to risk her life, yet again, but he was also risking his own life housing a Beastkin. What had come over him?

Raheem patted her shoulder. "I told you before, the boy is not all bad. I don't understand his reasoning any more than you do, but I truly believe there is good in him, Sultana. Perhaps there is a chance for him yet."

A sickly light of hope bloomed in her chest, one that was dangerous on all accords. She couldn't let it swallow her whole. The Beastkin needed her, rushing off to see her wayward husband who refused to see the importance of what she was doing would only hurt her in the long run. She couldn't let him do that to her.

"Sigrid," Raheem said quietly. "If there is a Beastkin you can help, then you have to go."

She shook her head.

"Yes, Sigrid. That is what you have chosen. It's your place to help these people when you put yourself as their savior. Go to him, take the Beastkin with you, but just..." Raheem swallowed, his face twisting with some strong emotion. "Talk to him? For me. Just let him know that it's never too late to admit he was wrong and to turn down another path."

She didn't know if Raheem was right. There would be a

point where even she couldn't forgive Nadir for his actions. If they ended up at war with Bymere, many would die. And she didn't know if those wounds on her soul could ever be healed.

But if he truly had a Beastkin who needed help, she couldn't deny him. She glanced down at all the good her people had already done, she felt something in her heart squeeze. This was the place for all those who were downtrodden, the weak and hungry.

The Beastkin race needed to heal. Everyone needed a place where they could be safe and lick their wounds. For their souls to slowly grow back into the bright beacons she knew they could be.

So instead of denying Raheem, as she would have liked to, Sigrid nodded.

But not now. She wouldn't go when there was so much at work here, when her people cried out for a war and she was going to give them one.

Maybe someday, when the world changed and the tides shifted, she could return to him. But for now, she must focus on war.

NADIR

THE SUN BEAT DOWN ON NADIR'S BACK. IT SANK UNDERNEATH the links of his metal armor plates, rolling in droplets of sweat down his spine.

He sat astride his steed at the forefront of the massive Bymerian army. A messenger had arrived only hours before, heralding the beginning of the war they'd feared. The Beastkin were coming in droves. An army of monsters, the messenger had claimed. They were bloodthirsty, clearing everything in their path like a great tide of death.

Let them come, Nadir had thought. Let them come and see that the Bymerians were waiting for them.

Armor jangled next to him, and he glanced over to see Abdul riding up.

"Sultan," his advisor said, nodding his head briefly. "The ranks are prepared."

"And the armored troops?"

"The elephants have been trained well, Sultan. They will

not flee, nor will they allow the Beastkin to sway them. However, we have no way of knowing if they can control animals."

They did have a way of knowing, but his advisor would never have asked Nadir's opinion. He still wanted to pretend that Nadir was more human than animal.

And yet, already the dragon wanted to break free from his skin. The anticipation of blood, screams, the horror of war all made the dragon male inside him rear his head. It was more than animalistic desire. Unlike some Beastkin, Nadir recognized that his beast wasn't just an animal. Dragons were far more intelligent than a horse or a leopard. They knew what war was. They recognized it as a playground for all they desired.

Death would fill the air with the metallic scent of blood. He would control himself, as he always had. No one could know what he was.

An elephant cried out and he tensed for a moment before realizing that it was one of his own. How were they to distinguish between the two?

Nadir glanced over his shoulder, checking the riders and the red banners fluttering from each elephant's tusk. There were thousands of men here, each in black and red armor that gleamed in the sunlight.

Deadly spears lifted into the air. The sharp tips would sink into flesh easily while the jagged edges would rend as they were removed. Scimitars were strapped to every waist, hastily forged and honed by all the blacksmiths of the city.

So many of his people hid within the walls of the Red Palace. They had arrived in droves, seeking sanctuary and praying that the sultan would cast pity upon them. The advisors said to leave them. He had declined their counsel and allowed them all inside.

No innocent would die to a Beastkin. Not today and not any other day in their future if he could help it.

Another animalistic cry lifted. This time from far in the distance. He stiffened and turned.

A wind blew toward them, unnatural in its force and dangerous in its speed. It could easily start a sandstorm, but that was likely the point. When a thunderbird came to battle, it never played fair.

The billowing cloud of sand and movement raced through the desert. His men shifted, armor creaking and filling Nadir with anticipation.

So, it would begin.

"Hold!" he shouted, his order carrying through the ranks and stilling their nerves. "Let them come to us!"

"Sultan," Abdul warned, "is that wise? Perhaps we should lead them away from the palace—"

"They won't get close enough to it."

"They're already close enough. You've taken in many from the outskirts of Misthall and beyond, it's too great a risk—"

"Abdul, enough." Nadir watched the approaching army with narrowed eyes. His vision shifted, becoming sharper and far more dangerous. With slit pupils, he flicked a glance to his advisor who paled. "Let them come."

Forms broke free from the dust. Lithe and lean, the felines lead the charge. Leopards and lions mostly, although a few dark shadows suggested that the Wildewyn panthers were in the ranks as well.

"Tell the armored fleet to prepare," he ordered Abdul. "And ready the catapults."

Abdul spun his horse with a harsh click of the tongue and wheeled away. Thundering hooves mixed with the approaching sounds of an army.

Nadir sat silent and still throughout it all. He'd trained for battle nearly his entire life, although his advisors had despised it. Raheem had somehow known this day would come. He'd always said that a sultan should know how to lead a battle. Now, he would have the chance.

He tightened his grip on the reins and watched the large cats as they stretched their long limbs. They were too far for most of his army to see, but his dragon eyes saw every detail. The sinewy muscles that flexed underneath their skin. The silken fur spotted with marks that were different for everyone.

What a shame they all had to die.

"Predictable," he growled. "You didn't listen to Sigrid, did you Butcher?"

The tell-tale creak of wood and rope filled his ears. The whoosh of flames called out to his dragon who he kept locked up tight within him. A flaming ball of pitch and fire launched overhead. It whistled through the air and landed in the center of the large cats.

Inhuman screams filled the air. Some of them were caught in the pitch, others tumbled in the sand as they tried to avoid the launched weapons. A large number kept racing for the armored ranks that stepped forward to greet them.

There wouldn't be many left as the catapults continued. One after another, fireballs rained down from the sky on the ranks of the Beastkin.

Nadir grit his teeth, stilling the guilt in his heart that these were people just like him. That he should be fighting, and dying, with them.

The remaining cats reached them. They slammed against the armored ranks with growls and snarls that filled the air until it was all he could hear. Their nails scratched down the metal chestplates. Their teeth gnashed at the air while yowls echoed from their throats.

And then the Bymerians began to scream.

Another blast of wind shook through his army. Men raised their hands to their faces, protecting the soft flesh from the glass-like shards of sand. Nadir stayed forward, disregarding the pain and ignoring the way his skin stung. The dragon reminded him that armored plates could cover his body with only a small release of power.

He held still, forcing his other form to calm. He kept his gaze on the swirling sands in the distance and waited for the exact moment when the rest of the Beastkin army revealed itself.

He didn't have to wait long.

Elephants and mammoths burst free from the storm. More lions, bears, birds, beasts of every color charged forward with a scream that echoed with every voice of nature. The ground thundered with the power of their stamping feet.

A man behind him gave a shout of fear and pointed to the sky. His heart clenched, but he looked up.

The thunderbird was albino like the man. It reared up and screamed, four wings spread so wide it blocked out the sun. Lightning struck the sand nearby.

"Dragonslayer!" he shouted. "Shoot that beast down!"

Pulling his scimitar from his side, Nadir kicked his horse and raced through the sands to meet the Beastkin army head-on. Hundreds of his men came with him. They all rode horses, where the foot soldiers would remain behind to clean up any that broke through the ranks.

Wind whistled past his ears, tangling in his hair as if he were flying. The others wore helms made of gold and rubies. They needed the protection, whereas Nadir could care less.

Birds dove from the sky, claws extended to pluck out eyes and scratch faces. Nadir bared his teeth in a growl and lifted an arm to keep them away. Others swung their swords wildly, catching wings and feathers easily in their haste.

An elephant charged by. It swung a great trunk, scooped up a horse and soldier, sending them flying into the distance. He heard an answering call, and then it locked tusks with one of his own elephants. The Bymerian beast's eyes rolled in their sockets, but the Beastkin was more man than animal.

The wild beast desired to live, and it would do anything to ensure its own future. The Beastkin cried out as the Bymerian elephant twisted and snapped a tusk free from the Beastkin's face.

A lion leapt onto his horse, digging claws into the shoulders and snapping its powerful jaws at Nadir's leg. He sliced his scimitar down, dragging it along the Beastkin's face and curving it under the throat.

The lion gave a gurgling growl and fell underneath his horse's stamping feet. His stallion staggered, blood seeping from the shoulder wound, and then fell to a knee.

Nadir slid from its back and pressed a hand to the wound.

"Be free, old friend. Run."

The wild look in the stallion's eye almost made him wonder whether it understood him. He wouldn't have been surprised to have a Beastkin looking out for him all this time. His life was made of surprises it seemed.

But the stallion lurched to its feet and raced away from the battle without a second glance.

He spun and raised his scimitar, catching a Beastkin horse as it charged. Nadir turned his head to the side so he didn't see the man's gurgling last breath. A scream echoed from the sky, and he looked up to watch a woman tumble through the clouds with an arrow through her breast.

This would be a war to end all wars. He would never be able to wipe these images from his brain.

Sigrid. Frantically, he spun, searching the skies for the woman who had changed him so thoroughly. Where was she?

Had she chosen not to fight? She hadn't wanted this war, but she would have stood by her people. Not unless something had happened, and the mere thought made his veins freeze.

"Sultan!" The shout echoed. "Sultan!"

He spun to see Abdul racing toward him on a black stallion. The advisor reached out a hand for him to take. Without hesitation, Nadir grasped the offered limb and swung himself up behind the advisor.

Abdul kicked the beast away from the battle, but Nadir could see that the Bymerians were losing. Though the ground was littered with animals slowly turning back into humans, there were so many more still coming.

Lightning struck the ground in front of them and their

horse lost its footing. Both he and Abdul were thrown over its head and hit the ground hard. Air burst from his lungs.

Stars danced in front of his eyes as lingering electricity made the hairs on his arms lift. But it was not his own safety that he thought of, nor that of his people or advisor. Even through the ringing of his ears, he listened for any sound of her arrival.

"The dragon," he croaked, reaching for his advisor. "Where is she?"

He didn't have to ask. The guttural vibration of her call filled the air with tension. Every soldier, man and Beastkin, paused in their fight to look up at the sky and see *her*.

Moonlight flesh reflected rainbows as she gently soared over them. She was beautiful in every sense of the word. Her wings did not beat; she did not scream or shout. Her call was a sad cry of mourning as she floated over the battlefield, silent as she flew.

"No," he whispered. "Don't do this, my love."

She was close enough he saw the sadness in her gaze as she tilted her great head and looked down at them with sky blue eyes. One of the Bymerian soldiers fell to his knees nearby, but Sigrid wasn't attacking the battlefield.

Her wings beat once, twice at the air and then she soared over the Red Palace where so many had seen her face.

Nadir stumbled to his feet, heart racing because he knew he couldn't forgive her for this. She couldn't. She *wouldn't*. Her heart was pure. Pain and death were not what she dealt.

If she did this, then he would have no choice but to fight her as well. He would *win*, because he was bigger and stronger, and he would not be able to control his rage.

"No," he said again, staggering toward the castle as if he might be able to catch her on foot. "No, anything but this."

Of all the things Nadir had prepared for, he had never dreamed that she would attack innocents.

Silence fell over the battlefield. Even the Beastkin stilled to watch. Had they not talked about this? Had they not used this as their secret plan all along?

He spared a moment to look at the eyes of the animals around him and realized they hadn't known she was going to do this. Even they hadn't thought she was capable of destroying so many.

Sigrid paused over the Red Palace and screams of innocent people filled the air. They weren't fighting. They were hiding, and still, she beat her wings. He watched her chest burn red as flames built in her chest.

She opened her mouth and released fire onto his home.

"*No!*" his tortured scream burst free from his chest, and he fell onto his knees.

Her great wing caught the edge of a rounded pillar and knocked it to the ground. Another tower fell under her great claws, and all he could think was how badly she had betrayed him.

A hand fell on his shoulder, and Abdul's voice shook with rage. "I will only say this once, boy, but now is the time to show our people *who you really are.*"

"They will not suffer a Beastkin as their sultan."

"They will rejoice at the God King who saved them from the demon who killed so many of their loved ones. Become the dragon, Nadir. Kill this monster."

He let out a coughing huff, the dragon rumbling to the

surface. Battle was battle, although it would never kill the creature it had already decided was its mate. But there was a lesson to be taught here, and he couldn't control it anymore.

Fire burned his lungs, but he managed to growl, "Get away from me."

Abdul staggered back. He nearly lost his footing, but finally was far enough that Nadir could let loose.

The dragon burst from his form so violently that he lost sense of space. He chuffed out an angry breath, shaking his head and digging red claws into the sand. Bymerians scattered, shouting in fear and awe. He already heard the cries shouting, "The sultan!"

It didn't matter. There were people in the Red Palace whom he needed to save. He rose up onto his back legs, stretched his wings wide, and roared. The sound shattered through the air, crackling with power and rage.

In the distance, Sigrid paused in her destruction and turned toward him.

His heart clenched. Even from so far away, her beauty nearly unmanned him. In this form, it didn't matter that she was killing people he held dear to his heart. It didn't matter that there was a war or that dead Beastkin and Bymerians scattered around him like fallen leaves.

All that mattered was that there was breath in her lungs and that he desired her more than anything else.

"The sultan is a dragon!" a shout lifted into the air from a nearby soldier who'd lost his helm. He was little more than a boy, just a teen who had somehow managed to join the army. He lifted his scimitar into the air and let out a gleeful shout. "We've our own dragon, men. Onward to battle! To the sultan!"

The war started again, and Nadir took to the skies.

Wind whistled through his wings. He'd meet her at the palace if she made him, but she'd turned. He knew she would come to him. She always did.

A shriek echoed from above him and claws raked down his side. Unharmed, he paused and stretched his neck to look at the thunderbird that plummeted from the sky again. Perhaps, Jabbar might have been able to harm Sigrid, but he'd never fought a dragon male before.

Fire billowed up from his chest into his mouth. Nadir let loose a stream of flames so hot it turned blue in the sky. Jabbar's scream was music to his hears.

Weight struck his side hard. He lost control of the flames and fell, catching himself at the last moment with powerful beats of his wings. He looked up and caught sight of Sigrid's spiked tail just before it hit him in the jaw.

The strike was so powerful that it knocked him even closer to the ground. The blasts of air from his wings made men and Beastkin fall beneath him. Angered, he shot back toward her.

His dragon took over. Instinct had him opening his mouth again. Fire poured from between his jagged teeth and flowed over her like a wave. She screamed. The creaking sound of scales reached his ears, then she blasted back her own fire that met his in the air.

A surge of triumph heated his blood. He got close enough to lock back feet with her and tugged her closer. Their wings fought for control, but he kept his claws curved together with hers.

She could fight him all she wanted, but they would remain together till the bitter end.

Let go, he thought. *You cannot win this fight, you foolish woman.*

They both lost their breath, and the flames died. He stared into her blue eyes, determination so easily read within their depths, and knew she wouldn't give up unless he made her. His lips curved into a snarl.

He gave a harsh twist, sending her spinning from his side. The sunlight gleamed off the gossamer membranes of her wings. Again, bitter resentment rose in his chest. Why couldn't she understand what he was trying to do? She should have left a long time ago.

Just as he was about to follow her, to grab her and shake her as best he could in this form, a whistling sound rocketed through the air.

Dragonslayer.

Time seemed to stop. He saw in his mind's eye the brutal arrow slicing through her body, and realized that even though she had done something so impossible to forgive, he couldn't watch her die. Not like this.

Never.

He twisted in the air and flung out his form until he managed to knock her to the side. A burning ache spread through his shoulder and wing. In shock, Nadir looked down and saw the jagged edge of the spear stuck between his scales. It had punctured them inward until it was his own body causing pain as well as foreign metal.

He tried to use the wing, but it folded against his side. Useless.

A soft growl escaped his lips and then he was falling, tumbling toward the sand and unable to stop himself. A thin stream of blood lifted into the air from the wound that slowly began to seep.

He looked up at Sigrid who let out a keening call that echoed in his own chest. He hadn't wanted to see her die. He couldn't watch such a terrible thing happen to someone he adored so much.

But now he was forcing her to watch *him* die.

SIGRID

SIGRID SCREAMED AS ALL HER WORST NIGHTMARES BECAME reality. He plummeted from the sky, a tangle of red limbs and mahogany wings. A cry escaped from her mouth, and she hesitated only a moment before following him.

Beastkin opinion be damned. He was a part of her, and she could not watch a piece of herself die. Not like this.

She folded her wings close to her sides and speared through the air until she was close enough to catch him. Her claws scrabbled at his, jerking his legs at the last second so that when they both struck the ground with a force hard enough to shake the earth, it would not be a deadly impact.

Sigrid was tossed from his side, rolling through the sand until she came to a stop. The air knocked from her lungs and she tasted blood on her tongue.

Shaking her large head, she lifted her neck to stare over at his still body and the red blood that streaked his form and stained the sand around him.

A shaking call escaped her again. The weak cry was little more than a whimper, a sad sound desiring little more than to know her mate still breathed.

The sounds of battle faded around them. She sensed the eyes of hundreds watching two great beasts of legend, fallen and wounded.

Rivals be damned. *She would not watch him die.*

Scales melted away into a cream, silk gown. Gold armor hammered into the shape of feathers stretched from her back, over her shoulders, and down to her belly She spat blood and pushed herself up from the sand.

"Nadir," she croaked, dragging her wounded and sore body to his side.

Sigrid slumped against him, pressing her hands to the overheated plates of his neck and following them up to his head. Blood smeared over her dress, leaving streaks of war and hatred that branded her very soul.

She sniffed, tears making it difficult for her to see.

"Husband," she whispered. Her hands shook as she smoothed them over his giant head, larger than her whole body in human form. "Wake up. Please wake up."

He didn't move. His large eyes remained closed, and she wanted nothing more than to see the golden color again.

"Please," again she begged. "Nadir, you can't leave me like this. Not now. *Not now.*"

She felt his large body move, shifting under her hands as his great head turned to look at her. He couldn't open his eyes the entire way, but he was alive. And that meant her heart started beating again.

"There you are," she said and swiped a hand underneath

her eyes. "We've to get that spear out of you, and then you can change back. I'll take care of you. You're going to be fine."

Hands scooped underneath her arms, lifting her from his side and yanking her backward. Pale and strong, she knew whose they were the moment she looked down.

Jabbar growled in her ear, "We have to go. The Bymerians have accepted defeat, but they won't for long. You're defenseless, foolish woman."

"Let go of me."

"Are you going to risk your life for him? Are you going to die just to make sure he lives? Because that's what they're going to do to you, Sigrid. They want to see you die."

She looked up and saw a wall of Bymerians with scimitars raised marching toward them. They were blood-covered and their numbers small, but she knew their intent. They wouldn't let her go, not when they saw her as the instrument of their destruction.

Her body fell limp in Jabbar's hold, and she let him pull her away. But her eyes remained locked on Nadir's yellow gaze that followed her. Tears slid down her cheeks, and she pressed a hand against her heart.

Though they both had fallen, she hoped he knew that her heart still beat for him.

She lost track of time and sense until she felt claws release and drop her into the waiting arms of her sisters in Woodcrest. They curled warmth and love around her, drawing her to their sides and whispering words of encouragement.

They stripped her of bloody clothes and sank her into a hot spring where they brushed her hair until it gleamed. They scrubbed her fingertips and poured ceremonial liquid over her hands and feet.

Golden and shimmering in the dying light, they dragged her out before their people wearing little more than a ceremonial wrap and metallic paint.

They waited for her in droves. Men and women with their faces painted, victorious. They reached out for her, stroking hands down her arms and touching the loose strands of her hair.

"Sigrid," they whispered, "our dragon."

She was numb to all of it. What had she done? What had she started in her desire for freedom and hope for a better life?

Jabbar, Brynhild, and others waited at a podium for her. In their hands, they held a golden crown of twisted metal that looked like branches and her gold dragon mask.

"Let it be known," Jabbar shouted, "that all of our history will sing legends of this day. The moment when Sigrid of Wildewyn felled the red beast of Bymere. Come, Sultana. Wear your crown with pride, and set aside your mask forever, knowing that you have saved us all, and that you will lead us through many battles to come."

Her stomach clenched, but she stood beside them and felt the crown heavy on her head. Today, she lost her title of Earthen woman and sultana.

So began the reign of the Warrior Queen.

NADIR

NADIR PLACED A FOREARM ON THE RAILING OF HIS BALCONY, looking out over his empire with a tired gaze. His shoulder still burned. They'd pulled the spear out, ruining muscle and sinew along the way. Though the healers thought he might be able to use the limb again, he wasn't so confident.

The battle had taken much from him. The loss of so many lives, the destruction of his city, and *her*.

Gods, he would never forget the look in her eyes as she left his side, or the words she had whispered in his ear. She still felt something for him, she still desired him at her side, and yet, she left without much complaint.

He'd never understand the woman, but there was something deep inside him that called out for her even now. Every inch of his person knew that she was meant to be at his side. Unfortunately, their fate had other ideas.

A door opened and closed behind him, footsteps following the sound.

"Sultan?" A soft rush of fabric suggested Abdul bowed behind him. "Shall we address the people?"

"Are they ready?"

"As they'll ever be."

When he turned, Nadir saw something like appreciation in Abdul's gaze. "It's the first time they've seen me since the battle."

"They have been waiting all morning to catch a glimpse of you."

He didn't ask if they were afraid of him. He knew they were, and they should be. A dragon was a fearsome thing to behold, let alone two battling in midair. He didn't expect them to accept him for what he was, but he knew that they had no choice.

Nadir had always thought he would bring about a time of prosperity for Bymere. He'd been wrong. All he had managed was a time of fear and loss.

He followed his advisor through the halls of the Red Palace, or what remained of them. Chunks of the walls were missing, pieces of armor and priceless heirlooms shattered on the floor. They'd tried to rebuild as much as they could, but he'd insisted that they rebuild the peasant homes before they focused on the palace.

After all that he'd done, he deserved to live in a ruin.

His bare feet crunched through the rubble to the same pavilion where he'd given so many speeches in his short time as sultan. First with his wife, second against his wife, and now... Now he didn't know what he was going to say.

Nadir stepped forward and allowed the remaining populace of Bymere to stare up at him. There was fear in their

413

eyes, he'd always known there would be. But there was something else there that he hadn't expected.

Hope.

Taking a deep breath, he pressed a hand against his wounded shoulder and slid it down to where his limp hand was strapped to his side. "My people. This is not the future I desired for Bymere."

His words echoed, and Nadir paused. He tried to get his bearings, to figure out what was the right thing to tell them but realized there were no right words. There was nothing he could tell them that would ease their minds of fear or soothe the ache of hatred.

And so, he swallowed all sense of pride and stepped forward to the very edge of the pavilion. Amongst confused murmurs, he carefully sat himself on the ledge and let his legs dangle down into the crowd.

He was closer to them here. Could smell their unwashed bodies, could see their confusion and worry. *They* could see him, his pain, his sadness.

His shoulder throbbed with its own heartbeat, and he winced.

"For most of my life, I have believed a sultan was not a person, but an instrument of your desires. What you wanted, I would fight for. When you needed protection, I would be your shield. When you required defense, I would be your sword. But I tell you now, I am just a man. More than that, I am Beastkin, one of the two remaining dragons to draw breath.

"I'll hide it no longer. I have chosen you, my people, time and time again. I hope you understand the depth of my pride for this kingdom and its people. You are the reason I draw breath each morning." He ran fingers through his hair and let out a huffing chuckle. "I understand some of you may wish for me to abdicate the throne, and I'll tell you now I have no interest in doing so. I intend to remain here until Bymere is returned to its former glory.

"I love this land, its people, even the sandstorms. I will stand by your side, protect you from harm as best I can. I hope, in time, that you will understand why I'm doing this. I don't want to hurt you. I don't want you to fear me. Understand, I am a boy king no longer. I'm just a man, fighting for his kingdom."

He fell silent, meeting the gazes of those around him. His arm felt heavy, even though he had no feeling in his fingertips. His legs dangled into the air.

It wasn't an adult who reached for him, but a child that slipped free from the front of the crowd and reached up to touch his foot.

Nadir stared down at the boy, all round cheeks and large eyes.

"Sultan," the boy said, "Thank you for saving us."

The sentiment was repeated until it lifted into the clouds. Nadir stilled his face, forcing tears to stay in his eyes.

And then, the words changed into a chant that would change his life forever. The Bymerians would no longer call him the boy king.

So began the reign of the God King.

EPILOGUE

SIGRID CLUTCHED THE SIDE OF THE RED PALACE, HER HAND ON THE edge of the crumbling balcony that would lead her back to where this all started. Her heart thundered in her chest, and she couldn't seem to catch her breath.

Would he still be there? Would he be happy to see her? She felt guilty for even thinking such thoughts. He didn't deserve them.

He'd made his choice, and it hadn't been her. Although she could understand where he was coming from, she couldn't forgive it. The Bymerians were his people and his past. She had simply hoped that she might be his future.

Her fingers flexed and she hauled herself up the cliff edge and onto the balcony. She landed in a crouch, the tight-fitting leather pants Brynhild had given her keeping her movements quiet. The soft leather had been a staple in the area where Brynhild was from. Most of the women had taken to wearing them, and Sigrid enjoyed them just as much as the others.

She blew a breath at her hair and tugged the scarf around her neck over her face. Now that they'd seen her face, she had to be even more careful. She couldn't wander around the Red Palace without being painfully obvious.

Barefoot, she padded to the door and pressed her spine against the wall beside it. She leaned carefully in the shadows to peer through the carved slats. Nadir's private quarters were just as she remembered them, and for some reason that made her chest squeeze painfully.

The pools bubbled in the corners, one leaking out onto the floor, his bed the same, even the desk seemed to have the exact same amount of papers.

Movement in the corner of the room caught her eye. A pile of silken fabric lifted, and for a moment her heart stopped as she wondered if he'd already moved a concubine into his quarters. But it was a little girl who lifted her pretty head. Her large eyes overpowered all her other features, and she crawled out of the pile to race to the desk.

She quickly ducked underneath the lip of it, hiding. Sigrid only had a moment to frown before she heard the door to Nadir's bedroom open.

The creaking sound echoed for a moment, but no footsteps entered. She held her breath, her eyes remaining on the child.

Who was she? Was this the Beastkin that Nadir wanted her to help, or was it a child he'd recently discovered was his?

Three footsteps then a pause. A very familiar sigh reached her ears and then Nadir said, "A'dab. I know you're in here. It's just me. You don't have to be afraid."

The little girl crawled out just enough to peek over the lip of the desk.

Sigrid leaned just enough so that she could see the grin on Nadir's face. His hair was disheveled, clothing far too plain to befit a sultan, but he looked well. His right arm was still in a sling, wounded from their battle.

"Just me." He held his good arm out to the side and waited for the little girl to come out from her hiding spot. "When are you going to trust me, little one?"

The frown on the little girl's face made Sigrid cover her mouth to hide a laughing huff of air. The child was a smart one, then. Nadir might have taken her into the palace, but he was still the man who was hunting her kind and supporting the people who wanted all Beastkin dead.

To Sigrid's surprise, the girl still moved forward a few steps. "You aren't bringing the guards?" she asked.

"I said I wouldn't. I've already reached out to my friend. She's going to help you."

"Are you sure?"

A shadow crossed his expression, but Sigrid waited to hear his words. "She wouldn't leave you here. Not with me."

Sigrid's heart stuttered as if he had taken it in his fist and squeezed. The sadness and regret she saw reflected in his eyes was nearly enough to send her to her knees. He hadn't wanted to make the choices he'd made.

And it made everything infinitely more difficult.

She stepped out of the shadows of the balcony and into the heated warmth of his private quarters. At first, he didn't notice her. Another flaw in his ridiculous protection that could easily end in the death of their sultan.

His gaze flicked up, and she froze in place. The heat of a thousand suns burned in those yellow eyes the instant they met hers. She felt as though flames licked up from her toes, and her own vision shifted as her pupils turned to slits.

It was strange how he still had that effect on her. After all that he'd chosen, the betrayal she'd felt when she left, Sigrid had thought she would feel nothing when she saw him again.

She had been wrong.

Nadir slowly straightened from his crouch. "Sigrid."

"Nadir."

The fire in his eyes burned brighter. "Little one, go sneak into the kitchens. You'll need food for this journey. Take whatever you want and make sure the cook doesn't catch you."

The little girl didn't need to be told twice. She fled from the room without a backward glance, not even taking the time to see who had entered the room through the balcony. Smart child. She knew not to look danger in the eye, even if that danger wasn't meant for her.

"You came," Nadir said, taking a step toward her.

"I did." But she didn't know how to feel about it now. He stared at her with such heat that she almost didn't recognize him. This wasn't the boy she had left. Nadir stood with a man's confidence and radiated a man's desire.

"For the girl," he said, his voice a low rumble.

"Of course. I couldn't leave her here, not with what's happening."

"The war?"

"Ending soon. My people have already won the first battle." She took a step back. "Why didn't you stop it, when only *you* could have?"

The simple question broke the chains that held him back. Nadir surged forward, his hands reaching for the loose fabric of her shirt, and yanked her against him.

His fingers crushed folds of cotton, his knuckles burning through the thin material until she could feel them against her ribs. He leaned down until his breath fanned across her face, his nose nearly touching hers, his lips so close their heat warmed her own.

She blew out a slow breath then inhaled his fireborn scent. "What are you doing?"

"I have no idea." He shook his head, pulling her closer until her hands were flat against his chest. One hand slid up her side, knuckles catching on the material, until he curved it around her neck. Ever so slowly, he dragged the material covering her face down until he could see all of her.

His eyes turned to molten gold. Burnished edges made them glow in the dim light of the sconces. Sigrid stared up at him and wondered why this hadn't happened while she was here. Why he hadn't pushed her for something more than the distant relationship they had fostered.

"I missed you," he murmured. He stroked the outline of her face, fingertips skating over her cheekbone, down to her jaw. "I didn't know how much until I saw your face again."

"We can't do this."

"We *have* to do this," he corrected. "Otherwise, we'll never know if all our dreams were true or not. All the restless nights we lay awake at night, thinking about a future that could never be."

"Were you doing that?" His exhale flowed between her lips, tasting of metal and perfumed lilies.

"Of course, I was." Nadir leaned closer until just a breath would have caused them to touch. "And so were you."

Gods save her, but she had been. She wondered what a future at his side would look like. What Bymere would look like if she had taken the throne as a sultana should have. If she had poured her life and devotion into this kingdom and changed it for the better.

Would it have changed? And more importantly, would *he* have changed. She'd seen him become something so much more than the boy king. He had become a man worthy of the throne. One with thoughts and ideas that would improve the lives of his people.

And then everything had shattered in an instant. Even a good sultan could still be a foolish one.

"Sigrid." He said her name like it was a caress.

She didn't know what came over her, but that was all she could take. She surged forward and pressed her lips against his even though she didn't really know what to do.

Kissing was as foreign to her as this world he lived in, but thankfully her husband seemed to know what to do. He wrapped his arms around her shoulders, crushing her against him, cradling the back of her head with his palm.

Nadir devoured her. There was no gentleness in this first kiss, as the world crashed down upon their shoulders and time raced forward. He branded himself on her skin so that she would never forget him, no matter where they ended up.

She curled her hands into fists against his chest, alternating between pushing him away and trying to pull him closer. Sigrid's mind whirled. She knew she shouldn't be enjoying this in the slightest. He was her enemy now. It was the fate he had chosen, and she needed to remember that.

But he tasted like sunshine and flames, and every fiber of

her being wanted to savor the rare golden taste. He was the other side of her coin. The darkness to her light, the sun that burned away all her moonlight.

Breathing hard, he pulled back enough to stare down into her eyes. "Sigrid—"

"No," she pressed her fingertips against his mouth. "Don't say anything. Nadir you can still stop this. You can return with me, to our people. The Beastkin will accept you. They are kind and good people. They'll understand why you did what you did."

"I can stop nothing. My people are here, my family name. My blood right is here, and I can still fix this."

"You're still choosing the humans?"

"I'm choosing Bymerians." He shook his head. "I don't expect you to understand this choice, Sigrid. But there is a chance here, and you must give me time. Do you really believe everyone in this kingdom wishes the Beastkin dead? That we are all evil? There is so much good here, so many people who would be welcome to change, they're proving it already. I just need you to *give me time.* Let me shake loose the chains of humanity and become the sultan they've always desired. Not a person, but a god king."

Her heart broke a little further with each of his words. There was reason in them. He had been raised to be a sultan, and he was following in the footsteps of the men who had come before him.

But she refused to believe him. "You're a person to me," she whispered.

"Why? Because we share the same affliction?"

"No. Because our souls call out for each other even in the

hardest of times. You and I understand each other." She took a step back, letting her arms fall to her sides. "You know it as well as I. Even now, when you choose to abandon your own people and live side by side with humans who would beat us, cage us, kill us. I understand why you're doing it."

His expression was troubled, the crumpled look something that tore at the fiber of her soul. "Then explain it to me, Sigrid. Because even I don't know why I'm doing it."

"A sultan is there for his people, you said it yourself. You've made yourself a sultan of sand and ruin. But likewise, I've made myself a sultana of beasts and monsters."

His fingers released the cotton of her shirt, and he stepped back as well. Sigrid wished that Bymerians didn't wear their hearts on their sleeves in that moment. She saw the exact moment his heart broke.

"Then be well, Sultana," he replied, his voice choked. "I wish you the best in your reign."

"I hope we can someday see eye to eye again, husband."

"Perhaps, when the stars realign in the sky, you and I will come together again."

She hoped it was the truth. The taste of him lingered on her tongue, and she felt more alive in this moment than she had since leaving. Even saving her people hadn't filled her lungs with air like this.

The door to his quarters creaked open, and the little girl slipped through. Sigrid watched her careful movements, the way she tip-toed as she walked, how she carefully closed the door behind her like someone would hear even the slightest creak.

It broke her heart to know the child had lived in such a way that she'd learned this was the way to stay safe. Children should be loud and boisterous. They shouldn't feel fear, worry about making sound, and walk as though someone might catch them.

The girl turned, A'dab she remembered, and held a small pack close to her thin chest. Nadir's shirt, and it had to be his, billowed around her. She'd rolled the sleeves up so far, they were little more than bulky lumps that still fell around her wrists.

The distrusting look on her face made Sigrid smile. In all this chaos of their lives, at least something good could come out of it. "Hello. I've heard all about you."

"Are you the golden lady?" she asked. Her voice was like that of a bird, light and airy as only a creature who had flown could make.

"I suppose, if that's what they're calling me."

"But you don't have the—" A'dab waved a hand over her face.

"The mask? No. I only wear it around people whom I do not consider family." She didn't miss the look A'dab flung toward Nadir. "He is my husband, little bird. He may see my face just as you."

"Husband? You're married to him?"

"I am the Sultana of Bymere. How did you think I got the title?"

A'dab lifted a shoulder and stepped closer to her. "The sultan said you were going to take me away. That you'd bring me somewhere safe."

"I intend to. Would you like to go on an adventure with me? It's very far away from here, but you'll live with many more people just like you. A kingdom of Beastkin. Men and women who can turn into animals at will, without anyone hunting us."

"It sounds like a dream," she accused. "I don't like being told dreams. I want to live stories, not listen to them."

Sigrid held back a smile, barely. "I'm not telling you a story or a dream. It's a real place, and I'd very much like to bring you there. I think there are many people who would like a spunky little girl like you. I cannot replace your parents, or even bring them back, but I can give you a new family."

Nadir cleared his throat and asked, "How many?"

"You know I can't tell you that." She shook her head and stood. "That's too much information, even though I somehow still trust you."

"I just want to know. To prepare."

Her heart squeezed again. There would be so much death in the coming months, and they both didn't know how to stop it. "A trade for information, perhaps?"

"What do you want to know?"

"Who taught them how to shoot me down?"

He blew out a breath, and she knew he was as affected as her. The pain in his expression shattered through the wall she was slowly building, and she knew she'd guessed right. He had helped design a weapon for dragons, or at least approved one. He'd taken part in the instrument of her death.

Nadir crossed his arms, staring down at his feet. "They call it the dragonslayer. I did not stop them."

She nodded, mirrored his posture, then frowned. "You created a weapon that could kill us both."

"I did."

He hadn't just designing a weapon that could kill her. That she might have been proud of him for. But he had helped design something that could kill *him*.

It was easy to forgive him for protecting his kingdom. It was not easy to forgive endangering himself.

"Not your finest hour, Nadir," she finally said, uncrossing her arms and holding her hands open at her sides. "I've already proven myself against your warriors. None will touch me on the battlefield."

"Except me," he replied with a wry grin. "Although I hope it doesn't come to that again."

She didn't want to know what would happen if they fought again. He'd proven himself formidable, his dragon much larger than hers. And yet, the feral part of her desired for the chance to fight him again.

Sigrid stooped and picked up the little girl. A'dab fit in her arms almost too perfectly. She was a pretty little thing, her dark skin a perfect combination with her own. They were a pair that should have been able to live on their own, in the wilds. Perhaps Sigrid would have adopted her as well. A'dab was the kind of child who could learn to be deadly.

She brushed a strand of hair away from the little girl's face. "What do you turn into, little bird?"

"How do you know I'm a bird?"

"I see the sky in your eyes. You've felt the glory of the wind racing underneath your wings. All creatures who can fly recognize each other. You know what I am, don't you?"

A'dab nodded. "You're a dragon."

"And you are?" Sigrid lifted her brow in a silent request for the little girl to fill it in.

"A dove."

"Ah, a symbol of peace. Fitting." The little one was everything that the Beastkin should have been able to lift above their heads and prove their worth. A child, a beautiful little child who could run through the streets with laughter on her heels. Sigrid frowned and glanced over at Nadir. "A girl?"

"Apparently, there are more Beastkin here than I knew about."

"You'll tell me when to collect them from now on, and keep them safe until I arrive." She made certain her voice was firm enough to convey how important this was. He might not abandon his kingdom, and so be it. But she wouldn't allow him to hunt her people anymore. Otherwise, she would return for them all and raze the city in her search.

He saw the fight in her eyes, because he blew out a frustrated breath and knowledge. "I'll do my best. I can't save them all, Sigrid. Someone will catch me, and then we'll all burn."

"A dragon cannot burn."

She turned on her heel and made her way back to the balcony. It was a long way down, but far enough that she might be able to carry the child on her back. A little one couldn't be expected to fly the entire way to Wildewyn. Perhaps she might even sleep a little. The Bymerian Beastkin had said her neck was quite comfortable on their journey.

A'dab tucked a cold hand into Sigrid's neck and stared up at the sky. "Are we leaving now?" she asked.

"We are."

"Sigrid," Nadir's voice drifted onto the balcony.

She set her teeth, telling herself not to look back. Only

temptation awaited there, and she had to go. But she glanced over her shoulder anyway.

Light silhouetted his form, turning strands of his dark hair red with fire. Yellow eyes stared back at her, and she knew what lingered in their depths. She would miss him, too.

But that was not their story.

"How many of you are there now?" he asked again.

"Hundreds. All the Beastkin in Wildewyn are now under my command. The Bymerians remain under Jabbar's."

"You know we call him the butcher here."

She nodded. "I've heard the name. I understand he's killed many of your people. Humans are very weak."

"He hasn't just killed humans. He's sacrificed Beastkin when the time seemed right. He doesn't care if people die, Sigrid. Ask him all you want; he'll tell you the stories. He's proud of them."

The words would likely haunt her, but she didn't have time to dwell on their meaning. She'd always known Jabbar may be up to something. She'd seen it in his dark gaze before. That didn't mean he wasn't the right person to help her lead. The men already followed him. And soon, there would be a council to help both of them.

If they made it that long. Her brows furrowed, fear settling in her stomach. "I'll ask him."

"Think hard if that's the kind of man you want at your side," Nadir replied. "As much as I'm leading this fight for the Bymerians, I don't want to see you harmed."

"Nor I you."

Sigrid turned before she did something foolish, like cry or return to his side. She perched the little girl on the balcony, and she seemed to understand what Sigrid wanted. With a flying leap, Sigrid vaulted over the edge and plummeted through thin air.

It was easy to let the dragon take over this time, even as she silently waited for a white dove to settle on her back. The dragon didn't feel as strongly as she did.

But, as she flew back to Wildewyn, even the dragon let out a haunting cry as she left her mate behind.

ABOUT THE AUTHOR

Emma Hamm grew up in a small town surrounded by trees and animals. She writes strong, confident, powerful women who aren't afraid to grow and make mistakes. Her books will always be a little bit feminist, and are geared towards empowering both men and women to be comfortable in their own skin.

To stay in touch
www.emmahamm.com
authoremmahamm@gmail.com